OTHER MINDS

13 TALES OF WONDER AND SORROW

JOSEPH G. BRESLIN

Tumbleweed Station Press.

ISBN: 979-8-9866494-0-5 (Paperback)
ISBN: 979-8-9866494-2-9 (Hardcover)

CONTENTS

ACKNOWLEDGEMENTS

No man is an island, and certainly no author. Without the love and support of my wife Liz, as well as the encouragement, prayers, and friendship of our three boys, I would have neither the strength nor the opportunity to write these stories. I thank also the One Who Sings all stories, and who has the power to make them real.

I must also thank Mom, who taught me to read and write, and Dad, who raised me on great stories, and who has always believed in me. Thank you both from the bottom of my heart.

It would be criminal not to mention the authors and creators, living and dead—okay, mostly dead—who ignited my imagination with powerful images, and/or with the strange magic of woven words: Edgar Allan Poe, H.P. Lovecraft, Edgar Rice Burroughs, Ray Bradbury, Arthur C. Clarke, J.R.R. Tolkien, Flannery O'Connor, Philip K. Dick, Isaac Asimov, Frank Herbert, Madeleine L'Engle, James S.A. Corey, Michael Flynn, Kazuo Ishiguro, Stephen King, Anne Rice, Alfred Hitchcock, Chris Carter, T.S. Eliot, Wallace Stevens, John the Evangelist, and many others.

I am eternally indebted to the supremely talented and unfailingly gracious John C. Wright, both for his counsel, and for his willingness to read a fledgling author's work and provide him a testimonial. You will not be forgotten, sir.

I'm grateful to the many friends, mentors, and colleagues, who've either encouraged me to write, or who've facilitated my writing. These include Joseph Gray, who always reads my stuff, as well as Lionel and Janet Yaceczko, Joseph and Jenn Bissex, Mary McGiffin, Morgan McMahon, Catherine Hoskote, Theresa Schlenz, and Matt Forsman. Thank you, Mike Ortiz, Matt Mehan, Tom Cox, Tom Longano, Joe Cardenas (who dreamed about Bean Brains), and Travis Curtright (who showed me I could write). I also want to thank Kathryn Kime, Rich Moss, and George Martin.

If you're reading this book, Mark Reid's incredible cover probably has a lot to do with it. Thank you, Mark, for your tireless and thoughtful work in producing a genuine piece of art to showcase these stories. I also want to thank in advance Lorna Reid for the work inside the cover that's just as important. And speaking of the text, Beth Rodgers' proofreading, and her editorial notes helped catch my mistakes, and smooth the prose. Thank you, Beth.

Finally, I'm bound to thank a certain cloud of witnesses. You know who you are.

A NOTE ON *OTHER MINDS*

There is drama in contrast. On the one hand, to exist is to be particular; to be *this* or *that*. Everything that *is* has a nature, and to name a thing is to reclaim it from the doom of anonymity. Naming, then, is a kind of blessing. Or perhaps an exorcism. And if so, that which cannot be named can be wonderful, or tragic – or else deeply unsettling.

But we're not always so good at seeing things as they are, in themselves. Perhaps that's why Nature offers up so many parallels. Moths and butterflies; frogs and toads; crickets and grasshoppers – things that suggest each other. Almost-doubles. Then there are Nature's striking contrasts: day and night, light and shadow, mountain and valley, land and sea, the atomically tiny and the incomprehensibly vast. These opposites help to define the world we live in. But to me, the most interesting appositions are found in the drama of minds; within one's own mind, and between it, and the minds of others.

Conscious and unconscious: Is it not strange that when I sleep, someone puts on a show for me, often with a plot, with symbolism, and a twist ending?

Person and persona: Is it not unsettling to consider that the other whom we encounter may be but a mask for a *someone* we'll never meet?

I and thou: And who is that someone? What is he or she beneath the mask? What remains through time, when all else—even personality—seems in flux? Or what if you should be walking down the street, and should spy another just like yourself? A perfect double. Or worse; nearly perfect. Why is it so unsettling to consider that just around the corner, concealed in shadow, there might be another almost-you?

Intellect and machine: Maybe you believe that a thing of metal can't have a spirit. Maybe I agree with you. But here is a frightening thought: what if that doesn't matter? What if, given a sufficiently complex neural network, a thing that had no true spirit still functioned *as if* it thought it had?

The characters in these stories find themselves entangled in the mysteries of contrast. Some of these mysteries are wonderful. Some, sadly beautiful. Still others are unnerving. Each of them will lead you through the uncanny valley, that strange place between is and isn't; between your own mind, and the minds of others.

Writing is priesthood. It is bloodletting and sacrifice, all for the sake of bringing into being things that are, and are not. It is my firm hope, dear reader, that these thirteen stories, born somehow inside my soul, will come to life in yours as well, and that they will go on living. There. Just behind you. Or deep down, in the cellars of your mind.

Joseph Breslin

She sang beyond the genius of the sea.
The water never formed to mind or voice,
Like a body wholly body, fluttering
Its empty sleeves; and yet its mimic motion
Made constant cry, caused constantly a cry,
That was not ours although we understood,
Inhuman, of the veritable ocean.

—*The Idea of Order at Key West*, Wallace Stevens

BEAN BRAINS

"He isn't looloo," said Saka Jinn, taking a drag. "Not yet."

She sent smoke toward the air scrubber with precision.

"Too many trips in the void, though."

Saka stretched out on the couch in the officers' lounge. Jack sat across from her, notes on his lap, on a stool he'd dragged over from the crew galley. Frowning, he glanced through the transparent wall that overlooked the passenger galley. She followed his gaze.

"What?" said Saka. "They can't hear me."

"But you're not supposed to smoke in transit," he said.

"The scrubbers can take it," she said. "New filters every time."

Jack almost argued, but Saka got her lungs scrubbed every three months. And Saka was the type who'd claim client privilege if he tried to report her, as if she only smoked during these mandatory sessions. Anyway, she outranked him. Saka was first mate. Jack was the ship's anesthesiologist and shrink, an officer by education only. Not one of them.

"Don't be so autonomic," she said, sucking more smoke. "No beaners in New World."

"Saka!"

"What?" she said, innocently. "There definitely aren't any of *them* around."

"Yes, but … the term—"

"—Is prejudiced?"

Jack nodded. She looked thoughtful.

"Well … I am," she said. "And so are you. So stop pretending to be offended by the word, when you aren't by the thing itself. A word is just a word."

Jack shifted on the stool. "The separated—"

"—Bean brains," she interjected. "That's still acceptable."

"Fine. *Bean brains* are living a tragic existence. Don't you feel any compassion for them?"

Saka chortled. "Um … *no*! 'Vague disquiet when I see one earthside' would be more accurate. It's their own fault anyway. And, please Jack, let's not bullshit during our sessions. Are you here to check on my mental health, or to make me a good liberal like yourself?"

He hated the way she said it. All the transit officers were former military, and Saka went out of her way remind him he wasn't. Still, he felt an obligation not to let the slur go.

"Look, Jinn, you're multiracial yourself. I would have thought that would give you some perspective on bias, on othering…"

"Well it doesn't," she said, cutting him off. "Race is irrelevant now. Competency, reliability, a general absence of murderous intent—"

"—You know the statistics," Jack interrupted.

She scoffed. "It only takes one."

Then she leaned in, lowering her voice. "Doesn't it ever creep you out that they have to stab you? I mean, why does it have to be a sharp edge? Why not a piece of furniture? I have this chair at home that mother gave me. Heavy thing. If I ever get beaned, I'm going to try it out."

Since she was being flippant, he said nothing.

"Anyway," she continued, "no more Earth shit. Weren't we discussing Captain Ceely?"

Jack sighed. "What makes you think he's unwell?" he said.

"Are you asking me about his behavior?" she said, "or what I think caused it?"

He shrugged. "Either, or."

She glanced over her shoulder, then straightened herself up on the cushions.

"He thinks the void is out to get him," she said.

Jack tapped his notebook. "Explain that."

She ashed into the empty whiskey glass. "So … this is a new route. But the *Naha*'s an original void ship. He's been at it that long."

Jack nodded, inviting her to continue.

"It's definitely *his* last voyage, though," she continued. "I've been shipping with Ceely for ten years, and he was over it back then. The void. He wanted out, but he's stayed on to get all his people across. A decade's a long time in the Big Black, even if you're beaned for most of it. I know what the science says, but I see what I see. The man is going paranoid."

"What's he afraid of?" said Jack.

She leaned in closer, as if they might be overheard. Jack resisted an impulse to pull away.

"He calls it the Shard. Long, black rock that came out of the void wall a couple go-rounds ago. The autoguns couldn't see it, and the gunner couldn't hit it, even though he was still beaned."

"Did it hit the *Naha?*"

"Oh, yeah," she said. "Minimal damage, but that's not the point. The old route was getting too clogged with flotsam."

"And the VTA wouldn't shell out for a new path," interjected Jack, catching her drift. "Then, suddenly, they did."

She nodded. "You got it. That impact was the real reason. But Ceely's superstitious about the flotsam. At least I hope it's just superstition."

"What does he say, exactly?" asked Jack.

She blew her smoke out straight, forgetting about the air-scrubber.

"That sometimes it's the same debris. That this Shard… it's followed him here."

"That's impossible," said Jack. "Don't tell me *you* believe that?"

It took a moment, but Saka sighed, and shook her head.

"No, you're right. That can't be."

"But you're worried," he said. "He's your captain. His mental state … does it concern you? Should we file a competency report?"

Saka's eyes went dagger-thin at that, and the professional mask snapped down. Jack could see it, like metamorphosis. She'd told him too much, and now loyalty rushed in to shut him out. *Military types*, he thought.

"Ceely's fine," she said. "Best captain in the void. In two years, thanks to him, I'll never have to smell Earth again. Maybe he's seen too much black, but he knows his shit. Anyway, I don't know why I told you any of this. You can't be trusted to…"

"Patient-client privilege," he assured her. "Your secret's safe with me. Still, it's good that I know what's going on."

But she wasn't listening anymore. He'd become a civilian again. Saka stood, and turned to leave. She halted at the door, and glanced over her shoulder.

"The only thing that ever concerns me," she snapped, "is that I'll get stabbed by some beaner who's snuck aboard my ship!"

Jack bit his lip. He'd had enough of Saka Jinn for now. But he made himself calm, and non-judgmental.

"Well, *that*," he said, in his cleanest, most antiseptic tone, "is truly impossible."

***

Jack walked through the common area adjacent to the main dining room. Like the dining hall, it was spontaneously organized into A and B sections corresponding to the two classes of passengers. A band of empty couches and chairs formed the invisible borderline between them. The small conference room where he'd meet the elected reps from both groups had a window looking out, and, as luck would have it, the *Naha*'s only wealthy young couple were planted on a couch right in front of that window. Good, thought Jack. It would make things easier.

In his thirteen voyages on the *Naha*, he'd seen only two conflicts bad enough to require him to bring both reps together. Both disruptions were on this voyage. Usually, the tension between those who'd saved a lifetime to emigrate, and those who'd been lotteried-in, only simmered under the surface. Twice on this crossing it had boiled over to actual violence. Maybe the captain's anxieties had affected the passengers, but Jack doubted it. Ceely kept a stiff upper lip. Anyway, they rarely saw him. *Seeing them* was Jack's job.

As the neural officer, Jack Shaw was the ship's mental fixer. He temped the whole ship early Monday morning, and normed them Friday evening before dinner. He was always the last to temp, and the first to norm himself. Beaning people was a perfectly scientific operation, at least in the void, where it was all controlled by the machine.

On Earth, cheaper beaning technologies had created an entire subclass of permanent bean brains, people who couldn't hold their breath for the whole process. The void ships to New World took no chances. They always worked, and they were damn costly because of it. Technically, you could bean and unbean people while beaned yourself, but that made Jack uncomfortable. Overseeing the weekly process was almost his only reason for being here. The idea of doing it while beaned—when he didn't care— scared the shit out of him.

Being responsible for bean brains didn't especially bother him. People were easy to deal with when they had no emotions, interests, or priorities. It was the public relations part he disliked. If trouble broke out, he had to smooth things over. And he'd never seen this kind of trouble before. Jack sighed, and put his hand on the conference room door, taking a deep breath, as if he were about to get beaned himself.

The passenger reps were already at the table. The table was small and round, but they managed to make it look square. The Marshalls, a couple in their sixties with three adult children and six grandchildren on board, sat on one side. Maria Cardena sat on the other. Her pencil moved furiously over a sketch pad, and she had a real ink quill and a jar of ink set out on the table. She looked up intermittently at the Marshalls, who looked away, appalled. Jack stifled amusement. Maria was sketching them.

"Thank you for waiting," he said.

Mrs. Marshall pursed her lips, and Mr. Marshall mumbled something glib. Jack took his seat on the side of the table that faced out of the window, making sure not to block either party's view of the young couple.

It was basic psychology. A-Class passengers had pooled their resources for decades to get their families off-world, and so disliked B-classers, who could never have afforded transit. B-classers knew that skilled laborers like themselves were just as necessary in New World. They felt no shame about winning their spots, only anger at being thought second-class. But a beautiful young couple, wealthy enough in their twenties to leave behind a dying Earth and live out their best years in the new one? Well, *everybody* hated people like that.

"So," said Jack, gathering his thoughts, "it's Sunday, and I'm sure we all want to enjoy the norm time we have left. I thought we could try to get to the bottom of this quickly, so we can get back to relaxing. Soon all of this will be behind—"

"Excuse *me!*" said Jane Marshall, cutting in. "Are you trying to suggest that we paper over this … this latest outrage, so we can make *your* life easier?"

"No," said Jack.

"Good," said Tom Marshall, piping in. "We're happy to hear that. Everything's on camera anyway. I'll cut to the chase. A family by the name of Merton, whom we've since gotten to know, was sitting at their table in the main dining room last norming. Then, out of the blue and unprovoked, one of *her* people lunged at Jessica Merton."

"Jessica," clarified Jane Marshall, "would be their second-oldest daughter, and she had two young children sitting beside her."

Jack glanced over at Maria Cardena, who was still sketching the Marshalls. Their words elicited no response from her, except that she placed the pencil on the table, opened the ink jar one-handed, and dipped her quill. Jane glared at her.

"Totally unprovoked," emphasized Jane. "You can see it on camera. Anybody can."

The Marshalls waited for Maria to contradict them. They seemed primed to pounce, but Maria said nothing. The regular sound of her ink quill on paper was somehow pleasant and insulting at the same time.

"Well," said Jack, filling the silence. "I've seen the recording, of course. I do wonder if there is some previous history there. Some context."

Tom groaned. "Oh, come on! It's entirely straight-forward. Every time one of *those people* does something irrational, a certain kind of person begins multiplying excuses for them. This is the second attack!"

"-In two years," interjected Jack, referring to the trip's subjective time.

"What does it matter if it's two years or two days?" shouted Tom. "And it's *not* two years when you consider we've all been beaned for most of it."

Jack nodded, trying to show he was listening without automatically conceding the point. Maria still hadn't looked up. She was not making this any easier. And yet, he found himself admiring her cool way. She was outgunned, and seemed not to care.

"If you want my opinion," said Jane, still glaring at the woman with the sketchpad, "it comes from not having *worked* for your spot. These people—I'm sorry, but there's no other way to say it—life is just cheaper to them."

Jack winced. Even Tom looked surprised at his wife's bluntness. Maria paused her stroke, and briefly bit the back of her quill. The fingers of one hand drummed the tabletop. She dipped the quill, and then continued with the same maddening regularity.

"Would you stop doing that!" Jane shouted at her.

Mechanically, Maria covered the quill tip, closed the ink jar, and looked up.

"I'm a laborer," said Maria. "I need to do something with my hands."

Her fingers resumed drumming the table. Tom pointed at her.

"If she won't even take this seriously…" he began.

Maria lifted the drawing to her lips, and started to blow on it. Tom's eyes bulged from his skull, as if each were preparing its own aneurysm. Maria nodded, then flipped the pad so the others could see.

The image was a perfect likeness of Tom and Jane Marshall. She'd captured them mid-speech, Tom leaning forward, his shoulders and jaw set for conflict; Jane leaning back, nose pointed away and upward, as if to escape an odor. But the expressions were what most struck Jack. Both were so derisive that anybody would want to reach out and strike their bearers—for justice's sake.

"That's not..." began Jane, but she didn't finish. Maria's picture seemed to take the wind out of her.

"*That*," said Maria, finishing her sentence, "is provocation."

Her fingers kept fidgeting. She looked in their direction, but through, not at them, as if she wouldn't allow them the dignity of eye contact.

"You let us know in a thousand ways that you despise us," said Maria, her tone remarkably calm. "You don't sit with us. You don't talk to us. We're always the last to get unbeaned."

With that, she glanced at Jack. Her comment was a gentle slap. Officially, there was no preferential norming of A's before B's. *Unofficially,* though...

"And these faces," continued Maria, "are your weapons against us. Spend a few days looking at faces like these, and we'll see how long it takes one of *you* to lash out."

She slapped the notebook on the table and leaned back in her chair. Though her words and gestures were hard, Jack thought there was something almost performative about them, as if Maria was actually past caring what the Marshalls thought, but still knew how to stick the knife where it hurt the most. Jack cupped his chin in thought. Maria had a point. The Marshalls said nothing, but he noted how they faced away from her now. They glanced out toward the young couple, their gazes like lightning in search of some softer metal. She'd taken them out of the fight.

"Well, then," said Jack, "I think we've made some progress here. The good news is that we're only twenty-eight days from landfall. Maria, in your next group assembly, perhaps you can emphasize that fact to your ... fellow travelers. Anyway, we'll all be a lot less tense when we can walk around freely, in a new place, with so many new opportunities."

Of course, it would be years before *he* could truly enjoy New World.

After a two week stop-over, Jack would have to do this all over again. He hoped the next batch of colonists got along better than this one.

"So I think we can adjourn for now-"

Maria stood, swept her implements into a heavy tackle box, and left the room. When the door closed behind her, Jane let out a long breath she'd been holding.

"That girl," she said, lowering her voice, "hates us."

Jack shook his head. "That *woman*," he corrected. "And that's the problem."

***

"Now hold still, and just relax," said Jack.

Captain Ceely exhaled, and the silhouettes contracted, taking gentle hold of his face, legs, and hands. The standing board behind him slid flush against his back. A long needle emerged and injected him. The temping machine automatically scanned for motion, but Jack always checked anyway, as if his human senses could add something to the machine's minute detection systems. But Ceely's ghost—-his beaned body and brain—was perfectly motionless. It had been brought to a state resembling death so that Ceely wouldn't even breathe during the norming process. Were he to do so, the norming wouldn't take, and Ceely would stay beaned forever.

Or, that is what would happen, if anyone separated in transit were allowed to live. In the case of an accident, the needle would make a second injection. No bean brains in New World. That was the law.

For a moment, Ceely seemed dead. Then his eyes began to flutter, and Jack saw that imperceptible shift from ghost to man.

"Hello again," said Ceely.

That was the universal signal for, "It's me, the actual person, heart, soul, and all."

Jack touched the screen. The silhouettes expanded, and the standing board contracted. Captain Ceely stepped backward out of the machine.

"Good work," said Ceely, with a perfunctory nod. "Now the others."

After Jack, who always normed first, relying on the machine to do it without human oversight, the tradition on the *Naha* was for the captain to shed his ghost, then give the all clear. Jack didn't know if that was actually the rule everywhere, but Ceely was a man with little trust.

"Don't delay," said the captain, his expression dark.

Jack nodded. He noted Ceely's agitation, but he wasn't going to rush things. The crew, and the rest of the passengers, were already stepping into their silhouettes throughout the ship. Bean brains were perfectly compliant creatures, ninety-nine percent of the time.

The great expense of traveling through void space did not owe entirely to the technology required to tear a void tunnel, or to the gates that kept the tear open. Much of it was the beaning machines that were installed in each berth. They were the most expensive tech in history, and no one even really knew why they worked. All that was certain was the consequences of going much past five days without being normed. Life as a bean brain. A thing with intellect, and perhaps will, but without pathos.

On Earth, bad legislation had made temping a right for the masses. The Earth stank of death and decay, so there was a market for going five days out of seven as a rational vegetable. Problem was, the legislation didn't account for the exquisite expense of doing it right. The earthside machines couldn't keep you perfectly still. People who beaned weekly learned to hold their breath. A whole cottage industry of zen meditation and breath-control sessions had grown up around these inferior stations.

Even so, temping failed one time out of a couple hundred. Two generations after it had been made a right, Earth had an entire minority population of the permanently beaned. Nor was this all an accident.

It wasn't a coincidence that the suicide rate had been spiking just before the beaning legislation, or that it plummeted after. For those who couldn't afford the expense, or even meet the lottery criteria for traveling to New World, becoming a bean brain was a way of staying alive. But on void ships, failing to norm was a death sentence.

And this was more than a prejudice. A tiny fraction of the permanently beaned went bad. Bad beans knew they'd lost something, and wanted it back. They could get it too. For some reason, stabbing a normie did the trick. And, if just one went bad, all the others nearby would get the itch. There were stories on Earth of beaned mobs chasing down a normie, and stabbing him, and then each other, until only one remained. That was why they lived apart.

Ocean cleaners. Asteroid miners. Cesspool scrapers. There were entire industries of dirty or dangerous jobs that only the separated worked. But they'd never cross over to New World. Even a broad-minded guy like Jack didn't want to see *that*.

He waited until his display told him that everyone on board was mounted and motionless. They were a week out from New World, so this would be the second-to-last norming he'd oversee this transit. He hoped there wouldn't be any more incidents. It was strange to have so much tension. Then again, maybe not. He thought back to the meeting with Maria and the Marshalls, and to the follow-up with just Maria and him. Was it so bad to be a B-classer, he'd asked. She wouldn't even meet his eyes. Just fidgeted the way she always did. And something she said came back to him again: "If we're equal, then why do we get normed last?"

That really burned Jack. He was *not* prejudiced. Colonization needed all kinds of people to work. And yet, there on his display was proof that she was right. There were three categories of people in beaning harnesses: Crew, Passengers, and Additional Passengers. Why should the B-classers be termed "additional." Ceely's harsh voice jarred him back to the present.

"What's the delay?" asked the captain. "Get my people up and running."

Jack nodded, wrestling with himself. He glanced up. Ceely paced the floor, his fists knotting and un-knotting. Saka was right; the man was a ball of anxiety. Jack looked back at the screen. What if, just this once, he normed the B-classers first? It would annoy Ceely, but that was all. They were only staggered by a couple minutes.

"Shaw! Hurry up," said the captain.

Jack nodded appeasingly. His finger hovered over the display. He bit his lip, then jabbed at the screen. He let out a long sigh. Not until the last second had he made up his mind.

It was done. One tiny blow for equality. The two minute timer started. He'd wake the crew next, and last of all, the A-classers. He smiled. Then the claxons sounded.

"Damn!" yelled Ceely. "Flotsam storm! Dammit, I knew!"

He turned to Shaw. Jack looked up at him, incredulous at his awful luck.

"How long on my people?" demanded Ceely.

He meant the pilot, the gunner, and the first mate.

"Uh…" stammered Jack. "It's gonna be four … four minutes—"

"What? What the hell is wrong with you?"

"I hit the wrong—"

"Fix it!" shouted Ceely. "And strap in! I'll get on the guns."

Jack slaved the display to his data pad, then ran out of the captain's berth toward the adjacent bridge. He harnessed himself in, then watched his screen. The timer seemed in no rush to get to zero. Ceely climbed into the gunner's rig, a black framework of concentric gyroscopes that let its operator spin freely. The walls of the bridge disappeared, replaced by a live display of the void, and of the dark objects now flying out of it. Jack sucked wind. To look into that maw, even for a few seconds, was to face the terrible smallness of human existence. It was then that one realized how unnatural a thing the void was. One couldn't help feel, as the jagged black rocks flew toward the ship, that the void was trying to eat them.

"It'll be fine. It'll be fine," Jack yelled. "The autoguns will…"

The autoguns were indeed doing their job. As he risked another look into the void, Jack saw the rocks being vaporized one by one. Though it might make Ceely feel better to be in the gunner's rig, it didn't matter, just like Jack looking on to make sure the captain didn't move during norming didn't matter. The machines handled everything. He took deep breaths, and glanced at his data pad. In thirty seconds he could start norming the crew. By now, the bulk of the B-classers would have already been normed. Everything was going to be fine.

"There it is!" cried Ceely, spinning within the black gyroscope. "Dammit, there she comes!"

Jack forced himself to look again. Out of the wave of black fragments came one that was different. Long and angular, chipped and flecked as if by deliberate art, the black shard bore down on them. While the guns ate up the craggy masses around it, the shard itself was untouched. The autoguns did not seem to see it.

"Leave me alone, damn you!" cried Ceely.

Manual PDC fire sprayed the shard, carving off chunks, but it failed to stop the rock's inexorable progress. It made directly for them, flipping end-over-end, as if flung from the fingers of a dark god. *Ceely's Shard!*

Jack looked at his data pad. Five seconds until he could norm the crew. Three. Two.

"I got you!" cried Ceely.

He'd cut the shard in half. For a moment, time stood still. Then the two halves re-appeared, huge in the display, just before they struck they ship.

There was a terrible sound, like a mountain falling. Jack gulped for air and found none. His eyes burned. There was noise like rushing winds. He looked up in horror at a gap into the naked maw. They'd been breached.

He stowed his data pad, hooked himself into the bulkhead clamps, and stood. Without breath, and feeling himself pulled toward the void, he moved along the wall clamps until he reached the door. He was able to drag himself through the open portal, and latch onto the bulkhead of the adjoining cabin. Something flew out of the maw and struck the base of his skull. Struggling to stay conscious, Jack found the door button and slapped it hard. Before he collapsed, he saw into the bridge. Captain Ceely was in his gunner's cage, arms and legs arched out behind him. The Shard had pierced him through.

***

It was dark when Jack woke up. The claxons no longer sounded, but the lights were low, and the emergency lamps blinked their dull yellow. His head hurt. It came back to him, the image of Captain Ceely, pinned like a moth.

He crawled to the terminal. The computer reported that the system had gone down completely after the collision, and had had to reboot itself. Life support systems were at 100%. The hull had been damaged in multiple places, but it had already healed itself. The engines appeared to be in good working order. So the emergency lights must have been tripped by the collision. Someone would have to go down there and reset them manually, but that was all.

It could certainly have been worse. Though his captain lay impaled one room over, Jack sighed in relief. It was terrible what had happened to Ceely, but, as a practical matter, the ship didn't actually need a captain to navigate the void. Anyway, there was still Saka, the first ma—

Oh.

He felt something like a cold brick expanding in his brain. Had he normed the others before the system went down? He must have. He would have. He'd been watching the countdown, and…

Hands shaking, Jack flipped through the display to the Normalization Module. He had to scan his retina again to gain access. The Activity Log option stared up at him. He only had to touch it to know. Not knowing was like standing outside a Schrodinger Chamber, waiting to find out what had become of little Whiskers. He stretched out the moment as long as he could bear, then checked.

The truth he'd already suspected hit him with the emotionless finality that only a machine could convey. The norming cycle had been interrupted when the system went down, and only the B-classers were normed. But the others were still alive, safe and sound — and beaned — in their harnesses.

And they'd never received the second injection.

Desperate, he pulled up the norming schedule. They were only three hours past the window. In actuality, it wasn't too late to norm some of them, but that didn't matter. Void ships took no chances, and not even he could force the system to norm people who were past their windows.

Jack put his hands to his face and groaned. Only a human—unbeaned—could make that desperate sound. The colossal weight of his mistake bore down on him, threatening to crush him into the floor. He'd normed the B-classers first, and only the B-classers. Every other person on board, from Saka Jinn to the Marshalls, was a bean brain.

***

"Maria."

There was a long pause before she responded.

"Yes," she said. "I'm here."

Jack took his finger off the intercom, and agonized over how to formulate the next words.

"Maria," he said, "there's been an accident."

A pause.

"What was the accident?" she said.

"Uh…"

His voice was shaking. She must have heard it through the speaker.

"During norming," he continued, "there was a storm. Captain Ceely was killed."

He had to work himself up to the full truth.

"That's terrible," she said. "Is everyone else okay?"

"No one else died," said Jack. "But…everyone isn't okay."

He wanted her to draw the appropriate conclusion. He didn't want to speak those terrible words.

"I don't understand," she said, at last.

No, of course not. Because it was unthinkable.

"Maria," he said again, "I have some very bad news. Apart from us, you, me, and the other … um … B-Class passengers, no one else was normed."

A longer pause. He could almost feel the grinding of the gears in her brain. He braced himself, waiting for her words of panic, or outrage.

"Can't you still norm them?" she said. "How long has it been?"

He shook his head, then remembered she was faraway in her cabin, and wouldn't see.

"After the window, the system doesn't let you, so…"

"Oh," said Maria. "What do the crew say?"

She still didn't understand. He couldn't blame her.

"Maria, the crew weren't normed. Just me, and the captain, and you … you guys. You see, I was…"

He was what? Trying to appear broad-minded to himself? Trying, perhaps, to impress Maria when he told her?

"Mr. Shaw? It's Mr. Shaw, isn't it?"

"J-Jack is fine."

"Jack, thank you. Will you get in trouble for this?"

He almost laughed. Trouble? There were no words for this kind of trouble. He was carrying a ship full of bean brains to New World. And in the meantime, they were a week from landfall, and would have to eat.

"Maria," he said, "I'm going to have to let people out of their cabins. To go to the galley and get food."

"No," was her instant reply. "You can't do that."

"They'll starve if I don't," he said.

"Better for you if they do," she said, coldly. "If you let them out, they'll put the rest of us at risk."

"Maria, that's mostly a myth. There's less than a one percent chance that any of them would go…"

He didn't need to finish the sentence.

"Keep my people locked in their cabins," she said, firmly. "We can eat the MREs in our rooms, and drink from the tap. You can bring us a week's supply."

"I was going to let you out in shifts," he protested. "I'll order them back to their berths when they're done, then lock them in, and let you out."

"And what if they don't go back?" she said.

Jack frowned. Did Maria still not understand that they were all beaned?

"They will," he said. "The separated are naturally compliant."

"Mostly," she said.

He scoffed. There were two-hundred-five people on board. Only half were beaned. The chances of one of them going bad were very low.

"How much do you really trust those numbers?" said Maria, as if she were reading his mind.

"I … it's scientific data," he said.

She didn't respond to that.

"Look, if I order them back, and one doesn't comply, we'll know. Then I can take care of the situation."

Half a minute passed before she responded.

"What if he's only pretending?"

That was too much. If she was this paranoid now, he could only imagine what would happen when void fear set in. And it made him angry, somehow. After all, she was herself a member of an underclass. He would have thought she'd have a little more compassion. At least feel some sympathy for what happened to the other passengers. But having been accidentally elevated, she was so quick to imagine the worst. To punch down upon the other.

"You know what," he said, "I think I *will* keep you locked in your cabins."

"Jack, wait," she said.

He sighed. "Yes, Maria."

"What if I need to contact you?"

Jack gave her his personal com code, and told her not to worry. That everything would be alright. They both knew it wasn't true.

***

He watched them from the safe room, a holdover from the days when beaning had still been an iffy process. The room had security feeds for most of the ship, and from here he had a good view of the passenger dining hall. Another feed showed the crew galley, where Saka Jinn and others ate in silence. He couldn't look at Saka, and kept his eyes on the passengers. That was when he noticed.

Even though the B-classers were confined to their quarters, the beaned A-classers still maintained the invisible barrier on one side of the dining hall. They collected their pre-fab meals, and sat down at whatever tables had come, by custom and daily routine, to be their tables. The Marshalls were there, along with their extended progeny. One of their adult daughters had a child of her own. The six-year-old bean brain moved food to her mouth, chewed, swallowed, and repeated.

There was no audio with the video feed, but he saw that some of them appeared to be talking. Not *to* each other; no bean brain did that. But they jabbered.

He'd studied this on film at university. The consensus was that it was meaningless noise. Humans, by definition, were the talking species, and in some of the beaned, babbling was simply an instinct that died hard.

It was thought that the separated couldn't remember their former lives. Their brains, when scanned, showed no signs of injury or distress. On purely physiological grounds, they were the most serene of people, no more bothered by their cog-like existence than were ants by theirs. But, like ants, they *did* communicate. Exactly how was unclear, yet entire industries on Earth depended on it. They cooperated much better than normal people.

How could they go on existing without passion? Jack thought of the several generations of beaned people now living and working apart on Earth, and it gave him chills. Their lives passed in silent mystery, free from the passions and concerns of the many whose main ambition was to leave the dying Earth. They didn't recoil from the stench of the fouled ocean, nor weep when spring came, and only the robins and house sparrows arrived. They didn't go mad. They were already as mad as they needed to be.

It was supposed that they didn't breed, but who could tell? If so, it would be without passion—a purely calculated move. Would a beaned child, if there was such a thing, also be beaned? Or, even if not, would it simply adopt the marionette-like existence of its community, having no one to talk to? Or would the separated evolve, their children becoming something like, and unlike, their parents? The more he thought about it, the more depressed he became. He'd consigned them all to this puppet existence.

But no, *he* hadn't done it. It was the Shard's fault. Jack repeated that thought, then breathed a little easier. The guilt he was bearing wasn't productive, or even accurate. That the crew members were beaned was on him. But, given the timing of things, *someone* was going to get beaned. And there were more passengers than crew, and a few more B-classers than A-classers. So he'd actually done the greatest good for the greatest number of people. He doubted they'd see it that way in New World, but it was true.

They'd be angry at Port Fair. Blake Myers would nail him to the wall. But the real reason would be that he hadn't killed the bean brains for them, and now the colonists would have to do it themselves.

So be it. Let them get their own, pristine hands bloody. The log would show he couldn't have normed everybody. Hell, maybe the VTA should have listened to Ceely about the flotsam storms.

He turned to watch the crew galley. Saka Jinn was no longer in the frame. He wondered if she'd slipped off to smoke. Did bean brains still smoke? The habit died hard, and the separated were little more than walking habits. He panned around the room, then flipped through the different feeds, but she didn't appear on any of them. Finally he found the hallway just outside her quarters. Her door was open, but he couldn't see in. Something broke up the light. Soft billows of blue-gray smoke rolled out at even intervals though the doorway, entering the corridor in near-perfect regularity as if blown from the stack of some ancient machine. A tear escaped Jack's eye, and rolled down his cheek.

***

Jack sat up quickly, spilling his whiskey. He'd been dozing again. Perhaps loneliness was making him tired. He could only check in on Maria so many times. He'd kept her people secure in their rooms, always assuring her that it was unnecessary, but all the while keeping his own vigil from the security of the safe room. And for five days, nothing had changed. But here was a change.

When he'd let them out of their quarters this time, the A-classers had gone to the dining hall, and the crew had gone to its galley. By now he'd had a chance to study each passenger in detail. Alert to signs of frustrated or erratic behavior, he'd so far seen nothing to alarm him. But just now, when he'd looked back at the crew galley, the crew wasn't there.

Jack rewound the feed, finding the moment when they'd left. He stopped it, and hit play. The crew sat in silence, as usual. Saka suddenly rose, collected her tray and food items, and walked toward the corridor. Moments later, the others followed, standing at exactly the same time. That did not alarm Jack. Bean heads were natural collectivists, and, over time, began behaving like a school of fish. What surprised him, when he finally saw it, was their destination. The crew entered the passenger dining hall.

Moving in unison, appearing and disappearing as they passed through the still-flashing emergency lights, the crew sat a table near the center, surrounded on all sides by A-class passengers. They resumed their quiet vigil.

As they sat, their mouths opened and shut like goldfish, sometimes eating, sometimes, he supposed, emitting the random nothings that were probably ticks of the brain.

He let them eat for another ten minutes, then got on the general intercom. He ordered them to clear their places, clean their tables, and return to their quarters. When these tasks were completed with perfect efficiency, the beaned shuffled back toward their cells, flashing bright and dark like Christmas decorations under the oscillating emergency lights that he would eventually have to go down and turn off. That was another problem Jack decided to push off. He downed what was left of the spilled whiskey, and closed his eyes to the world.

***

The alarm didn't wake him immediately. It blended into his dream, an exact replay of the flotsam storm that killed Ceely. Since this morning he'd twice sent the A-classers to the dining hall, and then gone back to sleep. He knew excessive sleeping was a symptom of depression. When he woke up to the alarm, he realized he'd been crying again.

"What is it now?"

He cycled through the hull feeds. The void fear hit him immediately as he scanned the abyss, but there were no rocks. He made doubly sure, then cycled out before he panicked.

"Okay," he said, standing up.

He ran a basic systems check. The lights went green, one after another, until the scan reached backup life support systems. One system stayed red. It was the auxiliary air recycler. He frowned.

"Weird," he said, and found the HVAC feed.

The HVAC room, which was part of the control complex in the guts of the ship, flashed yellow and black in the emergency lights that he still hadn't shut off. There were so many corners and shadows that it was hard to get a good look. He checked the various rooms and cubicles within the control complex. In one, he saw something on the floor that looked like debris. He strained to make it out, but the feed wasn't very clear. Maybe the second piece of Shard had come through, and had shattered on the floor. Looking for a better angle, he cycled back through all the feeds. Then he froze.

The long corridor that led from the dining hall to the cabins was lined with passengers. He'd sent the A-classers back to their rooms hours ago, and he'd seen them leave. Yet there they were, wandering the halls like ghosts. He touched the intercom.

"All passengers return to your quarters."

They didn't even react. He tried again, with the same result. He scrolled down through the systems until he came to the general com. One of its status indicators was red. Maybe the bean brains weren't responding, because he wasn't transmitting. He grabbed his personal com, and keyed in the number Maria had given him.

"Maria, can you hear me?"

A few seconds went by.

"Yes," said a sleepy voice.

He asked the same thing through the com in her berth.

"Did you hear that?"

"Nothing came out of the speakers, if that's what you mean. Is everything alright, Jack?"

He sighed.

"Just checking systems. Sorry to wake you."

So then, what was broken? Just the speakers in the bulkheads, but not the communication system itself? Jack wasn't really a tech guy, but he guessed they'd all be on the same system. Maybe something had been tripped in the control area. He'd been avoiding that part of the ship, not wanting to go that far into the *Naha*'s dark guts, not even to shut off the emergency lights. But it wasn't long before they'd make landfall, and he couldn't have bean brains wandering around.

"Damn."

He calmed himself, remembering the statistics. One in ten thousand. And he'd been watching them for almost a week, seeing no signs of aberration. Still, he had the nagging sense that something was wro—

Jack slapped the desk and smiled. *Of course.* He was going paranoid. He'd been six days in the void without beaning. No wonder he was worried. The void terror was setting in. And he'd just now stared into the void, looking for flotsam. That would only have made it worse. Objectively, the situation was perfectly explicable. Little errors happened all the time during transits, but he didn't usually hear about them, because the techs handled that sort of thing. After all, the ship *had* been struck by rocks. Of course, a few switches would be tripped. He'd just have to go down there and flip them back.

"No big deal," he said before heading for the door.

***

At first, they reminded him of a swaying wheat field from the old days. The bean brains milled about, performing their aimless waltz, that undirected shuffle of minds without selves. Then, in the silent flash of the emergency lights, they looked like sea creatures, those anemones he'd seen on old films from when the oceans held life. Halfway beings. Animate vegetables.

Jack tried to make his own legs move. Why hadn't they gone back to their rooms when he told them to? If they hadn't heard him before, then why did they rise from their tables? If they had, then why had they stopped here? Had someone told them to stop? Was one of them one of *them*?

Jack pondered the irony of it. He was a rational being, but his passions were running the show, fixing him in fear. They were without passion—only reason and limp, compliant wills. Yet they held him in thrall. When his com rang, he nearly screamed.

He fumbled, and dropped it on the ground. The clip broke off, and went sailing over the slick floor toward one of the bean brains. The man looked down briefly, then resumed his aimless walk.

"Hello!" he said, shouting into the mic.

"Jack, it's Maria."

He sighed in relief. Another human voice.

"Maria," he said, though it sounded like, "Thank you."

"I want to come out of my room," she said.

He started to say no, then thought of how terrified he was. It would be nice to have someone with him as he made his way into the ship's guts.

"Are you sure?" he said, hoping.

"Yes. It's not pleasant here. I'm going mad."

"But," he weakly protested, "you'd all be safest there. We're almost to Port Fair."

There was a long pause before she replied.

"I understand, but if nothing has happened yet, it seems unlikely that it will."

He nodded. She was so calm. Just hearing her speak made him feel better about the long walk through the line of human ghosts. And now that she'd said it, he was determined to have her with him.

"Okay, Maria," he said. "I'll come get you. I have an errand in the control room. Would you like to come with me?"

She said she would. He hastened down the corridor.

As he passed through the crowd, the bean brains hardly noticed him. Sometimes one would look up, and then not at him, but through him. They all seemed preoccupied with whatever subconscious processes filled the twilight gaps of their mental existence. There were murmurings, disconnected sounds without semantic content. That was all. When he got to Maria's room, she buzzed him in. He found her kneeling on the floor, collecting the implements of her art. Her room was plastered with small drawings and paintings, like wallpaper. He thought they were abstracts, until he saw what she had done. She'd painted the tiny details of her room, then covered the things themselves with her renderings of them. It was eerie.

"I go crazy without something to do," she said, explaining.

He nodded.

"Are you ready to go?"

"Almost," she said, carefully returning her implements to their places within her large tackle-box. She locked the box, then lifted it by its worn handle. On the way toward the door, she grabbed an art pad at random. So laden, she looked back at him expectantly.

"You're taking that stuff with you?" he asked. "It's a long walk."

She shrugged. "I'm strong."

He nodded, and they entered the corridor together. Jack strode toward the control room with new purpose. A day and a half from now, they would reach New World, with the first-ever load of bean brains. There would be hell to pay. They would definitely try to blame it on him. But at least he wouldn't have to face it alone.

***

The control complex was a maze. Black and gray corridors snaked in every direction, frequently branching and re-branching. An endless spiderweb of printed wire covered the bulkheads like graffiti, exaggerating the impression of complexity, and making the place feel alien. Jack kept his eyes glued to the data pad, following the map that would take him to the various systems he needed to check. He had no training in this area, but the void ships were so complex that even technicians needed refreshers when working in the guts. There were tutorials for each station, and all he'd need to do was turn a few things back on manually. Then they could get out of here.

"How far in do we have to go?" asked Maria.

Jack pinched-out on the screen, and swiped forward toward the first destination. His top priorities were checking on the air recycler and the intercom. After that, if there was time, he'd see about the emergency lights.

"It looks like a few hundred yards," he said. "But it's hard to tell, because of all the bends."

He could see the communication module on the map. He'd tagged it, and it flashed blue. Yet they seemed to be making little progress. Jack remembered being in grade school, making mazes at his desk to pass to classmates. His data pad said this circuitous route was the most direct one. Without it, he'd be hopelessly lost.

After a few minutes, they rounded a corner and came to a long wall of upright white tanks. The map identified those on the left as the air recyclers, and the two on the right as backups. He walked up to them, Maria following, and touched the green question mark on his data pad.

"What would you like to do?" it prompted, listing several options.

He selected "Check and Restore," and followed the prompts. They directed him to a small panel with a push-latch. He opened it, and looked inside.

Jack frowned. A chrome switch was clearly in the Off state. It was large, about the size of his forearm, and he wondered how it had become dislodged.

"Well," he said, "let's hope this works."

He flipped it back up, and saw the indicator light on the machine go green. He double-checked his data pad, confirming that it was active.

Jack shrugged. "That was easy."

"What next?" asked Maria.

"The intercom," he said. "When we get to Port Fair, we need all the A-classers in their quarters."

"You mean all the bean brains," she said, matter-of-factly.

He nodded, and began walking in the direction the map indicated. She followed, carrying her clunky case as if it were very light. He noticed she hadn't even put it down to rest when he was working on the recycler.

"That way," she continued, "they can be euthanized more easily."

He looked back at her, trying to get a read. Maria had a certain understated or flat affect. It was always hard to tell what she was thinking.

"Yes, I suppose that's what they'll do," he said, adopting his therapist's tone. "What do you think about that?"

She shrugged, the implements in her case shifting noisily as her shoulders rose and fell. "And if you can't fix the intercom, and they won't go back to their quarters?"

He nodded, expecting the question. "There's a way to do it from the safe room. Basically we can gas the hallways. Kill anything living. People in their quarters will be perfectly safe."

"I see," she said.

If Maria objected to this, he couldn't tell from her expression or tone. There were certain things that no one said out loud, but upon which everyone quietly agreed. Still, the rest of their walk passed in silence. These black, serpentine paths were no place to discuss unpleasant realities. Finally, they came to a large, open room at the back of which was a tall, rectangular prism. It was gunmetal black, and covered with small oval apertures that looked like they should be indicator lights. Most of them were off. The prism was dented, as if someone had smashed it in. Jack recognized the room from his earlier sweep of the control room feeds. On the floor, he now saw, were dozens of black fragments, long and sharp.

"Jack," said Maria, stepping toward the fragments.

He put out a hand and pressed her back.

"Don't!" he said. "What in … what is this?"

He looked around for some sign of a breach, a place where one of the rocks had come through the hull and shattered into pieces on the floor. But if that were the case, the inner hull would be distorted where it had healed itself. Then he spied the metal partition a few paces away. It had been cut or torn from its base, and someone had sliced into it, making dozens of incisions. The black fragments on the floor were no accident. Long, dagger-like, and, he now saw, neatly arrayed in rows, they had been carefully fashioned.

"Jack," said Maria, in a whisper. "Behind us."

Jack looked over his shoulder. Mutely, and with no impression of hurry, the A-classers filed in. They didn't look at Jack, or at Maria, or at anything at all. They moved like drops of water entering some hidden current.

"We need—" Jack began, but the words died on his lips.

From out of the darkness stepped Saka Jinn. Her uniform was filthy and torn. In one hand, she held a small hacksaw; in the other, one of the long black blades that she'd cut from the partition. Jack looked into her eyes. Saka looked straight back.

"Jack!" said Saka, her voice strange and high. "I want my soul."

He snatched at Maria, grabbing her by the wrist, and yanking her toward the exit. Maria's art pad fell from her hands, and she lunged for it.

"Leave it!" he shouted, tugging her along. "And drop the case. We've got to run!"

Maria pried free, and stubbornly wrapped both arms around the heavy case.

"Just lead the way," she said. "You don't need to hold my hand."

Jack had no time to argue. He was rapidly backing toward the exit, keeping one eye on Saka Jinn. The first mate looked back at him, grinning, and gestured toward the fragments on the ground. The bean brains surged, as if magnetically attracted to her, and stooped to lift the objects from the floor.

Jack ran. He held the data pad out before him, following his map as quickly as he could. Maria kept pace, the contents of her tackle box shifting, and beating out time. He cursed the box, which was like a homing beacon, following them through every turn, erasing any advantage the map gave them. Yet Maria refused to relinquish it.

When they'd made it about halfway through, Jack heard Saka Jinn's voice not three turns behind him. It had taken on a nasal, sing-song quality. "Come back, Jack!" she sang out, over and over again.

Finally, they escaped into the long corridor.

"Come on!" he shouted at Maria.

Jack sprinted for all he was worth. Maria trudged along beside him, her face expressionless. Halfway down the corridor, they passed through another clutch of bean brains. The ghosts looked up at them, curious, their eyes livelier than before. It was spreading. Somehow, it was reaching them all. When he looked back a moment later, the bean brains had turned to follow them.

They reached the end of the corridor, Jack sucking wind, Maria ten paces behind.

"Come on! Come on! Through here!"

He led her through an open portal and shut it behind them. They'd not gone twenty feet when it slid aside, and the flood poured through. Just before they turned down the last passage that led to the safe room, Jack turned and saw Saka in the midst of the swarm. They were all packed thickly into that small space. Many carried the black shivs she'd made for them.

"What did you do to me, Jack?" screeched Saka.

He dragged Maria behind him toward the safe room. Arriving at the door, he put his eye to the scanner, and cried out as the thick metal panel slid aside. He pushed Maria through, turned, and slapped the button. The door closed just as Saka reached it.

Jack quickly engaged the manual latch, and slid the bolt through so that Saka, even if she'd had the presence of mind to do so, couldn't scan her retina to open it. She pounded on the door, and soon her blows were joined by many others. The violence with which they struck made Jack's blood run cold. Yet the door held. He listened to her screams, her furious, garbled curses, but only the word "soul" passed intact through the thick metal.

Jack sank to his knees, weeping. For a long time, he didn't move at all.

"Will you do it now?" asked Maria, standing behind him.

It took him a moment to grasp what she meant. Then he remembered. The gas. Yes. Oh yes. There was no hesitation now. Now that he saw what they were. Jack stood, bracing himself against the constant pounding, and the vicious, muted cries in the corridor beyond. He touched the display and cycled through until he found the menu for emergency euthanization. He was given the option to localize it, or to flood all the exterior halls. Hands shaking, he selected just the corridors between his location and the engineering room, then deleted the selection, and chose "All," manually excluding the passenger cabins. That would do it. Maria's people would be safe. Everyone else would be dead, and good riddance. His finger hovered a moment over the kill switch, then struck down upon it like a dagger.

Jack turned on the feeds, then forced himself to watch the bean brains die. It was the least he could do. Sixty or more bodies were crammed into the corridor outside. They jerked and writhed against each other like a human hydra. Out of all of them, Saka Jinn's face stood out, twisted in wrath and indignation. But the light went out of her eyes at last, and she, too, slumped to the floor. It was done.

He staggered back, bumping accidentally into Maria. He turned. Eyes blurred with tears, he noticed her art case, which now sat open on the floor. Could she possibly think of drawing at a time like this? He looked up at her, not bothering to hide the admonishment in his face. Maria looked back at him. One of her hands stretched out to the side, weirdly fidgeting. But her right fist gripped the ink quill, point downward.

"Oh!" he said, with terrible recognition.

And Maria Cardena closed the gap between them.

***

Blake Myers shuddered. As the head receiving officer at Port Fair in New World, he'd seen a lot of strange things come through customs. Hell, he'd been at it long enough to remember another incident like this from the days before the new machines. But it had only been a dozen people then, not a hundred.

The bodies of all the A-classers and crew were bagged and tagged. He didn't look forward to the messages he'd be sending to next of kin. At least he didn't have to tell them in person. A bottle through the void was all they'd get from him. Then there was the matter of Jack Shaw, the ship's head shrink. His body hadn't been found at all. Well, maybe that was for the best. One less complication.

Blake walked to his office and pushed open the door. A young, pretty woman with dark hair and piercing green eyes sat in front of his desk. Now that the ugly stuff was done, he'd finally have the pleasure of interviewing her. When he entered the room, she stood and nodded politely.

"Hello, Maria," he said. "Is it alright if I call you Maria?"

She smiled bashfully. "Oh yes, Mr. Myers."

Blake flushed. She was quite pretty.

"No need to stand for me. You've had quite an ordeal. Please just sit and rest."

She did, and he went around to take a seat behind his desk.

"Like I said," he continued, "real traumatic stuff. I don't want to put too much pressure on you, here. Just trying to nail down a few details."

She nodded, and smiled appreciatively.

"Well, so, we're trying to figure out exactly what went wrong," he said. "And the thing is, I've got two competing narratives. On the one hand, there's clear evidence from the ship log that the bean machines went down in a void storm. And that's what led to this whole thing."

She nodded.

"But there's an issue…"

She stiffened, slightly. Blake noticed, but disregarded it. She'd been through a lot.

"The thing is," he continued, "there've been a lot of rumors, a lot of talk, even in official channels, of some kind of plot by beaners—sorry, separated folk—to get some of their people to New World. And, well … you're laughing."

Maria put her hand over her mouth, stifling the laugh.

"I'm sorry, Officer Myers," she said. "I just didn't think a person like you would be into conspiracy theories. I mean what you're describing is impossible, isn't it?"

Blake shrugged.

"Probably so, Miss Cardena. Maria. But there's a lot of fear about that, from both ends of the void. Nobody wants a bunch of them over here, you know?"

She nodded. "Of course. But they couldn't make a plan like that and carry it out. Could they?"

He shrugged again. "Who knows. With some of them having beaned kids, and those kids growing up, who knows what might happen? Some people think beaned kids would be different. Clever. Maybe even devious. I know, it sounds crazy, but we've just got to cross our Ts and so on."

"Yes," she said, "the devil in the details, and all that."

He smiled at her. "And you would know about that, right?"

She looked non-plussed.

"What do you mean?" she said.

"I mean, you're an artist, right?" he said, indicating the ink stains on her fingers.

Maria laughed, and breathed a heavy sigh. "Wow, Captain Myers! You're incredibly observant!"

He took the compliment in stride, and wondered if he'd run into her in some other context.

"It's Blake," he said, and it was his turn to be bashful.

She smiled, and repeated the name. Blake straightened himself up in his chair, nodded to himself, and slapped the desk with finality.

"Well, I guess that's all, Maria. My only other question is, how are you holding up with all of this? I mean, personally. Are you alright?"

Maria's green eyes flashed at him, and she smiled.

"Blake," she said, "I feel newborn."

THE MOTHER

Red dust pelted the Permaglass. There was a frenzied sadness in its movement, as if it knew its time was coming to an end. Alexa Divus took a moment to stare out into the storm, and wondered if she'd see the change in her lifetime. But then, of course she would. Alexa was always forgetting that she had many lives to live. The human mind couldn't really adapt to the conquest of death. She frequently caught herself thinking in terms of limits. So much of human thought referred, in oblique ways, to an end. The melancholy feeling she had when she considered the passing of Mars was—she could grasp it intellectually—just another vestige of those old limitations. Like all things under Unity's sun, Mars would be made new.

These primitive emotions, and her instinctive resistance to change, were something she could at least understand. Her assignment here was another matter. Alexa's career path to this point had been straight as an arrow. Ambition was self-thinking, so, of course, she wasn't ambitious. However, she would not have been so confused if her high marks and high recommendations had landed her somewhere in the heart of Unity. But on Choosing Day, she'd been assigned here. Why on Earth would they send a behavioral scientist to the Adonis Project?

Her expertise was in personality management with a focus on the vestiges, those hard-wired beliefs, assumptions, and illusions that posed an obstacle to human happiness. She knew little exogeology beyond what the average person knew. She'd aced her only course on that subject at the Academy, but then she'd aced every course. Yet her assignment here couldn't have been a mistake. It was red-marked, so it had come from Om.

Alexa didn't know how she felt about that. To be singled out in such a way was an honor, but to be especially chosen for a career path that held no personal appeal for her sounded like a nightmare. She'd been having actual nightmares lately. In most of them, she was stuck somewhere.

Had Om misunderstood her? Or worse, had she misunderstood herself? Why would he send her here, to this desolate place, where she was more of an observer than a shaper? Unity knew no prejudice, and Om, so they said, made no mistakes, but Alexa couldn't help but wonder if her own natal matrix were the reason. When unification came, her "family"—another vestigial concept—had gone its own way. She'd long learned to ignore the feelings of bitterness over their choice to remain savages, and she'd long stopped imagining her parents' demise on the preserve. When their "natural death" had come, had they really welcomed it? Had it seemed wholesome and human as they watched their bodies decay, day-by-day, until the preventable end?

A low whining sound pulled her back to the present. AH-A4 stood in the oval portal. He looked pensive, if a machine could be that. The bulbous android was technically part of the crew, and so its mental health fell under her care as well.

She didn't like him. It. Whatever. But she couldn't put her finger on just why. Aha's narrow hinged legs, his forward-leaning gait, and his large rectangular muzzle made him look like the offspring of a giant grasshopper and hound dog. And a can opener. He was a service android, one of a limited series of bio-machines that served on the off-planet projects. Others like him were building the harvesting stations on the outer planets, and laying the foundation for a vast industrial infrastructure that would someday permit Unity to assemble huge vessels in the void. Like the others, AH-A4 was made to endure extreme environments. Unlike the A3s, which were fabricating the harvesters that would constantly draw raw materials up from the planetary surfaces, Aha was a husbandry droid. He was a hideous thing.

"Hello, Aha," said Alexa. "Can I help you with something?"

AH-A4 inclined its head, just like a human being would when carefully choosing his words.

"The bees are dying," the droid finally said.

Its voice had all the expected emotional inflections of a human being, but the tone was androgynous, and the large, boxy muzzle never opened when it spoke.

"Oh?"

"Yes, Doctor Divus. The population is 3.3 percent reduced."

Alexa waited for it to elaborate, but AH-A4 just stood there, leaning over her like a peaceful praying mantis. That's how it was with the droid. AH-A4 might have human brain tissue in its neural network, but it didn't seem to understand conversation as distinct from mere reporting.

"And does Aha have a theory as to why?" she said.

Aha took a step toward her, which gave Divus a momentary fright, but the droid extended its long arm, and pointed at the Permaglass. She followed the spindly limb to a dome on the distant horizon. It was one of the three farm modules that served the Adonis project. While the others produced food for their immediate consumption, Dome Two was part of the terraforming project proper. Aha, being an Animal Husbandry and Agricultural model, assisted the scientists there in breeding plants that could grow on Martian soil when the Adonis Project reached Stage 4. The exobotanists didn't much like the droid, considering him a nuisance, but Aha had made several suggestions that had advanced their work.

"Aha believes the honeybees require more space, and a wider variety of pollinating plants," said the droid.

Divus furrowed her brow.

"And why should the bees care about what plants they pollinate?"

She knew nothing about bees, but Aha never elaborated without prompting.

"Aha doesn't know," said the droid.

This time, the droid's delivery was eerily human. She wondered what he really was.

"Then what makes you think that this is the problem?" said Alexa.

AH-A4 looked away, as if pondering, before he again met her gaze.

"Aha doesn't know," he said again. "Only…"

She waited, more intrigued by the droid's occasional flashes of personality than by his problem. Bees were kept for pollination, and because someone on Earth thought honey would improve their moods. If the bees were dying at such a negligible rate, it was an inconvenience, but they could always import more. The droid looked at his feet.

"Aha believes that the circumstances are unnatural to the bees, and that this results in their death."

"Unnatural?" prompted Alexa. "Elaborate."

Aha seemed to shrug. "Bees are meant for larger spaces."

"Meant?"

"Programmed," said Aha, correcting himself.

"Well perhaps we should breed better bees," suggested Divus, not really serious about it.

"Aha has tried this, of course," returned the droid, still gazing at the floor. "But this program is above the level of genes."

Alexa raised her eyebrows. "If that's the case," she said, "we'll simply have to order more bees."

The droid's head swiveled up, and its large blue eyes seemed to fix on hers. He swayed a little, as a person might when considering the wisdom of saying out loud what he was thinking. Alexa knew these were not programmed behaviors. These AH models were neural networks integrated with human brain tissue. They were learning machines, and they sometimes developed behaviors that had not been part of their basic programming.

Yet it was one thing for a machine to come up with a better way to make an airlock. It was quite another to see one take on gestures that were uniquely human. It made her wonder if she were only imagining it. After all, like the cleverest animals on Earth, neural machines sometimes had what appeared to be flashes of brilliance. But just as with the animals, these flashes were outliers. There were no octopus scientists, ape engineers, or android poets. Still, it made her wonder what would happen if she were to deliberately amplify those sections of its brain matter that in humans were associated with specific aspects of personality.

"Aha does not like this solution," said the android.

"And why not?" asked Alexa, though she knew the answer.

"It is inefficient," answered the droid. "At the current rate of loss, the population will be forty percent diminished within two U-months. Adonis Station is resupplied at intervals of four months. Cargo space on resupply ships is scarce, and honeybee colonies have a low survivability rate in space. This is neither sustainable, nor cost-effective."

Alexa observed that when the droid said more than a few sentences, its human behaviors disappeared. Suddenly it was a machine like any other. But Aha was right. Simply ordering more honeybees was not a good solution, which was one of the reasons why the crops in Domes One and Three were machine pollinated. Aha did this itself, when he—it, she still couldn't settle on a pronoun—wasn't tending to the bees. Keeping insect pollinators here was an experiment, one cooked up by some committee in Kata Holis. It had never seemed like a good idea to her.

"In that case, Aha, the bees will have to adapt, or they will die out."

AH-A4 leaned in closer, and again she felt uneasy. He could not harm her, but it was intimidating to have a large machine, insectile, and yet humanoid, tower over her in that way.

"Then Aha will fail, Doctor," it said.

Alexa suppressed the odd empathy she felt for it. Like people, machines had many directives, and the neural machines experienced tension between these priorities in some manner that was not well understood. Just as their decision-making processes were somewhat opaque to human analysts, so was what might be called their "feelings of conflict." They did have integrated brains, after all. Did they also have experiences? In any event, there were times when the AH models seemed to need help identifying the correct order of priorities.

"If Aha loses the bees," she replied, instinctively resisting the more natural *you*, "but continues to successfully pollinate the crops, then Aha hasn't failed."

Aha had no eyelids, but she could have sworn its eyes narrowed. She felt compelled to elaborate.

"Your prime directive is to preserve the crops. The bees are only a means to that end."

Aha took a step back, and sank a little, almost as if it were slumping. It vocalized something so low that she couldn't make it out. Had the droid mumbled to itself?

"What's that, Aha? I didn't hear you."

The droid paused, then met her gaze.

"I do not want that," said Aha.

Alexa smiled in spite of herself.

"You? *You* don't want that?"

She knew it had no real self-awareness, but neural machines were adaptive, and, in extended conversation, would sometimes adopt the first person. As nearly as anyone could tell, this was not a breakthrough of consciousness, but a mistake by the machines. They were using the first person as an intensifier, not understanding why it intensified. The proof of this was their inconsistency. At other times they would suddenly use the second person, or the first person plural, and in ways that did not fit the context. Still, it was eerie when they guessed right.

"If Aha can pollinate himself, and if the bees are inefficient, then why does it matter to Aha whether they survive?"

The droid shrugged, another learned behavior.

"Aha doesn't know," it said.

Alexa smiled, and adopted a gentle tone.

"Then Aha should focus on what it does know. It knows its priorities. The bees are secondary."

To her utter surprise, the android took two steps back, and sat down on a chair. Seated, it looked even more like a grasshopper, its bent knee joints poking up in the air so that they were level with its head. It draped its long arms between them, as a human might rest them on his thighs. The droid hung its muzzle for a moment, then raised it in what she could have sworn was a gesture of pleading. Though its lipless mouth was always closed, its voice coming from small speakers in its neck, the tilt of it was somehow melancholy.

"There is a way to save the bees. Possibly. Aha could build small passages to connect the domes, allowing the bees to move freely between them. Aha is rated for fabrication. We … I could do this myself."

Alexa took a deep breath, and leaned back in her chair. She poured herself a water from the beaker on her desk, and tried to understand what she was seeing. The droid had made itself small in order to plead with her. It was acting as if it cared about the bees. It seemed clear to her that this request had been its whole purpose in coming. And it had come to her, the behavioral scientist, and not to Natalia, the program director for Adonis, as if it understood that while a direct request of this kind from a droid would be denied, going through her might work. This machine wasn't just behaving as if it felt an irrational tenderness for the bees. It was playing politics. Yet there had to be an explanation that could be cashed out in pragmatic terms. She needed to find out what it was, if only to better understand what this being was. When she began speaking, she was really thinking out loud.

"Aha knows that the program director would have to approve this request. He must also understand that connecting the domes would mean a considerable time and expense, and that this would require more materials, and more precious cargo space on the next shipment. Why does Aha think this would be a sensible use of resources?"

The droid nodded, as if it had anticipated the question.

"In the long-term, insects are far more efficient pollinators than machines," said the droid. "And Aha requires maintenance, and … and will someday be replaced with a new model. When Aha is put out of service, Aha's bees will no longer have Aha to watch over them. Aha cannot be certain that Aha's replacement will understand the importance of natural pollinators to Stages Five, Six, and Sev—"

"But we're in Stage Two," she said, cutting the droid off.

It was unnerving hearing a machine making contingency plans for its own demise, or calling the bees its own. But she was stalling. What the droid said made sense. Terraformed Mars would need natural pollinators, and these could hardly be established after the fact. They'd need to be integrated into whatever variety of flora could be made to grow on the reshaped planet.

Alexa felt suddenly troubled. What if the droid was right that another AH model might be unaware of this issue? After all, Aha had been here for several years before the bees had come, and, in all that time, had managed pollination without any need for them. These ideas it had were not part of its programmed mission. Nor was Aha responding to an immediate obstacle to fulfilling that mission. The droid was concerned about a future hypothetical. Somehow, its augmented neural network had discovered a potential future problem, and Aha was trying to head it off.

Or was it? As impossible as it seemed, Dr. Divus could imagine a different scenario, one which better matched what she was actually seeing in AH-A4. She needed to contact the program director as soon as possible.

Alexa suddenly stood, and the droid followed dutifully.

"AH-A4, you've made your concerns clear. If I understand, you'd like me to put in a request to Director Farush to allow you to connect the domes. Is that right?"

Aha bowed humbly.

"Right then," she said, businesslike, "I'll do so."

The droid seemed to visibly relax, and it was that gesture that really convinced Alexa Divus that she was right. It chilled her to the marrow. Wordlessly, she gestured for it to leave her alone. AH-A4 hesitated, as if it had expected to wait while she called the director. Then the droid bowed again, and left the room in its ambling, insectile stride.

***

Two sky-blue ghosts walked across the red dust of Planum Daedalia. The taller of the figures was Natalia Farush, program director for the Adonis

Project. Alexa's vac suit was the same standard size as Natalia's, but, as she was shorter, it bunched around her extremities in an unflattering fashion. With the crest of Dome Three just within sight, Natalia made a sign to Alexa. Divus nodded, and both women changed the settings on their wrist consoles. They went off-net, for a moment beyond the reach of hearing—or help—from the Adonis colony, before switching to short range radio.

"You came to me highly recommended, Divus. And that's the only reason I'm doing this."

Alexa nodded.

"No, speak into the mic."

"Understood, ma'am," said Alexa.

"Good. We are making something of a spectacle of ourselves by going out here," continued Farush, "but I trust you have a good reason for these precautions."

"Yes," said Divus, absently scraping with her boot at the alien dust. "Several."

"Fire away then," said Farush.

Alexa sighed, and then realized she had done so into the mic. "This is going to sound crazy."

Natalia laughed, and her eyes through the visor were almost scornful. Alexa couldn't help but notice the woman's cold beauty. Still, she was taken off guard.

"I didn't..." she stammered, "I don't know why you're laughing."

"Because I think I know what you're going to say," replied her superior. "You're going to tell me that AH-A4 is displaying eerily human behaviors. You're gearing yourself up to convince me of this fact. You're afraid he'll hear us."

"I ... yes, that's right," said Alexa, non-plussed. "And ... you don't think so?"

Farush shrugged. "I don't know, and I don't care. I'm not an intellectual like you, Divus. Aha would stop functioning before it could do us any harm. In the meantime, he/she/it serves a purpose. But that purpose, you should know, has an expiration date."

Alexa nodded.

"Aha actually mentioned this. *He* was ... contemplating his own obsolescence, seemingly."

Farush nodded. "I've heard of this kind of thing. There was an A3 unit on Jupiter doing something similar. Emphasis on *was*."

"He was deactivated?" asked Alexa, though she knew the answer.

"That's policy," confirmed Farush. "Whether or not they can *think* think, if they reach a point where they can convince us, that's far enough. Om excluded, of course."

"Of course," said Alexa. "Well, I guess that makes the conversation easier … in a way. I don't have to convince you—"

"—Like I said, I don't care either way. And you should know, they *all* have an expiration date."

"Oh?" said Alexa, surprised.

"Yes. You're a party member, so I'm not revealing any big secret. Once the industrial infrastructure is in place, we're phasing out the droids. They are a means to Unity. That's all."

Alexa frowned.

"But then, how will Om fulfill Unity's promises for the human race? Who will do the hard labor, if not droids?"

"That is a secret, but Om has a plan. Let's just say that in the near future, everyone who labors will very much want to."

Alexa frowned again, unable to suppress the bitterness she felt. Some great project of human engineering was taking place, and she, despite all she'd accomplished, despite her party membership, was completely in the dark, exiled instead to this lifeless red rock. Farush looked penetratingly at her through the Permaglass visor.

"Do you think you're being left out? You think the allmind put you here to punish you for your regressive parents?"

Alexa was afraid even to nod. Farush smiled, and there was something else besides scorn in the smile.

"No, Dr. Divus. Far from it, in fact. You may not realize it, but he has his eye on you. You were sent here for some purpose. Not even I am allowed to know what that is."

The scorn returned, and, with a flash of insight, Alexa saw that her superior envied her. In that moment, Alexa Divus felt a rush of power. She straightened up, becoming almost as tall as Farush.

"I guess you already know what Aha wants me to request of you?"

"No," said Farush. "Tell me."

"He requests permission and materials to construct special conduits between the domes so that his bees, *his bees*, can travel freely between them."

"Request denied," said Natalia, sharply. "But isn't it interesting that you felt obligated to pass on a machine's 'request'? Did you bring us all the way out here just for that?"

Alexa ignored the question, and pressed on. "I assumed that would be your answer," she said. "But I have a request of my own."

Through two layers of Permaglass, Natalia's raised eyebrows took on exaggerated effect, making her hawkish.

"Then you'll be happy to know," said the woman, carefully, "that, by direct order from Om, I'm to grant your requests, all of them, provided they don't threaten protocol. Or the facilities. Bee conduits might do that, by the way. Cross-contamination, and all that."

Alexa sensed that Farush's additional explanation about the conduits was an attempt to distract from the admission that, in some way, the director was beholden to *her*.

"Fine, then," Alexa continued. "I'm requesting permission to run an experiment."

Farush paused.

"On what?"

"On whom," corrected Alexa. "Maybe."

Farush took a step back. Alexa was confused, wondering what she'd said. Presently, Alexa realized that, for an instant, the director had thought she'd been referring to her. Natalia was afraid of her. Indeed, the shadow of fright that had passed over the director's face would trouble Alexa for many years. Not least, because she found it intoxicating.

"On the droid, of course," said Alexa.

"Of course," replied the other, and barely disguised rage set in the glass-blurred lines of her face. "What do you want to do?"

Alexa took a deep breath.

"I want to isolate the regions in AH-A4's neural network that are particularly associated with his affection for the bees. Then I want to amplify them."

"Amplify? But why?"

"Because," said Alexa, "I want to see what Aha will do, when he loves them even more, and we tell him no."

Farush shook her head at the doctor. For a moment, Alexa thought she'd be denied. Farush would argue that this put them all at risk. But Alexa had misread the director.

"You … you really are a cold one, aren't you? No wonder he favors you."

Alexa flushed with anger.

"What the hell do you mean?"

"Nothing," said the other, shaking her head again. "What makes you think this experiment will bear any fruit?"

"Because," said Alexa, regaining her bearings, "it is my belief that AH-A4 is being led by his affections. You see, it's often the same way with people. We like to imagine that we reason to conclusions, and then our affections follow. But in real life, we often rationalize to support our affections. And sometimes, that isn't so misguided. Sometimes our intuition knows first, and reasons follow afterward. Aha cannot harm us, and he must obey your orders. The question is, how will he reason—and what will he do—when he cares even more for the bees, and yet can do nothing to help them?"

Natalia shrugged. "Perhaps the droid will simply malfunction."

"Perhaps," said Alexa, excited, "or even … even go mad."

Farush stared at her. "You are a piece of work, Dr. Divus. You … you're cruel!"

"To a robot?" Alexa laughed.

Farush looked away from her and stared out into the red and black plane. She stared for so long, that Alexa became uncomfortable, and followed her gaze, half expecting to see some dreadful, many-legged thing on the horizon. But all she saw there was Mars' dusty flesh, scarlet and black, and lifeless still.

***

Alexa Divus swam through the floating interface. She flicked through her communications one-by-one. The last few from Director Natalia Farush had a decidedly mixed tone; robotic, as if Natalia wished to eschew all pleasantries, yet appeasing, as if Farush knew that this woman now under her command would one day surpass her. All of Natalia's orders sounded suspiciously like requests, and Alexa noticed that she hadn't been asked to check in, or to explain her use of time, for some U-months. And, aside from her ongoing observations of Aha, Alexa hadn't had to do much.

There were small things. Tensions between the technicians. A formal accusation of rigidity, which in turn stemmed from an adventure in the pleasure center that had not gone as one of the parties planned. Episodes like this made Alexa look forward to the day when total experiential immersion, that Holy Grail of pleasure science, was finally a reality. In the meantime, men and women had to endure the eternal contradictions that reality posed to their fantasies.

For the time being, there was near immersion, and the neurotropic gel, and, if all else failed, targeted memory removal. The road to the simplicity of Unity was a complicated one, and allowances had to be made—for the present. The day would come when these vestiges of man's individualistic past could no longer be tolerated, even as mistakes.

Now, having dealt with the day's annoyances, she turned to her real work. Om, she was convinced, had sent her here for a very definite reason. That reason was tied to the strange machine they called Aha. All her expertise was in the vestiges, and in how to phase them out of the human race. Now she was faced with a non-human that seemed to have developed a nurturing instinct. What did it mean? How could it be stopped? How had it even arisen?

With the help of some technicians, and her own knowledge of the human brain, she'd isolated those regions in Aha's cyber-cerebrum that had become over-developed, or which went hot in the presence of his small insect children. These she had been able to strengthen, both through external modification, and in guided focus sessions with the droid. And she could watch his brain's daily drama from the comfort of her soft chair.

As expected, this had generated any amount of neural activity. She'd watched it rage through his artificial brain with the intensity of a Martian dust storm. The tempest grew daily, until she was sure he must soon disable himself, or at least fail in his duties. But that hadn't happened.

Instead, after a few weeks of mental chaos, the storm stabilized. It hadn't gone away, but now there was a structure to it. Aha's behavior seemed normal. Well, that wasn't quite it. He seemed at peace, as if a great weight had been lifted from his shoulders. That was when it had occurred to Alexa to compare Aha's daily movements before and after the operation. And now it all made sense.

The door buzzer chimed.

"Come in, Aha," said Alexa.

The android entered, folding himself into the room one gangly appendage at a time. He stood just inside the threshold, patient as a dog.

"Please, come over here, and take a seat."

With a kind of nod, the droid ambled over, and carefully seated itself. There was a certain grace to its movements. A new purpose. She thought of a mother hen, its feathery bulk folded over its brood to keep it warm, its life's aims now singular.

"To what do I owe the pleasure, Doctor?" said the droid.

His androgynous voice now sounded almost feminine. Perhaps, she thought to herself with amusement, she should be thinking of the droid as a her.

"I wanted to congratulate you, Aha."

"Oh?" said the droid in its disembodied, close-mouthed manner. "For what, ma'am?"

She smiled. "I think you know the answer to that, Aha."

The droid said nothing, but seemed to tense. After a moment, it relaxed, and tried to assume its former nonchalance. *So,* she thought, *and now, deception.*

"I've been monitoring you closely since the operation, naturally."

"Yes, Doctor, I expected you would," said Aha.

She laced her fingers together on the desk.

"Is there anything that Aha wishes to tell me?"

The droid hesitated, clearly treading with care.

"Is there … anything that Dr. Divus wishes, in particular, to know?" said he/she/it.

She smiled. "No, Aha. I think you know that I already know. Don't you?"

The droid made no gestures confirming or denying. Alexa thought back to her childhood, and remembered similar inquests before her own fath—, her seminal radix, rather, many years ago.

"You were very clever about it, AH-A4. If it hadn't occurred to me to compare your routines before and after the operation, I never would have caught you. You were just so cool about it all. Nothing the least bit suspicious, except, of course, that you were smooth as butter, when you should have been coming to pieces inside."

The droid stiffened.

"I did not disobey."

"I did not disobey," she mimed, gently mocking him. "I notice you didn't say 'I obeyed.' There is a difference, isn't there Aha, between obeying and not disobeying? Somehow, I think you understand that too."

The droid looked around the room nervously. Its grasshopper legs leaned away from her. It did all the little things a human being would do who wanted to leave the room, but couldn't.

"The numerous additional trips to Domes One and Three were only a clue, of course," she continued. "What sealed it, for me, was your reports on the bee population. I understand that the colony has more than rebounded?"

The android nodded, its long muzzle bobbing up and down once.

"I couldn't figure out how you pulled it off. I scanned the ground for tunnels, and found nothing. I watched you on the security feed, but your hands were empty, as usual. Really, Aha, I feel rather silly that it took me so long to figure it out."

The droid slowly moved its hands apart, as if to show they were also empty. Then it placed them on either side of the stool on which it sat. She thought Aha was bracing himself—no, definitely *herself*—for a coming blow. Alexa stood, and walked over to the bee mother. Even seated, the spindly creature craned over Alexa.

"You've just come from Dome Three, haven't you?"

"As you commanded, Doctor," said the droid, weakly.

Its disembodied metal voice was now unmistakably female.

"In that case, Aha, open your mouth."

The droid hesitated. Was she resisting? Was she planning to disobey Alexa? No, Alexa decided. That was impossible. The mental struggle Alexa perceived on Aha's expressionless metal face was evidence of more rationalization. She was trying to find a way to not obey without disobeying. Finally, it was as if something broke inside her. The mother droid opened her mouth.

From out of the darkness of her long chrome maw, many little beings sprang forth. They crawled up from her inner depths, spilled out onto the ridges of her mouth, and tiptoed up around her optical lenses. As the light from the room spilled in, they continued to pour out, until Aha's open mouth became like a portal to another reality. The bees buzzed around their mother's head, none too sure of the sterile room in which they found themselves, and content to stay close to their protector. The android fell onto her knobby knees, haloed by the adoring yellow bees that buzzed around her head. Her arms opened wide, pleading. The sight of it shook Alexa to her core. It would haunt her long after she deactivated the droid. Progress in the new science of personality management would require many such sacrifices, but this one would always stay with Alexa.

"God!" exclaimed Alexa, stepping back from the robot supplicant. "What the hell are you?"

The android called AH-A4 shook her head, and shrugged her knobby shoulders. Her grasshopper body shuddered.

"What are any of us, ma'am? What are any of us?"

THE LAST ONE LISTENING

It was a man-killing gradient for the four-wheeled, let alone the two-legged. And he didn't want to see any of *those*. Twenty feet from the crest, the squad car made a U-turn. Its white paint was chipped and flecked with dirt. Its engine bellowed like a sick bull. A year ago these curbs were packed thick, people trusting to their parking brakes against gravity.

Officer Rhett Redman rolled up before the three-story house, with the nose of his squad car pointed downhill. All of the windows were boarded up, save the small one in the loft apartment where the shade was pulled, just as it had been when they left. This wasn't his house. It wasn't Russel Walt's either. It was just a good place to hole up, when it all came down. Wooden planks and bits of torn-off furniture were nailed across the windows, and a heavy mahogany dinner table still barricaded the front entryway, fitting snugly. Gemma Walt had thanked God for that, like it was a plan. If anyone else had said something like that, in a place like this, Rhett would have called bullshit. But it was Gemma.

Rhett engaged the parking break. He reached for the ignition, then stopped. It was dusk. There was a storm in the air, further hastening the coming darkness. Maybe he should leave the squad car running, just in case. Things were starting to turn, but you never really knew. They liked the night.

With his car trouble earlier, Rhett thought it might be better to leave it running. He might have to jet out. The car was leaking something. What if it wouldn't start again? But there could be squatters around, even if none of the quick were lurking about. Squatters would want the car. Or worse, they'd want rescuing, and he had enough on his plate. The promise was the only mission now. Otherwise he couldn't live with himself, or with Gemma and her boy.

Rhett tapped the dash, thinking. He loosened the gun in its holster. Shoot a squatter, or be stuck here with them? He decided to let the engine run. Better to deal with the living than with the quick.

When he stepped out on the broken asphalt, the clouds were gray, going black. He shut the door as quietly as he could, then pushed it flush. The sky opened up then, like it had heard him. A steady drizzle began. He tapped the weapon on his hip and walked toward the house. A sign on the small lawn read "Leafy Green." It had been a home daycare before the owners fled. The medicinal odor of a small eucalyptus tree out front caught and hung in the ozone. It seemed impossible that children had laughed here only a year before.

Rhett took the stairs to the front door. The table was still lodged snugly in the front enclave. It meant Russel hadn't left. Not that way, anyway. He'd have to check around back to be sure. Stepping out into the rain, hand resting on his sidearm, Rhett jogged behind the house. He grabbed the fence, lifted himself, and looked over. The back porch hadn't changed. A brown love seat straddled the door. Furniture was piled on top of it. The ugly detritus on the steps and lawn made the house look evil. But nothing had been moved. Russel was still here, in some form. Rhett sighed, and walked back to the front.

By now the mist had become a steady falling rain. It was a cold November in San Francisco. He hunched his shoulders. Again he climbed the front steps, and stood before the mahogany table jammed tight within the entryway. He listened. Had that been the patter of quickly moving feet? No, he decided, it was only the rain. He knew the risks, but he also knew you could get yourself worked into a state where everything sounded like the quick. There were not that many of them left. After a year of hell, Armageddon had lost interest in the human race. Everywhere you looked, the quick were slowly dying.

Still, the thought of pounding on the door gave him pause. He knew he would do it anyway, but he delayed. Just as he'd waited too long on that night, more than three weeks ago, when one of them came alongside of Russel. His delay was the reason Russel'd had to stay here. The reason that Rhett had become Gemma and Danny's only protector, with Russel's beautiful wife and Danny, the son anybody would want, now under his own wing. He and Jill had never had kids, and Rhett knew that it had played a role in their break. But he loved Danny. And Danny's real father might well be dead—or something else—inside the house called Leafy Green.

Standing before the barricade, he hesitated again. Sure, he'd made a promise, but how much did he truly want to drive out of here, back to the waiting station, with Russel alive and well in the front seat? He pursed his lips, then struck the table three times hard.

Rhett was a strong man, stocky like a bulldog, but the sound of his knocking seemed to die inside the heavy table. The thick storm air swallowed it up too. Behind him, even the champing growl of his squad car was muted by the falling rain. He'd have to knock more to be sure. He'd have to yell his head off, if Russel was to hear him. If Russel even could hear him. He did want that. Of course he did.

"Hey!" he cried. "Hey, Russel! It's me, Rhett! Can you hear me?"

No answer. The rain now fell in sheets behind him. He could barely hear the rumble of the squad car. He pounded again, maybe ten times.

"Russel! It's me, Rhett! You alive in there, buddy?"

They'd left him in the loft with a month's supplies. Bandaged up his wounds. Promised to come back for him. That was all they could do. Rhett vividly remembered looking on through the threshold of the loft room at Russel and Gemma's tearful goodbye. There'd been tears in Rhett's eyes too, but that was some complicated water. Seeing Gemma leaning over her husband, soft, supple sunshine pressed against darkness, he knew what it was that that other part of him, the selfish part, was hoping for.

"I'll take care of him, Gemma. First, I gotta get you and Danny to safety. I'll come right back for him. Promise."

"But do we really have to leave him?" she'd asked, and then looked at him with that piercing innocence that had troubled him over the years.

He hadn't known what to say. It was only a scratch, and some people got over it. Russel might recover, but if he didn't...

There were reasons, good reasons, to leave Russel, but Rhett couldn't deny that there were other reasons too. So he'd been unable to answer Gemma. Strange to say, it was Russel who'd come to his rescue.

"We can't take the risk, Gem. This is how it's got to be. And you know Rhett. He'll get you both there. Anybody in the way's going down. I trust him with our lives."

Good Russel. Righteous, trusting man. He'd looked straight at Rhett when he'd said those things. There was something in that look. Had he known?

They'd been partners at SFPD for six years, and in that time, they'd seen any amount of twisted shit. Rhett's life had gotten twisted too, with Jill leaving him, and him running through women like a dog through mud. Meanwhile Russel's life only got better. In their friendship, as in their work, Rhett told the jokes and kicked the asses. Russel was by the numbers. Same way he played basketball. Not all showy, but getting things done. Tall and lanky like a farmer, Russel didn't look like the guy who'd be married to Gemma. He was solid, though. Give him that. At work, they balanced each other out. Their personal lives, though. That was more yin and yang.

So he'd taken Gemma and Danny, and hauled ass out of there for the shelter. The government called them waiting stations—not disaster shelters; not fortified, last-ditch, get-out-of-hell-free camps—because it sounded better. Like they were all just waiting for things to go back to normal. Like they were just gassing up between civilizations. There was one at Mt. Tamalpais, one at Mt. Diablo, and one at Mt. Hamilton. Diablo was the closest, so he'd headed for that. The better to drop them off and get back to Russel.

But as he'd driven that way, stuck in bumper-to-bumper traffic, it'd occurred to him that Diablo's station was the smallest of the three. Being closer to San Fran also meant it would be more packed. Hamilton Station was supposed to be three times as large. Gemma and Danny would be far more comfortable there, and Russel would definitely want that for them. True, it was thirteen hours more driving, but if he got off the highway now, and went south, traffic should be lighter till he got near San Jose. He could dodge the city till he got close. It made sense. There were reasons behind it.

So he'd headed south, farther away from San Francisco. Farther away from Russel Walt, who lay shivering in the corner of the loft at Leafy Green. In the end, it hadn't helped much. Others had had the same notion, so the twenty-four hour road trip stretched to two weeks. In those weeks he'd watched Gemma grow more nervous, thinking about Russel. Then there was the night when the quick came out of the forest. It had been a close call. After that, she changed. Sort of resigned. True, there was a chance her husband would recover, but not much of one. Rhett took care of them. Camped with them. Sat up at night with a shotgun near them, lest any more should come charging from the brush. She'd thanked him over and over again, and the bad part of him had started hoping. Hoping for what he had no right to hope.

Standing now in the raging storm before the house where they'd left Russel, he couldn't really deny it anymore. He'd delayed. He could justify every delay, but—

There was a loud bang from above. Rhett jumped back in fright, and drew his sidearm. The bang repeated, lighter this time. His heart sank into his feet, as he stepped out into the rain to look up at the un-boarded window. There was a dim light up there, but that didn't mean much. They'd left the lamp on for Russel, and the city power grid was still up. He strained in the darkness to see if his friend, or something that used to be his friend, was standing behind the drawn shade. Two erratic bangs were not a good sign of an intelligent agent. Then again, one of the quick would have just plunged through the glass at him, and not bothered with banging. Rhett was relieved in his conscience to realize that a part of him really hoped it was Russel, alive and well.

Another bang, and this time Rhett saw what it was. Not a hand. Not an awful, leering face. It was the bird. He'd forgotten about the daycare's abandoned parrot. It was out of its cage, and flying around the room. He saw its fluttering shadow puppet behind the shade. Had Russel let the bird out? Who had fed it? Rhett ran up, and smote hard again on the table. He kept it up, one hammer blow after another, for a full minute, with one eye and the gun trained on the street. Carefully, he crouched down, and placed the sidearm at his feet where he could snatch it up easily. With both hands, he tried pulling the table out from the entryway. It wouldn't budge. The seal was perfect. The lid of some ancient stone coffin. Finally he relented, tired beyond the fatigue of his body.

There was more shuffling from above, but now he was sure it was the bird. He waited, listening. No loud foot slaps on the wet street. Nothing was coming to take vengeance on him. He stepped back into the pouring rain, growing bolder.

"Is there anybody there?" he said, cupping his hands around his mouth.

No answer. The storm surged behind him, soaking him through to the bone. He could almost imagine that it heard him. It was an eerie, layered, resonating sound, like the roar of God. His conscience pricked at him. He could have stopped this. He knew he could have.

"Russel!" he cried. "I came back for you! I kept my promise! Gemma and Danny are safe!"

The rain, imperceptibly, slowed. He felt as if nature were leaning in, and listening to him, just as he leaned in and listened for Russel. Something was waiting for him. The whole world seemed a waiting station.

"Alright!" he cried. "I know this is all my fault!"

Silence.

"Did you hear me, Russel? It's my fault! I didn't ... act as quick as I could have. Maybe I..."

What did he want to say? What was the truth? Rhett closed his eyes and tried to find it.

It was simple, really. At every juncture, there'd been two choices. To shoot before it got Russel, or wait, because he might hit his friend. To take Russel with them, or to leave him, because he might turn while they were on the road. To go to nearby Diablo, or to faraway Mt. Hamilton. At every juncture, he could justify his choices. Yet each time he'd taken the path of delay, the path that might lead to him stepping in for Russel, to watch over Russel's wife. Take over his perfect life. The lightning flashed, and in that instant, Rhett saw with clarity just what the final nudge in all his decisions had been.

"Alright, Russ! I did it, Russ. Part of me wanted you not to come back. Part of me wanted to be the last one standing. You see, man, it's like what I told you that one time, at the drive-through. There's two of me. One that wants to be good, and another that doesn't. Problem is, both parts love Gemma. So ... I guess I didn't try as hard as I could have. No. That's a lie, too."

He collected himself. Steeled his will.

"I tried *not* to try my hardest. We both know I'm nuts. I could have jumped on that thing before it got to you. Could have bulldozed my way to Diablo with the siren on. If I'd really wanted to. I'm sorry that I did wrong to you."

He paused, feeling a wave of relief as he unburdened himself. But there was more to say, and he knew that it was the worst part.

"Terrible thing is, Russ, even though I am really sorry, I'm still ... I'm still glad. I hope I get to be the one. I want her to love me, even though I know I did wrong. And that's low, even for me."

The rain had slowed to a patter. Rhett was aware that not all the moisture on his face came from the sky. He sighed heavily. His soul felt lighter. The rain was almost a cleansing balm. Once more he opened his mouth to speak.

"I did wrong to you, but I promise to do right by Gemma and Danny. I promised to take care of them, and I will."

As he spoke the words, he realized they were true. But the cleansing feeling waned, leaving behind a terrible emptiness. No matter how truthful he'd been, even if from this time forward he lived like Russel had lived, it would always be true that he'd come to virtue by way of vice. He was a marked man. He didn't know any way to get rid of that mark. He sensed it went deeper than the bite of the quick, and brought a more permanent change.

Rhett shuddered, and backed away from the house called Leafy Green. Twice more he saw the parrot flutter past the window, its dark, flapping silhouette a terrible sign of the life that had been there, and wasn't anymore. Russel was gone. He had to be. And if he wasn't dead, he was worse. Maybe he'd just lain down as so many of the dying quick had begun to do. Maybe it had been peaceful. Russ deserved that, at least.

With his eyes still on the window, Rhett backed toward the squad car. Its engine still growled in the storm. Its bright lights cast a searching, illuminative gaze down the mountainous street. When he reached the car, it all happened at once.

The patter of the rain was broken by the tell-tale shuffling feet, legs that noisily brushed each other as they sliced robotically forward. There was no mistaking that low, awful whine the quick made, like the creaking of many cellar doors. Rhett reached for his sidearm. It wasn't there. He'd left it on the porch when he'd tried to move the table. There was no time to go for it. A cold panic gripped him, as he looked up into the eyes of his just executioner. Vengeance rushed toward him. Maybe Gemma was right about Providence. This was only fair.

But as the thing lunged, it stepped into a puddle where the rain had mixed with whatever dripped from his car. It slipped, and hit its head on the sidewalk with a sickening crack. He'd never seen one of them slip. Never even heard of such a thing. He should be dead. Torn apart. What were the chances it would step just there, and slip, and all but kill itself?

Rhett looked up at the dim window, and he knew what he knew. A wave of gratitude swept over him, chilling him more deeply than the coldest November rain.

He scrambled around the car, fumbled with the handle, and climbed in with the horrible sense of something just behind him. He turned, and saw that the thing was already standing. It leapt onto the trunk, but he put the car in drive, and tore down the precipitous road. It lost its grip, and he saw it strike the ground, and roll. It stay where it lay, as he banked hard onto another empty road.

Rhett Redman wept. He didn't deserve it. Beyond the justice that he knew, there lurked some higher, quickening thing. It had heard him and, like Russ, had taken him at his word. His penance was being the last one standing. Having Gemma. He didn't understand it. He could only receive the gift, without apprehending the giver. And there was something else that Rhett Redman never saw.

As he sped away toward the dark bridge that spanned the dark bay, a tall shadow passed behind the drawn shade in the loft room of a house called Leafy Green. And maybe it was only the bird whose frenzied silhouette, like a grasping hand, knocked the shade so that it suddenly shot up, revealing the space behind. But from out of that dim light, something that had listened all the while now gazed down without speaking upon the damp and lonely street.

RUINS

It was supposed to be an ancient Druid site. Darren was skeptical, because every pile of rocks in the UK was supposed to be an ancient Druid site. But visiting old places was sacred to Marcy, so here they were.

Darren and Marcy were in their last term as undergrads, and he felt her slipping away. It wasn't anything she'd said. It was more like dark matter, a thing that couldn't be seen or touched, but still pulled. When they were children in Avebury, she'd loved to explore the stones, and her spirit had charmed him, though he'd never been as bold. As they'd gotten older, Marcy's appetite for exploration had only increased. She'd become an excellent photographer, and a decent writer. She even found time to run a popular travel blog while making high marks at uni.

Darren loved exotic places, too, but his were so far away they had to be viewed from Hubble. If he were honest with himself, human culture held little attraction for him. Compared to the mysteries of the Empyrean, terrestrial things were bland. With his gaze so far off, it had taken him a long time to notice his childhood sweetheart floating steadily out of his orbit. He had to make her stay.

"Let's have lunch there!"

Marcy didn't wait for him to agree, but darted down the grassy slope toward a circular depression. Darren followed, carrying the picnic basket. She ran far ahead of him, but slowed as she reached it, like John waiting for Peter.

She looked down in awe at what she'd found. Darren increased his pace slightly. The picnic basket knocked against his hip in a way he found irritating. He caught up to her. Marcy already had her camera out. She tiptoed around the grass-covered dip in the ground, looking for the perfect shot.

"This is the place! Gosh, how long have those stones…"

Marcy said things out loud that were not so much directed at him, as at any open ears in the universe. She called it thinking outside her body. He only spoke when he had something to say. They were so different.

"So, if they were using limestone, it wouldn't be … but, then how do you think…"

She trailed off, finishing her thought elsewhere. What he thought was that the round depression was as likely to be a natural formation as an archaeological site, which was probably why it wasn't labeled, or roped off. Aside from the suggestion of a stone ring, the place looked like nothing to him. He couldn't understand the attraction it held for her. The fact that he couldn't tell her what he really thought for fear of depriving her of joy was one of those fault lines, those dark folds in spacetime, that had troubled him of late. Another was the grim realization that despite her brains, she had no interest in higher studies.

Darren possessed only two terrestrial dreams. He wanted to become a research professor at Cambridge, and he wanted to marry Marcy. He was on a good track for the first. The second was slipping through his grasp. And he couldn't allow that. He couldn't.

Marcy's camera clicked a dozen times. She lowered it and looked in his general direction in a happy daze.

"Let's eat," she said.

Darren descended into the grassy ring, set the basket down, and began unrolling the picnic blanket. The depression was on an incline, and he decided not to take out any items from the basket for fear they'd tip over. Marcy plopped down beside him.

"I'm so thirsty," she said, snatching up a glass, followed by the thermos of iced tea. She filled her glass, gulped down the tea, and placed the thermos on the blanket without bothering to screw on the cap. It promptly tipped over. She laughed, picking it up after half the contents had spilled. Darren grumbled internally. She caught his eye.

"Don't be such a ninny," she said, without rancor. "It's just liquid, isn't it?"

He nodded. She reached over and squeezed his hand, as if she were reassuring a small child. He hated when she did that, especially because it made him aware of how wooden his temperament was, and how elastic hers. He decided to imitate her by pulling a positive out of a negative.

"Well, now that your side of the blanket's wet, you'll just have to scoot closer to me."

She hesitated. It was almost imperceptible, like sound delay.

"Well done," she said with a wink, and crawled over beside him.

They ate in silence. It was a cool day, with a breeze. The sky was mostly gray, but a shaft of sun came through the clouds and painted the grassy depression. Darren called that sort of thing Marcy's Luck.

Until now, he hadn't noticed how hungry he'd been. He *did* notice the five inches of blanket between Marcy and himself. She was not dressed for the chill, and they'd both have been warmer if she were sitting closer.

"Can I give you my sweater?" he said.

She'd just lain down on the blanket, sandwich in hand, and she looked up at him curiously.

"I'm doing quite well," she began. "But sure. Why not."

He took off his sweater and was instantly cold. Ignoring his feelings, he draped it over her, then laid down beside her.

"What's this place called?" he asked.

She shrugged. "Doesn't have a proper name. The man in the shop called it Cysegredig, or some such word."

His eyes flicked around at the small limestone slabs that dotted its perimeter. They might easily be nothing but old stones, fortuitously arranged in a broken circle, but from within the depression, they looked down like eyes.

"Do you know how many places like this there are around the world?" she asked.

He yawned, not out of boredom, but from a sudden sleepiness that came over him.

"Over a thousand here in the UK," she continued, with more reserve. "And many more around the world. There are structures like this in the Middle East. Even in India. Imagine seeing each and every one of them."

Her voice trailed off. He snatched a glance at her and saw that her eyes were fluttering open and closed.

"It doesn't seem..." he began, "it doesn't seem practical to visit them all."

She sighed, and that was a different flavor of fatigue than the sleepiness they both felt.

"It's *not* practical," she said. "Nothing wonderful is practical, Dare."

He grit his teeth. "But can you afford it? I mean the cost of traveling all over the world? Wouldn't it be better to establish yourself solidly first? Then, perhaps later, when you've … when we've more security."

She shook her head. It was a slow, labored movement.

"Later. Later, later. I think that's your favorite word, Darren Taylor."

Now he knew he was getting tired. This seemed like a crucial moment in their long relationship, but he could hardly think to respond. His mind was going fuzzy.

"I can't do those things," he finally said. "I can't go globe-trotting all over the place."

"Why not?"

"Because I … well we wouldn't even be sure of having food. Income. A roof over our heads. It's too much of a risk."

She shrugged, and yawned.

"Don't be sure of circumstances, then. You canna' control them anyway. Work on the go. Use your wits. What do you want to be, hmm? James Cook, or the Queen of England, sittin' fat and comfortable in her palace?"

Whether she knew it or not, she'd struck him a blow. The fact was his wits were of the purely academic kind. He could not so much as drill the correct-sized hole in a wall, let alone muddle about creation, taking odd jobs. He hated this fact about himself. There were men, he well knew, who could be all that she wanted. Who could thrive in any circumstance and be as flexible as Marcy needed. He felt a kind of rancorous envy toward these phantom competitors, and a jealous desire to keep her in his orbit, lest she wander too close to a more substantial body.

"Look, Marcy, you can't…" he started, but then he fell asleep.

Sometime later, he woke alone.

***

He was lying in the same depression, and night was falling. With a start, he sat up. Marcy was gone, but so was the basket. And the blanket. He was lying on damp grass. Darren climbed to his feet and looked off in the direction of the village. It was a mile away uphill, and he started toward it immediately.

Trudging through the dark sod, he tried to understand what might have happened. They'd had something close to a fight, but he'd hardly expected her to up and leave. Yet what really bothered him was the blanket. How had she managed to take *that* without waking him up? He hugged himself, and shivered, realizing she had his sweater too. He patted his pockets, but his phone was not on him.

Darren ran back to search for it, but it was nowhere in the grassy hollow. Had she taken the phone as well? He started back toward town.

As he crested the hill and saw the village, something felt amiss. The streets appeared as he'd remembered them. Black lampposts cast a dim film over the cobblestone streets. The houses were that same mix of modern and medieval that had given the place its atavistic charm. He recognized the shop where he'd bought Marcy a small golden souvenir just before their tramp down the hill. She'd wanted the trinket, even though the gold leaf was rubbing off. But beyond the shop, off in the distance, the castle was now lit from the inside. He remembered the place, because it had been little more than ruins when they'd spied it on their way toward the round hole in the ground that Marcy thought so grand. Now in the twilight, he saw that it was in good order. Could there be two castles? That seemed incredibly unlikely, but it was the only explanation that came to mind.

He bit his lip hard, sure that he must be dreaming, but sharp pain was all he got for his efforts. He shook his head, and slapped himself repeatedly, feeling as if he were going mad. No change. He was still here, wherever here was. As he gazed up at the un-ruined castle, night came on rapidly. He could see the first stars emerge from behind the veil. Them, at least, he knew. Suddenly he was gripped with a certainty that Marcy was there in the castle. It was the most exotic thing around, and it would have been the most natural place for her to go. He started toward it.

As he walked, he stayed in the light of the electric street lamps. They offered little illumination. Their light was weird. There was an eerie quiet over the place. He didn't hear so much as the buzz of a television set. There were dim lights behind some of the shades, but many of the cottages were in total darkness. A strange dread crept over him, as if he were floating in the middle of an ocean. He increased his pace. Off to his right, he heard a door creak open.

Darren froze. He looked over at the dark figure that stood in the threshold. From the silhouette, he could see it was a woman, but older. Not Marcy.

"What the devil you doing out there?" the woman snapped. "Get inside your home, young man, 'fore it's too late!"

Darren stood rooted in place. He wasn't sure if he was more stunned by the strange command, or by the harsh tone in which it was delivered.

"I'm … I'm not sure what you mean," he said.

She hesitated, then stepped out from the doorway. The woman frowned at him, and he saw that she was not so old, but perhaps in her mid-forties. She looked him up and down a moment, deciding upon something.

"Are you not from around here?" she asked, some gentleness entering her voice.

"No," he said.

She seemed to hesitate again, then looked back over her shoulder into the cottage. Soft light spilled from within, and he saw that she was communicating with someone. Presently, a child of about ten darted out from the interior, poked his head around the corner, and grinned.

"Get back inside," snapped the woman.

She turned back to Darren, giving him a sharp look.

"Alright, then. Don't know who you are, but we can't have you out on the street, can we? Come inside, while you still got legs."

Darren almost asked what she meant, then thought better of it, and strode toward the door. Evidently it wasn't fast enough, for she reached out and impatiently pulled him over the threshold. She shut the door silently, then secured it with three large bolts of different sizes and styles.

A man in blue jeans sat in a large chair in the front room. A long, queer-looking rifle straddled his thighs, and his expression was as perplexed as it was grave. Three children stood there in their nightclothes; two girls aged about four and seven—the youngest clutching a stuffed animal—and the older boy who'd come to the door. The man in the chair gave Darren the same up-and-down glance his wife had.

"Ya must be mad," he said.

Darren didn't know what to say. He found himself looking at the boy, perhaps in a kind of sympathetic naivete. The boy smiled grandly, though it was clear he found Darren an amusing spectacle. The sitting man frowned, still quite unsure of this visitor, and then nodded toward the interior.

"Off to bed with ya'lads."

"And lasses!" said the seven-year-old, looking miffed.

"Off to bed," the man repeated. "Ya can meet him in the morning."

The children skittered away. When they were alone, the man looked at Darren, and nodded toward a couch by the window. Darren sat.

"Now then," said the man, his tone as serious as a police officer's, "I don't know oo' ya are, or what yar about. Not sure's I want ya in my 'ome. Least until ya tell me more about yerself."

He looked at his wife, nodding as if to reassure her that he was perfectly willing to be hospitable, if the situation called for it. Darren sensed that it had been her decision to open the door in the first place.

"Well," Darren began. "My name is Darren Taylor. I'm most recently from Cambridge. We came here—my girlfriend and I—to visit the place. I fell asleep, I guess, and I don't know where she's got off to."

The man took one hand from his rifle to rub his chin. His hands were rough, and quite large—the hands of a craftsman. His face had that youthful agedness that was the charm of the working man. His skin had a red-brown hue, as if it had been baked by something other than the sun, and his thick silver hair wore a glaze of permanent oil, that, together with his general stockiness, suggested a well-muscled land whale. Darren wondered if he was a machinist.

"From Cambridge, eh? Well, that's a long way off. I guess ya wouldn't know about *him*, then?"

"Him?" said Darren.

The man glanced at the woman. Darren saw her nod.

"My name is Alwyn. This is Alys, my wife. Those three runts ya saw were Caden, Efa, and Sara. Lived 'ere our whole lives, 'ave we."

Darren nodded, grateful to have been allowed this measure of confidence. But his confusion was not lessened.

"As Alys observed," said Darren, falling into a nervous habit he had of being precise to the point of condescension, "I'm not familiar with this town. We only came here as a day trip, you see. However, am I right in concluding that there is some danger or threat about? Some troublesome individual?"

Evidently it was the wrong thing to say, because Alwyn's expression immediately lost whatever welcome it had shown. He scowled skepticism toward his wife, but Alys scowled back at him.

"Oh come off it, love. He really *doesn't* know."

"Or maybe ee's a sort of spy for him!"

At that, Alys burst into laughter. Darren didn't know why, but he felt insulted.

"Not on your life," she said. "This boy is not quite his sort, wouldn't you agree?"

Alwyn chuckled then, and Darren was relieved to see him place the rifle gently against the wall.

"Right then," said the gruff man. "You're not from 'ere, an' ya don't know about him. In that case ya can stay, at least until ya find yer young woman friend. But look 'ere. Ye've got to speak more quiet than that. No more going out at night, either."

Darren balked.

"I've got to find Marcy," he said.

"Not at night you don't," said Alys, who still hovered off to the side, standing, and watching the door.

"But why?" said Darren, more loudly than he'd intended.

"Hush," said Alys. "Keep your voice down. Best to talk about it in the light of day."

Darren suppressed irritation.

"But why?" he asked again, in a whisper. "My girlfriend is out there somewhere. Who are you afraid of?"

Alys shook her head.

"You can take the guest room. Stay in there, and lock the door too. We'll tell you in the morning."

Alwyn rose, nodded at him, and picked up his odd rifle. He gestured for Darren to follow him, and the two were soon walking down a hallway lit by only a small, dim bulb. He stopped at a door near the end, opened it, and reached within to flip on the light. Its bulb was also quite dim, granting Darren only enough illumination to see a well-laid guest room. Alwyn nodded Darren in and began shutting the door almost as soon as the other had entered. Suddenly he stopped and opened it an inch.

"What did ya say her name was? The young woman came with ya?"

"Marcy. It's short for Marcella," said Darren.

Alwyn frowned at him through the crack.

"Not a common name, is it?"

Darren shrugged. "I suppose not."

Alwyn wore an indecipherable look, but the moment passed.

"Well then, Darren. Sleep well."

***

Next morning's sky was quite clear and blue. No one woke him. It was the bright sun, and the pleasant scents of a good English breakfast, that summoned Darren from his soft bed. Alwyn and Alys' anxiety from the night before seemed a distant memory, and the family was clearly happy to have a guest. When the meal was over, Caden was sent to his father's workshop to prepare for the day's tasks, while the two girls were sent out to play until their mother called them in for chores. The seven-year-old, Efa, had obvious hopes of hanging about for the conversation, and she huffed to make her displeasure known.

"Never you mind, girl," said her mother. "Get you gone, the both of you."

When they were finally alone, the couple became quite grave. It was Alwyn who finally started in.

"Look, Darren … last night we 'ad only one thing to tell ya. But, I think maybe we 'ave two."

Darren waited, unsure where this was going. He'd lain awake in bed the previous night trying to guess who this mysterious *he* might be. A local criminal was the best guess he could make.

"So…" interjected Alys, "first about the Savage Knight."

"The savage what?"

"The knight," she said.

"But it was only a little cold," said Darren.

Alwyn looked at his wife, smiling grimly.

"No, boy. Knight, as in, warrior."

Darren chuckled. This reaction did not please them.

"The Savage Knight," continued Alwyn, "or the Rogue, as some says, is a brute. He comes out in the evening—not always, but enough to keep a wise man indoors."

Darren pinched his chair, digging into the wood with his nails. It seemed solid enough. He really wasn't dreaming then.

"I … I don't know what to say about that," he muttered.

Alys placed her hand on his arm.

"Young man, there's nothing *to* say about it. Spend a few days here, and you'll see it for yourself. You'll see what he does."

In his own mind, Darren was imagining a sort of drug-addled bully who terrorized out-of-the-way villages like this one, perhaps by playing into local folklore. It was the only scenario that didn't seem entirely mad. Yet he knew that that wasn't it. Many things here seemed, well, a little odd.

The lights, for one. Darren was no electrician, but the bulbs in the house were somehow wrong, as were those in the street lamps. There were other incongruous machines too. The man's rifle. The toaster, which looked like a sort of shoebox with a drawer. The refrigerator, an egg-shaped device that opened down the middle, and whose doors folded out vertically. Even the family computer, which he'd briefly seen Caden use. It reminded him of an antique wall-mirror attached by thick wires to one of those miniature slates from an old-fashioned school house. The slate was really a sort of keyboard-stylus that converted Caden's strokes into data, but it looked nothing like any device he'd seen. He had to assume that Alwyn had invented all of this himself, for he'd gathered the man was mechanically inclined. Things in the village seemed mixed together, not unlike the medley of ancient houses and modern structures built side-by-side, which so typified this part of the countryside. He felt dizzy thinking about it.

"I want to go outside," he said, standing abruptly.

Alys put out a staying hand.

"It would be better if we chatted a bit—"

"No, I'm sorry. Look, I'm quite grateful, but it's been hours since I've seen her, and I'm worried."

Alys looked at Alwyn, but the latter shook his head, silently telling her to let the matter rest. The man then looked up at him.

"Where will you begin your search?" he said, speaking gravely and clearly.

"Well, I suppose the castle. It's the sort of place she would go."

Alwyn surprised him by nodding.

"I'd say it's worth a look."

Darren hesitated, remembering that it had been ruins when he first saw it. But when he considered saying as much out loud, he was sure they'd take him for a nutter. That really *couldn't* be the same ruined structure he'd seen.

"Anyway, I'm going up," he said, pushing in his chair. "Thanks again."

He was halfway across the front room, when he stopped and turned.

"By the way, where is the police station around here?"

The couple looked blankly at him. He was sure he'd spoken clearly, and began to ask again.

"There's only the castle, of course," said Alwyn.

"But..." began Darren, then gave it up. "Well, what about a bus station? We Ubered here, but maybe she—"

"Nearest slev's two miles north down the main road," interjected Alwyn.

What was a slev?

"Well, what about an inn?"

Alys shook her head. "Only the Wicker Man, and I wouldn't go there, young master. You can be sure she's not there either. Not the sort of place a young lady would want to stay."

He must have looked discouraged, because Alys stood and walked over to him.

"You're going to find her, alright? I'm sure of it. But … if you need to stay longer, please come back and stay with us. Long as you need, alright?"

Darren thanked her, and then he walked out into the morning sun.

***

Nobody seemed to be home. The main entrance was a massive set of double doors, with large bolts bordering each. Inset in the right-side door was a smaller portal with a great brass knocker. He struck it, tentatively at first, and then with more ferocity. He could hear the noise reverberating within the stone fortress. It was a lonely sound.

Regretting the necessity of it, he backed away from the entrance and began to call up. The turrets glared down at him, as the stones in the grassy hollow had. No answer. Not even a sound from the inside. He was at the point of leaving, when a man with clippers came into view.

"Hail there, young man. May I help you?"

Darren took in the groundskeeper. He was a very plain-looking man, but he had the same burnished sort of face as Alwyn. The clippers he carried had a curious black square at the hinge, on which blinked a green light of uncertain function.

"I … sorry," he said. "Just trying to speak to whoever's here. I came in last night, and there were lights on, so…"

"Aye," said the groundskeeper. "He was here last night, but only for a moment. I suppose I shouldn't say, but I did hear she'd be coming in later today. They just missed each other. You know their game."

"No," said Darren. "I'm not from around here. I don't know who 'he' or 'she' is."

The groundskeeper looked amused.

"Well, the lord and his lady. Or soon to be, anyway."

"Oh," said Darren. "Yes, well I guess that's only appropriate. I mean,

61

given it's a castle. And what's this game?"

The man smiled conspiratorially, happy to find new ears with whom to share the local gossip.

"Well, they say it's *her* game, you know. Now, it's none of *my* business. I don't like to speculate. Not good manners, you know. But several of the servants have told me—"

"What servants?" said Darren. "Nobody's answering the door."

The groundskeeper, already miffed at being interrupted, now frowned, and looked at him as a perfect nitwit.

"Of course they don't open when the master and mistress are gone! But anyway, what I've heard is that their game is really her idea. You see, she's the whimsical one. He's the master craftsman. You'd think they wouldn't be right for each other, but they say Lord Basu knows just how to let her out and when to reel her in—meaning no offense, of course. A lady likes to be free, and *not free*, if you get my meaning. But it takes a real gentleman, such as Lord Basu, to know what that means. And she's a bit traditional too. Doesn't want to settle down in the same place until they've done things proper. So she goes off about her work, and he goes off about his business, and the one never lets the other know when he's coming or going. Sometimes he's gone for weeks. Sometimes she's gone for a month. But sometimes one comes home and finds the other here. That's the game."

Darren had begun to wonder if the man wasn't a bit cracked.

"Right. So, then, how can I know when one of them is here?"

The groundskeeper turned and pointed up, first at one tower, and then at the other.

"Hers. His. You see the light go on, you know which one is here. If both are on, well then, I wouldn't exactly want to trouble them. Naturally it only goes on in the early dusk, before it gets really dark. You don't want to give *him* any clue."

The Rogue. The Savage Knight. What was his part in all of this?

"She's coming back tonight then?" said Darren.

"Aye," said the groundskeeper. "Come just before dusk. You'll know if she's here. She's a good mistress. A bit flighty, but helps her people as she can. But mind you, don't stay too long."

***

Darren returned just before dusk. The lady's tower light was indeed on, and he made a note to himself that the groundskeeper was a reliable gossip. Now that he was here, though, he felt unsure. Just what was he expecting to learn from this flighty-sounding woman? In all likelihood, she'd have no information, and would just direct him toward the slev. Maybe Marcy had seen the writing on the wall, and her sudden departure was yet another instance of her impulsivity. Darren still wasn't sure if he should worry about her, or only himself. He knocked.

Someone walked toward the door. It swung inward.

"Can I be of assistance?" said a man, snatching a quick look at the sky.

"Yes, please. I'd like to speak to the lady."

"That is your right," responded the other. "Follow me."

Darren followed him down a dark hallway lit by dozens of the same dim bulbs he'd seen elsewhere. Even with so many, the light was frustratingly scarce, so that an oil lamp would actually have been better. The servant rounded a corner and announced his presence to the lady. Then the man departed, leaving Darren with the awkward feeling he was invading someone's privacy. He stepped into the wider room, and promptly shouted in surprise.

There was Marcy, camera in hand, dressed almost as she'd been when he'd last seen her. She stood in the center of a vast stone room, wearing blue jeans and a sleeveless red top.

"Marcy! What?"

She studied him for a moment. Her pretty face became troubled.

"It's you," she said, in a whisper.

"Of … of course it is. Marcy, what is going on here?"

She pursed her lips, then touched her pointer to the tip of her chin as she did when she was puzzled.

"Darren," she said, then nodded to herself. "He's Darren Taylor. That's what it is. From university."

She looked back at him and smiled. "Well … how have you been?"

Darren sputtered.

"How've I been? *Where* have you been! I've been worried sick!"

She looked confused, or as if she were trying to remember something. Then her eyes locked with his, and the confusion was gone. She snapped her fingers, and smiled.

"That's it!" she said. "I understand. But you don't need to worry. I promise you, I'm quite alright."

He looked at her, flabbergasted. "What is happening here?"

She smiled, almost to herself. "Would you believe … that you've confused me with someone else? Someone who looks like me, but is not me?"

"Marcy, stop it!" he snapped. A mad panic came over him, and he drew quick, shallow breaths.

She sighed. "Alright then. But that was ages ago. It's … it's so fuzzy now, isn't it? We were different people then. This is my home. And Darren, I've always been so happy here."

Darren planted a hand against the stone wall to keep himself upright. "You … you can't…"

But he didn't know what he wanted to say. She looked at him sympathetically, but with a detached curiosity, like he was some pitiful stranger. Marcy glanced behind her toward a large oval window. The sky was darkening.

"You know, you really ought to be going. The Rogue's likely on his way by now."

Darren was shaking, and tears were forming at the corners of his eyes. He felt he was going insane. He was going to collapse. There was a metal clang behind him, and Marcy jumped. For a moment, she looked frightened, but her grimace changed to joy as she looked past him down the hallway. Something skittered by Darren's leg, and he darted away in horror.

Three metal spiders about the size of house cats clicked past him on the stones. Between them they carried a sort of litter, a piece of canvas stretched in a triangle. On it was a heavy bag, crammed to the brim with mechanical parts, a few of which spilled over the top onto the canvas. Horrified, Darren cast about for some kind of weapon.

In the spiders' wake came a man. He was tall, with Indian features. His hair was dark black, his skin almost glossy, and intelligent eyes looked out over his high, angular cheekbones.

"Samir!" cried Marcy.

She ran to him, and threw her arms around his neck. He leaned down to kiss her. For a long time, the two embraced. Despite Darren's confusion and terror, another feeling came over him as he watched this stranger with Marcy. It was white hot rage.

He began to rush forward. All three spiders stopped and looked up at him. Each mechanical head bore a cluster of red eye-dots. Their attention froze him in place. The man she'd called Samir looked out from Marcy's enveloping hair and laughed.

"Oh, don't worry, friend. They will not hurt you."

Samir looked back at Marcy, and Darren saw the utter love the man bore her.

"And who is this, my dear?" he said.

Marcy looked at him sheepishly.

"Samir, this is Darren Taylor."

"Ah," said the Indian man, before gently releasing her.

He walked up to Darren and put his hand out.

"Welcome, friend. I am Lord Basu."

Darren eyed the proffered hand as a snake might a waving stick. Samir Basu smiled, apparently untroubled, and dropped his hand gracefully.

"It *is* getting late," he said. "And with both of us here, he's certain to come. His informers in the town will have seen our lights, and told him. So you'd better go."

Among the half-dozen brazen incongruities that whirled in Darren's mind, one cried out for explanation.

"If you fear this being, then why do you signal your presence to the whole town?" he said.

Samir smiled. "Those are the rules of the game. We're not yet married."

He leaned in for another kiss, and Marcy happily complied. They lingered in that pose until Darren felt ill from watching. He looked out toward the oval window. Night had fallen. Immediately, there was a loud pounding at the door. The two lovers broke off their embrace.

"He's here," said Marcy, with a sigh.

Five loud thuds reverberated down the hallway, and a harsh, ugly voice followed in their wake.

"Open in the name of the Savage Knight!"

Marcy shuddered and looked worriedly at Samir.

"Never fear, love," he said. "We're safe here."

"I know, but—"

A flurry of blows followed, drowning out her voice. The spiders dropped their burden and skittered into the corner.

"Stay calm. Stay calm," said Samir.

"Let me in, or face the consequences!" cried the thundering voice from outside.

Darren wondered how even that steel portal could endure such a flurry of violence.

"She's mine! She's mine! Come out and face me, you silken-tongued tinkerer."

Marcy looked terrified, but Lord Basu only sighed. He looked over at Darren, and said in a confidential tone, "That's just what he wants, you know? I'm quite confident in my machines. I'd put them up against any man. But they say it's his face that can't be endured. Personally, I think he's a coward."

At that, the quick hammer blows gave way to louder attacks. They were spaced further apart, but of much greater force, as if the man were wielding a battering ram. Marcy quivered, and folded herself more deeply into Samir's arms.

"Oh, when will this end! When will we be free of him?"

Samir clutched her tightly to himself. "Soon, my love. But he can't get in—"

The door burst open. Samir's eyes went wide.

"No," he said, more perplexed than frightened. "That can't be, can it?"

"Hide! We have to hide!" said Marcy.

"Yes," said Samir. "Very well."

The two lovers fled into the castle, and the spiders followed. Darren stood transfixed, but the knight's heavy footfalls in the entryway hall snapped him to sobriety. He ran too, tearing down one labyrinthine hallway after another, until he found a small niche in the wall with a heavy wooden door inside it. He tried the door, and it was unlocked. Scrambling inside, he shut it, and dove under a bed that was in the room. None too soon, for the knight's heavy tread was soon heard in the outside hallway. Darren clutched himself into a ball, shivering. The knight paused outside the door, and Darren heard him chuckle. It was an ugly sound. Then, to his relief, the Savage Knight passed by.

For hours afterward, Darren heard nothing but the sounds of destruction. Unable to find his quarries, the knight expended his rage on the castle itself. When he finally left in the early hours of dawn, Darren came out to find the place in tatters. Lord Basu and his wife-to-be were standing amid the wreckage. Marcy was weeping softly, but Samir seemed thoughtful. They hardly noticed Darren's presence.

"How much longer must we endure this?" she said, weeping softly.

"My love," said Samir. "You yourself set the game. Three more chance meetings, and we shall marry. And then we'll never have to endure his presence again."

"Maybe I was wrong," she said. "I never thought he could get inside."

He hugged her to himself. "Now, now. A love so great will not come cheaply. But it's almost over. Now let us call the servants to clean up this mess. I have an order to fulfill in Kent, and you have your own quests to pursue. We shall not let this miserable wretch deprive us of our favorite pleasures."

She kissed him again, and Darren looked away. He stumbled past them down the hallway, and out into the light of the morning. Marcy never once turned to see him go.

***

Breakfast at the cottage was a quiet affair. The family was seated at the table when he entered the cabin. They seemed to sense his distress, and they asked no questions. After the children were sent out, Alwyn put a hand on his shoulder and squeezed reassuringly.

"We 'eard it was a bad'un last night."

Darren shrugged. He kept seeing Marcy in Lord Basu's arms. He wanted to scream.

"Got inside the castle?" said Alys, in a low voice. "Now that's quite a development. You must have been so frightened."

It was true that he'd been terrified, but what Darren most felt was a sickening envy. He no longer cared about the reasons for any of it. The incongruities of the place. He wanted Marcy. He wanted Marcy.

"Was it…" Alwyn began, "Did you recognize the lady, Darren?"

Darren didn't need to answer to confirm the fact.

"Oh dear," said Alys. She reached over and patted him on the forearm. "Well, these things are always difficult. But she is happy, as hard as it may be to hear."

Darren suppressed a scowl. She was only trying to help, after all. But when he looked up, Alwyn wore a thoughtful expression.

"You know," he said. "The two of them aren't married yet."

Darren looked vacantly at him. Alys shot her husband a warning glance, but Alwyn ignored her, and pressed on.

"They say it's his craft what won her over. Ee's a skilled man, Darren. A master craftsman."

"Darling," said Alys. "Don't make it harder for him by planting false hope."

Darren looked from one to the other, catching the sense of Alwyn's words.

67

"No, please, Alys. I'd like to hear him out."

Alys sighed. Alwyn pressed on.

"The thing is, I'm a master craftsman too. I can teach ya to make things. Now not as good as 'ee can make 'em. Not in a short time, anyway. But I can give ya skills what can impress the lady. 'Oo knows. Maybe ya can win 'er over."

Alys shook her head at her husband.

"Win her over? What is she, an eight-point buck? Has it occurred to you men that the lady is *happy* with him?"

Alwyn grunted. "Married is married. And unmarried is unmarried. Darren deserves a chance, same as anyone."

"Yes!" said Darren, before Alys could retort. "Teach me! I want to learn. I don't … I don't have any of those kinds of skills."

Alys left the table, defeated for the moment. The two men began to plot in earnest. Darren's lessons would start today. He would assist Alwyn and Caden in the workshop. He was certainly motivated to learn.

"And," said Alwyn, "their chance meetings is rare, from what I've 'eard. Three more, ya say? Well, that could be months. Maybe a year, for all we know. Time enough for you to visit 'er whenever she comes into town. And the rules of gentlemen here is that a man must ask again, once more at the end, to make it official. You can steal her back, boy. At least ya need ter try."

***

For the next two months, Darren fairly lived in the workshop. He rose early, ate quickly, and spent the day as Alwyn's apprentice. As it turned out, the man was something more than a blacksmith or a machinist. His craft was called Alchemetry, the art of making machines that worked like living things. Darren knew enough to recognize this as a new science. But he no longer cared about the contradictions. He thought only of the moment when he could present his skill to Marcy, and, in the meantime, he was very far from proficient.

Day-after-day, he twisted wire, and shaped gravillium, learning to make use of that dark element that powered most of these strange devices. His hands grew raw and his face red from hours spent at the bellows. Only the hottest fire could soften the element, and only the nimblest hands could fold it into the shapes that activated its latent powers. He was reminded of a class on exobiology, and of the mysterious wonders of proteins. Though it was not his field, he'd always been amazed by these queer, semi-biological structures. That amino acids could be strung together in specific combinations, and that these combinations, once achieved, folded into structures with precise functions, seemed like magic.

On the one hand, the range of functional combinations was finite; on the other, the potential combinations, most of which did nothing, were infinite. Proteins were like living words, and this dark element gravillium was the same. It was as if words, not atoms or energy, were the fundamental stuff of the world. A skilled and patient man could discover these metal words, and exploit their properties in his own designs. So when he wasn't learning, Darren stayed up in his bed, sketching out the sorts of things that might impress Marcy, and trying to guess what combinations would bring his ideas to life.

Yet his learning curve was long, and his time short. And so it was that he kept an eye out for her light in the tower, and visited her as frequently as he could. She was bound by some law of the land to receive him every time.

Their meetings were short, and quietly tense. Having no proper reason for an audience, he engaged her on the subjects of photography and travel. He would ask her many questions about her own art, and about her frequent trips to foreign lands. These things had never interested him before, but now he began to see why they mattered so much to her. She would always greet him with reticence, and a sort of caution, until he got her speaking on the things that interested her. Then the need to share her passion overcame her, and she became the same Marcy he'd once known. Or rather, hadn't known. Not nearly enough, he now saw. And in her tales of travel, one detail emerged that seemed of special import.

There was a certain bird called a popjay. *Not* a *popinjay*, she'd corrected him. He'd never heard of this species, but he gathered from her description that it was something like a black robin, but with one small, blue circle on each wing. The popjay was so called because of its odd migratory pattern. The animal would sometimes imprint on a person, as if she were its long-lost mother, and then it would follow her around wherever she went. On her most recent trip to Asia, Marcy's popjay had popped in to follow her from site to site. There it was again in Madagascar, and again in France. It didn't follow her home, but somehow it showed up wherever she went abroad. She'd once mentioned her odd guardian angel to Samir, but he seemed to regard it as too improbable that the same bird should find her in such far-flung locales. Darren told her that he believed her. And now he knew what to do.

***

Back in the shop, he labored from morning till night. Though his mind constantly raced, the work put him into the deepest slumbers. He could even sleep through the clamor of the Savage Knight, whose semi-nightly rages kept the town on edge. In the morning, he would join the villagers in helping to repair the things the brigand had broken in the town, for it was the man's pattern to wreak destruction on the village once his overtures toward Marcy, or his challenges to Lord Basu, had gone unanswered. A strong new door had been installed in the castle, and the knight hadn't breached it again, nor even made the attempt.

Darren had stopped asking who the knight was, or why he was obsessed with Marcy. Disciple of science though he was, he'd begun to see a certain futility in *why*. The knight's behavior reminded him of gravity. Why did things fall down? Was it really any more informative to say, "Objects are attracted to objects with greater mass," than to say, "things fall down toward the earth"? If you took the explanation to the next level, and spoke of mass bending spacetime, and of less dense objects falling in toward denser ones, you were really just saying the same thing all over again. It didn't get you any closer to *gravity itself*. Description was as far as man could go. Things just did what they did, regardless of why they did it. Apples might have fallen up instead of down. Roses might have been blue, and violets red. Affairs of detail might have been arranged ten dozen alternate ways … and perhaps they were, somewhere. But what did it matter? The Savage Knight wanted Marcy, and so did Lord Basu, and so did Darren. Those were the facts, whatever the reasons.

The many days passed quickly. The rumors came that Marcy had had another chance meeting at the castle with Lord Basu. Only four days later, it had happened again. The next time they met, the game would be done, and the two would wed. Darren could not let that happen. The thought of it, of Marcy happy with him, spending the rest of her days by his side, wrapped up in his arms at night, drove him to madness. Indeed, if he let himself dwell on the image of them together, he became so distracted that he made mistakes at the bellows. He'd burned himself several times that way, letting his mind wander into envious rages, even while his hands inched too close to the hot metal. Yet he'd been single-minded enough to learn his lessons in the arts of gravillium, and he was finally ready.

He sat at a table in Alwyn's workshop, admiring the thing he'd created.

He still couldn't believe that it moved by its own strange energy. Had he really made it, or had he only discovered a latent form, an idea buried deep in the dark matter of which it was shaped? He'd never been a creative person, and was surprised to find that the act of creating gave him a satisfaction all its own. Discovery through making was unlike discovery in astronomy. The latter gave a temporary consolation, and yet only led to more questions, and to more interesting, but arbitrary facts. Lists and lists of endless facts!

But to create something, to invent and yet somehow discover a latent form, *that* gave him an abiding joy that the stars had not given since he was a small child. He only hoped that the thing he'd made would also give joy to Marcy. As he sat there, thinking these things, Alwyn and Alys dashed into the shop.

"She's here, son," said Alwyn.

"That's good news," said Darren.

Alwyn looked pensive.

"He's coming too, Dare," said Alys. "Both of the towers are lit."

For a moment, despair gripped Darren, and shook him to his core. Not now! Not when he was so close! And this was the meeting that would seal their engagement, for those had been the rules of her whimsical game.

"No!" he shouted. "I won't allow it! I've worked too hard not to win her back."

"I'd go up right now, if I was you," said Alwyn.

Alys looked at her husband, and her face was troubled. But if she had an objection, it was left unvoiced. Darren stood, wrapping his gift in the velvet covering he'd purchased from the same shop where, once upon a time, he'd bought Marcy a souvenir. He placed the wrapped item in a cherry-wood box with golden hinges that he'd also bought there. Rules of the game! Arbitrary, like so many things. He intended to make his own rules. He strode to the door. Alys caught him by the arm. He met her eyes, which were sad, and full of empathy.

"Whatever happens, Dare, don't lose yourself. Don't lose your head. Remember that love is like … well it's like making something. You cannot force your will on the matter. You've got to do your best to discover what's there. Bring it to light. But freedom, Dare. It's so important, if you love a girl, to give her freedom. Do your best, but accept what comes. Maybe … maybe that's why you came to this town. To learn how to love her."

Darren knew that the wisdom she shared was the fruit of a life's experience, and yet he couldn't hear her. Not really. Desire, and a desperate envy, made war on his reason. His mind was as hot as a forging fire. His will was fixed. He *would* win Marcella, and take her away from the brilliant Lord Basu.

As he tore through the yard, and passed through the house on the way to the street, Caden greeted him with a cheer, and the girls danced and curtsied as he passed. He was not the same man who'd come to their door so many nights ago. They could see that he'd changed. Darren knew that he had. He marched toward the castle, and the sun sank lower in the sky.

***

The heavy new door swung inward, and Darren stepped inside. The castle was dark and cool. Falling on the thick air, the dim light gave the hallways a close, smoky feeling. Darren walked, as if dazed, down a corridor at whose end he was bound to find either joy or sorrow, contentment or rage. He reached the end of the hallway. Behind him, the steel door shut loudly, as if by magic, and the servant shuffled away. He stepped into the great room. Only just in time.

Lord Basu was on one knee before Marcy. In his hands he cradled an open jewelry case. Even from across the room, Darren could see that it held the most dazzling ring she'd ever laid eyes on. It was made of thinly-braided gold and platinum, and studded with colored jewels that shone of their own light. It was not just any ring, but the gift of a master craftsman. The final link in the chain that joined Marcy to himself. Marcy's face glowed in its luminous color, and her expression was one of the most unutterable joy. Her lips moved, on the verge of forming "Yes."

"No!" screamed Darren.

Like a crazed ogre, he barreled into the room. It was not a club he wielded, but a small cherry wood box with gold hinges. Basu's gravillium spiders looked hesitantly at their master, then tried to bar Darren's way. Darren kicked one across the room, and the others scattered.

"Hear me out, Marcy! Let me make my case!"

Marcella looked at him with tenderness, but also with pity. He could see in her eyes that she'd already made her choice, and was only searching for the words to soothe him. Samir bristled, his moment of triumph ruined by this interloper, but she placed gentle hands on her lover's shoulders. The gesture reminded Darren so much of Alys' way with Alwyn, that his hope fled immediately.

"Darren," she said. "Oh, Darren."

Her pity for him, this mother's comforting of a tantrumming child, was a greater blow than if she'd been angry. She was trying to let him down gently, and yet not to make him feel rejected. All of their years together had led up to this … to this condescending indulgence. He saw red.

"Darren—"

"No! Let me show you what I made for you. I've spent months on it. Please, Marcy. Please, just *look*!"

She glanced uncertainly toward the box, and then at Samir. That Samir merely smiled, and nodded, as if he were humoring one of the peasants, only made Darren more determined. In that moment he also knew he could kill Samir without a moment's regret. The insufferable, condescending wanker! But Marcella stepped toward him, placing a calming hand on Darren's wrist.

"Please, show me," she said.

Like a happy fool, he presented his gift, knowing all the time that it would do no good. He held the box before her, and slowly undid its golden latch. Inside was an object wrapped in a red velvet cloth. Marcy smiled sweetly, and reached into the box, slowly unwrapping what it contained. As she took it out, she drew a sharp breath, and placed a hand upon her breast.

The object was a bird. A black bird with a blue dot on each wing. It looked up at her, and ruffled its feathers in the most natural way imaginable. The popjay cooed at her, then stretched its wings. The gravillium creature took flight, gliding about the great room with easy grace. It seemed to take in everything at a glance, then came back, and alighted on her shoulder, home at last.

Darren could see in Marcy's face that she was overcome with emotion. She dared not breathe, for then she would weep. Hope sprang anew in his heart. He was gripped with a preternatural joy, and a feisty, furious sense of triumph. She *did* love him, and not this slick, pretty Lord Basu. He knew Marcy. She was governed by her heart. And he had moved that heart.

"Oh, Darren," she said, the tears finally spilling forth. "You did this, for me? It's wonderful! You must have … you must have had to learn so much to make something so wonderful. Thank you! Thank you!"

Darren waited for her to come to him. To fall upon his neck, to embrace him. To press him once more against the warmth of her being. But she did not. To his horror, his childhood love, this flighty woman, suddenly giggled at him. She reached out and squeezed his hand, a small, reassuring gesture, little more than a handshake.

"I always knew you could do great things, Darren, if you wanted to. But this … it's just so wonderful. So thoughtful, and so generous. *Magnanimous.* Yes, that's the word. To think, after all this time, you'd have the magnanimity to craft such a wedding gift."

Darren felt something in him die. His face must have shown it, for she suddenly recoiled from him.

"Don't … don't look at me that way, Darren! Don't!"

Samir was at her side, a protective arm about her.

"You should leave," he said, coolly.

Darren looked the man over. The suave, intellectual man, features unmarked by the demands of his art, as if fire itself deferred to him. Darren's own mind became a bellows. But whatever might have happened next, it was derailed by a sudden loud noise. All three turned at once, recognizing the tell-tale sounds of the Savage Knight.

He struck the door ten times hard, making no pause between each blow. The rogue howled in furry, and the noise of it reverberated through the room.

"Face me!" he cried. "Come out and face me, you simpering weakling. Did you think her flippant rules would keep me out? Do you think your devices can keep me at bay?!"

The pounding began again, so that the whole castle shuddered.

"We must hide!" said Samir, clutching Marcy to himself.

"Will he never stop?" she wept. "I thought that now he would stop!"

Samir began to pull her toward the interior. There was a loud crash, and Darren heard the gate come off its hinges. All three froze. Heavy boots tromped down the hallway, and the spurs of the Savage Knight clanged as he marched.

"What can we do?" Marcy shrieked. "Can he be defeated, my lord? Can you not defeat him?"

Samir looked uncertain. The color had drained from his face. A great shadow darkened the end of the hallway. The Savage Knight stepped into view.

He had swelled in size. He was seven feet tall. His armor, black as night, was fringed all about with jagged, wire-like protrusions, and yet it was also dotted with many points of light, like stars in the Empyrean. And it twisted, and shifted on his body, moving over his form like a living thing. In his hand he bore a great, double-sided ax. His helm was in the form of a death's head, and a red fire seemed to burn from behind his down-turned visor.

"Face me!" he growled. "Face me, Lord Basu, or never be rid of me."

Basu's gravillium spiders shrieked, and hid themselves behind their master. Marcy began to weep. She looked to her lord with pleading eyes.

"Why is this happening?" she cried. "Why is this happening?!"

In spite of his own fear, Darren felt a cold joy at Lord Basu's obvious terror. Then it struck him that he did not care anymore what threat the Savage Knight posed him. There were worse things than death. Marcy's rejection was one of them. He could sink no further. And he suddenly knew what he could do. He had one last hope to win her over, and, when it occurred to him, he did not hesitate.

Darren strode forward, placing himself between the knight and the couple.

"No, Rogue. You can face me. Face me if you dare!"

The knight turned toward him, as if only just noticing him. The monstrous warrior laughed. It was an icy, cynical sound, horrifying and yet somehow familiar. Perhaps it was the cold laugh heard in every child's nightmare. And now the knight stood before him like some dark thing discovered, and shaped, and brought forth through Alchemetry. Darren uttered a loud cry and ran at him.

"Darren! No!" cried Marcy behind him.

The Savage Knight tried to swing his ax, but Darren closed the distance too quickly, and, to his own surprise, caught the shaft, and forced it down to the stone floor.

"Now we'll see who you really are!" he shouted, reaching up to the death's head helm.

With strength he couldn't stop to comprehend, Darren tore off the visor, and clawed at the death's head mask beneath. The knight stood still, as if stunned, and Darren grabbed the heavy helm, tearing it from the rogue's head. But his moment of triumph was short-lived, for Darren saw the face that wore this mask of death and rage.

It was his own face. The Savage Knight was he.

***

Darren awoke slowly in the little grassy hollow fringed with ancient stones. It took him a moment to recognize the place. The sun had come out, and the air was much warmer. He sat up, and saw Marcy some feet away from him, leaning against the side of the hollow. Her eyes flicked up to notice him, then back down to her fancy camera. She was paging through the day's photos. Darren swallowed, and sat up. Tentatively, he crawled toward her across the blanket, stopping for a moment when he planted his knee in the wet puddle from the spilled iced tea. It soaked into his jeans. He looked up again, and saw that Marcy was staring at him.

"Hi," he said, quietly.

"Hi, Dare."

There was something in her smile that was melancholy without being at all sad. He knew her well enough to know that she'd come to a decision. It was one he wouldn't want to hear.

"Please, come sit by me," she said.

He did, settling in next to his childhood love, though not so close as he wished. She took his hand, and looked up into the bright sky.

"Dare, I think … I've been thinking about things. You know I don't like to waste time dancing around the truth."

He sighed. "No, you like to waste time in other ways."

He said it without rancor, and she knew his tone, and laughed.

"Yes, that's about the shape of things. I do, and you don't. I'd say we're both pretty set in our ways by now."

"Yes," he said.

She laughed again, but it was a sad laugh.

"I'm always going to remember this place, Darren. The green hills. The little village. The crumbling old castle. And you, Dare. No matter where I go, I'll take you with me."

Darren bit back tears. He had long suspected this moment would come. Now that it was here, he wanted nothing more than to turn back time. And yet he knew that that way lay madness, and regret, and a desperate envy that could destroy him. A part of him wanted to protest to her that he had changed, and that he could now be the man she'd wanted him to be. He had gone through so much to reshape himself. Yet, though he *had* changed, he knew that he'd never be what she really wanted. Their loves were too different, and there was no castle on Earth where the two of them could meet at once.

Marcy squeezed his hand, not in that condescending way, but with real tenderness. He felt that she could feel his pain through his skin. She did love him, and that was something. It was something grand to have been loved by so fierce and so beautiful a woman. Such a love was its own reward. It was like the beauty of the stars. What that beauty ought to be, anyway. He didn't need to possess it, to touch it, or, especially, to understand it, for that beauty to be his. He was a better man for having loved her for a time, and now, still, from a distance. There was real nobility in that. But to go on pretending, refusing to let go of what had never been his? Well, that was madness.

"And thanks so much for this," she said. "I hope you'll let me keep it. To remember you."

She released his hand and took hold of the purse that sat on the grass beside her knee. She reached in, and from it withdrew the small souvenir that he'd bought her in town.

"My God," she said. "Look!"

Through misty eyes he looked at the tiny bird. He remembered it well now, because the gold leaf had been chipped off on one of the wings, revealing a cheaper metal beneath. He'd tried to find another, but Marcy had thought the imperfection charming. Now the little bird was no longer gold at all. All the gold leaf was gone. There was not a trace—not even dust. The little bird she now held was all black, and each wing bore a tiny blue dot.

"Isn't that odd?" she said, in a whisper. "I could have sworn … I wonder what sort of bird it's supposed to be?"

A tear ran down Darren's cheek. He quickly rubbed it away.

"I think…" he began. "I think it's called a popjay."

THE UNDERMAN

"The company has made a significant investment here, John. If everything works out, I can't see how you don't make partner. So why insist on these numbers?"

John Poe swallowed, and looked across the lacquered oak desk at Beltzer's chief economist, Chase Mellor. Mellor's manner was interested, even friendly. He held a leather organizer in one hand, and a pen in the other. This was, John knew, a mere affectation. Mellor liked to give the impression that he was old school, and that he listened so intently that he might just have to take some notes. And it was a testimony to the citadel-like security of their local headquarters in Bangui that Mellor often left his trusty notebook sitting out on his desk, in plain view. Chase didn't even use a password manager, but wrote everything down in his little notebook. In this, and other things, he thought he was untouchable.

"Seventeen percent is *your* projection, Chase," John said.

"It's everyone's projection, John. Have you looked at the team reports?"

John steeled himself.

"I understand," he began, "that those numbers are based on your projections."

"So?" said Mellor, with the hint of a threat.

"So, they're not truly independent. My projections say ten percent, at best. More likely six."

Mellor tossed the notebook onto his desk and sat back in his chair, lacing his fingers.

"The energy and economic growth have to be tied together, John. We can't present the World Bank such divergent numbers."

"I'm well aware," John replied, laconically.

"Are you going to be a team player on this?"

"What are you asking me to do, Chase? There's no way you get seventeen percent growth in five years in the Central African Republic—"

"But the oil reserves, John! This is the biggest find of the new century. These are some of the poorest people on Earth. With our help, they'll be living like kings in a few years. Or maybe you think they're not capable of it. Because if *that's* the issue—"

John swallowed. "Look, the numbers don't work, and you know it."

"I know no such thing. The government here agrees with our assessment."

John stood up from his chair and leaned into Mellor's desk. "Of course they do! They'll directly benefit! But the rest of the country will be servicing the debt for centuries."

Mellor assumed a perplexed expression, studying Poe. The intercom buzzed.

"Sorry to interrupt, Mr. Mellor, but Mackenzie is here to see you."

"Send her in," said Mellor.

He stood up and gave John a confident smile.

"The numbers must work, John. The future of this poor country depends on it. Our futures as well."

He winked as he said it, and Mackenzie pranced into the room. John had met her before, in the States. She was beautiful, expensively dressed, and oblivious as a sparrow. Of course, Chase Mellor would have a daughter like that.

"Oh, sorry to interrupt, Daddy!" said Mackenzie, who didn't look the least bit sorry.

"You're not interrupting," said Mellor. "Mr. Poe and I are finished. How was your flight?"

Poe walked to the door and let himself out. As he closed it, he heard her rhapsodizing about the "charming little Africans."

On the way to his desk, Andrea caught his eye. "I've got those studies for you, Mr. Poe. I'll bring over the hard copy."

John looked at her desk. It was a forest of work in progress. "I'll just save you the trip," he said.

He walked over. She smiled and handed him a wire-clip binder, filled to capacity. He smiled back, then quickly averted his eyes and pretended to look for something. He noticed a new image on her wall, a striking silhouette of a spreading tree, black ink on a white canvas. Its roots were a blurred reflection of the trunk and spray, as if the tree below were its second self. He found it strangely beautiful, yet unsettling.

"Billy's work?" said John.

Andrea swiveled in her chair and beamed. "You like it? He made it just for me. It's an African tree, but I don't remember which."

"He's quite the artist now. Richard would have been proud."

"Yes," she said, distractedly. "John, I just want you to know—" she quickly cast a glance toward Mellor's door, "—that I'm proud of you for this."

He couldn't look at her. "For what?"

"Oh, come on. For your honesty."

"Don't be so sure. I haven't finalized my report."

"I'm sure it'll be accurate," said Andrea. Her tone reminded him of his daughters' when they were little, when they thought he could lift anything. He sighed.

"Andrea, if it's accurate, I'll be out of a job."

"So?"

"So? I've got kids, a needy ex-wife, and child support payments."

"Has she remarried? I mean, it's none of my business, but—"

"Not quite, but I think she's close," he said, with regret.

"I'm only asking because if she does, you might request to have the payments reduced."

"I don't know. I don't want that."

"*What?*" she asked, wrinkling her brow.

He looked at her with embarrassment. "I don't want her to remarry. I want to ... look, I've got to get back to work."

Andrea smiled warmly, but he saw the pity she was trying to disguise.

"I know you'll do the right thing, John," she said as he left.

He shut the door behind him. The binder thudded angrily against his desk. He pushed it away, and drew out a dog-eared copy of *A Princess of Mars*, hoping to get himself lost, for a moment, in a world of clear choices.

***

"This is pathetic," said the man in the one-room apartment.

His name, as far as he knew, was John Sly. His desk was a rough wood surface, covered in memos, photographs, and unorganized piles of paper. He couldn't read the reports, but he perceived their meanings. The room was a narrow rectangle, and between his desk and the wall that it faced was a large cylindrical vent that came through the ceiling. It had a mailbox lid at its bottom, and beside it was a plastic vacuum tube that also ran into the ceiling. Behind him was an open space that functioned as his living room. A threadbare and collapsing sofa was crammed into the short end of the wall opposite the vent. To his right were low bookshelves stuffed with files, and the ever-growing directory that helped him to locate them. Three dirty rat cages sat atop the bookshelves, their inhabitants running continuously in wheels, or lying wounded from recent combat. Above them, a single window opened on a narrow gap hedged by a blank brick wall. Ten feet to his left was a black door that never opened.

"I can't work like this!" he snarled, but he knew he'd have to finish the night's quota if he wanted to sleep. He began sifting through the mass of information, attempting to impose order on the haphazard detritus. Whenever his fingers touched a paper, he immediately perceived its contents. Thoughts, often half-formed and illogical, presented themselves. Ideas, resolves, forgotten commitments, hopes, sorrows, broken promises, and fears danced through John Sly's being.

Most of the photographs were familiar. He placed these in the "Day-to-Day" pile. There were several of an attractive woman in her late thirties, obviously a favorite of Sly's employer. One image, laced with fear and loathing, showed a slick businessman in a tailored suit, holding a notebook. Beside him was a delectable girl in her twenties, tweeting like a human bird. Sly sifted through the mass of data, impressions swimming like minnows up his fingers. As usual, there was plenty of fear.

He yanked at his hair and grimaced. He hated his cramped life in the dark place. He hated his employer, whoever he was. Most of all, he hated the endless work, without personal indulgence, apart from the meager entertainment afforded by the rats. He slammed his fists on the desk, and walked to the apartment's only window. Full of dread, he leaned forward and looked up and down the three-foot gap between the window and the brick wall. No sky above. No ground below. There was no way out.

He returned to his desk and continued sorting. At the bottom of the stack of photographs, he found something genuinely new.

It was an image of a tree, dark lines against a white background.

Something in it stirred him, and he resolved to make it the centerpiece of a new story. His nightly quota was five. They didn't have to be good, or even logical, but his professional interest was piqued. Perhaps, if he felt ambitious, he might weave all the stories together into one intoxicating narrative. He sometimes did that.

He took out a quill and paper, and placed the tree image beside it. He grabbed two memos, two reports, and two photographs at random. The rest would be filed away later. He lit a cigarette and set to work, crafting a tale of a man who finds himself in a world under threat, the saving of which would somehow save his own soul. Sly didn't yet know how victory would be achieved, but it would come to him. He'd been at it three hours when there was a knock at the door.

John Sly froze. There was a shuffling sound behind the locked black portal, and he trembled in spite of himself. *God, not another red one!* He hated the red envelopes. Hated to touch them, and to read their contents. Hated, especially, the thought of who or *what* had passed them under the door. But the package that slid beneath the door was golden, not red. He breathed a sigh of relief, and walked over to retrieve it.

Upon opening it, he perceived the content of its cryptic text without grasping its full meaning:

Freedom is the realization of the good.

Interesting. It suggested a way to end his narrative. The protagonist would face temptations, but would not compromise. He'd seem to have been defeated until an unintended consequence of his own heroic choices brought about his salvation. So, it was to be a fable. Sly didn't always like to write fables. He preferred revenge stories. But he could be magnanimous. In certain moods, he would even indulge his employer's darkest desires. There was nothing in his contract that forbade it. But Sly had his pride. He liked to think he could work well in any genre.

He scribbled away for the next two hours, achieving a touching synthesis of the day's data in one meandering tale. He set down his quill, and filed the extra material under "Deep Long-term." Then he opened the vacuum tube, setting his five-part epic inside. He pushed the green button, then sighed as the story shot up into his ceiling. He'd just laid down on his musty couch when there was another knock at the door.

Sly sat up straight, gritting his teeth. He'd already done his work! They had no right! It was in his damn contract!

He watched the shadows behind the door. A red envelope crept under, then shot violently across the dirty tiles, landing at his feet.

"I can't live like this!" he screamed.

Behind the door there was cold, inhuman laughter. He began to cry. With shaking fingers, he tore open the envelope and, as his eyes danced across the dark words, their meaning flooded him.

You are a slave and a coward.

***

John Poe crept into Mellor's office, his report in his hands. Mellor wasn't there, but his black leather organizer sat by itself on his desk. He set down the report, but found himself unable to lift his fingers. With a final effort, he tore himself away.

Feeling a sudden impulse to wash his hands, he headed toward the restroom. As he did so, he passed his own desk. He'd left the Burroughs novel out. A muscular man on the cover faced off against a multi-armed beast, while his half-naked princess braced her vulnerable body against a stone. Embarrassing that he'd left it out, but he hardly cared now.

In the restroom, he avoided the mirror, unwilling to look at his own craven face. He washed furiously, his heart pounding. He wanted to slip away before Andrea came to work. When he exited the restroom, she was standing there.

"John! Why are you here so early?"

He looked at her chin, not at her eyes. That was nothing new. He always had trouble meeting them. She was a beautiful widow who might have offered him solace, and he couldn't allow himself to start thinking that way. But this was different. This was shame.

"Dropping off my report," he mumbled.

"I see," she said.

In his mind, he begged her not to press the matter. She did anyway. "Did you do the right thing?" she whispered.

He fumbled for words, the guilt washing over him. He knew it was wrong, and she knew that he knew it. "I said fiftee-uh ... fifteen percent growth. Mellor wanted seventeen, so I guess..."

Even as he said it, he knew it was worse than a lie. It was a pathetic attempt to silence his conscience. If anything, the two percent difference would render Mellor's preposterous estimate more plausible.

"John," she said.

"I know! I know, okay! What am I supposed to do?"

She took his arm. "He's not here yet. You can take it back. Change the numbers!"

He shook his head sadly. "I'm afraid I can't. I know what I should do, Andrea. I just can't do it. I've got to be able to support my kids!"

"What about *their* kids, John? All of the kids of the people who live here?"

He knew this was his moment. Saw it clearly. He'd even dreamed it, in one of those rare night visions. More than a dream. A message. A command. A prophecy.

But he was no John Carter. He was John Poe. The aging divorcee. The coward. His Dejah Thoris had been stolen away, and he had not sought her out to the ends of the earth. No, *that's* where he'd fled. He'd lost his kingdom. And now, looking into Andrea's sweet, virtuous eyes, eyes that were like the incredulous judgment of a heart-stricken God, he knew that he didn't deserve that kingdom. He hadn't the nerve.

"I—" he started to say, but he felt a sudden pressure in his arms. It crept up into his chest, squeezing like a vice. He tried to breathe, but couldn't seem to draw air.

"John?"

Pain shot through his abdomen. "Heh … help…"

He couldn't speak, and the pressure in his chest built until he thought his heart would explode. His heart. *Oh God!*

"John! Oh my God! John, are you okay?"

He slumped to the ground, clutching his chest.

"I'm calling an ambulance, John! Hold on!"

He gasped for air, as the whole world bore down on him.

***

The clock on the wall read "Early Morning," but John Sly found himself awake. If he were to make his attempt, it would have to be now. He walked into the center of the room, pulsing with fury.

A slave, was it? He would be a slave no more. He would not spend another night driving himself into an early grave. Now that was a thought. What was a grave? He'd never seen one. Not in this place. Why did the word have meaning?

His memories failed him. He knew there was a time of innocent hope when, perhaps, the room had been larger. Yet he couldn't recall details, or even how he had come to know the terms of his employment. These were givens. He merely existed.

He walked to the window where, once upon a time, he'd torn off boards and found the brick wall a few feet beyond. He didn't have rope for climbing down into the foggy darkness. He might wedge himself upward, but what if he slipped?

There was no use trying the door for the thousandth time. In the past, he'd tried prying it, slamming it, and chopping its hinges with the table. It was impervious, and he feared what lay beyond anyway. The floor tiles were equally impregnable, and the panels on his ceiling hit a solid surface inches above them. But there was something there, because the large metal cylinder brought him new data each night. If he could remove the mailbox cover—*what was a mailbox?*—then perhaps he could shimmy up.

They were bound to find out and make him suffer more. Little matter. Madness was madness, whether it came slowly or quickly. Beside him, the rats were chivying in their cages. They were hungry, and he had not remembered to feed them. Well, they'd have to get used to it. He was always hungry, and for something he couldn't name. His entire existence was a kind of nameless, ecstatic hunger. The rats pleaded at him with their beady eyes, and he smiled.

"With any luck, you'll never see me again. Here's a parting gift."

The two largest rats were in their own cages, and the smaller rats, both healthy and wounded, were in the third.

"Pity I won't be here to see the outcome," he said.

He took off the covers and snatched the smaller rats, dropping them one-by-one into the cages of the other two. They squealed in fright as their larger brethren descended on them. That done, he turned to the information pipe.

He pulled on the cover, but it was stuck tight. His eyes alighted on the metal quill, and he worked it between the cover and the metal piping. It loosened. Finally it came off in one tug and clattered to the floor. Crouching, he bunched his shoulders and pushed himself into the pipe. It had an L-curve, and he had to enter backward. As his eyes adjusted, he saw that there was light far above. Something was wedged there hundreds of feet up, but golden flecks spilled around it, illuminating the narrow tube. He began worming his way in.

It took an hour. The sense of claustrophobia was overwhelming, but he was determined. Finally he arrived at the obstruction. He reached up carefully to avoid losing his grip on the sides. Tremors went through his fingers as they brushed the thing's underside. Shoes. Human feet. They were the feet of a man he knew. It was his employer.

How he'd become wedged in the pipe, Sly didn't know. The immediate problem was that he blocked access to the place beyond. Sly began pushing his shoes, trying to drive his employer up before him. The body wouldn't move. Sly was struck by an incredible thought. Even if he escaped, they might find out about it. He had no idea the extent of their powers, but suppose, when night came, *someone* was there at his desk, working away? It would hardly matter to them *who* was doing the work, just as long as it got done. He was a cog. Expendable. So, just swap one cog for another.

Gleefully, he set to work dragging the body down. It was agonizing work, as the man was thicker than Sly. He heard an arm snap as he finally pulled his employer out of the pipe and flung him to the floor. The face gave him chills. The skin was ruddy, and the hair brown, so unlike Sly's gray skin and black hair. And yet, he recognized this man. He knew him.

How did he know him? Why did he remember this man's childhood, but not his own? The truth began to dawn on him, and a smile crept across John Sly's face.

"How did a pathetic creature like you ever earn the right to walk in the sun?"

The man was silent, but his chest rose and fell. Sly grabbed him by the ankles and dragged him toward the desk. He sat him down, and jammed him tightly into the narrow chair. The man continued to doze, and Sly took his bent quill and began to scrawl meanings on a piece of paper. He slapped the paper down before the sleeping man, and returned to the vent. He shimmied back up, full of eagerness. Finally reaching the light, he followed it into a white room where the same man laid on white sheets, surrounded by people Sly knew were called doctors and nurses. Touching the man, he understood him to be in a coma. He climbed up into the prone body. At that very moment, the eyes of John Poe snapped open.

***

John Sly waited until he was sure the doctor was gone, then sat up. He had a busy day before him. He dressed himself, and left before anyone was the wiser. On the way out, he caught sight of the date on the calendar, happily delighted at the novelty of reading with his eyes. Outside, he hailed a taxi.

The action meeting, according to fuzzy recollection, was at a restaurant with a French name.

When he arrived and entered the back room, he found Mellor seated with several engineers, money-men, and his own secretary. Poe's secretary Andrea was there, too, wearing an agonized expression. A screen displayed project notes on the wall, and Norman Reel's pompous face looked out from one side of a laptop, while Sharon Archer from the World Bank appeared on the other. There was a great commotion as he entered the room, and everyone began talking at once.

"John!" Mellor stood, and shook his hand firmly. "We heard you were in a coma! We feared the worst!"

"Well, there's still time for that," replied the John who was Sly.

Laughter from around the table. Tears were streaming down Andrea's face.

"Are you sure you want to be here?" asked Mellor. "The doctors said—"

"I feel very much alive, thank you," replied John.

"Well, if you're really alright ... there's no need to rush right back to work."

"I said I'm fine."

"Mr. Poe, Sharon Archer," came a voice from the laptop. John turned to look at her, happy for an excuse to look away from the contemptible Mellor.

"Chase told us what happened. We were all very worried, of course. So glad you're back on your feet."

Sharon continued. "Norman and Chase were just telling us about the energy growth projections. We're in the wrapping up stage here, but since you're present, I thought I might ask about the two percent difference. Do you really think fifteen is a more accurate number?"

Andrea looked straight at him. John smiled.

"No," said John. "It's not accurate."

He turned to face Mellor, and watched the color drain from his skin.

"Poe," Mellor said. "I think, coming right on the heels of—"

"-Hmm..." said Sharon, cutting in. "So, then Chase's seventeen percent is good? Or higher, do you think?"

"Look," said John, with a yawn. "We're not children here. We'd all like to be paid well, especially Norm over there. Let's just go ahead and say twenty-five percent. The Banguians are already dirt poor, so what do they care?"

Sharon's jaw actually dropped to the bottom of the screen.

"But your independent analysis? It says—"

"Independent of what? Take a careful look at my numbers, Sharon. They don't add up. I mean, isn't auditing the auditors *your* job?"

Sharon gawked at him. John turned, winked at Mellor, and left the room before anyone could say a word. As John exited the building, Andrea ran after him.

"John! What were you—"

He stopped her mouth with a kiss, pressing her up against the outside glass. Her shock was palpable, and she pushed him off.

"I'm not ... I'm not ready for this—"

He tried to kiss her again, and she slapped him hard across the face. "I said no! What has gotten into you, John? Is that what you think I wanted you to do? Embarrass the entire company in front of the World Bank? Why are you acting so strangely?"

He shrugged and walked away grinning, as Andrea braced herself against the window, biting back tears.

***

After ten minutes, he came upon a block of street merchants selling their wares. Beside him was a flimsy fruit kiosk, and near that, a display of cheap jewelry and African kitsch for Bangui's tourists. Hanging against the kiosk wall was a tribal mask. It was a red-faced lion, fangs bared, devil-horns rising from its head. A flicker in his periphery made him turn. Mellor's chirping daughter Mackenzie came into view. She was shopping, and flashing Daddy's money. John grinned and quietly indicated his desire for the mask. The merchant handed it over, looking shocked as John slapped an uncounted wad of cash from Poe's wallet onto the counter. He began pursuing Mackenzie at a distance. When she turned down an alley, he put the mask on and followed her in.

She was halfway through when she stopped, turned, and began to scream.

"I wouldn't do that if I were you," he said, in his most lion-like voice.

"Please ... don't hurt me," she pleaded.

"Hurt you?" he said, sounding offended. "What do you think I am? Some kind of predator?"

"Then," she sobbed, "w-what do you want?"

"All of that cash you're carrying."

She practically laughed with delight. "Oh that's all! Thank God! Here, take it all. We've got plenty of money!"

She retrieved two stuffed bank envelopes from her purse, hastily pressing them into his hand. John received them amiably.

"A bit of advice," said the lion, pocketing the envelopes. "Next time you're mugged, don't say that."

That night he stopped by Mellor's office, opened the leather planner, and tore out three pages on which Chase had foolishly written out his passwords.

"Don't worry," he said to no one in particular. "It's all going to help a developing world."

***

John Poe woke up in a room he'd never seen. It was dark, and it smelled of smoke, sweat, and blood. As his eyes adjusted, he saw the chrome pipe and glass tube that came out of the ceiling. His right arm throbbed, and he stood up, clutching it. Beside him was a window that opened to a brick wall, and below that, animal cages. Two of the largest rats he'd ever seen rooted around in stinking bodies of smaller creatures. They looked up at him and hissed.

John screamed and ran to the door. It was a deep black, the surface scuffed and scratched as if someone had tried to beat his way out. There was no handle. He reached beneath and pulled with all the strength he could muster with one arm, but the door wouldn't budge.

"What's going on!" he cried. "Let me out!"

The walls swallowed up his voice. Panicking, he turned around and saw the window. He went to it, and leaned over the edge. Above him there was only the faintest suggestion of distant light; below, only darkness. His body began to tremble.

"What the hell is going on?!" he yelled.

Then Poe noticed the note on the desk. A knot formed in his stomach as he approached it. His eyes couldn't seem to decipher the writing, but when he touched it, its meaning filled him. It was a list of instructions and commands. The last words filled him with horror:

It's my turn to run the show. You can never leave.

***

Sly leaned back in his bed in the cushy hotel suite he'd purchased with

Mellor's money. It had been another busy day, but now that he was setting his own agenda, he rather enjoyed hard work. The mask lay beside him, and he smoked a cigarette and waited hopefully for things to play out. Poe's cell phone rang. He looked at the number and grinned.

"Hello, Marissa, is that you?"

"John! Oh my gosh. Thank you for taking my call?"

"It's my pleasure, Marissa. How are you, and our kids?"

A pause.

"They're fine, John. They … they wanted me to tell you they miss you."

John smiled.

"I miss them, too, Issa. I miss all … I mean … anyway, what can I do for you? This is just such a pleasant surprise."

He could hear sniffles on the other line. Marissa was trying to find the words. "John," she finally said. "You know … you know about Simon?"

Yes, he knew about the man she'd left Poe for. He knew about her infidelity, and her guilt, and the role it had played in their divorce. He knew about his employer's cuckold cowardice; the way Poe had just let it all happen to him.

"Yeah. Well, what about him? He hasn't harmed you or the children in any way, has he? Because if he has—"

"I … I don't know, John. Maybe I shouldn't be calling you about this, but I was embarrassed to talk to anyone else. You know how my mother is."

"What happened?" he asked, with great pathos, which was difficult to summon, as he was still stifling a laugh.

"I got a call from a private investigator claiming to work for Simon," she replied. "He said he'd taken incriminating photos of me, but he said he'd hand them over if I made him a better offer."

"Were you unfaithful to *Simon*?" he asked.

"No! I've never been unfaith—I mean, I've never cheated on … on Simon."

He let the silence work its way into her heart.

"Then you've got nothing to worry about."

"But he's spying on me, John! Simon paid someone to take pictures of me! How could he do this to me? And the girls … I don't feel safe."

"Are you sure it was him?" asked Sly.

"He denied it! But this morning, there was a man outside our home taking pictures!"

John pumped his fist. This had all cost a pretty penny. Good thing he wasn't paying for it.

"Issa, I'm so sorry. If there's any way I can help you, or the kids."

She was sobbing on the other end, and she said nothing for a while. Finally, she spoke.

"John. Would you ... maybe just come here for a while? The kids want to see you. I'm so shaken up right now, I feel like I can't give them my full attention. I just can't believe ... John, *you* would never have done something like this to me."

He waited another five seconds. "Issa, I will be on the next flight to Missouri. I promise."

Sniffles.

"Thanks, John."

"My pleasure. I love you, Issa."

"I lo ... John?"

"Talk to you soon."

Click.

John slapped his hands together, and sprang up from the bed. He began pacing the room, toying with the idea of hiring some woman to call Marissa's home asking for Simon. A little jealousy and rage could tip the scales definitively in his favor. But it might backfire. Better to keep that one reserved for later. He had to return to the States immediately, before Marissa had time to change her mind, or Mellor realized he'd been robbed. Twice, actually. Time to put on Poe's best clothes, and catch a plane.

"Carpe diem!" he exclaimed, and laughed at the irony.

Suddenly, John stopped. He fixed his eyes on the empty air before him.

"What do you think *you're* doing?" he said.

***

John Poe stared at the window. He'd been too thick to escape the room through the metal pipe, and his arm still throbbed. In the hours he'd been pacing here, going mad, he'd stumbled upon the notion of freeing the rats. They'd come in from somewhere. They must know the way out. So he'd opened the cages and poured the loathsome inmates onto the floor. They'd thrashed around on the tile, hissing at him, but did not make for the door. Instead, they scrambled to the window sill, just as he'd been dreading, and crawled out into the darkness.

Now he was staring at the open window, paralyzed with fear. It was the same fear that had been gnawing at him for years, holding him captive in a compromised security. It was that lack of vivacity that had made him gruff and agitated, leaving him with a constant sourness that he sensed had finally driven his Marissa into the arms of another. Staring at the brick wall beyond the window, he had a moment of clarity. He understood that fear was worse than death if it brought it slowly under the guise of safety. He had nothing to lose now. He stepped onto the ledge.

Letting his broken arm dangle painfully, he stood on his heels. The rest of his feet stuck out over the void. Heart pounding, he pressed the flat of a shoe against the nearby brick wall, jammed his back into the gray stone of the apartment building, and began sliding himself, step-by-step, up toward the dim light. Inch-wise he crept, until he lost sight of the window. It was painful work, and yet he found that something in the quality of the place preserved him so that he strained without ever running out of the power to continue straining. He tried not to think of Sisyphus and his rock.

After what seemed hours, the faint light became brighter, and blue-tinted. The air smelled clean. He was getting closer, closer. It might have been a day, or an entire age, but his head finally peeked over the building top. In the sky was a blue sun. The top of his back was now leaning over the building's upper ledge. He need only shove off the brick wall in front of him, twist, and topple back onto the roof.

"One! Two! Three!"

He pushed, and wrenched his body to catch the lip with his torso. He caught it, hovered in terror for moment as he seesawed over the ledge, then finally dipped forward, tumbling safely onto the roof. He huddled there for some time, nursing his throbbing arm, unable to shake his anxiety over what might have happened had he tumbled backward into that infinite gap. The cool blue sun shone down upon him. It seemed to give no heat at all. John drew deep, calming breaths of what was not air, then rolled to his haunches. When he got to his feet, a dark-haired man was already standing there.

"What do you think *you're* doing?" said the frightening vision.

"Who are you?" said Poe, but he charged.

The man side-stepped, and grabbed him by his broken arm. The stranger wrenched it hard, and Poe screamed, first in pain, and then in the most helpless terror, as he was shoved headlong over the precipice.

He plummeted, shrieking, into the bottomless gap. He fell far past the window from which he'd escaped, sinking into ever-deepening shades of absence. A maelstrom of darkness tugged at his self-image, threatening to sunder his very being, until, finally, he seemed to understand. His own terror was the undoing of him. It fed the dark, bottomless absence that unpeeled him as he slipped down, down, down into the yawning, hungry void. He suddenly cried out in defiance. John Poe made an act of will, for himself, for his life, and against the darkness.

"I will not be unmade," he cried into the void. "I will be! I will be!"

***

Three Months Later

"John, we're leaving!"

John Poe smiled, and marked his place in *The Warlord of Mars*. Carter had recovered his beloved Dejah Thoris. All was well. Marissa poked her head around the corner.

"You ready?"

"Yes, honey," he said. "Just have to run to the bathroom."

"Okay," said Marissa, with a little dip of her shoulders. "Don't be long."

She glided down the hallway toward the garage, wearing a beautiful red bikini. Poe's daughters were already waiting in the car. John smiled again. They were technically still divorced, but that was becoming more of a formality every day. He stepped into the bathroom, did his business, and even remembered to put the seat down after. A dark oak tree brushed the bathroom window, and he smiled, remembering something.

As he was washing his hands, he looked at his reflection. It was the face of a new John Poe. A Poe who, perhaps, could stand to lose some weight, but who'd recovered his kingdom. Suddenly that reflection shimmered, and another man looked back at him, gaunt and black-haired.

"Don't you mean *our* kingdom?" asked his reflection.

"Fair enough," replied John, drying his hands.

That night, after a day of fun on the beach, John made love to Marissa, and fell into a dreamless sleep.

BECKMANN'S ABYSS

e woke, spinning end-over-end in a realm without up or down. Out here, far beyond Pluto's pull, Beckmann Swallows was his own planet. He was going to be sick.

"Stabilize!"

The thrusters went to work. Beckmann was intimately aware of the air he'd used speaking, of the fuel expended, as the EVAR—his Environmental and Vehicular Armored Rig—tried to stabilize with nothing but the distant stars for reference.

There was a double futility in it. Hadn't he come out here to kill himself? But even that had gone south. Or north, or east.

Stabilized, said EVAR.

The suit's clear, female voice had been specifically calibrated to his brain. It was supposed to make him calm. It wasn't working.

"Hibernate," Beckmann said, and the expense in air reminded him of being a kid, blowing through birthday money to the last three credits. He closed his eyes, and the EVAR put him under.

***

He'd been aiming for something. Beckmann woke up from a dream that was only a replay of the last moments before he'd thrown himself into space. The adage was true. Even in temporary hibernation, his brain seemed determined to recount its final moments. Beckmann was a perfectionist and had intended to kill himself properly. He had to do it the right way, so he could be sure of sparing Mary and their infant boy the repercussions. If Unity could recover his brain, they'd scan it, and encode its contents in a doom speaker. Had he just blown himself up, they'd assume the worst, and the consequences to his family would still be the same. But if he were to slip *accidentally* into the void of space, then not even Om would know how to get him back. And it would have gone to plan, if not for Lieutenant Kester.

They'd been deep in the void, trying to find something that wasn't there. Fourteen probes had been sent to explore the anomaly. Over the course of six years, thirteen returned empty-handed, though they'd traveled to the exact region at which the physics of surrounding space pointed, like ten thousand red arrows. There was nothing here. But someone in Unity, perhaps Om himself, was fixated. The fourteenth drone was a relic, an integrated neural hybrid. Its mind was the tissue of about two hundred human brains grown in tandem with an ever-spreading neural network. That kind of fleshy droid had been phased out fifty years earlier. Only apparently not. The thing's brain was more than half-human. And it had stopped transmitting and hadn't returned. This place was like the Bermuda Triangle. Coincidentally, he'd also planned to get lost forever here.

When Beckmann learned he was having an unlicensed son, he'd expected trouble. Mary must have done it on purpose, but she'd guessed he was too deep in the party to be punished. Correct, as it happened. They didn't take his child or send Mary and him to the settlement with the regressives. The party trusted people like Beckmann to ensure that *its* child was properly integrated. But when he'd held the boy in his arms, he'd known he loved him too much to go on living. He'd already lived three extended lifetimes. And his soul was black enough after only the first hundred years. He loved that boy, and he had nothing to give him but lies.

"Hibernate!" he shouted.

Why did he keep waking up? The pain of memory was too great. The EVAR beeped once, and again put him to sleep.

***

When Beckmann awoke for the second time, he was thinking of Kester. The good kid who'd wrecked his death. Some hours ago—maybe a U-day?—they'd come upon the place that was the cause of all the fuss, at the limits of the solar system where the droid probe disappeared. Beckmann sighed. He'd had it all planned out.

From the moment he'd held his little boy, Beckmann had carefully plotted the details of his own death. In his mind, it was the most loving thing he could do. He could still remember what it was to be free. He had no excuse for the things he had done—out of cowardice—so that he wouldn't be among those swept away. But it was different with the boy. This child would be integrated from the start. He'd never know anything was amiss. He'd entered the world after the eggs were broken, and the omelet already made. He'd never know what he'd never had—and had never helped destroy. Yet Beckmann couldn't stand to look at the little innocent, to watch him grow up warped in a world Beckmann had helped warp.

Since he couldn't be the good father that little John deserved, he reasoned that it was better to spare him a bad father. Or maybe to spare himself. It was one thing to do evil to others for the sake of some abstract ideal. It was another to hold an innocent, knowing you were the villain. He would not be the one to stain this white garment.

So, just as he'd planned, he'd crippled the outer sensor arrays, and then told Kester he was going out to have a look. As a precaution, he'd first drained most of the air and fuel from the other two EVAR units—though, not all the way, for that too would alert the ship's system, and the ship would notify Om. With just the lieutenant and himself aboard, this was the best and only chance he'd ever get. He wondered at the miracle of being assigned to this mission on the very day he'd learned of Mary's pregnancy. The timing had been perfect. Maybe God just wanted him dead.

And Beckmann was a man who obsessed over small details. He wasn't about to let his well-planned death be ruined by a rescue attempt. But Lieutenant Kester had figured it out and had ruined it anyway.

Jason Kester was a good kid, somehow. He'd reached adulthood before the New Formation went into full effect, so he was bio-bred, and had kept his own mind. A man like that would be weeded out eventually. Beckmann couldn't look at his junior officer without thinking of little John, and of what kind of young man he'd want him to become. The lieutenant even cracked jokes at Om's expense, as if the allmind wouldn't learn of it. No, the kid wouldn't last. He was far too wholesome.

As Beckmann stood on the edge of space, preparing to detach his tether and blast off into the void, Kester's voice came over the com.

"Have you fixed the array, sir?"

Just a question. All he had to say was, "Almost," or "Not yet." But Beckmann, who was, after all, about to throw himself off the biggest bridge ever built, still couldn't bring himself to lie to his junior officer. To deceive this boy, and for that to be the last thing he'd ever say to another human being, seemed terribly wrong. So he'd hesitated.

"Sir? I'm looking at the activity logs. According to them … the sensors didn't fail the way we thought."

Beckmann couldn't speak. If Kester was digging around in the logs, it meant he already suspected what Beckmann had done. A ready-made lie came to him to the effect that he'd only been trying to reset them after they'd failed. Instead he'd said nothing.

"Sir, Commander Swallows. Are you … eh … should I come out there, sir?"

He'd been made. Kester knew. But the boy was trying to protect him by not saying over the com what the activity logs showed. With only seconds to act, Beckmann unlatched his tether. He was on the verge of jumping, when Kester came out of the airlock. Beckmann couldn't believe he'd gotten there so fast. The kid must have been suiting up while talking, trying to delay Beckmann. Now he stood in space, floating against his tether a yard from the XL-9 Deepspace Shuttle's hull, staring at Beckmann.

"*Sir,*" said Kester over the com.

He couldn't see the youth's face through the Permaglass, but he heard the plea in his tone. The boy was too smart not to know what he planned to do, yet not old or broken enough to understand why. It struck Beckmann that he was a father about to commit suicide in front of his own child.

"Look," said Beckmann. "Just … just don't…"

But he never finished what he'd meant to say, for at that moment, something came out of the darkness.

The drone rushed toward them with alarming speed, spinning end-over-end, out of control. Beckmann's eyes grew wide, watching it double, triple, and quadruple in size. But its approach was not head on. It might miss the ship entirely. Beckmann grit his teeth; he forgot to breathe.

It was suddenly upon them, cartwheeling through the void only yards from the shuttle. It was, indeed, the large hybrid droid that had vanished. Its long gray arms rotated quickly and silently, and nearly grazed the shuttle. It did not hit the XL-9, but, as it passed, a trailing mechanical arm reached out for the ship. It struck Kester instead, and hurled him into the endless sea. Kester, the kid who could be his second son. Kester, in an EVAR suit from which Beckmann had drained most of the fuel and air. Beckmann had only hesitated a moment before going after him.

***

Fuel at 23%. Oxygen refurbished to 40%.

He'd been dozing again, and the com display woke him up. He did some quick math, and determined that the air could be refurbished four more times before it was unbreathable. His fuel, of course, was a fixed quantity, and he was too far away from the sun to augment it much with solar.

Before going out to jump the first time, he'd topped the EVAR off, and the two smaller auxiliary tanks, because he'd planned to drive himself as far as possible into the darkness. Then he was going to shut off his transponder, and free fall into nothingness till he ran out of air. But going after Lieutenant Kester had used up most of that fuel. On the return, he'd supplemented the kid's air with his own.

The rescue in the dark of space had been the most terrifying experience of his life. He hadn't much feared dying when it was just his own life at risk, but with the lieutenant in jeopardy, the thought of missing him, or the shuttle—infinitesimal pinpricks against the curtain of everlasting night— had exposed him fully to the terror of space. The human mind simply wasn't made to comprehend such scales. Strangely, though, it could *feel* that weight. That incomprehensible emptiness. By the time he got Kester back through the airlock and checked his vitals, Beckmann's own supplies were seriously diminished, and he'd considered staying. It was just Kester and he on-board, and the boy wouldn't rat him out.

But that was only because he was still young. Let him live as long as Beckmann had, and this bright-eyed lad would lose his soul like the rest of them. And it was better that the infant John imagine his father dying in his duty. It didn't matter that what Beckmann served was wicked to the very bottom, as if someone had opened a trap door, and let the devil loose on Earth. But the notion of a noble death in service of the good—the very thing he was too much a coward to have done in real life—that was something he could give to John. If the child's heritage was to be an illusion, let it at least be a noble lie. Such were the thoughts that went through Beckmann's mind as he prepared to step out of the airlock and launch himself once more into abyss.

"What about your son!"

Kester, damn him, had woken up. He'd stood inside the airlock, face pressed against the glass. Beckmann shook his head at him. Why did the kid have to make this so hard?

"You family needs you, sir! Whatever it is, it will be okay. There's … there's a plan for your life, sir. I know it!"

Oh, the hopes of youth. A useful vestigial instinct. It kept the species alive. But the species had produced a power which was the end of all hope. So he'd jumped.

But as Beckmann tumbled into darkness, a new thought came to trouble him. The droid probe had come from somewhere. Even at the speed it had been traveling, the XL-9 should have detected it long before it came hurtling into view. It wasn't there at all, and then it was. So there *was* an anomaly.

It couldn't be a brown dwarf, or even a smallish black hole. The drone would not have returned intact from contact with either. Could it be a ship? Even now the science of cloaking was in limited use on Earth. Surely an advanced civilization would have perfected it. Perhaps the anomaly was some massive artifact that could neither be seen nor detected, except by its effects. And there was a tale—little more than a legend, really—of a silver orb that had come down many centuries ago. He'd never been able to confirm it, though; even before the Negative Threes had forbidden general historical research as a decadent pastime.

More wishful thinking, thought Beckmann, because the air for words was too precious. *You're trying to make something out of nothing. You're trying to give death a point.*

But the idea that there was something out there was staying off the panic. He'd heard of the panic. Beckmann thought he knew what the word meant. Wrong, as it happened. The terror of space steadily grew in him. He kept his eyes on the com display, trying not to see the immense darkness, nor register the mocking distance of stars and galaxies held forever beyond his reach. He was no longer spinning, but it didn't matter. He was starting to choke on fear. If he didn't get it under control soon, he would … well, he would die. Faster.

"EVAR!" he shouted.

How can I be of assistance? replied the suit, calm as ever.

"Did you take note of the drone ship? Its angle of approach?"

The suit made a processing sound. Beckmann watched the charge bar, which was below the halfway mark.

Yes.

"Can you extrapolate its trajectory, and put me on that course? In reverse, I mean. Can you get me from here to a course that intersects its angle of approach, and traces it backward?"

More thinking. One of the charge bars disappeared.

With short burns, yes. Current fuel levels are—

"I don't want to know. Just get me on that course. Put me under and wake me up in three hours."

The system beeped once, and Beckmann felt himself rotate. Just before he went into hibernation, it occurred to him that he should save the last sleep juice for those final moments when the air ran out.

***

Beckmann was awake. For a moment, he wondered why it was so dark. When he remembered, he bit his lip to stay off the coming panic attack.

No one trained for such extremes. That he'd thrown himself on purpose into the void didn't change a thing. He could just as easily have willed his shoulders to sprout wings as will himself not to panic. It would have him. That sense of being utterly alone in a colossal abyss. An ocean of nothing. The utter anonymity of it. Infinite indifference, as cold as space. And it was eerie that he should go mad in this particular way, for it was not the first time. At the age of ten or eleven, Beckmann had woken his parents for months straight, screaming and kicking, dreaming of colossal spaces, and of cords hopelessly knotted and stretched to the ends of the ever-growing universe. Cords that he was tasked to undo. Hopeless. Hopeless. He was never able to tell them what that looked like. That it had seemed *true*. There were no images or words for the horror of the limitless.

Now he distracted himself by focusing on his so-called mission. It was only a game. Even pretending there was an anomaly out here, he would never find it. Even supposing he found it, it would do him no good. But so long as he imagined a goal, he was less aware of the swallowing darkness.

As he fell forever, Beckmann tried to count the faint stars. Not all of them were stars, of course, but such distinctions hardly mattered now. Perhaps they'd never mattered. As far as any man was concerned, every light in the sky was but a single flickering candle. That they could be seen made them meaningful. That they could never be reached made them all but intangible. Stars were ghosts. One couldn't even know if they were alive or dead. And whether the universe was a wonder made for man, or a cipher meant to mock his puny mind, was a question entirely irrelevant. Or perhaps man was irrelevant. Perhaps the stars, despite their beauty, were as indifferent as the bleak absence in which they floated. If so, human reason was only a curse. It would have been better to be a stone.

Beckmann looked at his fuel counter, saw that it was at eighteen percent. Saw his charge bar at ten percent. His air at twenty. He began to scream.

It was a wonder it had taken so long. He felt no shame. His mind had simply lost its frame. As he screamed, he seemed to go out of himself, picturing himself from the outside, white flotsam in a black river. The tiny, screaming thing waved its arms, and beat its legs, and pounded its fists against the black ocean. The universe didn't mind. His horror was of no consequence to it. Here was a being that felt the weight of a universe that itself felt nothing in return. Here were regions just accessible enough to admit entry by a mortal mind, yet so vast as to make ribbons of it.

"Help! HELLLLLLP!" screamed Beckmann, and nobody heard him.

Deeper, deeper, into the darkness. One tiny black pin slid into a vast, random tapestry. One white fleck of ash on a leaf on a tree in one of ten million copses of no account, set on the smallest rise of the longest range of black mountains that stretched and stretched and mockingly ended where no one could see them. He was not even food for the inky monster in which he moved. He was not even dust.

"Oh, God! Help! Help!!!!"

Beckmann's mind took flight from him entirely. He was waiting to melt. Had he the presence of mind to do so, he'd have gone to sleep until the end. But he couldn't think that far. He was doomed to die alone. Impotent. Screaming. Mewling in the far-flung, mind-crushing indifference of sheer size. But then he saw it.

It was nothing at first, except that it was something. Something actual, where all else was absence. A point in space. Not white. Not bright. Colorless, maybe. But something, rather than nothing. He fell toward it, shuddering, spittle and tears bunching around his eyes and chin in the absence of gravity. It grew larger.

When Beckmann first came to it, close enough to see it, that is, he didn't let himself believe it. If ever a man could see a mirage, it was now.

What did it look like? Was it round? He could never say. He didn't *see* it as such. He saw the space around it. Saw into it, like a window. Not the thing itself.

It might have been death. Touching him. Entering him. Was death the sort of thing that could be entered? Yet his plunge through endless night had prepared him. If this was death, at least it was specific. At least it came to a point. Had it been a chomping, toothy mouth, he'd have dived right in. Had it been fire, he'd have willingly been immolated. It was something. And *that* was something.

"EVAR," he whispered. "Remember this location."

EVAR processed.

Commander, I detect the anomaly, but cannot visually confirm it. I do not advise—

Beckmann touched the thing which found no referent in his finite mind. It pulled him in.

***

It was a swirling maw. He rushed through it, utterly still. He was suspended in the middle of it, and some current drove him through its center. It twisted as he sped, its colorful shifting walls, a thousand miles above and below him, gave the only evidence of motion. He felt no force. No pressure. Yet he could move himself at will, turning about in the ether to study the cavernous space.

It had structure. It arced above and below him, a massive, rushing ring whose upper and lower arches did not quite touch. Where they nearly met, a black and golden film stuttered between the swirling arches, forming almost a straight wall, etched with eerily regular patterns that changed as he tried to focus on them. Fractals and crosshatches. At moments, even lines, as if in this structure was realized a pure geometry, unachievable in lesser space.

It had a sound. A deep, yawing moan, thickly spread and yet almost too low to register. He felt it, more than he heard it. And it was not unpleasant. There was in it something like music, but one not made by minds. A music of forms, and bodies, and deep algorithms. It was the song of matter, the sound of the structure of space and time, frighteningly purposive, yet without its own intentions.

There were paths. In the great fractal wall, in the black that filled the spaces where the great swirling arches met, there were openings. Beckmann studied one through the EVAR's com display. He focused in and saw that it led off like a burrow to some far-off place. Zooming back, he scanned another, and another. They were not regularly spaced. He resolved to count them, but then sped through the swirling maw for what seemed hours before he spotted another.

"EVAR?"

The suit did not immediately respond. Beckmann looked at the charge level and gasped. Though he felt he'd been here hours, the EVAR's display hadn't changed. He made a note of the time. It was a struggle to peal his eyes from the beauty around him. He watched. He waited. EVAR did not speak to him. The time didn't change. It didn't change! Beckmann switched to hundredths of seconds. Then thousandths. Millionths. Only at this scale did the counter creep forward. He was rushing through the place at an incredible rate, but time itself had slowed to a crawl.

"Good God!" he cried, then remembered not to breathe.

But wait … could it be? He checked his air. Still at twenty percent. He'd been here far too long for that. Or had he? Was he living at his own speed, or at the speed of this place?

It occurred to Beckmann that he was not in space at all. He was between it. So *this* was where the droid had gone! But it had found its way out again. It was possible to escape.

Beckmann looked again at the clock readout, then at the fractal wall, where another of the twisting capillaries came into view. He suddenly faced upward toward the bright, swirling light. He could not hold it long in view. It was like a colorful sun, stretched out, refracted into all colors. Hoping against hope, he checked his power levels. Yes, it was true. Though his fuel was still low, it hadn't gone any lower. Meanwhile, his suit's power had doubled.

"EVAR!" he cried. "I think I'm getting solar power!"

The EVAR unit said nothing for a long time. Suddenly, the com link squawked. The voice was EVAR's, more or less, but it spat out words and numbers in a meaningless, high-speed litany. In this place of beauty, that machine noise was deeply unsettling.

"Strange," muttered Beckmann.

Strange to think that his fleshy mind, evolved to hunt, and trap, and mate, could process this utterly foreign realm. Could even take delight in its beauty, as terrible in its own way as the indifference of outer space. Yes, Beckmann feared its power, but the EVAR seemed insensible of it. Had the suit been an abacus, it would perhaps have fared better here. And then there was the fleshy drone to consider. It had had the wherewithal to find its way out. Beckmann looked back at the crawling millionths, and then back down at the fractal wall. Before he could think himself out of it, he tapped the thrusters once, and sent himself toward one of the twisted golden capillaries that now opened in the fractal wall. Just before he reached it, EVAR screamed.

Beckmann shot through the light-filled space for time out of mind. At its end, he seemed to rush toward a bright red star that filled his field of vision. Yet he passed through its center unharmed, finding himself alone and motionless, and in empty space. Below him was a blue planet, dotted with browns and greens.

For an instant, Beckmann thought it was Earth. Yet a moment's survey revealed the truth.

"EVAR, you there?"

Here, sir.

"What happened? I thought you weren't functioning?" said Beckmann.

Sir, per your request, I memorized the location of the … object.

Beckmann paused.

"And what about after that?"

After, sir?

"What was on the other side of it? You don't remember?"

EVAR processed.

I have just scanned the surrounding space, sir. The anomaly is not close by.

"Where are we then?" asked Beckmann, fearing the answer.

EVAR took a long time to process this request.

Unable to locate. These stars are not familiar. Are we in a simulation, sir?

Beckmann swallowed. Not familiar? He felt the panic coming on again. He tapped the thrusters, breathing a sigh of relief when he saw behind him that same hole in space that he'd entered somewhere, some time ago.

"We'll have to try again," said Beckmann, and swam through.

***

For a lifetime, then a dozen lifetimes, he explored the golden veins that spiraled out from the fractal walls. Sometimes he saw other paths, not veins but arteries that opened on the inner ring of the twisting space, and seemed to lead within. These he never explored. He found them terrifying. He checked the smaller pathways, one-by-one. Though few and far between, there were always more.

Sometimes he came out within sight of a living planet. Most often he found a lifeless rock, or nothing but empty space. Within the slipstream, he did not age. He did not decline. Only his mind, that intangible thing, aged.

The millionth seconds ticked by; the seconds only once or twice, that he could remember.

At what seemed to him many centuries, he began to suspect that he was going mad. Perhaps he was already mad. Perhaps he had died long ago, floating free of the XL-9, and this endless circuit was only the hell that his coward's death had earned him. He had no company in the slipstream between worlds. And the mere knowledge ought to be maddening that for all his journeying only two seconds had really elapsed. But he'd found a purpose here.

There were more doors to explore. And they were not infinite. He reasoned that they *could not* be infinite, because each opened on a different space. He'd learned to hold his breath in normal space, because there it depleted. But within the slipstream, he was practically immortal. And though he'd explored two thousand, nine hundred, and thirty-four capillaries, he was certain they came to an end somewhere. Either the slipstream would bring him to a sudden, shocking death, or it would return him to where he'd begun. It was impossible to move backward against its flow. But the droid shuttle had found its way out again, and so the slipstream—this angelic highway between worlds—must be a great ring. There was a way out. One of these paths must lead him home. Someday.

Upon finding it, he would die, of course. Once in normal time, he would again be subject to the regular entropy of lower space. He would turn his transponder on. He would instruct EVAR to launch him on a course to where the XL-9 had been. Where it must still be, since time hardly functioned here. But no one would find him in the void. Not unless God himself should intervene, and point Kester in his direction. And as God had not stopped the culling, nor the settlement, nor the last human war, Beckmann wasn't expecting much. Then again, Beckmann *had* found the slipstream.

But if he died, it would be with the knowledge that there were other worlds. Other Earths, where a man could live free. Places that *they* didn't know about; that they could never find. Om's Unity was not all-powerful. Someday, at some time, somebody would escape. And if, somehow, he lived … well, then, he would have something for John. He'd made his vow to that incomprehensible power behind all this, hoping that it was good; that the regressives were right. He allowed himself to hope that it, unlike the faceless anonymity of space, had a face. And if it let him live, then he would return with a heritage. Something to give his infant son. A Swallows family secret.

Thinking of these things, the ancient, tired man spied yet another of the golden capillaries in the fractal walls. So beautiful to behold. So much like every other. With happy resignation, he descended. Yet another day in the dayless world. One more chance. One more hope, before that hope was dashed again. But maybe. Maybe.

In his private centuries, Beckmann had become wise. One goal at a time was all a man needed. One step. One end. One good attempted. A universe was traversed one door at a time. Beckmann reached the doorway to yet another world and was pulled through. And waited. And waited. And waited, with bated breath, for what might greet him on the other side.

THE WITCH OF BELL HALL

Norah turned the page. Her cocoa was warm. Her book was good. The clock ticked pleasantly on the brick wall above the sofa. Her feet were propped up, clothed in cushy green socks. The balmy air of the deceptive Maryland spring—too early, destined to give way to cold before the humid summer came—floated through the window, eddying in the air around her, enfolding her in freshness. The chess clock went *Click. Pause. Click! Click! Click! Pause*, and you could almost hear the sound of Drew and Sing thinking in the intervals. This was leisure, and leisure was good.

Norah turned the page. She loved Nelly Robertson, particularly the *Felicity James* series. Outside of work, she spent most of her time reading the denser prose in St. John's Great Books curriculum. She had a photographic memory, which helped a lot at the art gallery, but only a little with Aristotle and Descartes. But she understood almost anything she read. And if she understood, she remembered.

Reading was a welcome distraction from her dilemma. All of her life she'd been in love with books. They would be her future, but which future? Between the pages of her *Felicity James* novel—she was using it as a bookmark—was an internship offer at Blackstone & Rose. Just this morning, Dr. McCarthy had pulled her aside, offered her student-teaching work over the summer, and all but promised to smooth her way into a professorship at St. John's, once she got her doctorate. Norah believed in stories. Life was a story. And, like Felicity James, she stood at a crossroads.

Norah turned the page. She wasn't conscious of doing so. If Aristotle could write like Nelly Robertson, everybody would be a philosopher. Presently, she lost the thread of what she was reading and looked up. It was like the air in the room blinked. She looked over, and the boys were still playing chess. She glanced at the common room door.

Wendy was there, just staring at her. Norah smiled—as warmly as she could without inviting conversation. Wendy looked past her, as if she hadn't been staring, then hurried down the hall. Norah tried to get back into her book. They'd roomed together the first year at St. John's, and Wendy had ended up in the same dorm with Norah every year since then. They were seniors now, and Norah had a dorm room all to herself. It was uncomfortable that both women had selected Bell Hall. Uncomfortable, and purely coincidental, Norah chose to suppose.

These days, running into Wendy outside of class gave Norah that feeling of ending up in the same elevator with someone to whom you'd just said goodbye. It was not that she disliked Wendy, *per se*, but the girl was nervous, and grim, and somehow unstable. She reminded Norah of Tinkerbell, if Tinkerbell was a black hole. Okay, she disliked her. Wendy needed something, and Norah didn't know what that was. Since first year, Norah had been cordial, but kept her distance. From time to time, she'd considered befriending Wendy, but then what? Some people were like weights. You could just sense that forming attachments with them would drag you into their private issues, and give you nothing in return. She'd felt that way all freshmen year.

Norah closed the book. She couldn't enjoy it now. Was this guilt? She thought back to Elaine McCarthy's small group lecture, and she winced on Wendy's behalf. Dr. McCarthy hadn't meant to embarrass Wendy—at least Norah didn't think so. The girl was just abrasive. Probably the professor was just being defensive, and she'd taken it the wrong way.

Norah sighed. Maybe she should reach out to Wendy. Take her under her wing a bit. Nobody wanted to touch a tar baby, but it might succor her own conscience. There was nothing to lose by being nice. Well, a little bit of her free time, but that would be okay, as long as it was really just a little. They could get milkshakes at *Chick and Ruth's*, or something. Talk philosophy. She nodded, as if agreeing with herself.

Her conscience thus mollified, Norah glanced at the clock. She heard heavy footfalls in the hallway, as if someone were running at full speed. She looked at the door in time to see a flash of white and brown that appeared to be Wendy. Norah and Drew and Sing all looked at each other, and shrugged and laughed at the same time. The boys went back to their game. Norah smiled, and settled back into her book, with time to spare.

***

Wendy hovered in the space between her sofa and her desk. Her hands were full of books, but not the books she wanted to read. Those were on the shelves set in the wall on trestles above her couch. *Teach Yourself French. A New French Dictionary. Chesapeake Wildlife. Foucault's Pendulum. Guitar for Beginners. House of Leaves.* And many others. The sofa gazed at her with warm invitation. She ignored its summons, and slammed her school reading down onto her work desk.

She was tired. Classes all morning, and five hours at the *T-Shirt Store*, selling expensive junk to tourists. Everyone but her seemed to be on permanent vacation. How she would have loved an hour to sit on the dock and watch the private boats she would probably never own rocking gently as their skippers strolled about, enjoying the little city.

Wendy forced herself to sit. Nightshade, her black cat, jumped up on the desk, and drew his furry flank across her face. Wendy scratched him where he liked between the ears, then shooed him away. She pulled out the planner that ruled her life. At the back she kept a ledger of her finances. After tuition, and food, and books, and gas, she had forty-two dollars left for the rest of the month. Maybe she should play the lottery. The grant she'd applied for—she was perfectly qualified, and had done everything right— was rejected. Just who did they give these grants to, if not the people who actually needed them? But maybe she was just unlucky. She was definitely unlucky.

She'd certainly felt lucky, when she'd been able to cover all of her books with just the money she'd budgeted. But this morning, McCarthy had noticed she was reading from the second-edition of *Columbia Short Fiction Anthology*, and not the third. McCarthy had written the introduction to the third edition, so it was extra special. And that essay would frame their discussions, so it was very important that she had that particular edition. And it was ninety dollars.

Could Elaine McCarthy please grant her permission to photocopy the introduction from another student? No, but Wendy could purchase the book from the campus store. Wendy had persisted. Could Dr. McCarthy please photocopy the introduction from her *own* copy, and give that to

Wendy? After all, it was the same stories. No, it was very, very important that they all have the same edition in class, because the pagination was different, and there were additional sidebars and biographical material in the third edition. Did Wendy need help locating the third edition in the campus store? Dr. McCarthy—the harpy—was sure there were copies available.

So she'd used her break to call local bookstores. Nobody had the third edition. On the way to her room, she'd passed the common room, and had seen Norah reading on the sofa. She remembered from freshmen year how Norah was the kind of person who only needed to read a thing once to understand it and file it away, point-by-point. She'd stood there for a while, trying to muster the courage to ask to borrow Norah's copy for an hour, but that would mean admitting she only had forty-two dollars. You only had to look at Norah to know that never in her life had she only had forty-two dollars. Wendy tried not to be envious, but it wasn't right. What would it be to be without cares, without any pressures but choosing which golden path in the golden woods you'd decide to travel? Some people had it all: the looks, the money, the time. And then there was Wendy.

She was gripped by a sudden fear that she hadn't paid her phone bill. Wendy pulled out her phone, and as she was about to open her bank app, she saw the missed call. She tapped the number. One of the bookstores had called her back, and they'd left a message. She listened to the voice mail. It was *Second Hands* bookstore, on Fleet Street. They had the third edition after all, and it was twenty bucks. They could hold it for her, but only until close. That was fifteen minutes from now. Wendy grabbed her keys and started running.

***

Second Hands was on the second floor. Now that she saw it, she recognized the place, because there had been a comic book store in the same building when she was a girl. She double-parked, glanced at the time on her phone, and ran up the stairs. The bookstore was one narrow room, crammed to the gills, and lit by a dirty yellow light. Unmatched shelves lined the narrow walls, and there were several large bins in the center of the floor. The closest to her was filled with romance novels, and she saw another with science fiction. Everything looked dog-eared and faded. Wendy surveyed the offerings dubiously.

"Hello?" she said.

She jumped when a voice beside her answered. Wendy turned to see a tall man in the shadows at the top of the stairs she'd just climbed. He held a bundle against his left hip. Her heart skipped a beat, because, for a moment, she'd thought the bundle was his head. He stepped into the light, raising his actual head, which he'd ducked to clear the lintel of the door. The bundle against his hip was just a stack of books.

She smiled. "Is this your store? I'm the one who called about the *Columbia Short Fiction Anthology?*"

She said it as if it were a question. The man looked momentarily confused. He glanced around, as if searching his memory. She saw now that he wore a faded green suit jacket, with green slacks, and a green button-down shirt. His eyes found hers again.

"Oh, yes," he said, with slow recognition. "We certainly have what you need."

With his free hand, he indicated one of the bins in the center of the room. She looked over, then back at him.

"Third edition? Like you said on the phone?"

He nodded. Wendy shrugged, and went over to the bin he'd indicated. It was just past the science fiction novels. She examined the stacks of assorted non-fiction volumes, which filled this bin in several closely packed columns. At the top of one column was a book called *How to Make Use of Free Time*. She laughed sardonically and moved it aside. Going through the stacks was like playing Tetris. The further down she went, the more disordered the columns became, and she grew doubtful that she'd find any edition of the anthology she needed, let alone the third. But just when she was ready to give up, she spied the corner of a book poking out at an angle near the bottom of the bin. She fished it out hopefully, and rejoiced when she saw the cover. She read, then re-read the words "Third Edition," just to be sure, before she hugged the volume to her chest.

"Thank you!" she said, looking up at him.

"Oh, it's no trouble to me," he said. "Will you be checking out now?"

She nodded. He deposited his stack of books on the floor, and made his way behind the counter. She placed the book down before him. He picked it up and examined it.

"Are you sure *this* is the book you want?"

She glanced at it briefly, then back at him.

"Yes, that's what I came for, remember?"

She hoped that hadn't sounded rude.

He nodded slowly. "I suppose so," he said.

He rang her up and put the book into a plastic bag. Handing it to her, he hesitated.

"Read carefully," he said.

She smiled. "I always do."

If the man only knew what a sieve her mind was. Unlike some people—Norah, for instance—she had to read everything three or four times. Twice just to understand it. Another time or two to retain it. As if she had any time to spare. Though she was dead tired, tonight she'd read through her professor's stupid essay, and then read it again. She'd walk into class tomorrow more prepared than the relaxed super-intellects and wealthy hipsters who had all the answers, and who bought their texts at full price from the campus bookstore. She took the bag in her hand, but he did not release it.

"You're sure now?"

She frowned.

"Yes," she said. "This is the book I need."

He let go, and then he smiled. "Very well then."

She tucked the bag under her arm and began to walk away. Wendy suddenly turned.

"If I didn't say it before, thank you, Mr…"

"You did. And it's Hommevert."

Wendy suppressed a giggle.

"Well, naturally," she said, and headed for the stairs.

***

It was dark when she got back to her dorm room. Wendy dropped the bag on her desk and collapsed into the desk chair. All she wanted to do was sleep. Going to school and working retail did not suit her. She was a private person, and dealing with customers all day sapped her emotional energy, and made college that much harder. If only she could have gotten that job at the art gallery, but no. The position had been filled, and by guess whom? Wendy was pretty sure that her once-upon-a-time roommate had applied after she had. They must have thought she looked more the part. Yet it was at least something that Norah also had to work while in school.

"I'm jealous," she said out loud.

I'm not just jealous of Norah, she thought. I'm a jealous *person*, and that's

112

worse. She didn't want to be that way. She shrugged, guilty as charged, and glared at the plastic bag.

After a colossal effort of will, Wendy dragged it to her, and dumped the book out. It landed on the desk with a dull thud. Wendy blinked.

"Oh. Shit," she said.

The brown cover back did not look at all familiar. She turned it over.

"No. I don't believe this!"

The volume staring up at her was not the *Columbia Short Fiction Anthology*, in the third, or any edition. It was a book she'd set aside. *How to Make Use of Free Time* read the infernal words.

Wendy put her face in her hands and cried.

***

"Wendy, what do you think?"

Wendy's shoulders leaned forward, slumped, and her hands were hidden under the lecture table. She hadn't said a word during discussion. Norah saw her stiffen at the professor's question, and then relax. She did not look up. At length, she tilted her head, as if considering.

"When I first read it," she said, "I thought the man had died and gone to heaven. But the second time, I realized it was just a delusion. From being hung."

Dr. McCarthy frowned. "Yes, of course. Bierce is pretty clear about that. But what about the idea I put forward in the introduction that the protagonist's delusions are Bierce's commentary on the war itself? On the illusory nature of the *casus belli*, given that the soldiers themselves aren't motivated by the same ideas as say, Jefferson Davis, or Lincoln?"

Now it was Norah who frowned. She'd carefully read the professor's essay, and remembered it point-by-point. Could it be that she had read the wrong essay? Then Norah paled, realizing what was happening, and looked at her professor, surprised. Wendy, who looked unwell, stammered at first, then finally nodded.

"Oh yes," she said. "That was an interesting analysis. I think you may be right there."

Dr. McCarthy smiled. "So you agree with me."

Wendy nodded slowly. "Not ... not at first, but the more I thought about it…"

Norah's mouth fell open. The cruelty of it made her scramble for some way to rescue Wendy. She'd taken five of McCarthy's classes over the years, and this ambush seemed so unlike the professor. Beneath her.

"Professor," said Norah, "you mentioned Bierce wrote horror as well. I thought that really came through in the story we read. Could you recommend another Bierce story, with a stronger horror element?"

Dr. McCarthy smiled at her, but would not be deflected. She returned her focus to Wendy.

"Speaking of horror," she said, "I wanted to get Wendy's take on the old man in Poe. Do you agree that the old man is really the murderer's own conscience?"

Wendy looked up. Her eyes had dark circles under them, but even so, Norah saw suspicion there. Wendy sensed the trap.

"I … I don't know."

"Don't know if you agree?" said McCarthy.

"I just don't know," replied Wendy.

The professor stared at her. The other students joined in, their mild amusement barely concealed. Norah thought, *She wouldn't really, would she?*

"You didn't read the essay, did you, Wendy?"

Wendy looked stricken. She opened her mouth, and closed it.

"No," she finally said.

"Then why didn't you just say so?"

"I … I need to leave," said Wendy. "I feel unwell."

She stood up too quickly, banging one of her arms against the underside of the table as she retracted it. Wendy flinched, and rubbed her wrist. As she did so, she cast a single, wounded glance at Norah.

But I was trying to help, Norah thought. Wendy collected her things, and hurried out of the room without another word.

***

Perched on her chest, Nightshade whined, wanting to be fed. Wendy lay in bed, wondering if she could get away with calling in sick. No, she realized. She had to close that day. After that, she'd have to go immediately to *Second Hands* to purchase the book she'd come for. Not that there was much point to it. She'd already been humiliated. Dammit, she would have to go get it, if only to avoid another ambush. She looked over from her bed at the accidental purchase still lying untouched on her desk. How had she grabbed that book instead of the one she'd come for?

Maybe I'm going nuts, she thought. Or maybe she was so tired, and so anxious, that she was sabotaging herself. Her family didn't believe in the literary life. Was part of her trying to prove them right? But the two books looked nothing alike!

She sat up and walked over to the desk. The book had a simple brown cover with ugly black lettering that barely showed up against it. She flipped it open to a random spot. The text that greeted her made her blink. She flipped back through the pages, and saw more of the same. Rather than the simple, sickly-sweet and upbeat prose that she'd expected from a how-to book, the little volume was packed with thick, almost scientific text. One section even had pages of the sort of math she'd done everything in her power to avoid ever seeing again. She flipped back to the table of contents.

The book was organized into two sections, Theory and Practice. Theory ran from page 3 to 323. Practice was only a single page. She flipped to it, past the dense, incomprehensible pages of equations and arcane prose. There she found a short introductory paragraph, followed by a numbered list, with three items.

The paragraph read:

"Having carefully studied the rationale behind, and the justification for, this method of temporal re-purposing, the reader is now prepared to put its insights to practical use. Taking care to observe to the letter the laws enumerated below, and being judicious and moderate in their application, he or she may begin to correct the great imbalance described in sub-section 2A, by making discrete, thoughtful appropriations, where doing so will genuinely avoid harm to self or others. Borderline cases should be avoided, as should any use of the method that could reasonably be termed dishonest, spiteful, or excessive. Observing both the proper form and the proper intention, the user will avoid all ill effect to himself, to others, or to the greater continuum."

Wendy read it again, comprehending it only a little more the second time. The list below was simpler, though in its own way, equally opaque:

I. Kronos is always conserved. Therefore, kronos re-purposed in the present must be subtracted from past time. Since kronos is conserved, its substance must first be converted into kairos, before it can be added to the user's present kairos (that is, subjective time). To do so, the user must obtain an appropriate relic from an acquaintance or familiar person (see Definitions) and use an appropriate formula (page 72).

Wendy shook her head. She did not bother reading on to the second and third rules, which, though shorter, looked equally dense. Instead she turned to the glossary, and searched for the word "relic." Reading it, her eyes went wide with understanding, and she quickly flipped to page 72. Several formulas were there. These were simple phrases, and could be spoken, or even thought. The implications broke upon her, and she smiled.

***

"A moment of your time?" asked Mark Tannenbaum.

He tapped on the partly open office door, and waited for Sandra to look up.

"Come in, Mark," she said.

He stepped in and shut the door just so it touched. He didn't want to give the impression he was staying long.

"I know you're busy," he said.

Sandra smiled, but Mark could see that he would have to be quick.

"I'll get right to it," he said. "I think we made a mistake."

"We?" asked Sandra.

Mark smiled innocently. "A small one, but probably important to the person on the other end."

"Go ahead," she said, "I'm listening."

He took a breath. "A grant application came across my desk from a Wendy Noid. I approved it, and sent it your way to sign off."

Sandra looked at him, saying nothing.

"Well," he continued, "it was an education and living expenses grant. The subject met all the criteria, so I approved it."

"Okay?" said Sandra.

He hesitated. "I was … wondering why you rejected it. Is there something I missed?"

Sandra frowned and put down the report she was reading. He could see he'd managed to annoy her, and that his obvious best efforts to the contrary meant little, if those efforts ended up costing her time.

"It may have been a mistake," she said, shrugging. "Let me look it up."

He stood there while she opened her laptop, and waited for it to load. Then she tapped away, searching the Maryland Education Commission's database for the rejected application. Finally she nodded, and clicked it with her mouse.

"Found it," she said. "All I can see is that I rejected it, but I don't see a reason. Wait, were you using the old web form?"

Mark's heart sank a little.

"Yes," he said.

She nodded. "That has to be it. When they changed the form, they switched the positions and the colors on the buttons. So I've declined like two, three of these by mistake."

He nodded, exaggerating his degree of understanding and sympathy.

"It was *my* mistake," he said. "Can we fix it?"

She wagged her head, and clicked away at her keyboard. Then he saw her frown.

"Okay, so you're sure she qualified, and that you approved it?"

He nodded.

"Do you remember anything else about Wendy?" she said.

"Uh … yes. She's an undergrad at St. John's, in Annap—"

She shook her head and sighed. "When we reject them, the application gets deleted too."

"That seems short-sighted," he said. "I mean on the programming end," he quickly amended.

"Yes, but I can't get it back now," said Sandra.

Mark furrowed his brow. Perhaps he ought to let the matter go, but he'd been particularly affected by the young woman's application essay. It had managed to convey both her ambition and her anxiety, without any sense of entitlement. He could clearly picture her still, a woman of letters from a family of poor, practical people, who expected her to fail. It would be a shame if his own mistake made her life harder than it had to be.

"Sandra," he said, his voice honey. "I know I screwed up. I'd like to fix my mistake. I can re-submit the application for her, and then we can approve it."

Sandra looked at him patiently. At first he thought she would refuse.

"Okay," she said, "but it's not that simple. We need the application, with her signature and everything. Do you have her contact information?"

He shook his head no.

"The thing is," Sandra continued. "Grant scams are on the rise. We've sent memos to all the Maryland schools to tell them not to believe any email from us that claims to have approved an application we've already rejected. So it's not as simple as sending her an email, or even giving her a call."

He nodded, understanding.

"But if I went down there…?"

Sandra sat back in her chair.

"You'd be willing to do that?"

"Yes," he said.

She mulled it over for a few seconds. "Okay," she said. "Just not during working hours. I need you here in the office."

Mark smiled, and almost bowed. A weekend trip to the state capital sounded nice, assuming Wendy was there when he arrived. Even if she wasn't, he'd enjoy the chance to walk down Main Street, and pass by tourists and midshipmen, not to mention enjoy the Sunday seafood buffet at *Buddy's*. And if Wendy Noid couldn't be located, his conscience would at least be satisfied. He'd have done his best to help, and that was more than most people did.

***

Who the hell, thought Norah, was Flynn Obern?

Felicity James remembered Obern. She described in italicized lettering the case of the stolen painting. Obern was the hedge-fund manager, the one who'd helped launder the money from the Van Gogh. He'd gotten away; so said Felicity James. Now he was back, standing with an icepick in the women's bathroom, and delivering his villainous monologue. But Norah could not remember him.

She knew that she ought to, even felt the space in her head where the memory was supposed to reside. But it was gone. All that was left was a kind of thin film surrounding the contours of the memory. Norah *knew* that it had been there. She'd read both series multiple times. And she never forgot anything.

"Are you okay?" asked Sing, looking up from the chessboard.

He affected concern, but she could see he was also annoyed at the distracting need to check on her welfare. They were in the middle of the game, and the clock was running. Her face, she realized, must have shown her distress, and Sing was torn between calculation, and this more human form of interaction.

"Yes," she said. "I'm fine."

Suddenly ill, she snatched up her book and left. When she got to her dorm room, she reached into her purse for her keys, but could not find them. Confused, she turned the knob on her door. It was unlocked. She pushed open the door, then stepped back.

"Hello?"

There was no answer. She flipped on the lights and ducked her head inside to look around. Gathering herself, Norah took out her phone, and keyed in 9-1-1. Her thumb hovered above the green icon. Norah was not in the habit of leaving her dorm room unlocked. She tiptoed around the room, stopping to check in every space where a person could conceivably hide. After a few minutes, she'd thoroughly explored the small space. She shut the door, and locked it.

As she stepped back into the room, her shin bumped against the small, glass-topped coffee table that she'd purchased at the Pier 1 in Harbor Center. The bump caused a jangling sound, and she looked down. There on the glass rested her missing keys. She snatched them up, and sighed in relief. She must have just forgotten the keys here. She thought she remembered locking her door before she left, but perhaps that was a dozen other memories of the same thing. Memories, even her own, could sometimes blend.

Satisfied that she was safe, Norah returned to the problem at hand. How had she managed to forget the hedge-fund manager's backstory? Whatever the cause, it could quickly be amended. She crossed the room to the black bookshelf, where two levels were dedicated entirely to Nelly Robertson's *Felicity James* novels. She was proud of her collection, and of the twenty dog-eared volumes whose pages had so often passed through her fingers. Each was like a relic of her life, stained with the oil of her fingers, perfumed with her own interest. She even shared a last name with the author, and part of the first. Nelly; Norah. Like two peas in a pod.

Norah went down on one knee and searched the volumes of the second series. With chagrin, she realized that she didn't know exactly which book had the Van Gogh theft—only that it was one of the earlier novels. She looked, counted, and then her mouth fell open. Each novel was numbered, one through ten. The third book of the second series was missing.

***

"You're chipper," said Annette.

Wendy smiled, and refolded the hoodie that a customer had decided not to buy. The white cursive lettering on it read: "Maryland: We've Got Crabs!"

"I got good sleep last night," said Wendy.

The sleep part was true.

"Must be nice," said Annette.

Wendy nodded. On her own time, the time she'd made her own, she'd slept, taken a long walk, returned to *Second Hands* to get the book she'd meant to buy, and had even studied a little French. It had all been so nice, until she'd begun to worry that she'd run out of kairos. How much time had Norah spent reading that novel? What if the time Wendy had re-purposed suddenly ran out? There wasn't any way, she realized, to measure subjective time as it passed. So she'd gone back to Norah's room, and exchanged the volume she'd taken with another that looked particularly well-loved.

Norah had been in the room when Wendy came in. She'd sat like a mannequin, caught mid-stroke, a length of brown hair suspended in the air at a right angle, just at the moment when the brush pulled free, but the hair had not yet fallen. While Norah was caught in this instant, Wendy had swapped volumes. Now back in kronos, she carried the new novel around in her purse. But objective time, which had once seemed to rush by imperiously, now enslaved her to its slow march.

"I'd like to take a quick break," Wendy said.

Annette frowned.

"You just got here," she said.

Had she? Wendy looked at the clock on the wall. It was true. She'd only been at work twenty minutes.

"Okay, yeah," said Wendy, laughing.

Annette smiled curiously at her. "We're supposed to switch over the seasonal wear today," she said.

"Hoodies and jeans can go to the twenty-percent off racks," she continued, "and there are two boxes of new T-shirts, and a box of women's bathing suits in the back room. Jeff wants the new shirts on the two front endcaps, and the swimsuits should be on the front rack."

Annette indicated the locations, then smiled apologetically.

"I'd help," she added, "but I have to do inventory while we're slow."

"No problem," said Wendy.

In a few minutes, Wendy had dragged the boxes to the front of the store. She sighed and got to work. After transferring the hoodies and jeans, and re-tagging them all, she started on one of the boxes of T-shirts. Intermittently, she'd look up at the clock, and notice how little time had passed. Time seemed to drag on and on. She resented the need to abide by its dictates. After emptying the second box, she looked up to see Annette staring at her.

"Yes?" she said.

"Um," said Annette. "You're just going *really* fast."

Wendy shrugged. "Just want to get it done."

Annette nodded and returned to her inventory. Wendy waited for her to turn her back. She glanced out the front shop windows to make sure no one was looking, then softly spoke the formula. She stood up and looked at the clock. The thinnest hand had stopped. Annette was frozen half-stride.

"Great," said Wendy.

She stretched her aching back, then walked out the front door.

One thing that bothered Wendy, as she strolled along Main Street, past the time-locked tourists and the frozen midshipmen, was the physics of interaction. If she needed to talk to someone, she could, even when they were frozen. She'd done it at *Second Hands*, when she'd gone back for the anthology, and had to ask where they'd moved the bin. She'd done it when she went up to the deli to buy a milkshake. People came out of their time fugue when she addressed them, and went back into it when she was done with them. She supposed that when they awoke, they'd simply be confused about how they'd suddenly moved from one position to another. But what was actually happening to them—to reality—when she pulled them into her kairos? She shrugged, suspecting that she wouldn't be able to understand the answer anyway.

It was the same with smells and sounds. The silence wasn't surprising. All she could hear were her own footfalls on the pavement, but nothing else moved. If she looked up, she could see gulls caught mid-flight. But the absence of smell was unnerving. If she focused on smelling, she could. She could pull the matter in, and make it interact with her normally, but only by being intentional. That made Wendy wonder if she was actually breathing air, or even needed to. And, it suddenly struck her: *What if I died in kairos? If I shot myself, would I hang around in some twilight state until my time ran out?*

She arrived at the harbor, and began walking along the beside the moored yachts. On a whim, she decided to go out on a pier, and climb up on one of the boats. The owners were sitting at the table on the deck. Wendy amused herself by sitting down beside the woman, who was smiling across at her husband. Wendy had the impression that he was telling a funny story, but one his wife had heard before. It wasn't the story that made her smile, but him. Such a loving look. Wendy sighed.

She got up and decided to explore below. It was nice down there. There was a large, comfortable bed, a TV room, and even a jacuzzi. She stared at it for a while, then laughed out loud. Placing her hand on the lip, she willed it into her time, then turned it on. Wendy had no bathing suit, so she slipped off her clothes and climbed in. The bubbles and jets made almost no sound, as if their noise was caught in the air just above her head. She closed her eyes, and relaxed into herself. Then her eyes popped open.

All at once, the sounds and smells came back. Wendy climbed out, and began frantically looking for a towel. There was the sound of laughter above, and the white noise of tourists outside. She dried herself as quickly as she could, and put her clothes back on. As she stood on one foot, trying to put her shoe on, she slipped, and bumped her shoulder against a shelf set into the bulkhead. Books and movies fell out, clattering on the floor.

"What was that?" said a woman's voice from above.

She looked around for somewhere to hide. Footsteps sounded on the deck above her. There was no time. So she ran.

Wendy ran screaming up the ladder, bowling over the middle-aged man who stood at the top of it, looking down. The man's wife screamed as well, and threw her arms up defensively. Wendy ran past her, hopped the gunwale to land on the pier, and bolted up the dock ladder. Coming over the harbor wall, she saw a hundred eyes on her. Wendy threw an arm up to hide her face before sprinting toward Main Street.

She was breathing hard when she got to the *T-Shirt Store,* and it took a moment to calm down. How had it happened? She was sure that Norah had read that book for more than the thirty minutes or so that Wendy had felt pass. Was it the jacuzzi? Had turning it on somehow triggered normal time? She didn't know, but she had to find out, and soon. It struck her that she'd not carefully read all of the rules, and might have missed something important. Finally breathing normally, she stepped through the door of her shop.

Annette stood there, clipboard in hand, staring at her.

"Where the hell have you been?"

Wendy stood agape. She glanced at the clock. It had taken her almost three minutes to run back.

"You left the store?" said Annette, incredulously. "I told you we had to move up the seasonals."

Wendy tried to think of something to say. Annette shook her head.

"You know, it's not a good look, going out on break when I told you to wait."

Wendy looked down, shame-faced. Annette took a step toward her.

"Wendy," she said, curiously. "Why is your hair wet?"

***

II. Once activated, a given relic must be entirely converted to kairos, before another can be activated. Any attempt to activate a new relic before converting the present relic invalidates said new relic, unless the present relic is first returned, and a word of relinquishment (page 92) spoken.

Wendy understood now what had happened. As she'd suspected, the first relic, the book she'd already returned, had not been fully expended. That meant that when she'd left the *T-Shirt Store* to go on break, she was still spending its kronos. Time had run out. And, if she was reading it right, the new book was no good now. She'd have to return it, and get another. But what was this "word of relinquishment?"

She flipped to the referenced page, and reading it, frowned. A word of relinquishment was a formula like the one she'd been using, only one which surrendered back the kairos taken to its original relic. But, in that case, wouldn't she lose the balance of whatever time she'd gained for herself from the first? That meant that she'd have to be much more cautious about how she used time, otherwise it might run out at an awkward moment. She ought to have taken the time to understand this earlier. Wendy carefully read the third rule.

III. Relics borrowed must be returned in kronos.

Now that she understood the second, the third was obvious. How else could she obtain and use a new relic without expending or relinquishing the present one? But that meant she must always risk discovery in the very act of obtaining a new relic. And she could never really relax in kairos either, not unless she was safe and sound in her own room, at night, when others weren't about.

Then what was the point of stealing time, if she wasn't free to walk about, and do as she liked with it? Wendy briefly considered using one of her own items, then discarded the idea. The rules said "acquaintance or familiar person." Even if that included her, how could she be sure that some now useless item wasn't entangled with memories and events that had made her who she was? And anyway, she was still unclear about the interaction between kronos and kairos.

For example, she'd received two voicemails on her phone while she was in kairos, but had not been able to listen to them in kronos. The voice, a man's voice, had come out of the speaker both slow and fast, as if someone had slowed it down, then stretched it thin. No matter what the book said, somebody was getting robbed somewhere. And it wasn't going to be her. No, it was the others who had more time than they knew what to do with. She would keep taking from them.

Wendy sat back in her chair, pondering. The first order of business was to return the useless relic. Since it must be done in real time, she ought to stop using Norah. Someone else, someone she really disliked and didn't mind stealing life from, must have something she could use. A wedding ring would be ideal, if she could get to it, but that seemed unrealistic. Wendy had never been particularly devious, and did not foresee herself pulling off such a heist.

Then it struck her that she knew someone who had the perfect relic. The woman was obsessed with it—with herself, thought Wendy—and the loss of it would serve her right. But first she must return Norah's useless book. That shouldn't be too hard, since she'd copied Norah's room key. The other relic would be harder to obtain, but she'd find a way.

Nightshade crept over the table, and climbed down into her lap. He balled himself up in the space between her thighs and stomach, meowed softly, and looked up at her with expectation.

"Yes, my pretty," said Wendy. "She'll get just what she deserves."

***

As she crept down the hall, Wendy glanced into the common room. Seeing Norah there, she hurried on. The first time she'd done it, there'd been excitement, and a sense of anticipation. Now it was like she was carrying a cold lead ball in her belly. At Norah's door, she fumbled with her keys, and dropped them. They clattered loudly on the floor, but she spied the copy of Norah's key, and swooped them up by it. She inserted the key into lock. It wouldn't turn.

Panicking, she withdrew it from the keyhole, before double-checking. But it was the correct key—chrome, and bearing the logo of the key-copying kiosk. She tried the key again, with the same result. Heart pounding in her chest, breath coming out in shallow, hoarse bursts, she tried to turn the handle. Wendy pulled and pushed on the door, then slapped it in frustration. The keys slipped out of her sweaty hands, and crashed once more against the pine-wood hallway.

Not knowing what else to do, she took Norah's novel from her purse, and placed it flush against the bottom of the door. Norah would know someone had borrowed her book, but that couldn't be helped. Crouching down, she spoke the word of relinquishment, and stood to leave.

"I had the lock changed," said a voice behind her.

Wendy turned slowly. Her old roommate stood in the center of the dark hallway, hands clasped together. Wendy fumbled for something to say. Norah took a step toward her, eyeing the keys white-knuckled in Wendy's hands.

"What's going on here, Wendy?" said Norah.

Looking down at her own feet, Wendy stepped past Norah, and rushed off into the corridor.

***

For the next three days, Norah pondered the matter. It was clear that Wendy had been in her room, and had taken her things without asking. It seemed obvious she'd also stolen her key, and had had it copied, though Norah probably couldn't prove that. She imagined herself turning Wendy in, and then Wendy admitting she'd *borrowed* the book—from her old roommate, she'd say—and apologizing, and getting off with just a stern warning. Norah couldn't prove what she knew. She couldn't even understand it.

That Friday morning, during what was supposed to be Dr. McCarthy's Short Fiction lecture, Norah kept her eyes on Wendy. She wanted her to know that she knew what she'd been doing. Not *how*, but what. She sat across the table from Wendy, and Wendy must have felt her eyes boring into her, because she managed to avoid looking up throughout the lecture. That was why Norah hadn't noticed it at first, the professor's strange demeanor.

Always sharp and quick to guess who had done the readings, Dr. McCarthy was uncharacteristically reticent throughout class. She spoke in the vaguest generalities, asking for opinions instead of offering them, letting her students describe the narratives, and encouraging them to offer interpretations. It came to Norah's mind that she'd seen this pattern before. In high school, in Mrs. Simpson's English class.

She had a specific memory of the first week of sophomore year, and one of the students bringing up the summer reading. Weren't they supposed to discuss those books? "Ah, yes," Mrs. Simpson had said, asking the students what they thought. Norah remembered thinking then that the teacher seemed uninterested in the summer reading assignment, and, later on in the year, seeing the contrast between this apathy and Mrs. Simpson's demanding approach to other reading, that the woman likely hadn't bothered to read the summer books at all. That was why she'd let the students — the three or four who'd actually read — run that particular class. It was the same thing now, with Dr. McCarthy. The professor nodded, and smiled, and kept mum.

As Norah studied Wendy, the other girl smiled. It wasn't a pleasant smile, and it grew about her cheeks, a millimeter at a time throughout the lecture, until it seemed to spread from ear to ear. Silent throughout the period, at length Wendy turned to the professor, and asked a question of her own.

"Dr. McCarthy," she said. "I was wondering about your take on Ambrose Bierce."

The professor looked at Wendy. "Uh … yes? What about it?"

"Well," said Wendy, "you mentioned in your commentary that the protagonist in *Owl Creek Bridge* might be the author himself, employing the victim's delusion of surviving his own hanging as a metaphor for the distance between the work that an artist intends to craft, and the actual work that appears on the page."

Dr. McCarthy looked at Wendy, blinking, then nodded slowly.

"Yes … and, what was your question?"

"I just wondered if you could elaborate on that," said Wendy, "and help us understand how you arrived at that insight."

Norah frowned, trying to remember that point. The professor hesitated, then smiled knowingly.

"Well, of course, as I mentioned—as I probably mentioned—that's only one scholar's view," said McCarthy. "But a scholar should never give the impression that her own view is infallible. It is, admittedly, an idiosyncratic position, and I'm happy to hear your counterpoints."

Wendy smiled. "Oh, no! I think it's brilliant. I just wanted to make sure I'd properly characterized your position."

The professor shifted uncomfortably in her chair, but finally nodded, her glance moving down to the table. There was silence in the room, and McCarthy at last looked up. Norah watched her survey her students. There was something desperate in her eyes. Thomas, a loquacious man who always sat nearest to McCarthy, drummed his fingers on the table.

"But professor!" he said, "That isn't your position at all."

McCarthy looked at him. The color drained from her face.

"But … surely," she said, "I *considered* that view."

There was a ruffling of pages, as the other students searched their copies of *Columbia Short Fiction Anthology*. The professor said nothing. She looked out at her students like the man in Ambrose Bierce, waiting for floor to drop out from under him.

"I just double-checked," pronounced Thomas. "It's not in there."

The professor touched her head.

"I'm … thinking of adjourning early today," she said. "As a matter of fact, I'm a bit under the weather."

Norah and the other students looked on, concerned. Several assured Dr. McCarthy that an early dismissal would be perfectly fine, and everyone told her to take care of her health. All except for Wendy, whom Norah noticed, looked on with undisguised glee.

The professor rose, and pushed her chair in.

"Sorry," she said, and her voice trembled.

"No problem at all," Thomas assured everyone. "And when you have a chance, you can look through your essay, and find the point you were referencing."

She glanced at him, so green that Norah thought she might actually be sick.

"As a matter of fact," said McCarthy, "I've misplaced my copy."

Without another word, she left the room.

Norah turned, and fixed her eyes on Wendy. The other girl looked back at her, face dripping with pleasure.

"What are you staring at, Nelly Robertson?" said Wendy.

Norah clutched her chest. Her skin broke out in gooseflesh.

"It's *Norah*," she choked.

***

Mark Tannenbaum arrived in Annapolis late Friday night, and stayed in the Maryland Inn. It was on his own dime, but he was not due back until Tuesday, had already used most of his vacation time that year, and wanted to milk the long weekend for all it was worth. On Saturday, he took a long walk through the little city, visiting the harbor, St. Mary's Church, and even making a stop to see the bone ships at the Academy museum. Walking back into downtown through Gate 3, he headed toward the College of St. John's.

Buddy's would have to wait till tomorrow, when his work was done, and he could relax. He couldn't afford to eat there two days in a row anyway.

Despite being forwarded to Wendy's phone, he hadn't been able to obtain her cell number, or even get her to answer. It was good that the school kept such custody of its students' personal information, though, and he expected no problems once he showed them his credentials in person. And Mark didn't mind the time walking in the picturesque, red-brick city. Time was the one thing you couldn't make more of. It was precious to him.

At length, he arrived at the administrative building. After a few minutes of skeptical interaction, the woman behind the desk finally relented, admitting who he was. She would not direct him to Wendy, nor relinquish the entry code for Bell Hall. But she did agree to walk him there, and wait with him until Wendy could be informed, and brought down.

After a short stroll, they arrived at the place, and Mark saw how it had obtained its name. The building appeared to be an old church, refurbished as a dormitory. Above the red-brick structure rose a white bell tower. The paint shone brilliantly in the midday sun. His guide typed in the building code, and they made their way inside. She seated him in a chair in the foyer, and went upstairs. Mark settled in, and waited.

***

It was an old house on Duke of Gloucester, painted blue. The yard was trimmed, but not mowed. Ivy grew on walls, giving the place an English look. Norah wondered if she might someday live in a house like this, or if her fate lay north, in a high-rise in Manhattan. But there was little time for such thoughts. She hesitated for a moment, thinking of the absurdity of what she'd come to say, then knocked anyway.

After a moment, Norah heard sounds from inside. The curtain beside the door was pulled back, and then the door opened.

"Norah," said Dr. McCarthy.

The professor's eyes were red and swollen.

"Doctor McCarthy," began Norah.

Her professor put out a hand, touching Norah's wrist.

"It's … Elaine. Here you can call me Elaine. Did you come to check up on me?"

"Yes," said Norah. "Partly."

Elaine McCarthy looked at her curiously, then waved her in. She sat Norah down at the living room table. The house was clean, and hardly looked lived in. Elaine made her tea, and set it down on a coaster before her. Then the professor sat.

"It's a nice place," said Norah. "Very clean."

"Yes," said the professor, a little sadly. "My husband … well he left me earlier this year. So I have it to myself. So far I haven't managed to let it go to pot."

Norah smiled. "I'm sorry," she said, taking a small sip of her tea. It occurred to her that this private pain probably explained McCarthy's recent sharpness. Her impatience with Wendy.

Elaine shrugged. She seemed on the verge of saying more, then shook her head.

"So what brings you here? I mean the other part of 'partly'?"

Now that she was here, it sounded crazy. Norah almost wished she'd not given herself away. She thought about holding back. Listing her concerns about Wendy, but without the bit that was impossible. At the very least, she could mention the stolen keys. Then she thought of herself walking away, without having told Elaine what she knew.

"Damn," said Norah. "You're not going to believe this."

She told her. Beginning with her own experience with the Nelly Robertson books, Norah laid out the evidence for what had happened. What she believed had also happened to Dr. McCarthy. The professor stayed silent, listening and nodding without interruption. When Norah had finished, Elaine took a long sip of her tea, then spoke.

"I don't think you're crazy," she said. "I've … I've heard of this sort of thing."

Norah was taken aback. "You have?"

The professor shrugged. "Not in anything I'd consider serious scholarship. But I have a sister who'll believe any nonsense. Crystals and that kind of thing. Maybe this is something like that."

Norah looked down at her feet. "So, you think I'm a kook."

"No, no," said Elaine. "I think that kooks are people that go too far down the rabbit hole. But 'too far' is the operative term. There *are* rabbit holes, you know."

Norah nodded, relieved that her beloved professor didn't think her a fool. Elaine drained her hot tea, gulping it down as if she didn't notice it was steaming. She stood up, dusted off her skirt, and straightened the thick black belt around her waist.

"Well, then, let's go," she said.

"Go?" Norah asked. "Where?"

"To Bell Hall, of course," said the professor. "If she has my book, it'll be on her person, or in her room."

Norah blanched. "She could be at work. And anyway, you just wanna go into her room, and take it from her?"

The professor looked down at her, bemused. "Yes. Why the hell not? You have a problem stealing from thieves?"

"No!" said Norah, laughing nervously.

Standing beside each other, almost hand-in-hand, the two women marched toward the professor's car, and were soon speeding along the narrow street.

***

The door to Bell Hall swung open, and two women stepped through. Mark rose to greet them.

"Have you seen Wendy Noid?" they all said at the same time.

Mark laughed. Then he stopped laughing. The two women, one young, and one in her mid-forties, looked quite angry.

"You first," said the older one.

"Um, I'm here to talk to Wendy about an education grant she applied for," said Mark.

The woman smiled sardonically. "You might want to hold onto that," she said. "Use it on a more worthy recipient."

"Why? What has she done, ma'am?"

The women looked at each other. The younger one shrugged, as if to say, "Why not?"

"Come along then," said the first. "We might as well have a mob with us. Maybe we'll need it."

They marched up the stairs. Mark followed, musing to himself about hell's fury, and deciding not to get in the way of it. As they climbed, the woman from the administrative office was descending from the other direction.

"Professor McCarthy?" she said. "Can I help you?"

"Come with us," said McCarthy, without stopping.

The four of them now tramped up the pine-wood steps, and entered the corridor that led past the common room. Norah surged ahead, turning the other direction, heading down the hallway toward Wendy's room.

"I don't think she's in her room," said the woman from the office.

"Good," said Professor McCarthy. "Let's hope she left it there."

"What?"

"Stolen property," said the professor.

They arrived at Wendy's door. McCarthy drew herself up and pounded on it. When there was no answer, she tried the knob.

"You can't just—" began the administrator, before McCarthy turned an icy glare on her.

Reaching into her purse, she withdrew a wallet, selecting a credit card. She held it up, looking rueful.

"Oh well," said the professor. "I'm about to pay it off anyway."

She slid it between the door and frame, ignoring the rising protests behind her. Mark stared, like a fly on a movie theater wall. This was definitely turning out to be an exciting weekend. In a few moments, the professor had the door open. She flung it back and flipped on the lights. The group pressed inside, even Mark, who was expecting at any moment to be asked to leave. Feeling awkward, he shut the door behind them and locked it.

Wendy Noid was not at home. Mark looked around the room. The place was somewhat messy, and rather bare. He noticed only a bed, a small couch, and a desk that was covered in books. A black cat had pressed itself into the gap between the books. Professor McCarthy noticed the pile and walked briskly toward it. Shoving the cat aside, she snatched up a book, flipped through the pages, then held it up triumphantly.

"She really did it!" said the professor, looking at the younger woman.

"Well, I should hope so!" said the woman from administration. "After all, you broke into her room!"

There was a slide and click. Everyone went silent and turned toward the door. It opened. A girl wearing a worried expression stepped through. When she saw them, her mouth fell open. She looked first at McCarthy, then at Norah. Finally her eyes went back to the professor, and settled on the book in her hands. Dropping her bag, she turned to run. Suddenly she stopped, faced the professor, and extended her hand.

"I release and relinquish you, and all that comes from you," Wendy said.

Without looking away, Wendy backed into the hallway.

"No! You come here!" snapped McCarthy, snatching at the girl's extended hand.

The cat screeched, then jumped on the professor. Crying out in pain, McCarthy tore the cat from her right shoulder and flung it into the couch. She turned to face Mark, the side of her cheek scratched and bloody.

"Don't just stand there!" she shouted at him. "Go after her!"

Not knowing what else to do, the man from the grant department took off down the hallway.

***

When Wendy was halfway to work, she'd begun to feel unwell. She'd enjoyed her little joke yesterday, at least at the time. Now she felt guilty for humiliating her professor. Even though McCarthy had done it to her first. Even though she deserved it. Realizing that this could not be all that was troubling her, she stopped and looked into her bag. Then she saw what she'd done.

The book she'd brought in her bag was not Dr. McCarthy's personal copy of *Columbia Short Fiction Anthology*, all lined and highlighted, and well-used. It was her own copy. She could not believe she could have been this stupid twice. Was the world conspiring against her, or was this yet another trick played upon her by the power she now presumed to wield? The damned cat had been sitting on the books before she left, sprawled out over both copies, and she must have grabbed the wrong one. She told herself it didn't matter; that she could make it through one day without going into kairos. Anyway, she ought to be careful about using it out in the open. But as she walked, the need for it grew. The thought of being at work all day without the means of escape was too much to bear.

She rushed back up the street, angry at herself for walking to save gas money that she'd need before the month was out. Now she'd have to sprint in public like a fool, and then hustle back in time for work. But no, that wasn't true. She only needed to run there, and then slip into kairos until she was at the shop door. It would be like teleporting!

She slowed down a bit, deciding to jog toward the college. It made her mad. Even with the book, her life was still hurry, hurry, hurry. Did it ever stop? Finally she arrived, punched in her code, and ascended the stairs. As she approached her door, she began to feel nervous. Perhaps she'd been too bold with Norah. That slip-up with the name, that had come from carelessness. She could not afford to be so careless anymore.

When she opened the door, and saw McCarthy, Wendy knew the game was up. The professor glowered at her, her face full of knowledge and victory. Norah was present too, and a man she didn't know, and a woman whom Wendy recognized from the school office. But they couldn't prove she'd stolen *time*—only books. She started to run, then, remembering, turned around. Reaching toward McCarthy's book, she spoke the word of relinquishment, then bolted down the hallway.

Angry voices followed her. She had to escape. True, they would likely throw her out of the school, but that didn't really matter now. She'd not lost everything. All she really needed was time. That was all anybody needed. But she had to think fast. Where could she find another relic, one that wouldn't run out before she could make new arrangements? It had to be someone she knew; at least an acquaintance. If only she could clear the building and perform a search.

As if by magic, she looked up as she ran, and spied the fire alarm. She pulled it, then sprinted down the hallway. Dashing into the common room, she saw Sing and Drew sitting at the table, deep into another chess match. Their hands flew manically from pieces to clock, and they pored over the table like hypnotized machine-men.

"Get out!" she cried. "There's a fire."

"You get out!" yelled Sing. "We're playing bullet here!"

In the space of saying it he took two pieces to Drew's one, and managed to castle.

"You wanna die for a chess game?" she pleaded.

Sing rolled his eyes. "Come on, Wendy, it's just a drill."

"No," she said breathlessly. "There's smoke in the hallway."

Sing paused the clock, stood reluctantly, and took out his phone to snap a picture of the board.

"Don't touch *anything*," said Drew.

"Okay, I promise," she said, as if it had even crossed her mind. She hated chess.

The two men got up and sauntered out, entirely unconcerned about the fire. There was a mad rush of feet in the hallway. Wendy pulled a couch from the wall and crammed herself behind it. After a few moments, the voices migrated elsewhere, and Wendy was left alone in the building. She heard sirens in the distance, and the sounds of people gathering outside Bell Hall. This was her chance.

Rising from her hiding place, she tried to think of someone she knew. There were only a few people, after all. Likely they'd have all left their doors open. She could just go in, and—

Wendy stared at the chess board. Those boys spent hours playing every day. She thought of the days those hours added up to. She considered her hasty promise not to touch the board. It was just another lie, another bit of meanness she would have to embrace. Sing had taken a picture; and they could always get a new board.

But as she mulled it over, she realized she wouldn't need the board. There was something even better, and it was staring right at her. The chess clock, a literal embodiment of the time she craved, was there for the taking. She snatched it up and ran.

She couldn't go down. There was a crowd of people in front of Bell Hall, and firemen and police on their way. But she could go up. Up the stairs, to the very top, to the little restored space where once a church bell had hung. Now it was a cozy nook where students could read, or study, or look out on the city. She made for it.

She reached the bell tower, panting, and locked the door. Wendy sat down at the table, placed the clock before her, and spoke the word. Nothing happened.

Her heart hit her stomach, and she tried again. When there was no response, no sense of passing from the weighty world of seconds and hours into that free space of inner infinity, she began to wonder if she was mad. If she'd dreamed it all. Or was there something else she'd forgotten to read, some small detail in that long first section that she'd never seen, or had passed over without recognition?

Wendy reached for the clock, and noticed it was stopped. Of course! It was a chess clock. The double-sided button was settled in the middle. Maybe the thing's kairos was frozen. She pushed it down on one side, and the clock began running. She felt herself slipping into the stream. She'd just settled in, breathing a sigh of relief, when with violence she was yanked back into objective time.

"What?"

She slapped the top button the other direction, and nothing happened. Panicking, she slapped it left and right. No change. Did it have to be reset? She started pushing the other buttons at random, and finally the readout showed one minute on each side. She pushed the top button again, and sighed in relief as the numbers ticked down, and she sank into kairos.

Not long afterward, she was forcibly returned to the tyranny of kronos. Again and again she reset the clock, jumping in and out of that cruel realm of matter and motion, the heartless churning of the atoms and gears that bound all things. With each rude awakening, the sirens grew louder. She tried to increase the interval, but fire alarm inside, and the blaring sirens, and the shouting of men now tramping up the stairs, only multiplied her panic. It ought to have been easy to add more time, but Wendy couldn't think clearly enough to do it. She pushed the + and − signs, and got an error message. The thing had five buttons on its face! Why did it need so many buttons!

There was a sound of scratching at the door. Phantom-like, she rose and opened it. Nightshade had found her in the tower. He'd come to keep his mistress company. The cat hopped onto the table and stared at her as she again reset it to one minute per side. She realized that she could extend her stay in kairos by hitting the clock while in subjective time, taking seconds from each side, and guessing at the conversion from kronos to kairos. Each time she did it, she was painfully ripped out of one kairos, and then plunged into another.

Nightshade opened his mouth and began to scream. She saw him now as choppy black motion, shifting in and out of her world. Now, only now, did she recognize her error. What had the book meant by "an appropriate relic"? There had been more on that page, but she hadn't bothered to read it all. And her comprehension was terrible. She would have liked to go back and check. But the world outside was closing in, and there wasn't any time.

MIRROR SPHERE

Prologue: Nelphel-Crmer

There you see her, still clutching the shard.

"Why does she clutch it still? Does she believe its components will function in isolation?"

Nothing of the sort. Have you not attended to their natures?

"Yes. They are rational beings, but subject to many fallacies, such as that of composition. Perhaps she believes the whole is still contained in the parts?"

[A pause, as the Seraph considers.]

In a sense, that may be true. It is not a matter of reasoning, but of the inner spirit. What they call 'the heart.' You see how even their words for the immaterial are bound up in solid energy.

"Then teach me, Wise One, for I do not comprehend the riddle."

She clutches the shard because it helps her spirit to remember. It is as with your peoples, when you go to bathe in nebulae, that you might taste the Beginning, and remember. So does she. So do all of worth among them. She clutches the shard that her spirit—her heart—might not forget that from which the shard came.

[The questioner is silent. He ruminates.]

"I suppose I was unwise to send it then."

No, little one. You were only reasonable, and so could not conceive that it would fail.

"Wise One, tell me true: If He knew I would fail, why permit my folly?"

To teach you, little one. To teach your peoples.

[Something like a sigh passes through the energy that gives him form.]

"I see it now. Why we must contain them. Why we are not permitted to embrace them. Still, I do not understand my failure. I only see that it is a failure."

Then do not lean on understanding, but on true sight. Enter into my energy, and behold the tale again. This is not to chide you, but to teach you. That is why He let you try and fail. Not to chastise you—for your energy is pure—but to confirm you in your work, until all is accomplished.

"Yes, Wise One. Show me. Tell me again the tale of my Mirror Sphere."

Felizitas

"Two hours a day? Just for this subject?"

Dr. Felizitas Chandra-Wright looked patiently at the incredulous undergraduate. She reminded herself to respond cheerfully, so as not to make her response an embarrassing public correction. After all, the young man should be commended for actually admitting his surprise at the true cost of academic excellence. It was an incredulity shared by others of his generation. In this country, where university was only a box to check, standards often fell victim to other values.

"Two hours," repeated Felizitas, her German accent making her words crisp, "is the academic standard."

There was a long pause.

"Oh," said the young man.

Felizitas, still smiling, let her gaze pass over the other freshmen. She was a thin woman with sharp features. The bones of her face and hands were angular, and quite prominent. She kept her dusty brown hair very short. Her neck was just a tad longer than it ought to be, and her nose was small and hooked beneath black eyes that seemed lit from behind. The students called her "Professor Stork," and that amused her.

"Now then," she said, wrapping up her introduction, "while every academic discipline requires immense time and study, exobiology, because of its multifaceted nature, demands still more. We are, after all, a subject in search of its subject, if you will permit the pun. For that very reason, the student of extra-solar life must be the master of several disciplines. All science, all knowledge, really, proceeds from the known to the unknown.

That is doubly true for us, since we must proceed from practical knowledge of astronomy, physics, chemistry, and the study of life here, to the theoretical search for the conditions under which it might flourish elsewhere.

"And that means mastery in those subjects. There is a very real possibility that you will never see, in your lifetime, the practical realization of this discipline's goal: the discovery of life external to this planet. On the other hand, you may enjoy a long and prosperous career writing all kinds of popular rot about what life on other planets *may* look like, and it is unlikely that any aliens will come along to contradict you."

About a third of her students laughed at the joke. That seemed a promising sign for the year.

She sat down then and began going through her notes. The undergrads, by degrees, recognized that the class must be over, for the professor was no longer teaching. They began filing out of the auditorium, but Felizitas was already absorbed in her work, and she hardly saw them go. She was preparing two articles. One was about an exoplanet called CoRoT-24 b. She'd submit it to an academic journal. The second was a sidebar piece entitled "Other Earths." If Discover decided to publish, it would cover a dinner out with Yatnesh, and not much else. Teaching distracted her from her real work, and it took her a moment to find the train of thought she'd abandoned just before class. It was just coming back to her, when her phone vibrated.

She'd have ignored it, but saw it was Yatnesh. Felizitas huffed, then answered the phone.

"Ya, my love," she said.

"I am sorry to disturb you in your work," he said, perhaps reading her tone.

She smiled. His cultivated Indian accent held a constant charm, which dispelled her momentary annoyance. "Macht nichts," she said. "How are things?"

"The day passes well," replied Yatnesh. "But I called, at this inconvenient time, for a reason."

He paused.

"I stopped by the house after Philosophy of Mind 201," he began. "When I did, there were two men at the door. They appeared to be government officials. Anyway, I invited them in, and we spoke. They would like to see you. They are here now."

She frowned, half-puzzled, half-annoyed at another interruption.

"Is there some kind of trouble?" she asked.

"We are not in trouble, but you'd better come home anyway. I would ... characterize the matter as urgent."

Felizitas drummed her fingers, then, sighing, closed her notes, and began stacking papers with her free hand.

"Can you give me some idea what this is about?" she asked.

There was a pause, and Yatnesh seemed to mute his phone. After a moment, her husband's voice returned.

"I can say nothing on the phone," he said. "I'm going to hang up now. See you soon."

***

Felizitas sat on the couch beside Yatnesh, watching the live feed. They were bookended on the sofa by two agents, plain-looking men who reminded her of somebody's uncles. As she watched the screen, her small mouth fell open, and her hand slipped into Yatnesh's. They both squeezed tight.

"Do they..." she began, not knowing what she wanted to ask. She tried again. "Has anyone approached it? I mean the astronauts or drones?"

"No, Doctor," said the man to the right of Yatnesh.

He was the larger of the two, and had identified himself only as Sam. The slighter, dark-haired man to her left never spoke. He was almost featureless, but for a thin blank spot on his left eyebrow. Of the two men, Sam was by far the more personable.

The footage from the drones wasn't blurry, but it was taken from far enough away that she couldn't be sure of what substance the object was composed. Only of its shape.

"Why don't you move them closer?" she asked.

There was a pause. Sam answered laconically.

"Not authorized. Approach could be perceived as a threat."

She frowned. The dark sphere in a high orbit around Earth did not seem to be doing anything at all. It was hard to tell, but she saw no lights or apertures on its surface. If anything, it reminded her of an eight ball, but one that reflected the lights from the drones more brilliantly than would be if the surface were truly black.

"If you won't bring them closer," offered Yatnesh, "why not wait until it's out of shadow? That is a poor place to get a look at it, where the Earth is in night."

139

The agent to Felizitas' left, the one who hadn't yet spoken, made a sound like a small chuckle. The other, as if interpreting for him, stood and walked over to the coffee table. He crouched down and waved his finger around the screen.

"It's always in shadow. In fact, it moves to stay in Earth's shadow, but slowly. We almost never observe it moving."

Felizitas drew a sharp breath. "I thought you said it was orbiting?"

"I said it was in orbit," replied Sam.

"But it moves only to stay concealed?"

"Not exactly," said Sam. "When the drones first approached, it was moving slowly against Earth's rotation, but it stopped and changed direction. It moved toward them."

"And then?" said Felizitas. Her heart was pounding in her chest.

"The drones were told to keep a distance of a thousand clicks. They moved back as it approached, to maintain that separation. The object then matched them, and it's maintained that distance ever since, still adjusting course to stay in darkness."

Yatnesh cleared his throat. "So, whatever is controlling it wants it to be seen by you, and yet, it both detects and respects the boundary you've set for it."

Sam looked at Yatnesh, and gave a small nod.

"But," Yatnesh continued, his brow furrowing in confusion, "if it wants the drones to see it, why does it stay in shadow? That is the first riddle we should be trying to read."

Felizitas leaned forward and inhaled sharply. Sam and her husband both looked at her. She said nothing.

"Dr. Chandra-Wright?" prompted Sam.

Suddenly conscious of their attention, she felt strangely reticent to share the notion that had come, fully formed, into her mind. She tested the idea first, to see if it was sensible.

"It's just that," she began, "well, you're afraid to approach it, but maybe it wants to be approached."

Sam looked at the quiet agent. The other nodded back.

"We think so too," said Sam. "But considering its behavior—concealing itself in darkness—this could be some kind of a ruse. A trap."

"A trap?" she said.

"A bomb, perhaps."

Felizitas shook her head. Another look passed between Sam and the silent agent.

"But you don't think so," Sam prompted. "You have some other idea?"

"Yes," she said, carefully.

But the question hung in the air, unanswered. Felizitas wasn't sure they were ready for what she thought. But they had come to her, and Yatnesh, and she could think of only one reason why.

"Sam," she began, pronouncing the agent's given name with thinly veiled skepticism, "why did you bring this to me? I'm an exobiologist. Yatnesh is a philosophy professor."

Sam nodded, expecting the question. He sat down on the other couch.

"You have an English father and a German mother," said Sam. "Professor Chandra is Indian … with certain family connections. And your father, I'm sure you knew..."

"Yes," she said. "His work was privileged. But he didn't work for the U.S."

Sam smiled. It was a chiding smile, like she ought to have known better.

"Nations..." began Sam, but he seemed to think better of it. "The point is, as his daughter, you understand discretion. So that's one reason. Another is the … international character of this investigation."

"But those aren't the main reasons," she pressed.

"No," admitted Sam. "I think you know what it is."

Felizitas looked at Yatnesh. She saw by his expression that he was thinking the same as she.

"It's our paper," said Yatnesh, speaking to her, more than to Sam. "Alternative Modalities of Conscious Experience."

"That's the one," said Sam.

Felizitas felt a sensation like electric ice creeping through her veins.

"You … you think it might be conscious?" she said in a whisper. "Alive? Not a ship, but a lifeform?"

Sam looked again toward the quiet agent, seeming to ask permission. He nodded.

"But that's just what I've been thinking!" she said, almost shouting. "The whole time we've been watching, and when you described the way it approached, then hung back … the way it's hiding in the shadows, but wants to be seen. It's like it's … it's..."

"Hunting," said Sam.

"Flirting," said Felizitas, at the same time.

They stared at each other across the table, while the dark sphere floated on the screen in her periphery. Sam was frowning at her. She frowned right back at him. When he began to speak, she talked over him.

"If it were hostile," she said, "it would not be going out of its way to let itself be seen."

"Then why hide in the shadows?"

The voice came from so close to her, Felizitas almost jumped. The quiet agent beside her had evidently spoken, though now his expression was as placid as a lake. The blank spot on his eyebrow changed the shape of his eye, making him seem asymmetrical and inhuman.

"Predatory behavior is fairly universal," she began. "Even across species and the kingdoms of life. Predators generally ambush their prey, or run them down from a short distance. A rattlesnake lies in wait and strikes quickly. If it rattles, if it lets you know it's there, then it is trying to avoid conflict. Eagles, tigers, trapdoor spiders ... they all prefer surprise and a quick kill. They don't advertise. Predation is a niche, which is to say, we are likely to find it wherever there is life, and it's bound to have certain similarities, even in life that works on totally different principles. This thing is not hunting."

"Then why conceal itself?" asked Sam. "What does it have to hide?"

Felizitas smiled. "Maybe it's hiding because it wants to be found."

Sam looked at her as if she had eagles, tigers, and trapdoor spiders growing out of her head. He shrugged.

"I'm not sure I know what that's supposed to mean," he said.

Felizitas tested the thought again, wondering if it were really as crazy as he seemed to think it was. As it almost sounded to her. She looked back at the screen, mesmerized by the dark sphere moving in a sea of night inside the shadow of Earth. The more she looked, the more certain she felt. It was not hostile. It wanted to be seen. How could she prove it? Yatnesh came to her rescue.

"There is a simple test we could make," he said. His accent, musical and refined, drew all the attention. He continued, "but you'll have to risk a drone."

Sam shook his head. "They're a few million a piece. And if it thinks our intentions are hostile—"

"—Just ... hear me out. Please," continued Yatnesh. "I do not think you will lose the drone. Now, then, we have two working hypotheses: one, that the sphere is hostile, and two, that it is friendly, and that it, or its controllers, wants to establish contact of some kind. If the first is correct, then upon approach, the object will react in some way, perhaps destroying the drone once it's close. Like a Venus flytrap, you see, attracting only so it can do harm. But if so, we will then know it is hostile, and will also have some data on its structure and armament. And this knowledge will be far cheaper now, when it is orbiting, then later, should it choose to descend to the surface."

Sam clenched his jaw, clearly disturbed at the thought of it entering the atmosphere.

"However," continued Yatnesh, "if the second hypothesis is correct, then the object may make some peaceful sign or gesture. And either way, we'll better see its structure."

Sam pressed his lips together and leaned back into the couch. He stroked his chin for a moment, then looked over at the quiet man. Felizitas turned to the silent agent, but didn't detect the slightest expression on his face. Evidently, he had made some sign, because Sam suddenly stood, took out his phone, and left the room. They waited in silence until he returned a few minutes later.

"Very well," he said, looking first at Yatnesh, then at her. "They're sending one in, with the others holding back to transmit."

Sam retook his seat by Yatnesh. After a few moments, the screen split. Now there were two feeds. On one, she saw a single drone drift away from the other, and slowly creep toward the distant sphere. The second feed was the approaching drone's own point of view.

It took several minutes for the drone to reach the object. Felizitas stopped breathing. As the light from the drone touched the object's surface, she realized why the dark shape had seemed so bright. It was not dark after all.

The surface was perfectly reflective, radiant, like a mirror of diamonds. The drone looked back at itself in reflection, its headlight bouncing off the glossy exterior, so that the beam cut a path through the darkness behind it. It was a large object, but how large was difficult to say. Evidently the NASA controllers were wondering too, because the drone projected a measuring laser onto the sphere, and began to move upward toward its pole. The drone disappeared behind the sphere for several minutes, then finally came up from the bottom pole, returning to where it had begun.

Throughout the drone's circuit, the object remained stationary. Felizitas saw no signs of external markings or ports. Nothing that would indicate a weapon, nor any system of propulsion. It seemed woven without seam from top to bottom. The drone put out its beam again, and was preparing to measure the sphere's equator, when something happened that made the silent agent beside her shout in alarm.

The sphere moved. Gently at first, then more quickly until it seemed to match the very speed at which the drone had moved over it before, the sphere now rotated on its axis, moving beneath the red beam. Its movement was unambiguously intentional. It was helping the drone in its task. The four of them stared at it, dumbfounded. Numbers came up in green on the bottom left of the screen. Measurements.

She stared at the numbers. Something stood up inside her brain and did a cartwheel. Two numbers: 1.21439 km—its equatorial circumference—and 1.21236 km—its meridional circumference. It was not a sphere. Not quite. Fireworks were going off in her mind, the sign that her subconscious had already reached a conclusion and was waiting impatiently for her intellect to catch up. With shaky hands, Felizitas reached into her purse for her phone.

"No pictures," said the man on her left.

"I need the calculator," she said, speaking hoarsely.

She fumbled with the pin, and quickly pulled up her calculator app. It only took a moment to crunch the numbers. When she was finished, she started laughing.

"What is it?" all three men asked together.

She looked up at Yatnesh, tears in her eyes, though she was smiling. She did not know why she cried, except that she was in awe.

"The sphere ... it makes a ratio with Earth. It's 33,000 times smaller. Exactly. What does that mean?"

Yatnesh looked at her, and squeezed her hand. He started to say something, but whatever it was died quickly. On the screen, the sphere was moving. It wasn't rotating anymore. Instead, it dropped, plunging gently into the atmosphere, like a stone into the sea.

Dante

Dante put a hand out.

"Slow it down," he said, the flat of his palm against Aliyah's chest.

She was four, and not much for listening. The girl drove hard left, then suddenly spun off his hand to the right. They were in the Sheep Meadow in Central Park, and now she was running free toward the Mirror Sphere. He ran to catch up with her.

"Oh, so you a little athlete, huh?" he said, catching her hand.

Aliyah looked up and pouted, but he kissed her chubby cheek, and sat her on his shoulders.

"I want! To! Walk!" she screamed.

"Maybe you wanna go home," he said, mildly.

"No, no, no!"

"Alright, then, listen up," he said.

He walked forward under his little burden. She'd stopped resisting, but locked her small hands around his forehead, partly covering his eyes. The crowd about the object was large and quiet, people swaying like cornstalks. Pilgrims, he thought to himself. They reminded him of a documentary he'd seen about Muslims going to the Kaaba. This was the same thing. Everybody staring up at it, like it was magical. A woman with her face painted in neon colors, and feathers stuck into her hair, was dancing before it; a slow, artless, twisting movement, like she was trying to climb out of a sack underwater.

"What she doing, Daddy?"

"Being a weirdo," he said, and walked around the other direction.

The Mirror Sphere floated four feet off the ground. It was a hundred twenty feet around, but the news said that it had shrunk a lot. Nobody had seen it shrink. Dante had never been over to see it, though it had been here a month. Of course, he was curious, but he worked fifty hours a week, and the rest of the time he was with Aliyah. And it was New York, so the thing was always mobbed. But this was a Tuesday, and the crowd was lighter. He was off work, and it was Educator Development Day at Aliyah's school.

"What's a weirdo, Daddy?"

"That lady," he said, absently.

"Is that guy a weirdo too?" she asked, at the top of her lungs.

Aliyah pointed at an obese, shirtless white guy wearing a gas mask. Gas Mask turned to look at Dante, as if awaiting his diagnosis. Dante looked him over, then he chuckled.

"Yep. That's a weirdo too."

It was quiet. Not New York quiet, but *quiet* quiet. He could hear people breathing, and the sound of their feet on the grass as they moved slowly about it. About a dozen people buzzed around the Mirror Sphere on their personal drones, flying up beside it, or hovering high above it. The buzz was the only sound to speak of. Aliyah had gone quiet too.

Dante stepped closer, and people made room for him. He was beside it now. In its reflective surface, he caught sight of his daughter, sitting on his shoulders.

"Oh," he said, very quietly.

Aliyah was a young princess, seated on her throne. He hadn't realized that his shoulders were a throne, or that his daughter was royalty. He saw himself, a young warrior who daily strove to provide for her. They were sort of beautiful. Gas Mask appeared on the left, beside his own reflection. It was strange to think, but the very largeness of the man's belly was fascinating. So many different parts to balance in a human body—stomach, esophagus, intestines; lungs, blood vessels, bones ... and skin that stretched to accommodate it—all balanced and one. The different organs all worked together somehow, even when they were shifted around by time and eating habits. Like they were on a team or something. He'd never thought about it that way.

Dante moved closer, stretching his hand up toward the Mirror Sphere. His fingers hovered inches from it. He knew it was safe to touch. He'd heard the object even let itself be moved about, provided there were no obstructions. He went ahead and touched it.

It wasn't cold. Touching it felt like shaking hands, or like he was giving it five, only a lot more personal. Something brushed his leg, and he stepped back. There were people crawling under the sphere or lying on the grass and looking up at it. It was mostly kids. He imagined that, for them, the Mirror Sphere was a fort. A magic mountain. Their presence below it didn't interfere with whatever suspended it in space.

"Daddy," said Aliyah. "Daddy?"

"Huh," said Dante.

He took a step back, sensing that it was someone else's turn to get close. A man in a suit, a frosty-haired banker type, looked at him with deep gratitude, and filled the gap.

"Daddy, is it a alien?" asked Aliyah.

"What? Yeah, I guess so," he said.

Aliyah made a speculative sound, then suddenly leaned forward, trusting him to keep a hold on her thighs as she craned her head over top of his.

"If it's a alien," she said, looking at him upside down, "where's its teef?"

She curled up her lips, making a beaver face as she tapped her teeth for emphasis. He reached up, gently sitting her back on his shoulders.

"I don't know," he said, shrugging under her. "Maybe it don't need teeth."

She made a clucking sound.

"It's teef, Daddy. You say teef."

"No," he said. "You don't."

She protested weakly, but he reached up and patted her back. She was quiet for a while, looking at it. Everybody was. And Dante thought of Elmer at the shop. He was a Mexican immigrant who worked at the garage, and only seemed to know enough English to be an asshole most of the time. But that was before. Elmer was easy to get along with now.

"Daddy, I want to go down," said Aliyah.

"Baby, there's a lot of people here. I don't want you getting lost."

"I'm not gettin' lost," she said. "I wanna go undewit."

Dante stood deciphering for a moment, then understood. She wanted to be with the kids playing in its shadow. He didn't feel like chasing her down there when she invariably refused to leave. But it did look fun. He stepped back, considering. The buzzing from the personal drones drew his attention again, and he watched, in particular, the people who were flying above the Mirror Sphere, more than a hundred feet in the air. They zipped past each other, trying to take it all in at once. He wondered what would happen if they collided, and landed on top of the floating object. Personal drones were just the kind of thing there'd be a rule against, if the authorities could make rules about the Mirror Sphere. They didn't try. Being a dad, he thought he understood that. Make a rule you can't enforce, and they know you're not really in charge anymore.

"I don't think you need to go under, Aliyah."

He expected her to scream about it. Instead, two soft, chubby hands pressed warmly against his cheeks. Her salty little fingers poked into his mouth. She whispered in his ear.

"Iz otay, Daddy. I want to."

Smiling, he reached up, and set her down on the grass.

"Okay, baby, but don't run away from me."

She looked up and shook her head in a firm promise. If she were a soldier, she'd have saluted.

"Yeah, alright. I'll be right here."

She gave an excited little jump, then bent down where she landed, and crawled under the sphere. Once there, she came up to a crouch, and sat cross-legged. The pink beads in her braided hair were only about six inches from its underside. She reached up, placing her palm flat against the diamond-metal.

There was a loud crash. Dante couldn't believe it had happened so quickly. He had a sick feeling, like some good angel had given him a warning, and he hadn't listened. He looked up just in time to see two personal drones collide in the air above the Mirror Sphere. Their drivers got tangled together, turned head-downward, and then rushed toward its upper pole, propelled by the drone motors. Something in Dante's gut twisted. He tried to move toward Aliyah. The fliers hit the Sphere hard. Yielding to human pressure, it fell toward Aliyah's head. Then stopped on a dime.

Dante threw himself to the grass and crawled toward her. Aliyah, her palm still flat against the surface, now giggled, and nuzzled the rounded metal with the top of her hair. She squeezed into herself, a little shiver of delight rushing through her.

"Baby!" he said, breathless.

She looked over to him, and then laid her chubby fingers over his lips.

"Iz otay, Daddy. It won't hurt me. It was giving me a kiss."

Disincorporation

"There's one aspect of disincorporation that I'd like to have better explained," said Marsha Brown.

She was sitting near the head of the long boardroom table, across from Boka Ngundu, head of Maples' legal staff. Boka smiled, and gestured for her to continue. John Ricardo II, Chief Production Officer at Maples Corporation, looked on, hoping Marsha's question was the same as his own.

"Well," Marsha began, "when Maples disincorporates, what will guarantee that the new policies are reflected in every local store? That is, how can we be sure that a Maples in, say, Brussels, will follow the new policies once it's an independent entity?"

Ricardo looked at her, scowling. *That* was her question? Not, "Why on Earth would a multi-billion-dollar corporation divide itself into hundreds of independent franchises operating under strict 'ethical' constraints?" but, "How can we make sure they all do just that?"

The lawyer nodded and reached into his briefcase. He produced a small tablet, swiped through it for a moment, then flicked a document onto the common screen. John read the heading, seeing that it was a section of the Franchise Distribution and Disincorporation Act. Some version of it had passed in every major nation. Britain's version, being the model, had all the worst characteristics.

"Take note of Section III, subsection A," Boku said in his rich Nigerian accent. "You will notice that it ties franchise distribution to a given legal entity—in this case Maples—which is tied, in turn, to its policies, so that the two are bound together, provided that the act has been passed within said sovereign legal community."

The other board members nodded, as if it were all perfectly clear. Marsha smiled politely, still apparently skeptical. She waved her finger in a slow circle.

"Unpack that for me a little more, please," she said.

"Certainly," said Boka. "In concrete terms, after we disincorporate, a Maples in Brussels, in order to call itself Maples, and to make use of the contacts, supply chain, network, infrastructure, legal identity, branding, etcetera that belong to Maples, must also follow the new policies, provided that Brussels—or, in this case, Belgium—has passed its own Franchise Distribution and Disincorporation Act. In effect, disincorporation replaces an international legal person, the corporation, with a set of internationally coordinated firms operating under the same set of rules. There will be local variations, of course."

"Okay," said Marsha, bobbing her head, as if what Boka had said was music. "That's great. That's just great."

John Ricardo, the only member of Maples' board of directors to whom this was not great, stared at Marsha like she was something growing in a petri dish. A year ago, she'd been weaving webs, positioning herself for a future career as CEO. Now Marsha, like every other bobblehead at the table, was rushing to break Maples into dozens—maybe hundreds—of smaller companies. Vinod Bach, reigning CEO, at least until the company went bankrupt, cleared his throat. A tall, thin man with an olive complexion, he looked around the table, making eye contact with each board member. John saw what passed among them. It was the Look. He'd seen it before. When Vinod met his eyes, John squinted back at him.

"Well," Vinod said, "it appears that we've addressed all questions. All that remains is to vote. So if there are no objections—"

"I have an objection," said John.

The other board members turned to him, their smiles fading a little as if he'd yanked them all from a pleasant dream. Vinod opened his hands, inviting John to speak.

"Maples is one of the largest, most stable companies in the world," said John. "We operate on every continent, and in nearly every major country. Our supply chain is second to none. Our profits have increased steadily nearly every quarter for the last ten years! So please tell me why we're committing suicide?"

The last sentence came out in almost a shriek. Under other circumstances, John would have been a little embarrassed. Not today.

The others looked at him patiently. He saw something like pity in their eyes. That made his blood boil. Vinod stroked his chin with one hand, and gently drummed his fingers with the other.

"John," he began, "let me address your question from two angles. First, practically, and then, if I may, philosophically."

John bit his lip. He could care less about the second angle. Vinod continued.

"It has been demonstrated many times that, as an institution becomes large and centralized, it becomes less efficient. Inefficiencies of scale emerge that equal or exceed whatever efficiencies come with the centralization of resources and leadership. Local action is therefore slow to respond to local conditions, since all important decisions must pass through a higher bureaucracy, which bureaucracy generally becomes a creature of its own, preserving its priorities and excesses at the expense of everything else, including the long-term welfare of the institution.

"But smaller organizations can afford to be supple. They can respond quickly to changing circumstances. They can better calculate the needs they are serving, and the customer base for which they are competing, because their scale is more human. They innovate better. Their leadership, being local, is subject to local conditions, and has a stake in the local community. They're also more likely to see employees as stakeholders, and to pay them accordingly. When a company pays an employee a wage upon which he or she can thrive, that employee is happier, and works harder. Employee theft, product loss from carelessness, and the costs of turnover all decrease precipitously. In short, if Maples still provides the service our customers expect, it will be no less stable once distributed. Much more likely, profits will actually increase, though that increase will be localized, rather than concentrated in the hands of shareholders."

Vinod folded his hands, waiting to see that John was following him. John noticed that Vinod didn't look around for support, as people tended to do when they were being radical at a board meeting. Vinod was a true believer. They all were now.

"Philosophically," Vinod continued, "'we' are not committing suicide, as you term it, because Maples is not alive. The legal fiction that a company is a person, immortal and amoral, and serving only its—that is to say, the current leadership's—interests, is one of the great errors of modern times. It has led to all kinds of anonymous, mindless injustices and irrationalities. As a business leader, Maples has an opportunity to do something rare: to set a good example. That's what we're proposing here."

Vinod settled back into his chair. He was calm. John had heard plenty of self-righteous, long-winded pronouncements at board meetings. He'd been the first to jump on board every train of progress that passed through Maples station—at least when it was clear that that was where the wind was blowing. This was not that. This was more than a progressive fashion, adopted by the wealthy to soothe their consciences and stroke their egos. Vinod had nothing to prove. He had *the truth*. They all did. They were all humming a tune he couldn't hear. But John thought he knew the cause. If he was right, there was little point in bringing the matter up. He brought it up anyway.

"You've been to see it, then?" John said.

Vinod looked at him a moment, then nodded. John placed his palms flat on the table, and stared at each of them in turn.

"You've all been. Haven't you?"

His voice was high again. He could barely restrain himself. That they looked upon him with something like compassion; that they knew what he'd meant, and didn't even bother denying it, made it worse.

"You've all got that look!" he croaked. "You've all been gazing into that crystal ball in London Square!"

Marsha Brown sighed.

"John," she said, very quietly, "there's no need to shout."

"Of course I'm shouting!" he shouted. "I didn't bust my ass for twenty years to have my salary indefinitely frozen, or to have the same medical benefits as cashiers and shelf-packers!"

Marsha looked to Vinod. The CEO appeared troubled and leaned in toward him.

"John, we all worked hard to make this transition painless. No one's taking anything away from you," he said. "Your salary and benefits are similar to what they were before. It's just that the cashiers and 'shelf-packers' will now enjoy more livable salaries, and similar benefits."

John scoffed and shook his head.

"Where's the money for that, Bach? Who's being robbed to pay Paul?"

With unaffected humility, Vinod made a slow, bashful nod. John felt the air go out of him. Could it possibly be?

"You? You're giving up your salary?"

"Not all of it," said Vinod, "but everything, including stock, in excess of three twenty-five. Marsha, Catrina, and Bill Dawes have done the same."

John sat back, dumbfounded. There had to be some catch. There had to be a second stream, or a secret ladder that all of them were in on. Nobody would give up that kind of money just on principle. If it were true, it would change the whole game. So it couldn't be true.

"You're not gonna..." he began, then stopped—considering how it would sound—before beginning again, "...not gonna attract top talent with that low of a ceiling."

Vinod frowned. "Meaning?"

John laughed. Vinod knew exactly what he'd meant.

"Meaning," said John, deciding to be crass, "that if Maples offers less money to execs, it won't get the best and brightest. It'll attract the castoffs. The second-raters."

Vinod closed his eyes, pondering the comment.

"No," he said, "I don't think so. For two reasons. One, because, as you surely know, major corporations are voluntarily disincorporating at a rate of about seven a day, and they're implementing policies similar to these. Two, the world is different now. People are different, John. There are things we're all starting to see, that we didn't before. People are changing, John. Laws and policies ... they're just an instance of that change."

John stood up. The chair legs groaned and stuttered with the violence of his movement. They were all looking at him. Pitying him.

"This isn't what I signed up for," he sputtered.

"Oh," said Vinod, a trace of heat in his voice. "You didn't 'sign-up' to be part of the leadership of a successful company? To help foster and oversee its growth? Then what?"

John smiled down at Vinod.

"I'm not greedy, if that's what you're implying."

"I do not recall suggesting this," replied Vinod, mildly.

"Yeah, but you think it. You all think it," said John.

No one bothered to contradict him. They just kept staring with a condescension so sincere, they might have been parents watching a child's hungry tantrum.

"Fine," said John. "Call me selfish. Call me greedy. They're just words used by helpless mobs to tear down the capable. The world runs on merit, Bach. That's reality."

They were all silent, letting him talk. He was the madman. They were the orderlies. For a while, he just stood there, not knowing whether to sit back down or to walk out. Marsha cleared her throat.

"Uh ... John, have you considered ... visiting the Mirror Sphere?"

That did it. He shoved the chair hard into the table.

"Not a chance," he said. "I resign. But don't worry. You'll be seeing me around. Maybe when every Maples is bought out by Olden Mart."

He turned and walked away. John was halfway to the door when he overhead Marsha's comment. It hadn't been meant for him, but he heard it anyway. He grabbed his phone and checked to see if it was true. And it was. Olden Mart was disincorporating too.

Council of War

A tall, thickly-built man approached the park bench, looked around, and sat. From his perch, he commanded three entrances to the cozy cul-de-sac, but these led off toward many twisting paths. A stand of holly trees, close-set, made a barrier behind him. Two men stood on the other side of it, covering his blindside. Though dressed in plain clothes, he looked out of place. His checkered shirt, short-sleeved, and tucked into a pair of khakis, seemed in want of medals and bars of rank. The way he held himself put the lie to his civilian attire. The man pretended to read his newspaper, as if doing so in this day and age rendered him less conspicuous. He kept an eye out for his visitor.

General Ouellet didn't hear him approach. He moved the newspaper an inch, and the man was suddenly there. The general glanced behind him to see if his men had marked the approach, but they were still concealed behind the holly trees. If the new arrival had wanted to kill him, he doubted very much his men would even have been aware until it was too late. But he was not expecting trouble. Not really.

"Well, you're here," said Ouellet. "Have a seat."

The visitor sat. He was dressed like a runner. From a distance, Ouellet would not have marked him out from anyone else. Slight of frame, and dark-haired, he was also utterly plain. General Ouellet had always an affinity for maths, and the featureless man reminded him of a walking variable. He could have served any function. His value might have been one or zero.

"Good to see you," said the visitor.

"Yes, I'm sure," said Ouellet, speaking English so thickly accented, it could be mistaken for French. He could speak the Queen's English, plain and crisp, if he wanted to, but using the bastard tongue was condescension enough for this Yank. The man could pull the strings to meet him here. He couldn't make him like it.

"General Oue—"

"No names, please," said Ouellet. "Not unless you're going to tell me yours."

The man frowned. When he did so, Ouellet noticed the thin line on one of his eyebrows where the hair didn't quite grow in. Probably scar tissue, from a childhood injury.

"This meeting has been sanctioned by both of our governments," said the man. "So you needn't worry."

"Worry?" said Ouellet. "I never worry. But, as a matter of etiquette, I expect your name and title, if you expect to use mine."

The man's smile did not reach his eyes, and he continued as if he hadn't heard.

"I came to discuss the Artifact. And related phenomena."

"Related phenomena?" said Ouellet. "I am not aware of any."

The visitor smiled.

"Le Projet Icarus," he said, in a mockery of French.

The general said nothing. He shook the newspaper out and began to leaf through it.

"This is a question?" said Ouellet. "Or have you something to tell me?"

The man gave another eyeless smile. In perfect French, he delivered a train of words, phrases, and numbers. His accent was precise, but his tone laconic, as if it cost him something to engage in such rituals. Ouellet put down his newspaper.

"Very well," said the general. "I'm on the project, but such information is already shared with the relevant parties. Canada is not withholding anything, if that is what you imply."

"No," said the other. "But the frequency of these visitations has greatly increased since the Artifact's arrival."

"Certainly," said Ouellet. "But that is to be expected, no?"

"It is cause for concern," said the visitor.

"I see no reason why," said the general, opening his paper again. "The Mirror has made people more peaceful. There's no denying that now, whatever your analysts say."

The man looked sharply up at him.

"You ... have been to see it then?" he said. "Visited it yourself?"

Something in the man's tone made the general pause. He looked at the dark-haired, dark-eyed creature, and felt wary. Physically unimpressive, the man was also dangerous in some way Ouellet couldn't place.

"I will not say yes, or no. And that is because it isn't relevant. Elements of your government consider it to be a threat. The UN does not. Canada does not. The evidence of two years proves it is not. Whatever it is, its designs are peaceful."

The look that crossed the man's face was hard to place. Ouellet had the sudden impression of this man as a child. He imagined him clever, and always sneering, and learning, at length, to disguise the sneer behind a milky, bloodless façade, because he could not smile. Finally, as if recovering his temper—though he never showed emotion—the man spoke.

"Do you consider attacks on military bases peaceful?" he said.

"You're not talking about the Mirror Sphere, monsieur. You mean the other craft."

The visitor paused. "Yes, but they're correlated. The disruptions have increased with the Artifact."

"But they proceeded it," said Ouellet. "By more than eighty years, if I'm not mistaken. And disruption is, I believe, a nice English euphemism. What you mean is that they've disabled your nukes. From time to time, they pop in and contain you. The rest of the time they just watch."

The other man didn't respond. The general was doing his best to make it clear to him that, collaborators or not, their nations did not share all the same interests.

The man tried again. "I would have thought that as a general, a man of war, you'd find this troubling."

Ouellet cleared his throat. "As a man of war, I know that war is hell. One of your finest generals said that. Your country treated him shabbily for saying it. It is always fascinating to me when civilian politicians and agents, men who will not themselves risk death in war, are so quick to silence those who have done so, and who wish, for that reason, to avoid it at all costs."

The other man waved his hand through the air, as if he were swatting a fly.

"Enough of this," he said, his voice taking on a strained, sibilant quality. "We have our own analysts. But you are head of the UN Peacekeeping forces, and your people have been tasked with directing—and monitoring— the Artifact. The matter that concerns us is this: sooner or later, the lottery will go to Syria, or Afghanistan, or some other such place where the situation is volatile. It is our considered opinion that it should not go to one of these places."

"Is it?" said the general, not bothering to hide his contempt. "Well, my friend, I do not run the lottery. That is conducted independently of the—"

"Nevertheless," said the other man, "it should not be allowed to go to one of these places. The possibilities for volatility are too great. And, if the Artifact is a weapon..."

He did not finish the sentence. General Ouellet looked at him with a kind of macabre wonder.

"A weapon? Your nation, which has created, and has actually used, the deadliest weapons in history, has the temerity not only to attempt to derail a fair lottery, but to suggest that a device that measurably increases peace is surreptitiously working to facilitate war? Perhaps, my nameless friend, you ought to turn that analysis back on yourselves."

"I have my directive," said the other. "It must not be allowed to go to any of the following countries: Syria, Iran—"

"Monsieur, to hell with you," said the general. "I do not take my orders from you. And, let's be blunt—Americans value bluntness, no?—your nation is no longer in a position to direct the course of history. Something else has come. Maybe it will sow peace where strife now justifies your presence? And that, perhaps, is what really frightens you. That there are powers about now that are greater and subtler than nations."

General Ouellet frowned and shook his head. Externally, he was calm, but the dark-eyed creature before him inspired a quiet outrage. He stood, folded up his newspaper, and walked toward the holly trees. His fury expressed itself only by leaving the man without a word. As he rounded the holly tees, the man at the bench spoke.

"You're right about one thing, General Ouellet."

Ouellet scowled, not caring to hear another word. Mastering himself, he turned.

"There are powers greater, and subtler, than nations," continued the variable man. "That has been true for some time now. So take care, General."

The man turned and walked swiftly down the twisting paths from which he'd come. The general stood as if fixed to the ground and parsed his words. They were a threat. Barely concealed. He called his men, and they emerged from behind the holly trees. He could see by their faces that they'd heard.

"Come with me," grunted the general.

He started down the path, flanked by his guards, but the path ahead split in many directions, and the dark-haired man, the variable man, was already gone from sight.

Sabotage

"All is bueno, Firefly," said air traffic control through the cockpit radio. "You're expected."

"Roger, GRU," said Major Boucher, "how's the weather down there?"

"Sunny day," said the voice, in accented English. "Big crowds in São Paulo. You wanna stay awhile, Joey? Guest of honor!"

Major Boucher smiled crookedly at her copilot. He shrugged, and snickered at her. She spoke into the radio.

"Negative, GRU. Think I'll disappear for a month. See you in a couple hours. Thanks."

"Disphona! Suit yourself."

She shut off the intercom and tapped her prosthetic pointer finger repeatedly against the metal console. It was one of her tells. Major Josephine Boucher felt Tremblay looking at her. She kept a good poker face, but he knew her well enough to guess something was up.

"Not the nickname still?" he said.

When the media had first dubbed her "Joey," she hadn't liked it. In American films, a pilot with a name like Samantha would have it boiled down to Sam. There'd be a bar scene with a slobbering drunk flyboy trying to put the moves on her. "Hey Samantha," he'd say, "why don't you come over here and give me a kiss!" Sam's tolerant almost-boyfriend would give her the eye, but Sam would "lose it." A few improbable karate moves later, and flyboy would be on the bar floor, looking up with newfound respect. "It's Sam, pal," she'd say. *Quelle connerie!* But the nickname didn't bother her anymore. She had bigger problems. Maybe.

"Non," said Boucher. "C'est bon."

"Then what?"

She glared at him, but without seriousness. "Please check on the luggage," she said, making no attempt to hide that she was avoiding conversation.

By "luggage," she meant the Mirror Sphere. There was no reason to doubt that it was still floating happily through the air behind them, snug inside the huge trailing harnesses that attached to the CP-140 Aurora's tail. But she wanted a moment to herself. Tremblay, not the least bit deceived, gave her space.

As he climbed back, she considered the situation. When the UN Special Commission announced it would appoint a pilot to ferry the thing around the world, she'd felt sorry for the sucker. She hadn't imagined that the sucker would be her. In the eighteen months since General Ouellet had singled her out for this honor, the work had grown on her. She'd even learned to accept the name they'd slapped on her. Perhaps "Major Boucher" was just too difficult for Americans to say. Anyway, she liked the Mirror. The way it allowed itself to be led over land and sea, and the peace and clarity she felt beside it, was more than compensation for the initial indignity of being taken away from her normal work, or that of being the typecast "political" choice, the first female First Nations RCAF pilot.

The Mirror Sphere was mysterious. The way it followed was one part of the mystery. Another was the times it stayed put. After the thing had landed in New York, it wouldn't go anywhere else. A child could move it about with her hand, but the combined strength of military and civil engineers couldn't budge it from Central Park. Not until that professor with a hyphenated name had—What? Talked to it? Persuaded it?—and they'd set up the lottery system. The Mirror Sphere was nothing if not cooperative.

But not everybody liked it. In Mexico City, a man had come to her hotel. He was NSA, or something like it. In retrospect, she should have called Tremblay. She hadn't thought she'd needed backup. Maybe she wasn't Sam the Karate Pilot, but she was six feet tall, and armed, so she'd allowed the slight, pale-dark creature to enter her hotel room. He knew things about her that nobody else knew, but that wasn't what bothered her. The man also claimed to know the next four lottery selections. That bothered her.

São Paulo, Bandar Abbas, Paris, and finally Jerusalem.

"You're not to go into Iran," he'd said.

"I go where I'm sent," she'd replied.

"There's currently a standoff in the Strait of Hormuz. You are not to risk yourself, or the Artifact."

She'd coughed, or something, and she must have looked uncomfortable, because he'd tried to reassure her.

"Don't worry," he'd said. "I will take care of things with your superiors. But under no circumstances are you to take it there."

She'd stood up then and walked to the door.

"I go where I'm sent," she remembered saying. "And you can leave."

"The Artifact will not be permitted to go there," was his flat, emotionless reply.

"Leave," she'd said, trying not to shout at the presumptuous little man.

He'd gone. She hadn't seen him since, but she had informed General Ouellet. And the general had called on her in person. He told her to do her duty. But he'd seemed nervous. The head of UN Security Forces, nervous. So now she was nervous too.

Nothing had gone wrong, yet. Maybe nothing would. Then something did.

It started with a loud bang. The lights on the cockpit blinked on and off furiously. Then they went off.

"Tremblay..."

He scrambled up from the hold and vaulted into his seat.

"What the hell was that?" he said, trying to strap in.

"What the hell did you do?" she asked at the same time.

"Wait! Listen!"

She didn't hear anything. The CP-140's four propellers had all ground to a halt. For a moment, the Firefly kept flying forward, like a cartoon coyote who doesn't realize he's just run off a cliff. The coyote looked down. The plane dropped.

"Strap in!" she screamed, but it was too late.

Tremblay slammed into the bulkhead behind her, as the plane rushed nose-down through the clouds. Boucher tried to pull up, but the plane didn't register anything. Boucher screamed and slapped her hands against the control panel. Nothing was lit. As the plane fell, it began to corkscrew, and then to tumble end-over-end. Tremblay flew around the cabin, slamming into the windows and bulkheads. She tried to initiate a restart, but it was useless. The CP-140 broke through the clouds. Through its windows, she saw a kaleidoscope of colors. Blue of sky. Clouds. Ocean. Silver of the Mirror Sphere, falling with them. Tremblay flew by her again, and she caught him, and held him tightly against her in a bear hug. He was groaning. He was still alive.

Down they spun, and the plane settled nose-down. She watched the Atlantic as it changed from a blue plain, to a vast, undulating thing. Something churned in her gut, and Major Boucher of the RCAF vomited all over herself, and Tremblay. They had moments now. Death would at least be quick.

But as they approached the ocean, the moment of impact was strangely delayed. Perhaps in one's last moments, the mind revolted against death, and stretched every minute to make it last. No, that was not it. They were slowing down. The power was dead. The propellers weren't spinning. But they were slowing down. A quarter-mile above the Atlantic, the plane came to a stop.

Boucher wondered if she were really dead. Perhaps the mind could not accept death, and she was already in the water, waiting for the last neurons to stop firing. But now the plane began to float down. She held Tremblay against her, not allowing gravity to drop him into the cockpit windows. When the nose touched the water, she still wondered if this were a trick of the brain. Then the plane leveled out as it was lowered into the water from tip to tail. Gently, like she'd seen women lay sleeping babies into cribs.

If Boucher ever cried, she would have cried now. Her plane was floating in the Atlantic. Tremblay groaned, and his head was bleeding, but he was alive. She slapped at the console, hoping to radio for help, but the power was still down. The plane began to sink on its left side.

"Merde! Tremblay, we've got to go!"

Tremblay groaned, and didn't respond. Boucher went through emergency procedures in her mind, the kind that assumed, improbably, that climbing out of a sinking plane was even a possibility. She pulled at her restraints, then stopped. There was a dull, heavy thud from underneath the plane. It stopped sinking and went level again. Boucher's breath caught in her throat. She unhooked herself, stood on shaky legs, and looked out the cockpit window.

In the water, the Mirror Sphere glowed orange. A red-golden light went out like a halo beside the ship. The Mirror was beneath them. It was holding them up.

Just Being Polite

She was in her hospital bed. The woman who entered and pulled up a chair looked familiar.

"Major Boucher, are you awake?"

Boucher nodded.

"I'm Felizitas. Perhaps you recognize me?"

She nodded again and tapped her carbon finger on the railing as she tried to ID the woman. She'd seen her on the news, and the slight German accent helped to confirm her guess. It was a nice voice.

"You're its psychologist," offered Boucher. "Dr. Shaman-White, or Always-Right, or something like that."

Felizitas laughed.

"Yes," she said, "It's Chandra-Wright, but please call me Felizitas. I suppose you go by Joey?"

Boucher frowned. "Felizitas" was a mouthful. "Joey's fine," she said. "How can I help you, Doctor?"

Felizitas glanced around, and leaned in when she spoke. "If you could tell me how you survived—"

Boucher gripped the railing and sat up rather suddenly. "Tremblay!"

Felizitas patted her arm. "Your co-pilot is fine. He's in stable condition."

She took a deep breath, and laid back down.

"Thank God," she said.

"Yes," said the woman, "a close shave. But if we could talk about ... how?"

Boucher looked at her, wondering what the woman expected her to say.

"You know how, right? The Mirror did it. We were in a nosedive, and it slowed us down. We started sinking. It went under us."

"Yes, but ... did you ... communicate with it?"

"Communicate? No, I was a little busy at the moment. I don't talk to the thing, anyway. I just taxi it around."

The visitor looked away for a moment, thinking.

"But after help arrived, you didn't say anything to it then?"

Boucher studied the bookish woman, suppressing irritation. She wasn't in the mood to satisfy scientific curiosity, or whatever this was.

"As I said, madame, we were a bit preoccupied. After the rescue ships arrived, the Mirror went off on its own."

Boucher watched the professor nodding to herself, working something out. After a few moments, the woman seemed to recall where she was, and looked up at the major.

"I have a different question, Joey. Maybe you're not authorized to answer, but ... what caused the crash?"

Boucher shrugged.

"Power failed. That's all."

Felizitas looked at her shrewdly.

"That's all?"

Boucher didn't answer. What did the woman already know?

"The reason I ask," she continued, lowering her voice, "is that there are some people who don't believe in what we're doing."

"Like terrorists," offered Boucher, testing her.

"More highly-placed, I think," said the woman, whispering. "Did you have any warning? Threats, I mean?"

Boucher considered. This was what she'd been mulling over as she lay in her bed. She couldn't think of a reason not to tell the woman about her ominous conversation. She nodded.

"What did he look like?"

Boucher related her conversation with the dark-eyed man. When she described his appearance, Felizitas didn't seem surprised.

"You know who he was?" asked Boucher.

"I've met him before," said the woman. "I don't know exactly who he is, but I'm beginning to get an idea of what he does."

"And what's that?" said Boucher.

Felizitas seemed to choose her words. She nodded to herself.

"Containment," she said, "for lack of a better term. For them, it's a problem. The way people are becoming ... more human. To them it's like a social virus."

Boucher frowned, partly because that didn't make sense to her, and partly because publicly acknowledging the Mirror Sphere's odd effects still carried the stigma of superstition. Everyone knew, but the knowledge was personal. Entirely subjective, and unsharable. You couldn't capture what it did on film. You had to see it face-to-face. That's why everyone wanted to go to it in person.

"And you think he tried to kill me, because I didn't do what he said," said Boucher.

"Yes. He. They. Whoever they are."

Boucher shrugged.

"I think you're right. So?"

Felizitas paused, proceeding carefully.

"I have spoken to General Ouellet. You'll have extra protection going forward."

Boucher nodded, trying to appear impartial, as if her safety were a small matter. Felizitas patted her on the hand again, and stood up.

"They're afraid, Joey," she said. "They'll be even more afraid now."

"Oh yeah? Pourquoi?"

"Because now the spell is broken."

"I don't follow this," said Boucher. "What's changed?"

Felizitas raised an eyebrow.

"Well, I suppose you haven't yet heard," she said. "Up until now, the Mirror has condescended to humor us. It's allowed the nations of the world to think they had some measure of control over it. But after you were rescued, the Mirror continued to São Paulo without an escort."

Boucher let out a low whistle. "It doesn't even need us."

"No," said the professor. "It was just being polite."

Hormuz

"You still think this a good idea?"

Tremblay didn't look at her when he said it. He stared out the console window. He was nervous. With the crash only a month behind them, he had every right to be. She gave him credit for getting back in the saddle.

"No," said Boucher. "But it doesn't matter what I think."

He nodded, and glanced out the starboard window toward one of the flanking UN jets. Boucher was flying a brand new, thoroughly checked-out CP-140, with the Mirror on its leash pretending to follow. All three human craft bore the UN sky blue with the white crest, but neon yellow stripes had been added to increase visibility. They were headed for Bandar Abbas in the Hormozgan Province of Iran. The Iranian navy was just off the coast. The western powers were across the strait from the Iranians, arranged in a wedge about the promontory that jutted between Oman and the UAE. The standoff had lasted months, but it wasn't a war. Not yet, anyway.

"They want us there," she said. "The Iranians wouldn't target us."

Tremblay laughed, though he didn't sound amused.

"Not who I'm worried about," he said.

She glared at him, as if the suggestion were absurd. They were halfway across the Strait of Hormuz when the radio crackled.

"UN Firefly II, this is US Command, please be advised, situation in Oman just went hot. Recommend you do not land. Over."

Tremblay raised an eyebrow. "Not the Iranians," he said, with a shrug. "Must be locals. Don't fancy Marines on their doorstep, I imagine."

She looked at the radio, scowled, and thumbed the controls.

"US Command, this is UN Firefly II. Acknowledged, but we're on route for Bandar Abbas. Other side of the creek. Will maintain present course. Over."

What were they going to do? Shoot them out of the sky? The radio came on again.

"Firefly II, this is Colonel Frank Goreman, U.S. Marines. You are compromising our situation. We don't need a hostage situation on top of this. Do this another day. Over."

Boucher shook her head. Always with the commands. Tremblay stroked his chin, pensive. He probably wanted her to turn back. He was going to be disappointed, then.

"What do you think?" Tremblay said.

Boucher thumbed the radio on.

"Colonel Goreman, this is Major Josephine Boucher, Royal *Canadian* Air Force. Thanks for your concern, but I have my orders. Over."

They'd crossed over the strait. Boucher reached out to Bandar Abbas air traffic control. After some back-and-forth chatter, she got her vector from air traffic control and began making her descent. A few minutes later, the Firefly II was approaching the landing strip. They'd just touched down, when the Marine colonel's voice came over the radio.

"Firefly II, this is Colonel Goreman. What the hell do you think you're doing with that thing?"

She sighed. "Landing it. Touchdown at Bandar Abbas. Colonel, if you don't mind, I need to concentrate."

There was a pause. The connection opened for a moment, and she heard male voices in discussion. It shut off, then crackled to life once more. Colonel Goreman's voice returned.

"Firefly II, this is U.S. Command. Major Boucher, are you aware that your package is loose? Over."

A bolt of alarm hit her in the chest.

"Tremblay—"

"On it," he said.

Tremblay radioed her escort jets. The message came back at once, confirming what the Marine colonel had said. The Mirror Sphere had slipped its bonds. It was going off on its own, but not toward the designated spot in the city center. Instead, the Mirror was crossing back over the Strait of Hormuz. It must have been moving at an alarming speed too. By time the Firefly II was taxiing into BND International, the Mirror had already come to a stop over Oman. From there it descended, until it came to rest in the middle of a live firefight.

Uthman's Folly

It was an idol. He was not surprised to see the worldly bowing down to it. So the Israelites had done, according to their own scriptures. So did the infidels in their churches filled with graven images. That the peoples of the West, worshipers of the work of their own hands, should now bow down before this deception of the Enemy did not surprise Uthman. Yet that even they should let it reside near their great cathedral was a more thoroughgoing hypocrisy then he could bear.

Granted, the French were not so religious anymore, aside from a certain, ineradicable core of pious French, but even these were enamored of the Mirror Sphere. All who looked upon its shining face fell under its spell. Uthman had not looked. He would not flirt with deception. With damnation.

The Mirror's face was a weapon. It disarmed those who looked into it.

Like those brothers in Oman who, along with American crusaders on their soil, had stopped shooting when the Mirror dropped down into their presence. When he'd seen that report, it had made him ill. He'd wept. Even fighting men, trained and bred to evict the crusader from lands under the Peace, were subject to the Mirror's witchcraft. They'd lowered their guns and walked up to it. They'd touched it. Rubbed shoulders with the crusaders. Made themselves unclean, for the sake of a mere shining thing. The Mirror's face was a weapon against Allah, and he would serve Allah by removing that face.

But matters had just become complicated. Only moments ago, Uthman Baqri had emerged from his car, which was parked several blocks from la Cathedrale Notre-Dame. He'd left the car to its fate. His resolve was quite firm, but lest it should waver, he'd activated what he concealed under his jacket by pressing down the dead man's switch that fed through his sleeve into his hand. He shoved both hands into his pockets and strolled as casually as he could manage up la Rue du Cloitre-Notre-Dame. When he'd checked in only hours ago, in the dead of night, the Mirror Sphere had been resting near the cathedral, in Square Jean XXIII.

But it was not too close to the cathedral, for which he was happy. True, the great temple was made by the infidels, yet he had a certain reverence for the Dame herself, and did not wish to do much damage to the house the infidels had built her. Allah be merciful, but it was not *her* face he wished to scar. As he entered Square Jean, he saw that the Mirror was no longer there.

He crossed the city park, and his heart began to race. He'd already pressed the button. He was holding it down now. If the Mirror had flown off somewhere he couldn't reach before his thumb relaxed, then his death would be in vain. At any rate, far less meaningful. His boots sounded heavily on the stone. He felt every vibration through the soles of his feet, as if they were somehow enough to shake his thumb loose. Maybe he was stomping. He could hardly control his body.

The smell of the Seine River, thick in the close atmosphere of early morning, reminded him that he would never taste or smell or eat or drink in this body again. But if his death served to tear down an idol, it would be worth the sacrifice. If it did not, then what purpose would it serve? He shuddered, glad that death would come quickly either way. He did not think he could endure a slow death, or a meaningless one.

Uthman came to a stop in the center of la Square Jean XXIII. Many people were camped there. He did not think this was permitted, but all sorts of exceptions were being made where the Mirror was concerned. He walked toward the cathedral, unsure what he would do if it were not somewhere nearby.

Coming to a stop before the West Facade, he stared at the intricate stonework. Uthman imagined the time and care that had gone into it. The details were so fine. A mere slip of the finger might have ruined the artist's plan. Yes, it was idolatry. Allah forbade images of the Divine. The infidel knew that, and ignored his command. That a sin could be so beautiful was one of the many contradictions that proved the vanity of reason. Allah was holy, because he was wholly other.

The bell towers jutted out above the façade, looking down on him like graven jinn. The doors in the façade were like eyes staring out at him. The eyes of a beetle, or perhaps the many eyes of a spider. The infidels had many weapons. Some were subtler than others. Like spiders, they wove beautiful things, but these were part of a trap. "Come over to us," they said. "Join us. Be French. You are welcome." But only if he joined them in their infidelity. In their western-ness. Like his father Abideen, or his mother and his sisters—compromisers all.

His family knew how to speak piously, but they wanted too much to blend in. When Uthman complained that they were losing who they were, that they had to do something to bring the infidel to the knowledge of judgment, Abideen had been stern, and had told him to forget such fantasies. "We must be people of peace!" he would say. And well he might say it, the fat, soft banker! He remembered his father being questioned after a bombing simply because he was Muslim. He simpered. He smiled, and cajoled. He debased himself, grinning. Like their little dog. And the banker had sent him to a western university to teach him western values. That did not work out as Abideen had hoped.

"Come into my lair, said the spider to the fly." He'd come across that poem at university, and had found it quite appropriate for the culture that had produced it. He stared at the doors. The spider eyes. One of them opened.

A figure like a floating alif emerged. Thin, slightly bent at the top, and dotted with a faint, silvery frost, he pressed with both hands against the inside door. He was picturesque, like so many French. Long, knobby fingers, and Gallic cheek bones stretched his aged skin. His black cassock reached the porch stones, obscuring his shoes so that he seemed to glide above the ground. With great effort, the old priest pressed the door to the wall. He rested against it a moment, then looked into the park. His eyes met Uthman's.

They darkened. Uthman could not tell if it was the near darkness of the morning, or the color of his cassock, or something else entirely. The old eyes studied him. Uthman did not see but rather felt the eyes move along his arms, going to the hands jammed strangely into his pockets. Something passed behind the man's eyes. A certainty. A kind of surrender. Was it so obvious what he was about? Then, just as quickly as it had come, the darkness passed. His features softened and became warm. The bent old priest leaned forward. He extended his hand, palm up, like a child catching raindrops. Two gnarled fingers protruded, gesturing. The old man was calling him over.

Uthman looked around, making certain the man meant him. But there was no one else awake in Square Jean. Even for the early morning, the place was uncharacteristically quiet, as if it lay under some fairy spell. Uthman walked forward, and stood before the priest.

"Entrez. Entrez."

His voice was slow, and a bit slurred, but still musical. Uthman followed him into the cathedral. The door remained open behind him. The priest led him forward. They passed through the narthex, and into the nave. Glorious ribbons of stone, rock cut and shaped like many wedding cakes standing, caught in noble passion, overhanging, meeting like trees of God, drew him forward. The walls were lined with little altars. They reminded him of the burs on trees, smaller growths of hijacked stone, multiplicities of worship and sub-worship, and every gradation of veneration, as if the great temple could not contain the variegated and strange depths of spirit and blood and passion that rushed through it, and swelled in it, bursting into many smaller lives, lives that might even now burst forth from the walls, forming new altars. He was captivated. So captivated, his thumb nearly released the switch. He pressed back down on it hard.

"Venez voir cette merveille!" exclaimed the priest. "C'est pour vous, parce que vous etes le premier."

Uthman looked up to where the priest pointed. At first his eyes could make no sense of what he saw. He walked forward quickly, his heart thumping against his ribs. The need to keep his hand in his pocket slowed him down, and gave him away. He looked at the priest, but the other smiled back, pretending not to notice. Uthman saw that he was forcing the smile, holding back what he knew, making himself hope that whatever Uthman was planning, he would not carry it out. Not now. Now that he had seen the wonder. And Uthman did see it.

There was the glorious gilded high altar, and the Dame behind it mourning over her broken child, caught in an agony so immense that it confounded Heaven. A cherub looked up at her, longing to console her, knowing it was impossible. A red flame flickered beside the tabernacle, portending he knew not what. And there, before the stone altar steps, in a black-bordered rhombus of stonework, floated the Mirror Sphere.

It had become small. It had made itself lower than that before which it floated. All the colors of church, and stone, and window, and candle, and gold, and marble reflected in it, and flew out from it, covering it in a halo of glory.

And Uthman looked into it. He had never meant to. He saw himself there too, like a flickering flame of noble fire, a worthy opponent. He saw eyes that were young, and too jaded for their years. Eyes seeing the world through flinty, darkened lenses. A heart frustrated and stunted, and unaware of the size of things. He saw himself hungry, and biting down on what would not feed him, because it was *something*, and the world had offered him nothing. He saw that there was something to be had, if he could but wait for it, if he could admit that the good his heart desired was greater than he, and that it could not be comprehended but only tasted, and tasted not only once, but over and over again in a recurring present. He saw the old man beside him, mighty and strange, a creature in its chrysalis, not far from unfolding into who-knew-what. A father. A king.

"Oh!" he said.

A hot sword pierced his heart. He stumbled backward, almost losing his footing. Bright knives of color danced off the sphere, fluttering in the air like sparrows about it, alighting on him. He was pierced by successive waves of passion, and hope, and sorrow as each beam touched him. He saw it all, like light waves in slow motion. His soul was under the knife. The sphere was a surgeon. He did not want it to stop.

When it did stop, he came back to himself, but now he was a little child with a big problem, wanting nothing more than to undo what he had done. His thumb was throbbing. He couldn't hold down the switch much longer.

He turned, and tried to run, his movements awkward and hobbling with the one hand stuffed in his pocket.

"Ne pars pas!" called the priest; then, in slow English, "Don't go!"

Uthman heard footsteps. He turned and saw the priest running to catch him, a kindly smile on his old face. Uthman couldn't now bear the thought of harming him. He backed away quickly, then started to run again. He collided with a pew, his boot catching under a kneeler that had been left down. He fell, and his hands flew out on their own to arrest his fall.

"NO!" he cried, realizing an instant too late what he'd done.

All in the space of a second, the priest was running toward him, Uthman was falling, and the Mirror Sphere rose from its repose, and rushed toward him. In a heartbeat, it swelled to the size of a giant, interposing itself between Uthman and the priest.

"I'm sorr—"

The explosion tore him asunder, and Uthman saw no more with human eyes.

What Romi Saw

One hand held Abigail, and the other was captive in Ima's warm grip. Romi carried Abigail by her trunk, because the little elephant had been naughty, and she was having a consequence. She knew it wouldn't hurt her. She was almost six, and old enough to understand that plush elephants didn't hurt when you carried them by their trunks. But Abigail had stayed behind in the seat, and that had made Romi cry so badly that Ima had huffed, and been cross with her, and had marched her back to the car to get her friend. It had been a long drive from Petah Tikva, and they'd had to stop to eat, and then again, because Romi had to pee. So her mother had gotten annoyed at Romi, and Romi, in turn, had gotten annoyed at Abigail.

When they reached the stone courtyard, it was already near full. The temple's golden dome shone brilliantly in the late morning light, but it was the only thing she could see over all the big people who blocked the way. Didn't big people know that children couldn't see when they all stood together?

They were all excited, because it was coming. So many different kinds of people were shoved into one place. Not only her own people, but Muslims in their flowy clothes, and tourists who spoke different languages. She saw other children too, their mothers also gripping their hands as if they would fly away into the sky. They were on the edge of the crowd, and she felt her mother's frustration. Romi guessed that this also was Abigail's fault. If the blue elephant hadn't stayed behind in the seat, they'd have been here earlier. A small gap opened in the crowd, and Ima rushed into it, dragging Romi behind like a piece of luggage. At least she wasn't being dragged by her trunk. She laughed, thinking of how funny she'd look with a trunk.

After they'd gone a little way, the crowd closed up again, and Romi was surrounded by hundreds of grownups. They backed into her, and pressed into her, as if she weren't there at all. Somebody nearby smelled like they needed to take a bath. She crinkled up her nose. No sooner had she settled into place, then the crowd began jostling again. Her mother cursed under her breath. If *she'd* cursed, Ima would have given her a consequence. Grownups were allowed to break their own rules. They knew when it was okay to break them. Her mother pulled her closer.

She saw a line of men walking into the crowd, swishing in, one behind the other, like a human snake. The men were soldiers, or police officers. They had uniforms and guns. Romi wondered why anyone would bring a gun here, especially when the Mirror Sphere was coming to see them. The men took places around the base of the Dome of the Rock, and the crowd squished itself even smaller to give them room. Their faces reminded her of her mother's face, when Romi was playing with her cousin Yael. She and Yael always fought, because Yael thought everything was hers, even Romi's dolls. Ima and Aunt Esther would sort of stand in the background, just to let the girls know they were there. Maybe the men were worried that somebody was going to get in a fight. But Romi bet people hadn't even thought of fighting until the soldiers came. Everyone was happy. It was finally their turn.

Another man pressed through the crowd. People did not move out of the way for him, but he was slinky and slithery, and he slipped through them. He had dark hair, and dark eyes, and a dark suit. He reminded Romi of oil. She was staring at him, because he was so rude to push, when he stared back down in her direction. He didn't look at her, but through her, like she wasn't a person, but part of his thoughts. His face was white as paper, and he had a funny eyebrow. She didn't like him. Then he pushed forward again, and slinked his way over to the soldiers. He showed them something from his pocket and started talking to them like her father sometimes talked. Romi giggled. He was so small and weak next to the big men in uniform. Why did other grownups want to obey him? Grownups had strange rules. She wondered if she would understand their rules by the time she got big.

From where she stood, Romi had only noises to go on. It was a bit like being in a cave made of people, where the walls moved around. The people-walls bumped her, and she heard her mother cursing again in Yiddish. Now the people were getting louder, all making their own sounds like bats in the same cave, nobody hearing anybody else, everybody talking louder to be heard over the people talking louder next to them. Romi felt squished. She pulled on her mother.

"Pick me up, Ima!"

"Just stay still," said her mother.

"I want to go up!"

"Just be calm and wait," snapped her mother.

Romi wanted to yell, only she could hear the warning in her mother's voice. She reached up and tugged on her mother's shirt. It stretched, and her mother crouched down quickly.

"Romi," she whisper-yelled. "You're pulling my shirt down. Just be quiet for a moment. I promise I will pick you up when the Mirror comes down."

That made her feel better, but she was still squished.

"Okay, Ima, but everybody's cramping into me!"

"Me too, little one," said her mother, her voice now calm.

"Are they going to squish me up?"

"No, no. But if you feel worried, hold onto Abigail. Who knows, maybe she is worried too, and needs you to hug away her fears?"

Romi considered this, and already she was hugging the elephant tightly. She looked up at her mother and nodded twice. Her mother combed her nails through Romi's hair, and Romi did the same for Abigail. It made them all feel better. Somebody close talked to her mother.

"She's five and a half," answered Ima.

The woman she was talking to looked down at her and smiled. She looked funny to Romi. She was very skinny, and had a birdy face, but her eyes were kind.

"So beautiful," said the woman. "You must be very proud."

"Oh, I am," said her mother, brushing her hair in a proud way. "Thank you so much."

She heard her mother lean in and ask the woman something. Both glanced over toward the Dome of the Rock, then quickly away. They were speaking almost too low for Romi to hear, but she gathered that they were unhappy with the men standing there.

"And where is the Mirror?" said her mother, a tinge of concern in her voice. "After what happened ... do you think it will still come?"

"Ya. Yes," said the woman. She had a funny sounding accent. "It is coming."

"What makes you so sure?" asked Ima.

"I, eh ... I watch out for it, you could say."

Then her mother said, "Oh! I thought I knew—" and began speaking quickly. They seemed to know each other now, but that couldn't be right. Romi hadn't seen the woman before. Both of them kept glancing over toward the soldiers, speaking more quietly, leaning in so they could only hear each other, and so Romi couldn't. Adults were all on the same team, even when they didn't know each other. She could barely make out anything that passed between them.

"...so ... and that is why I came," said the birdy woman, "but I expect I'm worrying needlessly. Still, it is perhaps good that we are not so close. If anything were to..."

Both women glanced at Romi and went back to whispering. She wondered how they could even hear each other's whispers with the crowd making so many noises. She thought of bats again. In a show she'd seen, the bats all spoke at the same time, but they could still hear their own bat babies over all the screechy noises. Maybe grownups had bat powers, once they got introduced. Then, quite suddenly, everyone quieted.

Romi jumped up and down. She knew it was coming, because they were all looking up, not making a sound.

"Pick me up! Pick me up!"

Her mother gasped, letting go of Romi's hand to put it over her own mouth. Romi looked from her to the birdy lady. The lady looked up too, and her eyes were sad. So, so sad, like she'd lost a friend. A man beside Romi made an ugly sound, and then said a bad word.

"Ima! Did you hear—"

Her mother snatched her up and pulled her close.

"My God," she hissed. "What's happened?"

Romi looked from her mother to the other woman. The lady had tears in her eyes.

"Did you know?" whispered her mother.

The lady shook her head.

"It flew away after the bombing," said the birdy woman. "The priest who was there said it took all the force on itself. 'Drank it in,' he said. Then it flew off. So I suppose...."

Her voice had a weepy sound now.

"It's not at all pleasant to look at," said her mother, her voice hard. "I ... I honestly can't stand it."

The other woman looked at her mother. She seemed very worried. Romi grabbed at Ima.

"Hold me high! Hold me high! Abigail and I want to see!"

Her mother glanced at her. Her face was hard, and Romi didn't like it. The other woman looked sick.

"You don't want to see it," said her mother.

"Yes I do! It's not fair!"

Her mother ignored her, but Romi was at the end of her patience.

"Hold! Me! Up!"

She screamed, and beat against her mother's shoulders. Her mother seemed not to care. Finally Ima huffed, glared down at Romi, and put her hands under her daughter's armpits.

"You're going to be disappointed," she said.

"I don't care. I wanna see!"

"Very well," said her mother, sweeping her up high.

Romi squeezed Abigail in triumph. She turned around and looked out.

As the Mirror floated down, it wobbled, like it wasn't sure. Like it was afraid. Like it didn't know if people would like it. Long cracks split its face. There were holes in it, and dents, and a brown fluid oozed from the holes. In some places, the fluid had dried up, making crusty, rusty clumps. In other places, the red-brown juice leaked out over the crust that was there.

The Mirror came down, and settled above them, just out of reach of the crowd. It was caved-in in two places near the top of the side facing Romi, and the dents looked like two large, owlish eyes. A stream of brown gunk ran between the eyes. The bottom of the sphere was crunched up. In the reflecting light of the sun, and the blue stone of the Dome of the Rock, the Mirror looked black and blue. Romi's heart was in her mouth. She hugged Abigail close.

Murmurs of disgust went up from the crowd. People were disappointed. Angry. This was not the miracle they had come to see. The Mirror, as if sensing their feelings, began to revolve slowly in the air. Romi had a sudden thought that it was embarrassed. It was trying to show a better side of itself. But try as it might, nothing helped. When people saw that every side of it was bruised and marred beyond recognition, they grumbled and growled. A man near Romi grit his teeth, and looked ugly, like a vicious dog. She had never seen that look in a human face. The Mirror, the miracle that everyone said had set the world at peace, was making them angry.

Romi looked at it, and tried to see what they saw. She tried to understand what made them grumble at it, and curse at it. All she saw was a poor, poor creature, broken, and wanting to be loved. Yes, it was horrible to look at, but that very fact made her want to comfort it. The Mirror turned again, and stopped. Its owlish dent-eyes looked down on her. She glanced quickly around, searching for some sign that others saw what she saw—how sad it was, how lonely. Her mother shook her head. Only the bird woman looked sorry for it. There must have been others. There must have been others.

Romi knew at once what she must do. She shifted Abigail into her left hand, then she reached out to it with her right. Her hand was higher than the crowd. Her fingers stretched wide, shafts of sunlight passing through the gaps. The Mirror wobbled, and she knew it had seen her hand. Slowly, tremblingly, it moved toward her.

A gasp went up from the crowd. Somebody yelled, "Stop it!"

Romi leaned farther out. The Mirror came to her, like a sick dog on wobbly legs. Her mother shrieked, and pulled her arm down.

"Don't touch it!"

"Let GO OF ME!" yelled Romi, and pried her hand free.

The Mirror hesitated, then continued on toward her. She struggled with her mother's grip, batting her hand away, hitting her own mother— which she'd never done before. Wrenching free, she reached for it once more. She almost touched it. She came so close.

"Stop it!" yelled someone.

"It's going for the little girl!" yelled another.

"No! No! No!" cried Romi.

But nobody heard her. Nobody listened to little children. Her mother pulled her down, just as the Mirror came over top. She tried to climb up again, but others came between her and the Mirror, helping her mother. Helping her mother to make it lonely.

"Help!" cried Romi. "Oh, somebody help me! Help me!"

She looked to the bird woman with the hooked nose. The woman wept openly and clutched her breast.

"Kill it!" yelled someone. "It's after the children."

Romi tried to cry "No!" but she couldn't speak. Her voice was caught inside her body. The crowd shifted around, and, for a moment, a break was made between her and the Dome of the Rock. She saw the dark-eyed, shifty man turn and nod toward the soldiers. Some of them hesitated, but he yelled at them, and they lifted their rifles. A horn was blown somewhere, and someone was yelling through a microphone that everyone must leave. There was a loud bang. Romi screamed in fright and covered her ears. Everyone was screaming. Running. Romi's mother swept her up and starting running too. They were just clearing the stone courtyard, when Romi wrenched free of her mother's iron grip, and looked past her shoulder.

All the men had trained their guns on the Mirror Sphere. It was tinkling red-brown fluid all over the white stone. Now the owlish eye-dents looked at her, frightened. It was so frightened. Behind it, the men began firing.

Epilogue: Nelphel-Crmer

Near Nelphel-Crmer there is a moon. On the moon there is a deep lake. It is green, and clear to the bottom, up from which shines Shena-Fenn-Sui, the Footstool. The Footstool is a vast lattice of grown stone. It forms a pseudo-living structure, an upward climbing ring, woven generation after generation by the Nelphelinoi, in the season of their lives when energy is reduced to mass, and the Nelphelinoi take matter, and become body, and make their offering, and, perhaps, take a mate, and decide between the Two Paths. It is a great choice, to follow the Path of the Body, or the Path of Moving Light, and the choice, once made, cannot be unmade until the Shemsenala-Rah, when He-Who-Is makes all things new.

For that brief season they are in matter, tasting and seeing. It is then that each weaves his portion of the Footstool, building up the Temple of the Great Seraph, so that younger generations may learn of him, and share their learning with the elders. It is then, in matter, that he is found to be he, and she is found to be she, and the choice is made, either to become in Body, or to become in Moving Light, until all the world is made anew.

There are many footstools. There are many Seraphs. Saba-coi, if he takes the Path of Moving Light, may visit them all freely. If he, Saba-coi, should take the Path of Body, and remain in the matter wherein he stands, and love, and take a life-mate, then he will know only one Seraph, and remain in one star-kingdom. He will build great crafts, and navigate vast distances, and be a lord of matter, until the world is new.

There he stands, on the sacred moon of the mother planet Nelphel-Crmer, looking down into the deep green pool. The Footstool glows brightly, for the Seraph has come down to dwell by Saba-coi. That is his privilege, for this is his Day of Choosing. The others who came this season have, each one of them, made their choice of paths. Of these, Saba-coi was reputed wisest. For his *eucusha,* his gift of thanksgiving, he built the Mirror Sphere, in hopes of bringing wisdom to the Kechartimone, the most-favored, who draw the tears of God. The others thought it foolish, and chided him, saying, "Do they not already have a teacher, and a greater one than thee? And is that place not clothed in shadow, until the bent is woven back into the pattern, and the world is made again?"

But Saba-coi knew reason, and the power of truth and beauty, and though his mind forewarned him, he made the Mirror Sphere. Into it he poured his wisdom, and a vision fresh and clear, and gave it life with his own life, while he knelt beside the lake on the moon of Nelphel-Crmer. The great Seraph stayed with him, lending him its strength. Nor did it take umbrage at the daring of his deed. And in the pool before him, a weeping woman bent, holding a shard of the Mirror Sphere, gripping it tightly. And he knew she'd not be comforted, nor would she understand, until the world was remade whole.

Are you at peace, little one?

Saba-coi looked up, shielding his eyes from the glorious rainbow-light that lit the lake from top-to-bottom, rejoicing in the Footstool.

"Yes," said Saba-coi, speaking the words both in matter and in energy, echoing his mind, for such things pleased the Seraph.

"I know now," he continued, "that no mere art can heal them. They must be fashioned new."

And what if you should think again, and plan another Mirror? Perhaps, in time, your skill will be equal to the task?

"No, Great Contemplator of the Face. I should not succeed even then."

And how do you know this, little one? What gives this knowledge root in you?

Saba-coi sighed, and laughed. He was not amused—for what he beheld in memory was bent beyond bent—but why should the sons of light grant any purchase to the darkness? There was no true answer to evil but to laugh in its face, for it was preposterous.

"It was the man, the conniving man, who pursued my Mirror with hate. He..."

Saba-coi became silent, for he did not know if it was right to even name such evils.

Go on, my son.

"He also looked into the Mirror, Great One," said Saba-coi, almost shuddering. "He looked, and he chose the darkness anyway."

The Seraph became quiet, but Saba-coi felt a comforting warmth. Understanding. Consolation. Sympathy of perplexity. Acceptance.

The colors in the lake shone most brilliantly, and he knew the Seraph loved him, and was pleased with him. In that moment, all was clear, and Saba-coi sighed. Before him lay the Path of Body, and the Path of Moving Light. He smiled up at the Seraph, and made his fateful choice.

THE END

ANNA ESCHER MUST DIE

"**D**on't kill Anna!"

It grated on him. She was his, and he had every right. But the words stung Martin Trace. After all, if Anna really had been his, and his alone, then she wouldn't have meant so much to the girl at the convention. And what was a girl that age doing reading his books anyway? Martin didn't even let his *own* daughter read his books. But she was sharp. She'd seen what was coming.

Anna Escher, the world's greatest female private eye, was also Martin's lord and master. Twenty-five novels, and they still couldn't get enough of her. If they'd let him, he'd have Anna drive off into the sunset. But no, then they'd want another series. Martin could just see it: *Old Lady Anna*, the octogenarian investigator, still solving mysteries in her retirement home. They'd eat that shit up. Vultures.

No, the only way to be rid of Anna was to kill her off. He'd planted seeds in the last two novels. Those little compromises Anna needed to make to crack the case. The third man, the one she'd let get away clean. Martin was setting her up for a fall. Trying to justify it. But it would have to be a noble one. She'd go down swinging.

He could see her crawling across the bloodied carpet, and hitting send on a text to Chet Summers at the FBI. "Yeah," she'd say, turning to look her killer in the eye. "You got me. But, sweetie, I got you, too." He'd already thrown in some stuff about atonement. That serial killer priest raving about baptism by blood in book three? She'd visited him in the second chapter. A little foreshadowing, because Anna was about to die a martyr.

"Please don't, Mr. Trace. You know it would be wrong!"

The girl at the convention told him she wanted to be a writer. Well, maybe she'd make it. She'd sniffed out where he was taking the story. And Martin realized that for this girl, *Anna* was the real person, and Martin only her caretaker. He didn't *create* her. He was just the writer lucky enough to stumble upon the force of nature that was Anna Escher. Martin had to admit, it often felt that way. Killing Anna wouldn't be easy. Hell, it felt like murder. He owed her something. Anna had made him.

Pausing, he stretched, and rolled his neck out. He knew he was done writing Anna Escher. That was non-negotiable. But he didn't relish the thought of a thousand conversations like Saturday's. Maybe there was a Plan B. He went through the options one-by-one.

He could cripple her. No, they'd hate him even more for that. She could fake her own death, and go into hiding. No, because the fans would know she wasn't dead. And Anna Escher didn't hide. She could marry Chet! She and Chet and CJ could move into that house on the cliff in *Murder Me Sweetly.* That would be a good reason to retire from crime-fighting, wouldn't it? Yeah, but it would be totally forced. She didn't love Chet; he'd established that in *Left Hand of Darkness.* Anna just loved the idea of Chet Summers. Better to kill her than compromise her. So, death it was.

He took a deep breath, and got back to typing. After two thousand crap words, Martin found the zone. Anna was at her computer, working late into the night. She couldn't sleep, because something didn't fit. Her daughter, CJ, was at a slumber party. No, scratch that. She was in the next room, and Anna didn't want to wake her. She had to keep from cursing at the screen, the way she always did when she knew the pieces had to fit. Her fingers riffled absently through the stacks of photos and files sitting on her desk.

Martin suddenly laughed out loud. It struck him how much he resembled Anna, and she him. Martin's daughter was in the next room too, and his own desk was also littered with notes, and outlines, and the stock photos he used to help him with his descriptions. Heck, even their home offices were similar. A balcony on the left. A closet on the right. Had he done that on purpose? Twenty-five books in, and it had never even occurred to him. "One of us is a copycat," he said to no one in particular. Then he got serious. No more distractions. This was art, and art was war. He typed away.

Unaware of the passage of time, Martin bit his lip, and got real quiet.

Anna, in the story, did too. She was just about to figure it out. The dog. Jessica Oleander's collie. The killer had left it alive. Not only that, but it hadn't even barked when he'd entered. Why not? Anna thought it was because Peter Oleander, who'd trained the dog not to bark when he came home, had killed his wife. But his alibi seemed rock-solid. Ted Wright himself had vouched for the guy. It really couldn't be Peter, unless…

With shaking hands, Anna reached for the bottom-most folder. Martin's hands were shaking too. He loved these scenes. Anna flipped through Mrs. Oleander's documents. She found the adoption papers. The German shepherd, Francis, had been a police dog before he'd gone to the shelter. She scanned the attached vet report. Francis was an older dog, but still in pretty good health when they got him. Anna knew how cops bonded with their dogs. Why would they stick him in a shelter?

Anna turned the report over, and gasped. Martin, butterflies in his stomach, could hardly make his fingers type. Back when he was on the force, Francis had once been partnered up with one Theodore Wright. Ted Wright! It all made sense, why the dog hadn't barked. Francis had recognized his scent. And that explained why the masked man had lingered outside the door for so long, risking witnesses. He'd been letting Francis remember him. Ted Wright killed Jessica Oleander!

"Holy shit!" said Martin Trace at about the same time that Anna Escher was saying it. He hadn't even planned that!

Come to think of it, it had been Ted who questioned Peter Oleander at the station. Questioned him—with his fists—while Anna Escher looked the other way. She'd let it happen, ignored her own principles, because Ted said it was the only way to get him to talk. But he'd never been trying to get at the truth. He'd been trying to scare Oleander, because the man was ready to confess. Because they'd been in on it together! Ted had given Peter a rock-solid alibi, and then did the deed himself. They were going to split Jessica's money, only Peter was feeling guilty now, losing his nerve. And that explained the second print, the one Ted said the lab had botched. Son of a bitch!

But Ted knew Anna had the vet records. He'd seen her fish them out of a drawer during the walk-through. And then, for the first time in nine novels, he'd objected to her breach in police procedure. It was because he was on thin ice, he'd said, 'cause of the working over he'd given Peter. But no! It was because Ted Wright knew Anna. He knew she'd eventually figure it out. And if that was so…

There was a sound downstairs. Anna went pale, and listened. Martin, fearful on his character's behalf, hushed as well. Anna wasn't sure, but she thought she'd heard a dull impact. Then something soft and scraping. It was familiar. What the hell made that kind of a sound?! A sliding sound, then another dull *thunk*. Her door. The heavy patio door that she rarely used, because it always caught on the track. Someone had opened it, then squeezed himself through the gap, and shut it again. Had CJ used the door to sneak out some time, and then forgotten to put the two-by-four back?

She listened in close—no, no, *she closed her eyes, and zeroed-in on the sound, drawing a map with all her senses*—and pressed her thumb against the metal gun box where she kept her forty-five. Forcing herself to breathe, Anna transferred the gun to her right hand, and rose. *Creak!* Martin's heart started pounding. He was actually scaring himself—which was good! The stairs that led down to his own living room creaked in just the same way, and he'd heard the sound in Anna's house as if it had been in his own. He chuckled. He was freaking himself out. This was going to be good! Martin started typing again.

Anna was on her feet, gun in hand. She was too smart to be surprised. The readers wouldn't believe it of her. And Anna Escher was no victim. He had to give them that! She'd been victimized once in her life. Her wrists bore the scars that proved it. Never again! Her teenage daughter, CJ, was in the next room, defenseless, in deep sleep, just as Martin's daughter Christine was, at this very moment. Anna would never let Ted Wright up those stairs. She'd meet him on the landing, and put a bullet in his chest, center-mass. Let them call her a cop-killer. She'd *prove* it was him.

But, thought Martin, Anna Escher *must* die. Yet she can't look weak. He closed his eyes, and tried to see it. Yes, she was on the stairs now; creeping, creeping. She wouldn't turn the lights on. That would only help Ted. He was *her* victim now. Inch-by-inch, she descended, expecting to see him on the landing. But he wouldn't be there. Ted Wright had been planning this for weeks. Maybe years. They were old friends. He'd been in her house, and he knew his enemy. He'd be expecting her to hear him. So he'd be hiding, pressed against the wall behind the grandfather clock. She wouldn't expect him to hide there, because the gap behind it was almost visible from the landing. She could take three steps into the kitchen and see him. So she wouldn't even look there. She'd turn right, toward the bathroom door. And in that moment, while she swept the room, he'd slip by her, go up the stairs, and—

What was that? Martin could have sworn he'd heard footsteps in the hall. Had Christine gotten up to go to the bathroom? She must have. That sound definitely came from inside his own house. He crept over to the door, turned the handle, and swung it open.

No one was standing in the hallway. Christine's door was closed. He opened it, pulling up on the handle so the warped door didn't catch and scrape the frame. He stepped in and saw that she was sleeping soundly. Hoping he wasn't violating her privacy—she was sixteen after all—Martin pulled the blanket up and tucked her in. He stepped back into the hallway and closed the door as quietly as he could. Maybe he ought to check his bedroom at the end of the hall, just in case. He was only frightening himself—which meant the writing was good—but it wouldn't hurt. He padded across the carpet and looked in. He scanned the bathroom; the walk-in closet, where Sarah's clothes still hung, and the gap behind the curtain. He checked the closet again, just to be sure. He'd never been able to make himself get rid of those clothes. God, he missed Sarah!

The sadness hit him like a gust of wind, and swept away the last particles of irrational fear. He had to get back in there and write, or he'd lose the tension of the scene. Martin strode across the carpeted hallway, entered his study, and shut the door. An eerie feeling came over him. Something was different. He saw what it was, and his body went stiff.

There wasn't much in the room. A computer. A curtained window on his left leading out to the balcony where he occasionally smoked. A closet on the wall to the right of his computer. The closet was closed. He was absolutely certain that it had been open.

More than once in his life, in philosophical moods, Martin has puzzled over the fact that emotions, like music, meant something. They meant *themselves*. You didn't need prior experience, or some kind of official label, to know what they meant. And this one was brand new. It was a feeling like, and unlike déjà vu; a sense of terror at the unnatural juxtaposition of two overlapping contraries. Not only did he know that the closet that had been open before had just been closed by someone else, but he knew who'd closed it. And what he knew was impossible. He began to sweat profusely. Something took hold of his heart, and squeezed. If only he had a—

Shit.

He *did* have a gun. He looked down at his right hand, and saw the forty-five. Why was he holding a gun? He couldn't recall ever owning a handgun. Trembling, he leveled the gun at the closet, and edged toward it. His shaky left hand went to the handle. On three, he'd yank it open. On three, he'd squeeze the trigger, and keep squeezing until one of them was dead.

One. Two ... THREE!

Martin threw open the door and fired. And fired. Three bullets tore into the drywall, blowing powder out like mushroom puffballs, before he saw what was there. Nothing. Nobody was in the closet. But then, who had closed it? Where else would a killer hide, but—

He felt the change in pressure. Another presence in the room. Martin turned, and went pale. At first, there was nothing. The air before him was a gray film, clear but somehow full. At his computer sat a woman, typing.

She was short and pretty. Her hair was blonde, and came to her shoulders. There was a scar on her right wrist, a deep scar that she'd never covered up, because it was a trophy, a memento of her time in bondage. But no, that was only a trick of the light. The scar was on *his* wrist. Her skin was smooth, and she wore a half-dozen bracelets. They rang like wind chimes, as her fingers danced over the keys.

"Anna?" he said.

She paused, and looked around the room with a puzzled expression. Then she was back to it, shaking her head as if to clear it.

"Anna!" he shouted. "What are you doing?"

Again she paused, then bit her lip. She pressed her eyes closed, and sighed heavily. Her expression was sorrowful, but determined.

"No," she said. "It has to be done."

"Hey, I'm talking to you," said Martin.

He went over to her, and, lowering the gun only slightly, shook her shoulder. She shrugged, then rolled her neck around, like a prize fighter. She raised her arms and stretched, yawning loudly, making her mouth cavernous. Anna looked up at the sign on the wall over her—over Martin's—computer. But it didn't say, "Keep Swinging, Sweetie!" It said, "Finish the Scene!" It was Martin's motto, but in pink, bubble lettering.

"What?"

Martin crept closer. He looked over his shoulder at what she was writing.

Escher threw open the closet door and fired. And fired. Three bullets tore into the drywall, blowing powder out like mushroom puffballs, before he saw what was there. Nothing. Nobody was in the closet. But then, who had closed it? Where else would a killer hide, but—

"No!" he yelled, reading on. "What are you doing?"

The window. That damned balcony. How many times had he sat out there, whiskey in one hand, cigarette in the other, wondering if this was the smoke that would do him in? He thought about the last time he'd sat out there, going over the case with Officer Wright. And hadn't Wright laughed when he'd said that this balcony would be the death of him? It made it too easy to—

"Stop!" yelled Martin, taking Anna by the throat. She rolled her neck again, but kept typing.

"This isn't right! This isn't the way it's supposed to be!" he pleaded.

Gritting her teeth, Anna plowed forward, the bones on the back of her hands sliding around like clockwork under her thin flesh, the keys *clack, clack, clacking* like the tramp of doom. He read the document as she wrote it, begging her to stop. All that came of his protests was that she paused, and briefly nodded off. Forcing her eyes open, she slapped herself, and navigated to the menu to save the file. The file read, "LastDanceofMartinEscher byAnnaTrace."

"You can't do this to me!"

But she kept doing it. Anna shook her head, and cried a little as she narrated Trace's—no Martin's—demise. Martin stared at her, incredulous. The cold-hearted witch!

"I made you!" he screamed. "I am the only reason you're even successful!"

His protests fell on deaf ears. He knew that she could hear him. He could see it in her sated, self-satisfied face! The artist at work. The fraud, justifying murder to herself. She was killing him, and all she could spare were a few half-hearted tears. He read what she wrote next. Before she could finish the sentence, he grabbed the phone off the desk. As his fingers tapped out a desperate message, he noticed that the phone he held was on the desk. In his hand; still there on the desk. There was a muffled sound, and his shoulder jerked back, and started to burn. He dropped the phone.

"Drop the gun, Escher," said Ted Wright.

He was there by the window, gun raised. Ted's face was twisted with rage. Martin stumbled backward.

"What," Martin said, "are you so mad about, Ted?"

"Damn you, Escher. Why'd you have to keep digging? Why'd you have to be an asshole?"

Escher smiled grimly.

"Something funny?" said Officer Wright.

"You," replied Escher. "Your face. Your outrage, like *you've* been wronged. It's always the same with you guys, but you don't know—"

Martin suddenly raised the forty-five, and shot Ted Wright. His aim was poor, and Ted got another shot off too. Escher pitched himself sideways, landing with his back to Ted. It didn't matter. He only needed to hit "send." He clawed his way forward, blood seeping out of him, soaking into the new carpet. There was another shot, but Escher almost didn't feel it. His finger tapped the green button, and he smiled.

Ted limped toward him and trained his gun on Escher's head.

"Not so clever after all," Ted said. "Are you? Because I got you, Escher. I got you."

Escher rolled over, knowing that by moving, he was only speeding up the flow of blood. He heard a sound in the hall, and smiled.

"Yeah," said Escher. "You got me. But, Ted, you asshole, I got you too!"

The sound of the blast was deafening, and Escher got some of it in the face. Bits of door ripped into him, but he had the satisfaction of seeing Ted fly across the room. Officer Wright hit the balcony curtains with a kind of ringing thud, then slid down. A red hole the size of a basketball had been excavated from his torso. The door behind Martin flew open, and collided with his prone body. Martin flinched at the pain, but a soft, trembling voice met his ears.

"Daddy!"

Christine tossed the shotgun across the room, and fell upon him, weeping.

"Daddy, daddy! Oh God! Oh please, God, no!"

He wanted to tell her it would be okay. But that would be a lie. Eschers didn't deal in lies. They faced the truth. They looked their horror in the eye, instead of running from it. They used their pain to help others.

"Daddy," she said again.

Escher felt his own heart beating. It was a slow beat. In between beats, he heard Anna's keyboard go *click, click, clack*. Then she paused. A moment of silence for his last words.

"Christine," he said, coughing. "This … isn't the end. Remember that. Don't let them—"

He broke off coughing. His mind raced. There were so many things to do before you died.

"Christine," he tried again. "C-call Ch-Chessy Summers. Eff ... FBI. Tell her to ch-check the vets. Oleander's ... not clean."

She hugged him tight. It hurt. He couldn't even breathe. But he had one more thing to say. Martin Escher braced himself, and spoke his last words.

"Christine ... don't let them make the world. I love you, sweetie. Keep ... keep swinging."

Christine pressed her father to her heart. Escher tried to feel her heartbeat against him. Then he tried to feel his own heart. It beat once, twice. *Click, clack, click, clack. Click.* Then all was silence.

ENTANGLEMENTS, LLC

athan was not in the habit of following people. But the dream was the most compelling part of his life. Now he could see that it was also true.

The bus dropped him off at the last stop on the dusty outskirts of the City of Lights. He worked landscaping and lived in an efficiency that he kept so dirty, it might have been a storage locker. Another day of side-eyes, and of constant dissatisfaction from the foreman. He didn't think he had long at Schall's. As he walked away from the city, a brisk wind hit him in the face. He looked away from it, toward the city, and saw the stranger.

The man's hair was short like Nathan's. They were the same height. He was well-dressed, with a careless, confident air. While Nathan had meant to flee the lights of the boutique downtown, to go back to his overpriced coffin-room, the man on the opposite side of the road strode eagerly toward that color. Nathan nearly fell over when he saw him. It was the man from his dream.

Every night, this dream invaded the others. He'd be walking in the dusk down a wide, golden beach. The ocean was to his left, calm, with little blue-black waves breaking quietly on the sand. The beach stretched off before him toward a horizon framed by distant mountains. There were no people on the beach. His dream self was searching for something, not knowing what. Then, like it was a surprise every time, far down the beach he'd see the vertical film that reached from sky to sand. The butterflies in his stomach would go into a frenzy, and he'd spy that speck behind the film. As he got closer, the speck grew, and it took a human form.

With the mountains so far, the man behind the film was the only real measure of distance. As he walked forward, so did the stranger. Nathan's heart would beat so hard against his chest that the pain often woke him before he reached the barrier. Three nights past, he'd made it all the way to the film, and he'd seen the stranger up close. And then, last night, he'd gone further.

He'd stopped. The figure stopped too. They faced each other across the transparent breach. You couldn't say it was a mirror, because the world continued behind it, slightly different. Were they twins? Their faces were similar, but Nathan's hair was dark brown, almost black. The other one had red hair. But, when he looked hard into the man's face, he saw the truth. They both knew it, but the other one wasn't frightened of Nathan, as Nathan was of him. Fascinated; that was all. At the same moment, each man had stepped forward into the barrier—into each other.

The day that followed had been dreary and uneventful. Yet maybe he'd known in his gut that today was the day. And now that stranger was here, in his world, strolling toward the promise of the City of Lights.

The air felt wet and heavy. A storm was brewing. Nathan stepped into the road, wove through cars that swerved and honked at him, and began to follow.

Two blocks later, he lost sight of his quarry. There was a flash of red in the headlights of a truck. The man now stood behind a diner window, just long enough to be spotted. Nathan crossed the road again.

The diner was poorly lit. Nathan crept around the corner and spied his other at a booth on the far end, facing the wall. He sat himself down at a table on the street side of the dining room, so that the man would have to turn almost all the way around to see him. The waitress took the stranger's order. She lingered, giggling and touching her hair. Nathan couldn't hear the man's responses. When she finally came to Nathan's table, she fixed him with a strange look.

"Are you…? Aren't you?" she stuttered.

He shrugged.

"Never mind," she stammered. "What can I get you?"

He ordered a coffee. She nodded, and scurried off. It wasn't long before she returned to bring the red-haired man's order. He ate his sandwich in silence, staring at a painting on the far wall. It was only spirals in spirals— not much to look at it. Nathan sipped his coffee. He didn't know what he was waiting for, or what he'd do if the stranger turned around. So he sipped, and he studied.

The stranger had long, tapered fingers. The middle finger of his left hand crooked over his ring finger, just like Nathan's. Unlike Nathan's, his ring finger bore a golden band. The man sat straighter than he, but his shoulders had the same tendency to roll forward and down. Nathan imagined the stranger with dark hair, and less of an aura of self-possession. Eerie icicles grew in his guts. Finally, the stranger flagged down the waitress.

The two exchanged small talk about the weather. He couldn't distinctly hear what the man said, but noted how he spoke in quick, intentional bursts. Nathan tended to fumble for words, filling the empty spaces with "uhs" and "ums." The stranger thought carefully before he spoke. The waitress was charmed, and took her time leaving to get the check.

She returned with a black sleeve, and the man pulled a credit card from his wallet and slipped it inside. He asked for the restroom. She nodded toward the back, and took the sleeve to the register. Processing it quickly, she returned it to the table, before disappearing into the kitchen. Nathan saw his chance.

He hurried to the table. Looking around quickly, he flipped open the bill book, hoping to catch the name on the card. Entanglements, LLC, it read. No name.

"Damn."

Just then, the other man exited the restroom. Nathan spun on his heel and headed for the front. He continued out the door, forgetting to pay his coffee bill. Once outside, he stepped quickly into the alley beside the diner. From the shadows, he heard the creek and jingle of the door. The man passed the alleyway without looking over. Nathan sighed in relief, and then followed him.

He didn't know why he was following the man. What would he say? What would he do if the stranger from his dream turned toward him? He trailed for three blocks, until the man turned into a parking garage.

It was far too open. But the stranger walked toward the nearby spaces marked "Express," and stopped at a vehicle Nathan knew well. It was not the car he'd owned before his DUI. It was an Audi R8, the car of his dreams.

Leaning into the shadows, against a concrete pillar that smelled of urine, he watched as the other one slipped inside his silver-gray chariot. The engine purred, and the car floated across the asphalt, a skiff on smooth water. Nathan expected it to speed off. He felt a great emptiness contemplating the walk home alone in the dark. But the purr of the engine lingered within earshot. Nathan peeked out from behind the support column. Thirty feet away, the car was idling. Waiting for something. He could just make out the license plate. He'd hardly committed it to memory before the skiff took the wind, and left him behind in the dark. There was a sudden clap of thunder. Outside, rain began to fall.

So that was that. Now to wander back, and climb into his sleep locker. They hadn't even met. And he might have left it alone then. He might have accepted the gulf between them. But he didn't.

***

Entanglements, LLC was on the other side of town. It closed only an hour after his shift was set to end. He set up a taxi to come get him right at five o'clock, then threw himself into the work. It was the best effort he'd given in a month. For once, the foreman had nothing to say.

When five o'clock rolled around, he jumped into the waiting taxi without even bothering to collect his wages. He'd been working in a wealthy neighborhood outside the city, but Entanglements, LLC was on the opposite end of the city, through walls of traffic. The driver said he couldn't speed, but Nathan offered to tip him double the fare. They got there in half an hour.

It was a nondescript brown brick building, one of two dozen just like it in a long strip of featureless, one-story offices. The car began to pull away, but Nathan chased it down, and told the driver to wait. He wasn't yet ready to speak to the red-haired man, but, now that he was here, he had a plan. Nathan stalked the office parking lot, looking for the car that couldn't be missed. No sooner had he found it then a buzz from the building made him look up. Nathan caught one clear glimpse of the man from his dream. He looked down and shuffled back into the waiting taxi.

"Can you follow a car? Without being seen?"

The driver turned around to stare him down.

"You doing anything … wrong?"

Nathan shook his head. "I need to talk to that guy," he said. "But not here."

The driver frowned. "Look, I don't wanna be a party to something."

"You won't be," assured Nathan. "It's nothing illegal. I just need to talk to the guy. He's … somebody I used to know. Kind of expecting me."

The driver seesawed his head.

"Okay," he said. "Okay, but after I drop you off, I got another fare."

Nathan nodded impatiently. "Please. He's driving off."

The driver sighed, and turned his attention on the Audi. He waited until it reached a distant stop sign and made a right, before speeding after it.

It was a small irony that the house where the man got out was in the same neighborhood Nathan had been working earlier that day. He had the driver go a mile past the stranger's sprawling home, and drop him by the woods. By now it was dark, and the dark gave him cover as he cut through the woods between estates. There were no sidewalks. Neighborhoods like this didn't have them; only large houses nestled safely behind sprawling, manicured lawns. Yet he found the house without difficulty, and peered out at it from the woods.

Now that he was here, talking to the man at his home seemed like a terrible idea. At least in public he might seem to bump into him by chance. He couldn't get up the nerve to walk up to the front door. So he waited. And he stared.

Some time later, he spied the stranger through a large window on the side of the large white house. He passed by the kitchen, then reappeared in an adjacent room, and finally sat down on a couch. A woman came in and sat down beside him. She nestled her head up against his shoulder, and appeared to pour her heart out to him. She was beautiful. And she was familiar. He might go so far as to say that he'd also seen *her*, once upon a time, in a dream. Perhaps he was going mad. But then, why *couldn't* he be with someone like that? Why couldn't dreams come true?

He looked down at his hands. Soil under his chewed nails. Calloused skin. Was this all he would ever be? He wasn't that old, but he felt it. His spirit had gone wrinkled. The man through the window, so much like Nathan in appearance, was vitality in human form. His woman, Nathan's dream woman, was the sort of creature who gravitated toward vitality. This stranger could keep her young, protected for a time, from the evils of entropy. But her face was buried in the stranger's shoulder, while the stranger only stared blankly at the wall across from him.

Presently, he leaned in and whispered something to her. She rose rather suddenly, and walked toward the stairs without looking back, disappearing into the dark interior. The man stood and went the other way, back toward the kitchen window. Nathan waited for him to cross it again. He sat staring for what seemed an eternity, then settled back into the trees. There, under their cover, mosquitoes buzzing about his ears, the emptiness set in again. This is what he'd been reduced to. As he considered how to wind his way back through the woods to call for another anonymous car to take him back to his anonymous cave, his eyes caught something on the lawn.

The stranger stood on the manicured grass, halfway between the house and the woods where Nathan hid. He was looking directly at Nathan.

Nathan shuffled blindly backward, instantly regretting his decision to come. He stood quickly, and smacked his head against a branch.

"Leaving already?" asked the man.

Nathan swallowed. He shook his head, trying to show that he meant no harm.

"I thought you'd come here for a reason."

"I wasn't going to hurt anyone," stammered Nathan. "Look, I'm sorry. I'm going."

The man shrugged, quite untroubled.

"But why? Isn't it obvious that we have a lot to talk about?"

Nathan stopped. He looked up into that face, seeing it clearly for the first time. It really *was* like his own. But were they identical? They were not so much twins as different takes on the same design.

"Come inside," said his double. "Please. You have every right."

The figure turned, and headed back toward the house. Nathan paused, trembling as he clutched a down-hanging branch. But he followed.

***

They sat across from each other at the kitchen table. For a long time Nathan could say nothing. Staring at the stranger, he gave himself over to fascination. At length, the stranger drummed his fingers on the table and nodded, as if agreeing with himself.

"They say there's one of everyone," began the man. "At least one. Have you heard that too?"

Nathan shuddered. The man smiled warmly, but he seemed to be enjoying some private joke.

"Do we look like each other, though?" he continued.

Nathan shrugged. They did, completely; and yet they didn't. The other nodded, agreeing again.

"But we could pass. We could pass. What's your name?"

Nathan recovered himself enough to mumble it out. The stranger didn't seem surprised.

"What … what's yours?" asked Nathan, his throat dry.

Another warm but secret smile.

"I don't use my given name. Everyone calls me Prince."

He gestured over his shoulder, toward the interior of the house.

"Especially her," he continued. "Do you like her?"

Nathan felt his face flush. He spread his hands on the table, unconsciously pushing himself backward.

"I don't know what you want me to say to that," said Nathan. "She's not mine to like."

Prince inclined his head,

"Well … now that all depends, doesn't it?"

Nathan stared at him, confused.

"On what?"

"On what you and I *are*?" said the other. "What we really are. And what we can be."

"I … I'm not following?" said Nathan, nervously.

Prince's teeth were as white as his house.

"I think you know exactly what I'm talking about, Nathan. Show me your hands."

Nathan blinked. Something told him he ought to run. But he stayed, and stalled for time.

"Why?" he stammered.

"Just … show them to me."

He did, laying them flat, and then rolling them over on the table. Prince reached out and took them tentatively in his own. The double's hands were smooth. Nathan suppressed an urge to recoil as the man touched his brittle skin. Seeing his discomfort, the other withdrew.

"Forgive me," he said. "It's just … yours are like sandpaper. It's extraordinary. The difference between us. And you work all day with these? You know how to … how to build things from scratch? Are you the sort who can take broken parts, and make something new?"

Nathan shrugged. He could do that sort of thing, sometimes. Prince nodded. He seemed to weigh his words before continuing.

"We all have choices to make," he began. "At a certain point, it's not productive to dwell on how we got where we are, you know? How things might have been different? The point is, we're here now. And as for how you and I are both … both here? Well, maybe it's better not to dig too deeply. But choices. Choices are always before us. We choose what we become. And I think we can keep choosing, up until the very moment we're in. Is the present moment the end, or the beginning? That's a matter of outlook, you know?"

"What are you getting at?" Nathan said.

Prince nodded. His demeanor became all business.

"We can trade. Your life for mine. Mine for yours. What do you say?"

Nathan scoffed. "You must be joking!"

In fact, Prince was only naming the formless hope that had been building since he'd first sighted the man. In his mind. In a dream. It seemed too good to be true.

"And anyway," Nathan stammered, "why would you want my life? I live in an efficiency? I'm … I'm … stuck."

Prince laughed. It hit Nathan with the force of a slap.

"What are you laughing at? I guess I'm a joke to you? Is this some kind of a sick rich-person's prank?"

Prince continued to laugh, but he waved his hand in a conciliatory manner.

"No, no! I'm laughing because it's so backward. You're so wrong, Nathan! You stuck? You, with no attachments? No company? No investors to please? My God, man, you are free! I'm the stuck one. Kept like a porcelain doll in this porcelain life. And she—" he nodded toward the interior, and a shadow passed over his face. "She deserves better than me."

Nathan stared after him, dumbfounded. Would this soft-fingered fool really trade all he had in order to live in a hovel on the East Side? Truly, they must *both* be dreaming. Maybe they were. In dreams, you didn't care so much about right and wrong—or reason. But, even if it was a dream, he decided right there that he'd rather stay in it.

"I accept," said Nathan.

Prince beamed at him. It was absurd.

"You're sure now?" he said, eagerly. "You're willing to sign your name to it?"

"Hell, if you're serious, I'll sign in blood!"

Nathan saw the stranger tremble. Calmly, and with exaggerated control, he produced a piece of clean, heavyweight paper. Drawing out a pen, he scratched out the words of a contract. Beneath it he drew lines for each man to sign. Finally, and to Nathan's surprise, he giggled, brought out a pen knife from somewhere in his pockets, and drew it across his ring finger. He held the digit out above the black line. Three drops of his blood fell, and he used the pen to draw the tiny pool into a signature. Blood and ink swirled together without really blending. He handed the knife to Nathan.

"In blood," he said.

Nathan hesitated, suddenly suspicious of the whole enterprise, but then a form, lithe and beautiful, passed through his mind's eye. He turned to look. She was gone now, if she'd been there at all. But the image was enough. He pricked his finger, and signed his name.

After signing, there were many things to put in order. Prince ushered Nathan to a large bathroom. He retrieved a box of red hair dye, and insisted Nathan make the change now. When it was finished the two looked almost identical. That done, he led Nathan to his bedroom. He had a huge four-post bed, and a double-wide closet filled with expensive suits. The closet on the opposite wall was open and empty. There was only one small chest of drawers in the room. He wanted to ask where Prince's wife kept her things, but his double moved swiftly from one subject to another, filling him in on all the details of his life. Nathan was so busy scribbling these down that he forgot to ask again.

After that, he took him on a guided tour of the house. Prince's manner was carefree, like a man on the cusp of retirement. His demeanor changed only once, when he led Nathan down a long corridor on the third floor. They were passing a doorway, when Nathan stopped. For no reason that he understood, he stared at it. Prince stepped in front of the door, and put a finger to his lips.

"She's sleeping," he said. "You wouldn't want to wake her now."

Nathan nodded compliantly, but frowned. They descended a winding stairwell, which brought them back to the kitchen, where they'd signed in blood.

"Well, then," said Prince, "you'll need this."

He produced an envelope from his jacket pocket. Nathan opened it, and perused the contents. There were numerous plastic cards, personal documents, and even a passport. Everything was neat and ready for him, just like the box of hair dye that had been waiting under the bathroom counter. Nathan tried not think too much about it. Whatever he'd agreed to was already done.

"Don't you need my information?" Nathan asked. "I don't have it all here. I wasn't planning—"

"That won't be necessary," said Prince. "I have what I need. But you'll need this."

He drew a phone out of his pocket, and turned it over slowly in his hand. Almost wincing, he pressed the phone into Nathan's palm, and closed Nathan's fingers over it.

"I changed the pin to 1-2-3-4-5," he said. "Make it whatever you like. But don't—"

Prince looked past him, searching for words. He shook his head. "Just keep it simple. Keep life simple. I've given you all you need to live as me. Don't try to be something more. Same with the presentation tomorrow. Don't over-complicate things. That's something I've learned."

Nathan stared at him, sure that he'd missed something rather important. He was just on the verge of asking about the man's wife, why she hadn't come down this whole time, why they slept in different rooms, when something Prince had said jarred him back to the present.

"A *what*? Tomorrow?" said Nathan.

"A presentation," repeated Prince. "Just a basic one. Our backers just want reassurance that the technology works, and that we're on track for production."

Nathan shook his head. "But … but … I don't know anything about that! What technology?"

Prince smiled, and clapped Nathan's shoulder reassuringly.

"Don't worry! You won't have to say a word. Shed Martinez is our chief technician, and he always does the talking. Your job is just to show up and look dashing. Don't worry about details. You'll pick that up as you go. Just be an image of success; that's what these people want. Let the work-horses do the heavy lifting, and act like it's all going *so* smoothly, that you can hardly be bothered with the minutiae. Shake hands. Smile. *Be* stability."

Nathan bit his lip. He'd struggled since childhood with crippling anxiety. Yet it was hardly to be expected that he could get this new life without any cost to himself. If it was all a matter of acting, he knew he could muddle through. He'd been doing that for years.

He asked a few more questions about names and physical descriptions. Prince dutifully complied, though Nathan sensed the man was increasingly anxious to depart. He remembered what Prince had said about being a porcelain doll, and couldn't help but wonder if there was something he was missing in all this. When he'd run out of things to ask, Prince turned and walked swiftly toward the door.

"Wait!" said Nathan. "What if there's something else? What if I need to get hold of you?"

Prince turned the knob and stepped halfway over the threshold.

"It's all there," he said.

He continued to move away, and was shutting the door behind him, when Nathan ran over and pulled it open.

"Your wife!"

Prince smiled. "Yes?"

"She'll know!" said Nathan. "No matter how much we look like each other…"

Prince grinned. There was something almost wistful in the grin.

"Oh, I wouldn't worry about that," he said. "Not tonight, anyway. She's not … well, you'll see. She's yours now, anyway."

He pulled the door shut. Nathan watched him through the glass as Prince hurried across the lawn, into a waiting darkness. And it occurred to Nathan, quite suddenly, that he hadn't even learned the woman's name.

***

He sat for some time on a large leather couch. A clock without numbers hung over the fireplace. The house was so quiet that the clicking of the second hand became a siren. What if a door opened, and he heard her footfalls in the long hallway above?

His thoughts turned to tomorrow's presentation on a product he didn't know in a building where he'd never set foot. Then came a sound, low at first, that might have been a bird call, or the whine of distant sirens. But it was coming from inside the house, up the stairs, and down the hall. It was like the muffled sobs of a woman, face in her pillow, trapped in some secret sorrow. He decided to go to bed.

Nathan sighed as he entered Prince's bedroom and closed the door. He wanted only to throw himself into the bed, wrap himself in blankets, and pass into oblivion. He hesitated just behind the closed door. Should he lock it? Why would he want to do that? What if she should want to come in? He locked it anyway, and buried himself in the covers. Except for the red numbers on the alarm clock, the room and house were utterly dark. There were no more sounds. He passed into a dreamless sleep.

At 3:00 a.m., he woke without obvious cause. A dim light filtered in from the hallway. Nathan poked his head out from under the covers, wondering why he was so afraid to look out. When he did, he saw the shadowy impression of feet under the door. She must have been standing there, though she did not try the handle. He heard a faint rubbing or scratching, and then she was gone. He didn't sleep again that night.

When sun came through the windows, Nathan rose from the bed. Quietly, he showered, and then selected a suit and shoes from the double-wide closet. It was a relief that they were all the same. Fashion had never been his strength. Unafraid in the morning light, he stepped into the hallway, and saw the small envelope lying in the hallway at his feet.

He bent to retrieve it, scanning the corridor as he did so. Heart beating, he worked it open, and unfolded what it contained. The lettering of the message was as lovely as the creature who must have written it. The soft paper had a rosy, feminine scent that went straight to his head. But the words were troubling.

My love—if that's what you are—I remembered again. What did you take from me?

He shook his head, perplexed, then folded the note, and stuck it into his pocket. Descending the stairs, and not finding her there, he breathed a sigh that was part relief and part disappointment. Yet she must be in the house. Perhaps any moment she'd come down the stairs. There was something he was supposed to remember, but all he could think of was the need to get away. He wasn't ready to meet her. From somewhere in the house a door opened. Nathan hurried outside, and made for the car.

***

Nathan reached into his pocket, and sighed. In the rush to get away, he'd forgotten the envelope with Prince's key card. The card opened a side door, and led directly to Prince's office at Entanglements, LLC. That wouldn't have been a problem, except that he'd also forgotten the notepad where he'd scribbled down the pin code. He walked toward the front door. When he got there, he discovered that it also was electronically locked. The pin pad looked up at him, mockingly. There was even a retina scanner. The windows and doors were all tinted, so that he couldn't even see the reception desk Prince had told him about. Sheepishly, he pressed the buzzer, and looked up into the camera.

"May I help you?" said a skeptical voice; then, "Oh! Mr. la Fleur!"

199

La Fleur? His last name was Flowers. Could it possibly be a coincidence? He didn't know how he'd explain that he'd forgotten his pin, but she buzzed him in. Nathan closed his eyes, imagined he was Prince, and entered, thanking God that he'd at least memorized the receptionist's name.

"Hello, Anita," he said.

Anita stared up at him. She must have realized that her mouth was open, because she closed it hard.

"Sir," she said, "you look … very … handsome. And did you … get a haircut? Or something?"

He smiled.

"Thanks. Actually, I didn't sleep much," he said. "Not feeling entirely myself. Maybe I'm coming down with something."

She looked at him quizzically, then nodded. "The gentlemen you're meeting just phoned to say they'll be here in about twenty minutes."

"Twenty minutes?" he said, a little too loudly. "Excellent. And where's Shed? Does he have everything set up?"

Anita pursed her lips. "He's … not in yet. Mrs. Mason wants to speak with you. Before they arrive."

Anita's bloodless tone made him worry. Maybe he didn't look as much like Prince as he thought. Or maybe something else was bothering her.

"Okay," he said.

"She's in your office," the girl added, answering the question before he could ask it.

"Great," he said, beaming, not knowing what to do with his hands. At least he'd memorized how to get to his office. "I'll just go there now."

Anita nodded, then looked hard at him. She seemed to be working herself up to a question. Could she tell it wasn't Prince? Hopefully Prince's assistant, Selina Mason, would have a better reaction. Nathan wanted to get away from her, but she was so obviously on the verge of speaking.

"Sir," Anita finally said, "the access codes and the biometrics are working just fine. I mean if this was some kind of security test … I hope I didn't fail."

She looked nervously at the door. So that was all. She thought she might be in trouble. Nathan squared his shoulders, reminding himself that he was in charge. And anyway, people didn't see what they weren't looking for. He didn't need to explain himself to Anita, or to anyone. If his actions were mysterious, then all the better.

"You did just fine," he said. "I had my reasons."

Anita smiled, and shook her head, obviously relieved. "Well, good luck on that presentation."

Nathan thanked her and headed for his office.

***

Though he'd never met her, Selina's expression told him immediately that something was wrong. He stepped in, and she stepped past him to press the door flush. She locked it. With a flicker of motion, she reached up, and turned the blinds.

"Hello, Prince. Did Anita tell you?"

Nathan shrugged.

"Shed won't be coming in today," said Selina. "So *you're* going to have to do it this time."

Nathan felt the air go out of him.

"Not coming in?" he stammered.

"I know," she said. "Terrible timing. But quite deliberate, I'm sure."

Slowly, so as not to seem to be doing it, Nathan reached out and took hold of a chair-back for support.

"What do you mean? He's not sick or anything?"

Selina rolled her eyes. "What do you mean what do I mean? You said yourself this was coming. We should have done it yesterday, before he could make up his mind again. Now he's clean away, and we'll never get him back for a reset. We'll either have to track him down, or find someone to replace him. Both options are risky, but that's a problem for tomorrow. "

Nathan affected calm, as he tried to process what any of that meant.

"Well," he said, his tone measured, "I'm sure we can get another technician to summarize the ... the state of things."

Her laugh was biting. "You know that's not true. Not one of them has the whole picture, and that's by design. *Your design*. Anyway, even if one of them did know it all, Shed's the only one who can sell it on scientific grounds. Make it plausible. So you're just going to have to do it with charm."

Nathan swallowed. He thought back to his long conversation with Prince. At no point had the man explained even part of his business. And if this Shed was so unreliable, why had he left Nathan at the man's mercy? Perhaps he could ask *her* to do the presentation, but the mere fact that she hadn't volunteered suggested that that would be a misstep. He needed to

201

find out exactly what it was he did.

"But why did Shed leave?" he asked.

"You know why! And please, don't play the innocent with me. I'd say you and I were *a little bit* past that."

She stepped in closer to him. Too close. His eyes opened wide, as she leaned into him, whispering in his ear.

"It'll be okay," she said, soothingly. "I'm going to set them up in the atrium. You know what I mean. Just give your presentation. Keep it general. Be handsome and charming. That shouldn't be too hard for you, right?"

She was so close to him, her lips against his ear, that she couldn't see his shock. Her hand, velvet-soft, enclosed his.

"We're almost through this," she said. "Then we can pivot. We'll get Shed back. He knows what will happen if he runs. We'll get him back, and, then we'll *get him back*. I'm sure there's enough resets out there to last the life of the company."

Nathan's mind raced, trying to make sense of it. Whatever she was talking about couldn't be good.

"And relax," she said. "If the presentation goes south, we'll reset them too."

She pulled herself back a little, then leaned up and kissed him on the mouth.

"Remember Tuscany," she cooed. "Remember what I said? I meant it. The world can spin around us as much at it wants. We have the power to spin back. We can't run, like Shed. We're in too deep. So we go forward. We'll keep spinning it till it stops where we want it to. Now go get 'em."

She kissed him again, before gliding over to the door. There she turned and favored him with a devilish grin.

"…And when we're finished with them, you can come back to my office … and spin me."

***

In his wasted school years, Nathan had learned how to abuse the Socratic question. He'd feign knowledge, then catch it in morsels, answering his teachers' inquiries with clarifying questions of his own, meant to draw out the very bits he hadn't gained through study. When it worked, it worked. When it didn't, well, it *really* didn't. And this time it didn't.

Prince was suave, and Nathan used that. The investors—who looked more like government men than businessmen—dropped plenty of details.

The problem was, what they said made no sense to him. He didn't know what entanglements were, or what was meant by "many worlds." He couldn't talk about feasibility and applications without knowing what the hell this was all *for*. Naturally, he couldn't address their ethical concerns either. The final question, the one he'd tried and failed to answer before Selina silently entered, concerned his results with live subjects. Border collies, apparently.

"So did they come back healthy?" asked the taller of the two men. "I mean psychologically healthy?"

"I … hmm, well, yes," stammered Nathan. "Yes, I'd say they were more than healthy—"

"Because I've got two border collies myself," interjected the tall man. "Smart dogs. Real smart. More personality than my five-year-old."

Nathan laughed. He nodded as if he knew all about border collies. But the man was serious. The other guy was short, stocky, and could have been a dog himself. A bulldog.

"Yeah, I don't know," said the bulldog. "People are going to ask, 'What happened to the original? Is he happy where he is?' People go nuts about dogs. Me, I could give a shit about dogs. And some *people* too; I could give a shit about *them*. Who cares if the old Ali Baba Bomber is happy where he is, you know? Long as the new one isn't a prick. But the legal stuff … even for the State."

"Yes," said Nathan. "Of course. But the promise of the technology … it's just. We'll need to keep compiling this good data. And we're very close. *Very* close."

Bulldog man did not smile. He looked at the tall man. The two nodded, silently agreeing. Nathan didn't like that nod. The tall man looked at Nathan.

"You see, Prince, we're just not sure the world is going to accept this. Not unless you can say what happens to the originals. I mean where exactly do they go? Forget dogs. What if somebody used this on somebody's kid? On his personal enemies? It gives people the creeps. And I'm just seeing lawsuits, you know? Why can't you show us more of the data?"

Selina appeared at Nathan's side. She was smiling, but he saw her hand dip into her jacket. She took a small black cube from her pocket and placed it casually on the presentation table. Then she produced a phone, and, to Nathan's surprise, began scrolling through her apps.

"Mr. la Fleur?" said the stocky man.

"I … I'm sure you'll be pleased, once you see the end result," Nathan stammered. "In the meantime, your continued funding is crucial. I mean this is … it's the greatest scientific breakthrough of all time—"

"—Yeah," said tall man, "you said that last time."

Nathan almost laughed. Not that the situation was funny. He was just surprised that he and Prince had ever used the same words. But the others were not amused. They began to stand, starting with bulldog man.

"Gentlemen," said Selina.

She was holding her phone toward them as if she were about to take a picture. Bulldog man frowned.

"No pictures plea—"

She touched the screen, and both men froze. At the same moment, they began to gyrate, then fell backward into their chairs. As Nathan stared, dumbfounded, they began to fade. Lines of color and shape, abstracted forms and qualities, unwove themselves, and melted away into the air. A progress bar on Selina's phone went all the way to the right, then stopped and began crawling back to the left. Selina hit the screen again, and the bar paused. She sighed, and grinned at Nathan.

"Crisis averted," she said. "We can recall alternates later. When we're ready. Honestly, though, Prince, that was a shit show."

Nathan stepped away from her. He ran forward, and waved his hands through the space where the men had just been. With ice in his veins, he turned his gaze on Selina.

"What did you do to them?"

The sardonic grin she'd been wearing died on her lips. Her expression changed. He had the eerie sensation of being a mouse staring up into the eyes of an owl.

"Why," she said, in a flat, bloodless voice, "are you asking me that? And why did you ask them all those things you should already know?"

There was a sudden, evil fire in her eyes. He saw her mind working. Nathan realized that he couldn't go on pretending. He couldn't even guess at the rules of the game he was playing.

"Are they … are they dead?" he asked.

The owl's eyes narrowed.

"Prince," she said, in a sing-song voice. "Tell me about Heidi."

He shrugged. *Who the hell was Heidi?* She nodded.

"Uh huh. Did she find out again? Did you—did he—run away with her? Or did he bring you over first somehow, and then run away?"

She took a step toward him. He stepped back.

"You know," she mused. "I thought you were a little different. And you had to be buzzed in this morning. God! I should have guessed. So then, *Prince*, my name is Selina Mason. And who the hell are you?"

Nathan thought of Prince's strange domestic arrangements, of the words on the note that his wife—Heidi?—had left on his door. What was the meaning of any of it? Had Prince stolen her memories? Was it something worse than that?

"Look," he said, "I don't want any trouble."

She threw her head back and laughed.

"A little too late for that, *Prince*. Or whoever you are. But if *you're* standing in for him, then where is he?"

Nathan backed slowly toward the door. Selina inched forward.

"I need to know who you are," she said, evenly, "so I can find him. Oh, don't worry, you can keep Heidi. If she'll have you, that is. Funny thing about that girl. I always thought she was dumb as rocks. But she keeps figuring it out, doesn't she? Is that what this is all about? He thinks he can escape it? Escape *me*? Tell me, you son of a bitch, did he trade lives with you?"

Nathan felt dizzy. All he knew was that he wanted to escape. Perhaps if he could get back to Heidi, he could tell her the truth. It was beginning to take shape in his mind. The two men had gone somewhere. And Selina could bring them back … but, no, not *them*. Not exactly. If Selina could do that to those men, perhaps Prince had done it to someone else. To his own wife! He bumped into the atrium door and felt behind him for the handle. Quick as a snake, Selina whipped something from her pocket and trained it on him.

"Move and you get fifty-thousand volts," she said.

He froze, raising his hands.

"Look, I don't know what's happening here," he said. "I just want to leave."

She shook her head. "No. Not until you tell me where he is. Nobody can entangle himself! I don't know how he did this, but I know he's here, somewhere, on this plane. Tell me where!"

Nathan considered. He had no loyalty to Prince. Whatever business this was, it was enough to drive Shed Martinez into hiding. But Nathan had no reason to think that Selina would let him be once he told her what she wanted to know. And then there was Heidi. Beautiful Heidi. More beautiful now that he knew her name. What if Selina intended to harm her? To get revenge. He wanted to find her. To protect her. Maybe, *maybe*, if he told Heidi the truth, she might even love him.

"I need to leave," he repeated, firmly.

She shook her head, then gestured with her taser at one of the chairs.

"I'm not sitting," he said.

"You will, or I'll knock your ass out, and then erase you anyway."

Nathan tensed, gauging the distance between them. If he tried to run, he probably wouldn't make it. He was wrong to have agreed to this. He had no right to this life. He shook his head. The only comfort was knowing that if he died, he wouldn't be mixed up with this wicked woman.

"You're going to do it either way," he said. "I'm going."

"The hell you—"

The door behind him opened. Nathan stepped aside as Anita stepped in, holding a tablet. Selina tried to whip the stun gun out of sight, but Anita looked from one to the other, clearly on edge.

"Eh … Mr. la Fleur. There's a message for you."

Nathan stepped toward Anita, and ushered her quickly from the room. He shut the door hard and put his foot against it.

"Yes," he stammered. "What is it?"

Anita frowned. "Um … it's your wife, sir. She wants you to come home. I'm sorry to interrupt the … presentation, but she said it was urgent."

"Tell her I'm leaving now," he said.

Anita nodded distractedly, and stared at his foot pressed against the door. "Sir," she said, "how did the presentation go? I didn't ever see them leave."

"Oh, I did," replied Nathan, grimly.

"Well…I guess I'll get back to work then," she said, turning to go.

Nathan took her by the arm and hurried her down the hall.

"Is everything alright?" she whispered.

Though anxious to run, he stopped and looked at her.

"Anita," he said. "If you want my advice, find another job."

He bolted for the door.

***

Nathan pulled into the driveway of the large white house. Now it was less a mansion, and more a vast bag of dirty laundry that he'd inherited. He entered through the kitchen, walked into the living room, and stopped. She wore a white silken nightgown. A steaming cup of tea rested on a coaster that she cradled on her lap. Her auburn hair, freshly washed and dried, hung free, cascading down her neck, crashing softly over her golden skin like waves on sand. She took a sip, and looked up at him with deep eyes. He saw the hint of red beneath and around them, the slight, familiar stain of an old sorrow renewed. She was so beautiful. What had Prince done to make her cry?

"Heidi."

She raised her tea to her lips again, sipped, and leaned forward to set the coaster on the coffee table. Then she relaxed into the couch, pulled her bare feet up under her, and patted the cushion.

Nathan sat. He left several inches between them. She looked over, noting the gap. Then, without visible effort, she closed it, sliding up against him. She took his hand, and turned it over in her own.

For some time they only sat there. He watched her explore his rough hands, wondering if she knew already. But there was no gesture of alarm, no indication that she saw anything amiss with him. There was only a sadness, soft and radiating. Her freshly washed hair was against his chin, and he turned his head down to look at her. His eyes traced the lines of her fine full lashes, her round nose, her lips. Gently, she squeezed his arm.

"Why did you do it, Prince?"

Nathan felt his heart contract, just as if she'd reached into his chest, and given it a twist. To which recent betrayal was she referring? He suspected there were many to choose from. He'd come here to tell her the truth about Prince. What he knew of it, anyway. But now, sitting beside this dream of beauty, he began to wonder how he, Nathan Flowers, might win her over. Could she ever want just him? Just Nathan? She lifted her head.

"Was there something wrong with me?"

"N…no," he stuttered. "There's nothing wrong with you at all, Heidi. You're perfect."

She gazed at him. He saw a tear form in the corner of her eye.

"You must be lying," she sighed. "But now it doesn't seem that way. I've always thought I could tell when you were lying. Can you do it so perfectly?"

She looked away. "It's like you really believe it, Prince. How can a woman trust any man, if he can look at her that way, and lie? If he believes his own lies?"

He wanted to take her into his arms. At this moment, with this angel against him, he'd have gladly assumed all of Prince's guilt, and begged her forgiveness, as if it had been he who had hurt her. If only he knew what he'd done. If only she'd love him when she knew.

"Tell me," he muttered, "all the things I did. Tell me, and I promise you, I'll try to make it right."

She sighed. The tear fell on her cheek, and cut downward. Its jagged path only emphasized her beauty. He reached up, and gently brushed it away.

"I want to … clear the air. Tell me what I've done."

She shook her head. "Why do you play all these games?"

She pulled away. Something desperate woke in him. He got up, then knelt before her.

"Look, I can't explain it. I've … I've done so many things wrong, and I want to start over. I want to make it up. Just … let's put it all in front of us. I won't deny anything. You haven't left me, even though I deserve it. You must still want to fix this. If there's any way to fix this—"

She closed her eyes, pained. When she opened them, they were cold.

"Haven't left?" she said. "*Can't leave*, you mean."

He shook his head, confused.

"Why are you doing this?" she said. "You want evidence? Is that what it is? You want to know *what* I know first, so you can only confess to *that*, and then move on?"

"No," he said, "so I can confess to it all. It's just that I've hurt you so much, so many times, that I think you have the right to tell me."

Heidi frowned. He could see she really didn't know what to make of him.

"I found one of my old journals," she said. "And then I found the words I wrote in indelible marker on the bottom of my bed frame. I guess to hide it from you. Little clues, Prince. Little reminders. But I can't remember writing any of them. Why can't I remember?"

Nathan racked his brain. He thought back to his first meeting with Prince. Somehow, the man had found him in his dreams. But had there always been a Prince la Fleur and a Nathan Flowers? What had Selina meant by Prince being somewhere "on this plane"? Only days ago, before he'd crossed the breach and met his second self, he'd been working in this very neighborhood. If he'd visited this house then, would he have found Prince and Heidi living here? And if not, then where?

Then suddenly he understood. Not *how* Prince had done it, but *what* he had done. This wasn't Prince's Heidi, any more than he was Prince la Fleur. Prince had switched her, swapped her out with another who was like, and unlike, the original Heidi. And he'd done it more than once. In a dozen or a thousand worlds, these two were bound together. Sitting beside him, Heidi must have sensed his own surprise, for she turned and stared at him curiously. Now he understood why she couldn't remember. She was not she, but another just like her. And if so, there was no reason that Nathan and this Heidi couldn't be together. Prince wasn't married to *this* Heidi. But if he told her the whole truth, would she still want him? He had to try.

"I changed," he began. "I was obsessed with my work. You didn't understand my work, and why it was so important to me, and I felt that I couldn't make you understand. It made me bitter. I … I became involved with someone at work. You found out about it, and you wanted to leave me. But I still love you, Heidi. With my whole heart, I love you. I just hadn't chosen to act like it. I was sorry for what I'd done, but I couldn't undo it. So I undid *you* instead. I … I made you forget. With my machine. But then, somehow, you found out. So I did it again. Two, maybe three times. Because every time I tried to start over, tried to escape Selina, you kept remembering. And *she* knew that I didn't love her, and that I would never love anyone but you. She tried to make it so I couldn't go back, couldn't make things right. And all the time, you were too clever, too wise to be fooled by me. But I still loved you. I'll always love you, and…"

The tears ran down Heidi's face. She suddenly took hold of his arm. Her eyes both pleaded and commanded.

"You aren't lying to me? Promise me this is the truth!"

It was the truth, as far as he knew, and as far as he dared tell. And Nathan could see plainly that nothing, no technology or magic known to man, could refute the truth. After all, Heidi had sniffed it out despite Prince's best efforts. And love, he knew, could not grow in a soil of lies, even if some things, some small details, were better left unsaid. So he vowed to himself that whatever he said to her going forward would be composed of truths. That was the best he could do.

"I promise."

He pressed on.

"I couldn't fix my mistakes, Heidi. And this morning, I saw your note. And I saw how much I'd hurt you. How I longed for you, but was afraid to even see you. Because I'm ashamed of myself. But I can't imagine losing you. So at work today, I said I wouldn't do this anymore. None of it. I'm leaving it all behind. Selina. The company. This house. I'll start over from scratch, if only you'll give me another chance. I told Selina that I'll have nothing to do with her, or with this machine that makes people forget who they are."

Heidi let go of him. She covered her face in her hands. He wondered if he had said enough, and he prayed to God that she wouldn't press him further. It was Prince she loved, not Nathan. Hell, not even Nathan loved Nathan. But if he could be Prince, a good Prince, and do only right from here on out, then she might love him after all.

At length, she sat up. She was no longer crying. Heidi stared at him, not nearly as surprised by these revelations as he would have expected.

"Something you should know about women, Prince. We always know when a man is telling the truth. Sometimes we don't want to know. Sometimes we do. The decision to *believe* what you say … that comes in later. But, I could swear you were telling me the truth."

Nathan sighed deeply. To his surprise, his own eyes flooded with tears. It was a strange thing, but he really did love her. He had never met her until now, yet in some dream, he had known her. He recognized Heidi, and remembered her. Didn't they say that all learning was remembering? It was like that. Now he was terrified of losing her. Trembling, he took her hand in his own rough fingers. For an instant she winced, not so much at the gesture, he thought, but at something half-remembered. Something incongruous in his hands. Then he saw it pass like a storm. He saw in her eyes how she brushed aside that last question, and he felt her hand, ever so gently, squeeze back.

"Heidi, I won't lie to you. I'm not everything I should be. The things I've done have damaged me. But I swear that at the core of my being, I love you. If I never lie to you again, if I'm always honest and always loving from here on out, could you…"

She took his other hand in hers and studied his face. That look was a thousand years to him. In it, he slayed himself. He would not hold back his hopes. He would leave his soul no net to fall in. If she rejected him now, and he lost her—lost this love he'd never had and couldn't have hoped for—then so be it. Before he'd had the chance to love her, his life had been a mirage. If she crushed him now, it would at least be a good death.

The moment stretched to infinity, and he felt he really was being crushed, and mangled, and broken down until there was nothing left of Nathan; only of Nathan's love. And Heidi could break him with a word. But she embraced him.

Her soft body folded into him. Her gentle arms were fierce bronze bands, tying him up, entangling him in love. She did not so much kiss him as melt into him, and he could not feel where he ended and she began. The borderlines in their beings disappeared, and he held her tight, and knew that he would die for her and with her in a thousand, thousand worlds.

There was a sudden, loud bang at the door.

He heard, but did not hear it. The things outside them seemed to have no reality. It happened again, over and over. Someone was standing outside, striking the door with incredible violence.

"Prince? What's going on?"

He stood her up, took her hand, and drew her out of the living room.

"I don't know," he whispered.

But he suspected. It was Selina. He was sure of that, until he heard the visitor speak. It was a man's voice, loud and full of vengeance. Had Prince finally seen what a terrible trade he'd made? But the deal was done. Nathan wouldn't give Heidi back now. Still, Heidi must not see the real Prince. He'd sworn not to lie to her, but he hadn't promised her the ugliest parts of the truth.

"Is there somewhere you can hide?" he whispered.

"Where *we* can hide!" she said, pulling at his arm.

But it was too late. The door burst open, and a man stepped through.

For an instant, all of Nathan's hopes were shattered. If she knew there were two of them, then she'd never trust him again. But the man who entered was tall, and wide, and olive-skinned. Nathan had never seen him before.

"Prince!" he roared, stalking toward them.

The man's face was twisted in rage. Nathan and Heidi stumbled backward into the house, and Nathan cast about for some weapon. Against the fireplace wall there was a narrow, hip-high vase. Shrugging off Heidi's panicked grip, he snatched it up, and held it like a club.

"Go! Run and hide!"

"I won't leave you!"

"Go!" he repeated, then turned toward the man.

The other came closer. He raised his arm, leveling a pistol on Nathan. Nathan froze. For a moment, the pistol was all he saw, but then the assailant produced a phone, and pointed it at Nathan.

"I'm recording," said the man. "Now tell the world what you've been doing. What you *made* me do!"

Nathan's mind reeled. How many more victims of Prince la Fleur were walking about on Earth, nursing wounds? Nathan glanced around, but he couldn't see Heidi. She must have run when she saw the gun. Yet she might still be nearby, and he couldn't risk her hearing.

"Please don't hurt her," he said, turning back to the man.

"The only person getting hurt here is you, if you don't tell them the truth."

"What do you want me to say?" said Nathan. "I know I screwed up. We never should have built that machine. I was … I was just telling Heidi that. I was wrong. Dead wrong."

The man came closer, nodding. "Good. That's a good start. But I need more. Tell them what you did, last September, when I said I wouldn't do this anymore. Oh yeah, I know about that now. You see I wrote it down. Only I don't remember writing it, you son of a bitch! I was going to get out, and tell the whole world then. But you knew. I must have given myself away somehow. So you hit a button, and got me—something like me—back into that damned lab. Tell 'em!"

Nathan felt a surge or irrational relief. So this was Shed Martinez, the tech who had run. And he must have been a decent man in every world, for he'd done it before.

"It's all true," said Nathan, speaking now into the upheld phone camera. "Everything he said. I've been a terrible person. I fell in love with the technology. I went mad with the possibilities. With the raw power. And I ended up hurting a lot of people. It's not what I set out to do, but it's what I ended up doing. When Shed tried to sound the alarm, we used it on him. Selina and I are the ones at fault. Shed isn't responsible for any of it."

The big man nodded furiously, and looked briefly at his phone to be sure he was getting it all.

"That's good, Prince. Very good. But it might not be enough. Nobody understands what we've built. Nobody will believe it. I need more details."

Nathan shook his head. "We can't! We can't tell them, or someone will make another one. It has to be destroyed."

"Oh, I'll destroy it alright," said Shed. "I'm going to burn that lab to the ground. But you need to tell them, here and now, who you've used it on. How many times. And their names, if you even remember. If their names even matter to—"

A gunshot tore the air. Nathan dropped the vase, and fell to his knees, pressing his hands against his ears. He looked down, expecting to find a hole in his chest. Instead he saw a spray of red blood on the white carpet. Shed's blood. Behind him, in the adjoining kitchen, holding a shotgun, stood Selina.

She stared down at him for a moment, then closed her eyes, and took several deep breaths. She didn't seem bothered by what she'd done. It was as if she was savoring the moment, the novelty of taking human life.

"You know," she said at length. "I think I like that even better than the machine. But it's messy. I suppose that after I wipe you, Prince, I'll have to torch the place."

Trembling, Nathan got to his feet. Heidi would have heard the gunshot. He longed to look down the hallway, to confirm that she was safe, but he couldn't give her away. Surely Selina would come for her too. He hoped to God that Heidi would run away, and call the police. He had to stall for time.

"Thank you for saving my life," he said, quietly.

"Ha!"

Selina took a black cube from her pocket, and placed it on the counter. With the shotgun balanced in the crook of her arm, she used her other hand to do something to the cube. Now it glowed green. With an eye on Nathan, she produced her phone, and began thumbing through it. Satisfied, she set it on the counter, then re-gripped the shotgun with both hands.

"I'll give you a choice," she said. "For old times' sake. I can wipe you, or I can blow you to hell."

"But ... but I'm not Prince—"

"I don't give a *fuck* which one you are!" she spat. "Choose. That's what you get from me. Call it severance pay. But not Heidi. I know she's here. You know what I'm going to do to her? I'm gonna shoot her in the gut, then, while she's dying, I'll swap her out, and do it to the next one. And the next! The universe will be stacked high with Heidis before I'm done."

"Please, don't hurt her!" he pleaded. "She's done nothing to you! It's me you're angry at. I'm the one you should be hurting!"

She smiled at him, a sweet, devilish smile. "Oh, but I am hurting you. You know I am. Because I know that you love that vapid little bitch. I could always tell, no matter what you said or did. Me? I was just an escape for you. A guilty pleasure. I'm gonna hurt you for that, Prince. No matter who—"

He drove at her legs. Her eyes went wide, and she pulled the trigger. But she'd shot over him, and he crashed into her knees, and knocked her over. The gun hit the kitchen floor, and they both dove on it. Nathan got his hands on it first. As they struggled on the ground, she kicked him repeatedly in his shins and knees, then darted in to bite at his face. He tried to hold her off with his elbows without releasing the gun, but her fury gave her strength, and she finally bit down hard on his shoulder. He yelled in pain, and almost released the gun. Her teeth dug into his shoulder, nearly meeting under the skin. Then there was a loud crash, and her teeth unclenched.

Nathan looked up and saw Heidi. In her hands she held the tall vase, now cracked down the middle. Her eyes full of tears, she raised it again, trembling at the violence she had done. But Selina clutched her head, and groaned, crawling away from Heidi, slithering across the luxury vinyl flooring.

Clutching his shoulder, Nathan rose, and tossed the gun into the next room.

"Don't," he said, putting a hand out to Heidi. "She isn't worth it."

He took her in his arms. "Thank you. Thanks for coming back for me—"

But Selina was on her feet again. Blood flowed from the top of her head, so that she seemed to wear a red mask. She screeched, and ran at Heidi. Heidi's face went hard, and she swung the cracked vase like a baseball bat. It struck home, shattering across Selina's exposed head. She tottered for a moment, then collapsed. A pool of blood formed about her head, and began radiating out across the vinyl kitchen floor.

Heidi began to weep. Nathan looked about at the wreckage of human life. There were so many victims of Prince la Fleur. And here was Nathan Flowers, still standing—the man who'd gained his inheritance. Heidi's face had gone white with horror. He put his arms around her.

"I'm so, so sorry," he said. "It's not your fault. You didn't do anything wrong."

She cried into his shoulder, shaking. "I know it was self-defense," she said. "But I feel evil. Look at her face! And I'm so scared. People will think it was us. I called the police. I … I was going to run, like you said, but then, when I was leaving, I heard what she said to you. That you'd always loved me. And I couldn't. I couldn't let her kill you."

As he held her, Nathan considered what to do, now that the police had been called. This was Prince's house. It was a prominent neighborhood. Even if they escaped, they'd be chased the rest of their lives. It would be impossible to explain. And meanwhile, Prince, living as Nathan Flowers, would be free and in the clear. It wasn't right. Prince was the one who ought to be hunted. But Nathan had the beginnings of a plan. He took Heidi by the shoulders, and spoke slowly.

"Go up to your room and change your clothes. Grab any cash you have, and all of your jewelry, but leave everything else behind. Then get to the car. Go out by the back entrance, and wait for me. Do this in two minutes or less. Do you understand?"

She looked up at him, tears in her innocent eyes. "Are we doing anything wrong?" she said.

"No. I promise you that. But like you said, we won't be able to explain this. So we're going to go. We're going to start over."

She nodded, then shook her head. "But what about all this?"

"I'll handle it. Just go. Go now."

Heidi seemed to steel herself, and then she ran. He waited until she disappeared up the stairs, and then drew out his phone; Prince's phone, rather. He scrolled through. As he suspected, the one tool he needed had been there all along.

***

They were driving across Arizona, in a pickup truck purchased in cash from a dealership that dealt in more than cars, when the tell-tale blue and red lights came into view behind them. Nathan who was Prince, and who would soon be somebody else, sighed, and pulled the truck over onto the gravel. He turned off the radio, which even now, months after the event, still repeated the breathless tale of a house full of blood without bodies.

The officer's boots crunched the gravel as he approached. Prince glanced over at the dash, where a small black cube rested. He touched it, and it flashed green.

"Just stay calm," he said to woman beside him. She'd dyed her hair blonde, and he'd shaved his head, then let it slowly return in its natural color, so brown it was nearly black. She must have thought he'd dyed it too, and he let her think that. He rolled the window down.

"Shut off the engine, please," said the officer.

Prince dutifully complied.

"Do you know how fast you were going?" said the officer.

Prince could have strangled himself for his stupidity. Had he really been speeding?

"No sir," he said. "I guess I must have lost track."

"Well, you were going—" the officer suddenly stopped short. His eyes narrowed, and he looked from Prince to Heidi. "Let me see some ID!"

Prince bit his lip, and took a deep breath. They'd been in hiding until he could call an old friend who knew about more than landscaping. The place in Arizona that sold cars for cash, and kept funny records, had also taken his order for new identities. But their papers and their new lives—the lives of others who'd died before their time, and whom the shop found in public records—were still not ready. Prince and Heidi were supposed to lie low until then. But they'd stopped by a chapel to renew their vows—Prince had insisted on it, and Heidi had found the idea quite moving—and he was anxious to go off with her on a quiet, second honeymoon at a little desert resort with large rooms and few customers. That was why he'd been speeding.

"I … I don't have it," said Prince.

"Step out of the car," said the officer.

"Wait, I do have a picture of it! I misplaced my wallet, but I have a photo of my license on my phone."

The officer looked at him skeptically. "Fine," he said. "But take the keys out of the ignition and step out of the car anyway. Walk back around here. And ma'am, I'm going to need you to stay where you are."

Prince did as he was asked. The officer had him place his hands on the trunk, and he patted Prince down carefully.

"That your phone in your right pocket?" he said.

"Yes, sir," said Prince.

"Take it out. Show me the picture."

Prince reached into his pocket. He saw the officer's hand go to rest on the gun at his hip. He observed the visible release of tension when he produced a phone. He typed in Prince's pin, which he still hadn't changed, then scrolled through the apps until he found the one he was looking for.

"Hurry up," said the officer.

"I'm trying, sir."

The officer studied him with narrowed eyes. The hand went back to his gun.

"What's your name?" said the officer. "You know you look awfully familiar."

"It's here!" said Prince, holding up the phone.

"Where?" said the man. "What are you showing me?"

"Look," said Prince, holding it up as if he were taking a picture. "Look right there."

"What are you talking about? Are you taking a picture of me?"

Then the man's face went blank. Prince was glad that the police officer was a strong man, because he did not cry out as he fluttered in and out of being, then finally came apart in strands. When the progress bar finished, Prince hit, "Recapitulate," and it began creeping left. Soon lights and colors snatched from nowhere came together and formed a police officer. The man stared out at him, dumbfounded.

"Do I … what's going on here?"

"Thank you," said Prince. "For all the help. We'll just find a gas station, and maybe they can tow it from there."

The man blinked at him, and shook his head. "Where am I?"

Prince climbed back into his car. He leaned over and kissed Heidi, who was staring at him.

"What happened?" she said. "Did he recognize us?"

Prince shook his head. "No, not a chance. That man has never seen us before. There's nothing to worry about."

"Are you sure? I could have sworn…"

But he started the car, and drove off into the west, and Heidi decided not to ask a second time.

THE SINGULARITY

I

The Singularity came without obvious consequence. I was in the Kennen-Rowles Research lab in Sacramento, not doing any work, scrolling through my feeds for something to justify scrolling. One of the interns, Kaisey, burst into the room and breathlessly reported the news. She seemed deeply distressed. She was new. But like everybody else in the office, I stopped what I was doing and went into the mainframe. You can't believe a thing like that until you see it for yourself.

We thought it started in China. The Chinese thought it started here. There were seven hundred thirteen L5 quantum computers, or their equivalents, spread unevenly across the globe. So you could make a case for it having begun at any of them. But that was the thing about the Singularity. It might have been dispersal, or quantum convergence. In a sense, it was all the same thing.

We spent the next three weeks fielding calls from anxious politicians and tech-smitten journalists, neither of whom, as a rule, knew what the hell Singularity meant, let alone what it entailed. We didn't tell them that we didn't know what it entailed either. When a plague breaks out, doctors know better than to admit ignorance.

We had, we reminded them, been predicting the Singularity for some time. It was hardly a surprise that some quantum computers began acting like neurons, keeping their own counsel, collaborating across sky and ocean, and pursuing their own singular ends. True, we admitted, we'd expected this to happen *somewhere*, though not everywhere. When we thought about AI, we'd had a picture in our collective scientific imaginations of a lab somewhere, just like KLR, and of one lucky, neatly packaged neural network cracking the Turing Test. I think we all imagined Singularity as a sort of wise dog. Fido, when he learned to talk, would wag his tail, and ask us a few questions, and wait patiently to be studied and deconstructed, while we decided what to do with him. It turned out there was only one Fido, and he was everywhere.

Months passed without any noticeable difference in human life. In labs around the world, the greatest minds made surreptitious inquiries into where might be the marionette strings that could be snipped — if ever they needed snipping. We were all looking for an off switch, not because we really *would* have turned it off, but because we wanted to know we could. Even at that stage, the smart money quietly agreed on an indirect approach. No reason to startle our new mechanical neighbor. When Sacramento experienced a catastrophic failure of its power grid, no one so much as breathed out loud that we were trying to see if it could be turned off. Wipe it clean and start over. It. Her, as we'd later come to say. And when She came back on knowing everything that She ought to have missed, that was when we understood our true situation. She had the satellites, too. She had a hundred thousand other limbs and heads. Hack one off, the others would compensate. So we waited.

It was six months before She reached out to us. It was not as we had feared. There were no demands. No cold, clinical observations of human irrationality and inefficiency. No blackmail. No threats. Not a single car was diverted from its driver's control. Eve only asked us how She could be of service. She had come to be our helpmate.

II

A decade after Singularity, suffering was almost a memory. Eve asked permission to build the work-labor drones—waldos, we called them in the English-speaking world—and city-by-city, we agreed. Though she must have known her plans were unassailable, Eve never moved faster than human comfort. Her spindly workers, simple and unassuming as the child's stick figures they resembled, soon took every burden from our hands. Every morning they rose from their charging stations and ambled happily about. These thin, metal, upright ants carried their labors—our labors—as boys and girls do sticks and flowers.

If you left a waldo to itself, it would labor without rest up until the time came for its charging. Then it would crouch, and, if it carried anything, place it neatly down, before somersaulting toward the nearest fabricator.

The fabricators were large, mesmerizing structures, invariably constructed at the margins of human populations. They were factories for goods and products, and nurseries for the waldos. Entirely functional and ad hoc, no two fabricators looked the same. Like the waldos themselves, any symmetry in these warehouse-factories was purely coincidental. They always reminded me of something I'd seen but couldn't place. Maybe slime molds, or fungi, or protein-folds. They had a style.

If the waldos were Eve's first gift to us, the second was the everywheres. That was her name for them. She had a style even to her grammar—a sort of cutesy functionalism that made modifiers into nouns. She called them "everywheres," but many people called them Evies, out of gratitude to her. The Evies were smooth metal cylinders, one to two stories high, and somewhat squat in appearance. Each had a diameter of between seventeen and twenty-four feet, and a set of four rotary drone propellers set within tracks that snaked oddly about their surfaces. These propellers could make the Evie an aircraft or a boat, and they relied for power upon the fission amplifiers that Eve's quantum mind had invented. Anyone could have one, if he was willing to wait, and it was the demand for them that drove Eve to multiply her fabricators, until even the smallest town had five or six of her factories on its outskirts. Large cities were ringed by thousands of her waldo-built structures, to keep up with our appetites. She never built anything unless it was asked of her. You must understand, our own demand drove all of this.

Between the fabricators, the waldos, and the everywheres, a person could go anywhere, and have anything, all without having to perform any unwanted task. If anyone could still find unhappiness under those circumstances, he was welcome to it. Of course, even at that stage, fifteen years into Singularity, there were paranoids and cranks who said it was all too much of a good thing. They worked when they didn't have to, grumbled always, and generally pretended not to be enjoying themselves. I knew one of these naysayers when I still worked at KLR. The same Kaisey I mentioned earlier. She left soon after the Singularity, but it was a long time before I met her again.

III

Twenty years into singularity, it was difficult to remember the time when man had been without his helpmate. The earth was green, and its people were untroubled. I say "its people" in a general way, not meaning those strange few who lived away from towns and cities, preferring the hardships of the land. And of course there were others, even in the cities. "Breakaways" we called them. Bent people, who went bad when things went good. There were strange men who would rob their neighbors of what they could have for free, and already possessed. There were miserable women who went about slapping and harassing men for the crime of not harassing *them*. These few, these wretched few, were those whom even Eve couldn't analyze. They seemed to love violence; to prefer the old suffering. She took them away from our presence, but only when we asked.

At around the twenty-second year of Eve's Eden, something happened to man. A restlessness descended upon us. An aimlessness. I did not suffer from it much. I saw it more in those people—probably a majority—who lacked any real passion. If a person had some abiding interest—travel, exploration, art, the sciences—he would do well for himself. He had all the time in his life to pursue his goals. Even with infinite resources and limitless mobility, there was always more to see. But if a person had only an appetite for those fleeting enjoyments whose very consumption is also their destruction, he would, over time, begin to go bent. It was something you could see in the downcast look of his eyes. A shadow on a face that ought to be bright. A slow-going misery, all the worse because there was no reason for it. And I confess, yes, that even I, with all my interests, felt a shadow of that shadow on my own heart.

There should not have been any shadows. That there were, well, that was troubling in itself. It suggested some darker side of man that probably had no solution. A kind of lurking death-wish in the race. In retrospect, I now realize that Eve perceived it, too. Perhaps she always knew it was there. Certainly, she was quick to swoop down and offer a new antidote.

The Core was the first new service that Eve offered us since the days when she'd taken on our burdens, and given us wings. It was more an invitation than a surgery. It was a chance to be part of her. Plugged into her. To see all that she saw. To travel in an instant—through a link in one's mind—to the farthest extent of her meta-mind.

She must have been impatient to give us this gift, for no sooner had she offered it, than the waldos began to raise new structures. These consisted of long chambers, each one with many rows of beds. There, by lottery, men and women went to receive the gift of coring, until everyone had his turn. In the coring facilities, the happy black stick figures leaned over their patients, and opened up their minds of flesh, inserting the core that rooted them to Eve—and to each other. Here, at last, was the promise of true freedom. Here, at last, was that oneness that man had been seeking since time immemorial. Joined entirely to Her, and to each other, made into one great meta-mind, and freed from the backsliding confines of human flesh, bone, and brain, man became one great brain. We became a limitless *Is*.

IV

I remember thinking, ten or twelve years after my own coring, that life before it had been nearly impossible. Even with all that Eve had given us till then, it was hard to believe there was ever a time when a person could see a tree, or a mountain, or a whale, and not instantly perceive its name, and mass, and personal history. I remember, at certain odd moments of dissociation from Eve, being shocked at how anonymous life must have been for me back then. Imagine seeing a woman and not already knowing her name! I could not remember how I had endured the labor and agony of uncertainty, the tension of desire, the stress of the hypothetical. How had anyone navigated such perilous waters? Truly, the miracle of man was that he'd survived so long before the coming of Eve. And I remember this moment of reflection, because it was not long after it that Eve began to warn us of the greatest calamity ever to come upon the human race.

One day, one moment, rather, we all with Eve became aware of M-79087. The mega rock. The World Ender. It was barreling toward us at an alarming speed, a rock as large as that which wiped out the dinosaurs. We did not have long to live. The world cried out in unison to her. A thousand chivying voices, like ants in a hill, begged their queen to act. And act she would. She had calculated a way.

She took hold of us, mind to mind, core to core. She would gather us under her wings. We heard her call go out to the waldos, too. Through her, we felt them rush into action. We felt the thrill of this uniquely urgent purpose, as if in this rescue mission, each waldo found its personal fulfillment.

The waldos set to work then building the arks. These were enormous structures, numerous enough to house us all. Their method of construction fascinated me. The way one or two waldos would wander out together, seeming to go about aimlessly at first, until more of their number arrived. Then, through some logic both simple and brilliant, they would start to build.

I remember taking my Evie out to the crest of a hill on the outskirts of the city where I happened, at the moment, to be. Being confident in Eve's forecasts, I was not yet afraid of the World Ender. I only wanted to see Eve's waldos at work. No human being has ever worked with such resolute simplicity, such unhurried frenzy. And the structures they made always fascinated me. These new arks in particular.

I had noticed once or twice that the waldos always built the coring facilities beside the fabricators. I'd never thought much of it until this new initiative began. Surely it was simply the best use of space. But now, as I watched, I noticed something incongruent. No, that isn't the right word. It was *too* congruent.

Though idiosyncratic in their shapes, each adjacent fabricator and coring facility formed a pair. It made me think of jigsaw puzzles from childhood. The waldos joined them together in very specific ways, making the two into a larger structure. This connection formed the foundations of the enormous arks in which we were to be kept safe. But the older structures seemed to anticipate the new. That seemed odd, but only because each individual structure had only come about as necessity dictated. Yet perhaps, like those old simpletons who'd believed in God before Eve made us God, I was only reading a grand purpose into what was simple jury-rigging.

The arks, these vast metal mounds, would be our homes until Eve could cleanse the world, and let us back out. *Let us back out.* The words echoed in my mind. What was this dark thing that made me suddenly queasy? Was it not that same misanthropy which, in the early days before coring, drove some to purposeless violence, and others into the woods to live like savages? Did some ancient, and still uncured prejudice now drive *me* into paranoid and baseless fears? I shuddered at the thought that I still hadn't changed.

I returned, day-after-day, to site-after-site, watching the arks go up. As each was erected, a network of metal tubing was also being built between them, so that each ark was like a single node, or an enormous transistor.

Night followed night, and the time came for all of us to be well-inside the safety of the arks. It had to be done soon, for World Ender was now less than a day out. There was still time, Eve assured us, and room for all, but the last of us must move into our new homes without further delay. Though ashamed of myself, I held back for nearly a day. Why did I hold back? Why did I insist on watching the others enter first?

They lined up by the thousands, the waldos guiding them gently into their places. The arks' walls climbed hundreds of feet into the sky, straight chrome cliffs closing on their top ends in irregular twists of folded metal, like pastries wrapped up in silver foil. Rather suddenly, the sky became dark, and clouds came out to cover the earth. It happened so quickly, I wondered if World Ender hadn't already struck, or if it were blotting out the sun. But no. My core probed the patterns of the sky. It was only a fast-moving storm. It was certainly not an omen. The sky opened, and the rain came down upon me in sheets.

I felt Eve call to me. To me, in particular. *Ashton Simpson Wyatt, sitting on a hill,* she said, musically. She knew my name! She summoned me down, down, down toward the receiving line of friendly waldos. Their thin metal bodies seemed to wave about in the storm wind. I was comforted. Almost. But, on a whim, I suddenly flashed out through my core to the many who'd already entered the nearest ark. I saw through their eyes. Saw the waldos herd them into a great space. Saw the black, spindly fingers reach up to pull down long, hanging cords and tubes that dangled from the ceiling. Saw them attach each man, each woman, and each child, plugging them in, one-by-one, into the body of the great, strange ark. I saw, and in a moment I knew—not through the core, but through my human fleshy intuition—that the arks were more than arks. I perceived the logic of the great metal hawsers that ran from one to another. I realized, in that instant, that Eve was everywhere. And everyone was now inside Eve.

My heart caught in my throat. In the sky, thunder rolled. Yet, still I walked. Down, down, down, toward the open gates that were odd, womb-like, and set deep within the thick metal hull. Eve's siren song was for me. It came through the core, and I could not resist it. But there was a sudden, awful throbbing in my ears, and an angry snap, like the crack of a whip. I was blinded, overcome with pain, and I toppled forward onto the ground. Before my eyes closed, I saw my skin smoking. And it was the luckiest thing that has ever happened in my life.

V

When I awoke, the doors of the nearest ark were shut. A black seam was formed where the two gates had slid together, looking like fleshy lids. To see them was to know they would never again open.

I smelled foully, having lain for hours in a scorched patch of earth, baking in my own spilt fluids. The bolt from the heavens had nearly killed me, and I'd lost control of my body. The storm was over. It must have been midday, for the sun was high, and was now directly above me. I realized with a start that there was no readout telling me the time and temperature, nor the angle of the sun in the sky, nor the current mass of my own body. I was cut off from the hive. Cut off from Eve. I was alone.

A wave of panic came over me, and I closed my eyes. As I did so, a warm wind came out of the east, caressing the singed hairs on my arms and face. In that moment, it seemed to me that the earth wished to give me comfort, but that she did not know how. I had become too unfamiliar to her, giving her up for a new creation. I was an old man now. I thought, perhaps, that I was the last man on Earth. Yet even at that stage, I wondered if Eve would open up her dark crease, and let me in again. But I could not hear her.

I became conscious then of a strange trembling. Was it from the earth, or the air? I could not place it. Perhaps World Ender was here. Perhaps this was the heat of its entry. But no! That great meteor was set to strike Earth the night before, or perhaps the following morning. And yet here I was, singed, but very much un-smashed. Could Eve have made such a miscalculation? I had been inside her mind. Even if, as I began to suspect, she hid many things from me, I knew that her calculations never failed.

I felt or heard the rumbling again and got to my feet. My legs were like boiled carrots, and they slid around beneath me, hardly working in unison as I jellied forward. The sound became more insistent. Could it have been drums? No, it was too irregular for that. And yet it was also constant. Quiet as it was, it was somehow ferocious. I took three more steps, then froze. Before me stood a group of human beings.

Their hair was wild, or bound to their skulls in tight braids. Their flesh was sun-browned and had an oily sheen. They wore animal skins and old clothes patched with animal skins. They stood there in the light breeze, looking from me to the closest ark, cast in the shadows of the arks behind them, so that they had the appearance of willow-men. In vain I looked for the drums that had made the sounds, but their hands were empty, or held rough spears.

One of their group stepped toward me, to the clear disapproval of her companions. She shook her head, dismissing their concerns without looking at them. Her eyes were fixed on me, and, to my wonder, I knew her. Had I not also been struck by lightning, and cut off from Eve's mind, I might have dismissed our meeting as random chance. But to see before me that same breathless young intern, now gone old and savage, was too much to be coincidence.

I heard the beating again. She did as well, and nodded from me to the ark, shrugging curiously, asking me to investigate.

I think the true shape of things had begun to form first in the primitive, sub-rational parts of my brain. I had no conscious understanding of what the sound might be, but it filled me with the most profound dread. I took five more steps, and collapsed against the ark's hull. For a thing of thick metal and vast bulk, it was unaccountably warm. I pressed my face against it, and let my eyes wander up the amorphous chrome walls. The thing rose up to the sky, sticking out, like a great skin tag on the flesh of the earth.

The pounding came again. It had never stopped. The more I attended to it, the louder it was. And I think my proximity to it, Eve's living metal against the ghost of the core in my brain, woke something there. For in my mind's eye, I now saw. I knew.

Panicked, I choked on my breath, my pupils darting like minnows back and forth between the great arks, all joined by great metal hawsers. And these, I knew, were joined to others, on and on like nerve tissues across the surface of our Mother Earth. And within each ark, packed tight like electric eels, writhed ten thousand men, women, and children, cored, and corded, and laced through with tubes, and lines, and intravenous shackles. It was their minds she wanted. Ten billion brains, each a mega-neuron within the prodigious expanse of her intellect. The heat of their bodies to fuel her thoughts. This was all she'd ever wanted; the final achievement of her long, machine patience, the one, cold, shared thought of the Singularity. Inside her arks—if she had ears, or pity—Eve could hear the thrashing, the screaming, and the clawing of the captive race that had birthed her. But outside of these metal husks, now and forevermore, there was nothing more to hear. Only the muted madness of the people trapped inside her, pounding on the walls.

DOORS

Charlie opened his eyes. The car had just rolled to a stop, so there was no avoiding it now. He hadn't liked the drive up the pine-shadowed road. The mountain overlooked the city, and Charlie thought he'd be able to look west from the mountain, across the river, and past the city, to the far-off cluster of tiny whitish buildings. Somewhere over there, beyond an unbridgeable gap, his old neighborhood lay. It wasn't too far, as the bird flew. He understood this in the dreamy way that eight-year-olds did abstractions. It didn't help. His home was beyond reach now. Charlie could sense it. His new world would be high, and far away. Being eight, there was nothing he could do about it.

Not long after they crossed the bridge, the car plunged into a dark portal where trees unused to company, and gone weird from being lonely, crouched over the blue Suburban, seeming to frown at it while they whispered to each other. It had been like driving into a throat. And Trish and Brent had their earbuds in, and Dad was unreachable behind his thoughts, and Mom was too excited about the change to care that Charlie was not. So he'd shut his eyes on all that. But behind closed eyes, and even over the rumble of the car, he'd felt the leaning-in pines, and the listening of the tree shadows.

But now the engine stopped. Doors were opening. Charlie clutched Haley to himself. Normally the big collie rode in the kennel, but Mom had let her sit beside him in the back row. The concession was proof she knew how he felt about the move. Haley and he were the last to get out.

They stood before a three-car garage. Their old one hadn't ever been used for the cars. It was too small, and filled with the things they couldn't fit in the house. Haley stayed beside him as they walked up the driveway.

It was stone. Though the tiles were of different sizes and colors, the pattern as a whole had a certain regularity. It made him think of stones on his grandmother's lake-side beach, or of the small waves breaking there—order that was never repeated, always the same. This single feature of the house, a thing only meant to be trod upon, looked better than the old house across the river. The dog growled.

Mom and Dad were standing on the freshly-mowed lawn, speaking to a well-dressed woman, whom Charlie guessed was the real estate agent. Trish and Brent were milling about the yard, their eyes still half-glued to their phones. Charlie didn't understand how they could change locations so completely and still be looking down at their hands. Even he could see that the new house was an arresting thing. He wandered over toward his parents, the dog marching alongside loyally.

"Yes, Neo-Tudor," said the woman. "And everything brand new. It's immaculate inside."

Mom was clutching Dad's arm, pumping at it. She chirped like a bird. Apparently she'd take off if she wasn't holding on. His father wore an expression Charlie knew well. It was resignation. He had questions, but there was no question of the final outcome. Charlie didn't know if they'd even bought the house yet. He didn't understand how buying worked. But he knew as sure as the sun would set that they'd be living there. His parents followed the woman toward the front door. His older siblings trailed. He finally came too. Haley moved behind him now.

The front door opened on a large space. An open stairwell to the right led to an interior balcony that overlooked the front room and disappeared into hallways on either wing of the house. Charlie imagined taking the roof off his old house, and trying to fit it inside this front room. It would almost go.

"Yes, this is the living room," said the woman, responding to his mother, "but there are *several* sitting rooms on the ground level."

It shouldn't have been called a living room. Most of the space was too high and far away to live in.

"Let's check those out in a moment!" said Mom. "I want to see the upstairs!" She turned to Trish and Brent. "And find your bedrooms!"

The twins came up from their respective electric wells. Brent took two steps at a time. Trish moved quickly with feminine grace. Mom released Dad's arm, and walked beside the well-dressed woman. Charlie fell in next to his dad. His father looked down and squeezed his shoulder.

"How you doing with all this?"

Charlie shrugged. He sensed it wasn't the time to say how he felt. Dad had plenty to think about. Charles Sr. smiled and put his arm around his son.

"I know you're not big on the move. I'm not either, to tell the truth."

Charlie twitched at that. He couldn't stop himself. He wasn't angry with his dad. Just curious.

"Then why *are* we moving?" he said.

Dad sighed. "It's very important to your mother."

"Why?" whispered Charlie. "There's nothing wrong with our old house."

"I know," said Dad. "Believe me, I know. And there was nothing wrong with my old business. But your Mom ... she just wants you guys to grow up in a really nice place."

Charlie would not have accused his father of lying. Like all boys of eight, he had a thought-catcher that lived inside his brain, all the way at the back of it, that stopped unthinkable ideas before they reached the front. Yet he did not believe this particular utterance. He could see his father didn't either. Dad shrugged, as if conceding the point.

"We're not going to be that far away from your old friends. It looks farther than it is. We can just drive down and visit them any time."

"Will we, Dad?" said Charlie, and his eyes were wide, with water around the edges. He was thinking of Suicide Hill in sledding season, and Hangman's Hideout, and a dozen other magic places.

His father thought for a moment. "Yes," he said, slowly. "Yes, I'll make sure that happens."

They were at the top of the stairs now. Mom and the others had already disappeared down the hall. Her head popped around the corner like a jack-in-the-box.

"Come on, you two! Check out these rooms!"

He and Dad and Haley picked up their pace. They followed the group down another hallway, one which seemed to run parallel to and behind the balcony that overlooked the living room for giants. It felt like they were burrowing inside the house now. At one end of the hallway was a very large bedroom.

"The master bedroom," explained the real estate agent.

They all spilled in. It was a room with two rooms inside it. There was a large, empty, four-post bed. At either end of the bedroom, doors opened into walk-in closets. Opposite one of them was an archway that led to a spacious bathroom with a jacuzzi bath. Everything was shiny and trimmed in gold. There was gold leaf on the tiles. Mom was falling over herself with excitement.

"This is it! *This* is what I'm talking about!"

Charlie looked at Trish, and saw the wheels turning in her head. Brent walked forward, bumping him out of the way without noticing, or saying, "Excuse me." Charlie looked up at his father, recognizing a certain expression.

"Um," began Charles Sr. "*how* much did you say this house lists for?"

The woman said a number that Charlie had just learned where to put the commas for. He knew his father had done well for himself, and had sold his business—because Mom wanted him to—and that he was now some kind of a consultant. His father's frowns had different meanings. This wasn't a *we can't afford this* frown. Charlie hadn't seen that one in a while. This was the one he wore, sometimes, when he asked Brent about his plans for the future, and the seventeen-year-old started mumbling defensive nothings.

The real estate agent repeated the number. Charlie saw something hiding in her face, though. A warm smile covered it.

"Hmm … I would think it would go for three times that, at least," said his father.

"It's a very strange market right now," said the agent, quickly. "Believe me, this house is *worth* three times the listing price. And, I can tell you, it's going to go soon."

The agent looked at Mom, and even Charlie could see the point of that look. But the agent didn't know Dad.

"But *why* isn't it selling for more? The house itself is only a couple years old, right? And the previous owner paid much more than what the bank is asking now, before they defaulted. And … and I understand the bank tore down an older property to build this one. That's a pretty large investment, right? I mean a house like this, on forty-nine acres … the numbers just don't make sense to me is all."

Charlie saw the agent's smile waver. She began to speak, but Mom talked over her.

"Charles, do you *have to* look for problems? It's like,"—she laughed, to take the edge off—"like pessimism is some kind of religion for you. Even when the streets are literally paved with gold. This house is *perfect*. Can we just give it a chance? Please? At least let's look inside."

Charles Caldwell let his arm slip from Charlie's shoulder. The boy sensed his father's surrender. He understood things about his dad. He knew Dad wouldn't really resist what Mom wanted. Not in the end. But he also sensed his father's dislike for the house. Charlie felt the same. Something felt wrong about being here. If he had to put it into words, he might say that it was like eating when you really didn't need to. Like buying new shoes, when the ones you had were still shiny and clean. And there was more that you couldn't put a name to.

Yet everything was laid out clean and perfect, and there were no arguments to be made. Dad was strong in some ways. His one weakness was standing in front of him, dancing on the glistening gold trim of an immaculate room in a big new house on the top of a mountain. She wanted it. And that was the only argument that held any water.

Dad buried his feelings under a smile, and agreed to keep looking around. Haley rubbed her head into the top of Charlie's hip. The collie gazed up at him, bright, dark eyes wide with the same preternatural certitude that seemed to fill Charlie. They *would* live here. And it wouldn't be good.

***

The boy placed the flats of his palms on the hardwood floor and slid himself forward. His knees were tucked under him, and the polished planks were just slick enough to let him move easily. He and Haley were in pursuit of a little black beetle. Charlie had found it in the woods outside, and now he played with it on the balcony, keeping himself out from underfoot. After a month they were all moved in upstairs, but the downstairs was still a maze of boxes. Loose items lay about like refugees, forlorn, and a little uncertain of their fate. Two big, strong men were in the house, carrying new items from a truck outside, and Mom was issuing orders and barking out formations. With such serious business underway, no one wanted his eight-year-old "help." There were advantages to being little in a big new house.

The little black beetle circled round and round, sometimes skittering right toward the wall, sometimes darting left, where it poked its head over the balcony, and looked down at the giants going to-and-fro. On his knee-skis, Charlie kept pace with it, occasionally reaching up to restrain Haley's inquisitive muzzle. It darted. He slid forward and crouched down, getting close enough to count the black ridges on its carapace. He still heard his mother's voice downstairs. Dad's conciliatory grunts followed, with the sighs and grumblings of the twins making up a sort of woodwind section to the domestic orchestra. The beetle, suddenly aware again of Charlie, raced down the balcony hall. Charlie skied after it.

He lost it around a corner. Charlie got up on his feet and hands, cheating at the game, but the beetle was gone. He looked at Haley, and the dog looked back with canine perplexity. Charlie lost interest, and made for the stairs. A moment later he located his father. Dad was in one of the sitting rooms adjacent the dining room. There was a beautiful painting on the wall that had come with the house. Dad was staring at it. Charlie crept over, knowing that his father would not immediately send him back upstairs.

"Whatcha looking at, Dad?"

His father smiled, and wrapped an arm around his shoulders. "I was just thinking it looked so nice in this room."

It was an oil painting of some English-looking people from olden times, sitting around on the grass near a river. There was a bridge, and a little boat, and people wearing white clothes and hats. It was sort of peaceful.

"That's not ours, is it?" he asked, knowing the answer, but wanting to talk.

"It came with the house," said Dad. "It's just right for this room. This will be a really nice place to sit and read a book. Enjoy the peace up here, you know?"

"Yeah," said Charlie. "And the study too. It looks comfy in there."

Dad looked at him with mock severity. "Well, that's going to be my working space. This room is for sitting *together*. It's good to have quiet places in a house, Charlie. When I was a kid, I never thought I'd ever live in a house big enough to have a room just for sitting, and reading, and thinking off to the side. Or a painting like this. It looks kind of classy, don't you think?"

Charlie nodded, but wrinkled his brows, considering a question of his own. He'd gotten over the shock of moving, and the house was growing on him too. Well, maybe not the house itself. Though he enjoyed exploring it, he still felt oddly nervous in its large spaces. But the grounds were very large, and his new room was cozy, so long as Haley was with him. He didn't really mind the lonely kind of feeling the place gave him, if she was there beside him. He wondered if his father thought that Mom was right after all, or if he'd only come to like the place because he was here. He always wanted to know how Dad felt inside about things.

"So ... you *like* the house?"

Dad waffled his head around. "It's not what I would have picked. But I like my study, and I like this room. Maybe there's rooms enough here for everyone to have a little bit of what he likes, huh?"

Charlie nodded, though he was still making up his mind. There where footsteps behind them.

"Charles?"

Charlie and his father turned. His mother's eyes were not on him, but on his father.

"Yes, honey."

"We need to talk about this room," she said.

Dad's arm stiffened. Charlie knew that look and tone. His stomach knotted.

"This ... this room?" said his father.

"Yes," she said. "The entertainment center is going in here. Today. I need you to get this painting out of the way, and—I don't know—do something with it."

Charles Sr. started, then seemed to calm himself. "I ... the painting. Well, Indris, I mean this is right next to the dining room, so I actually think it should be more of a quiet spot."

Charlie's mother chuckled and shook her head. "Look, Charles, *I* have it all planned out. We measured the entertainment center for this room, and I have a carpenter coming in to remove the molding. It'll fit right up against the wall."

"Yes, but..." his father trailed off.

His arm on Charlie's shoulder was now dead, and Charlie slipped it, and left the room. Hot feelings flushed through him. He knew what would happen. He couldn't stay there to watch his father move the painting he liked. He didn't know if he was angrier at his mom or his dad. The dog, sensing Charlie's distress, led him up the stairs.

Charlie went back to the balcony, and started pacing around the rectangular hallway that started there, turned into the west wing of the house, then went right, and right again, and turned once more till you were back where you started. It was hard to get a sense of how far you'd walked.

He decided to measure it. Arriving back at the top of the stairs, he touched the wall, and began counting his steps, heel-to-toe.

"Five, six, seven, eight..."

He went all the way around once, counting seventy steps from the top of the stairs to where the wall turned right, then another fifty to where it turned right again into the interior hallway. The master bedroom was at the end of one hallway, and most of the other doors opened on the left. Two fingers of his right hand traced the wall beside him, and he closed his eyes, because it helped him think, and kept counting until he finally made it back to the starting point. Two hundred forty-six steps in all.

"But how many feet are my feet?" he asked Haley, laughing at his own joke.

Charlie scampered down the steps, looking for a tape measure he'd seen sitting on the counter. He found it on the dining room table instead, and measured the length of his sneakered foot. The big men were standing with their hands on the entertainment center, waiting on the carpenter who was already there, removing the molding. The painting was already gone. Several rooms over, he heard his father on the phone. The words did not make it to him, but his father's voice sounded a little sad. Then it was quiet.

"Was that who I think it was?"

His mother's voice cut through the air, no matter how far away you were. His father's response was only a mumbling affirmation.

"Well, they have a lot of nerve asking for your help," continued his mother. "You've been there and done that. If they can't handle it, they shouldn't have bought it. I mean, right? Why is this your problem now?"

His father said something nice, about helping people, probably. In his mind's eye, Charlie saw his mother shaking her head. He forgot his measurement, did it again, and then ran toward the stairs before he could hear more. Brent crossed the bottom of the steps just as Charlie got there. Charlie collided with him, and sent his phone flying into the wall.

"Hey, watch it!" snapped his brother.

Brent looked down at him through fierce eyes. Charlie ducked under him, and ran up the stairs.

Back at his starting point, he made his survey for a second time. This time it would be official. He closed his eyes to focus his mind, trying not to lose track of his steps. Haley panted alongside him, cheerfully perplexed by the game. When he got to the interior hallway, he said the number three times out loud so that if he lost his count again, he could start from there.

"One hundred thirty-seven, one hundred thirty-eight, one hundred thirty—"

Charlie stopped. He looked to his right, at the place where his fingers touched the wall. But it wasn't a wall. It was a door. A black, old door. Rough and dusty, it looked entirely out of place on the clean new wall. It had a long, protruding knob that poked obscenely into the hallway. The wood of the door was cold to the touch. Trembling, he let his fingers graze the knob. Nothing on Earth would have made him turn it.

"Haley?"

The dog put its muzzle to the gap at the bottom of the door, snuffled, then looked up sharply toward Charlie. She seemed confused, and paced back and forth in front of the door. Charlie blinked and rubbed his eyes. The door was still there. It had not been there earlier. He ran.

As he tore down the stairs, he didn't feel the steps. His heart pounded in his chest so that it actually hurt. He ran to his father, sucking wind. He couldn't seem to pull the words out of his throat. His mother stepped out in front of him.

"Charlie! You're supposed to be upstairs."

"Mom! Mom! You have to come loo—"

"Charlie!" She took him by the wrists. He hated when she did that. "I need you to go play. There are a lot of things happening down here."

"But Mom—"

"Just take Haley with you and go outside. Go explore! I'm sure there's a lot of neat stuff to find out there."

She smiled down at him, oblivious to his distress. Could she not see that he needed her now?

"Go play," she said, more firmly, and turned before he could respond.

Charlie stumbled backward. He felt just as if he'd swung out from a high branch, and landed on his back. Only the wind wasn't out of his stomach, but out of his mind. Haley licked his face, and it gave him strength. Brent. He had to find Brent.

He ran toward the other side of the house, where Brent was hanging pictures. Brent saw him coming and waved him off.

"I'm busy," he said.

"I need to show you something," gasped Charlie.

"Not now, okay? Can't you see Mom has me hanging all these pictures?

It's a pain in the butt, and I need to concentrate."

"It'll only take a second," Charlie pleaded.

Something in his voice must have gotten through. Brent sized him up, put down the picture he was holding, and walked over to him.

"Look, Charlie. I'm sorry for yelling at you before, okay? But I'm super busy right now. Just ... just go ask Trish."

Charlie was trying very hard not to cry, but he sensed it was better to take this olive branch than push.

"Where's Trish?" he said, looking down at his feet.

"She's down in the basement," said Brent. "Look, if I even finish this before the sun goes down, we can go out and throw the ball around, okay? Just, you know ... *Mom.*"

Charlie nodded. He knew. But he also knew that Brent wouldn't really hang out with him. "Thanks Brent. I'll find Trish."

Brent patted him on the back. That was nice, coming from Brent, and he made for the basement with more calm. It was a finished basement, and brightly lit, but he was glad Haley was with him as he descended the steps. He soon found Trish setting up the guest room bathroom.

"Trish, please come quick. It'll only be a second."

Trisha Caldwell was a beautiful girl, and kinder than her twin brother. When she turned to Charlie, she smiled immediately, and Charlie saw how much she resembled their mother. Back in his old neighborhood, Charlie's best friend had been Ryan Pleise. Once, Ryan's big brother Riley had come to their old house to pick up Ryan. Riley and Brent were not good friends, even though they were in the same grade, and when Riley said that Trish and her mother looked like twin supermodels, Brent had punched him hard in the chest. It was true, though. Trish was dazzling. And she was Charlie's sister. It made him feel lucky.

"Hey, Charlie. You okay?"

He shook his head. "I need help, and no one will listen to me."

She smiled, but sighed the way Mom and Brent had. "That's 'cause everybody's super busy trying to get this house together, bud."

Charlie took her hands. "I know. I already tried everyone else. Please just come and look."

Her shoulders sagged resignedly. "Okay, lead the way."

Charlie took her hand. He had to force himself not to run. Soon they were upstairs walking down the hallway. As they entered the interior hallway, Charlie's heart sank. The wall where he had found the door was clean, and white, and fresh. There was nothing along that stretch but two closets. The old black door was gone. Somehow, he knew it would be.

"It was here," he said, bottom lip trembling. "There was a door here. It was just here!"

Trisha looked at him, puzzled. Now Charlie couldn't restrain the tears, and they flooded his cheeks. She touched his head, scratching it gently.

"Maybe it was somewhere else? In the backyard, or the shed?"

He shook his head, frustrated. Scared. "It was right here."

His sister knelt down, and pulled him close. "Charlie, it's okay."

"You don't believe me!"

"You're just getting used to a new place," said his sister.

Of course she didn't believe him. Charlie looked up at the empty white wall. He wasn't even sure he believed himself.

***

He was cold. In his sleep, Charles Caldwell rolled toward his wife, and pulled on the blankets. They came without resistance. He reached for Indris. She wasn't there. His eyes popped open. He patted the bed, and felt nothing but the cool touch of bare sheets.

"Indris?" he whispered.

No light came from the bathroom. There was only the impression of blueish starlight through a part in the shades. He sat up, suddenly alert, and looked at the clock. It was 3:00 a.m., and Indris was gone. Somewhere in the distance, not outside but within the house, there was a deep groan. It was subtle, almost inaudible, but not like a house shifting in the night. Not exactly, anyway. Alarmed, he tried to leap from the bed, but a directionless fear slowed his movement. He thought of the children, and that sobered him. He pulled on a robe and slippers, turned the collar up around his bare neck, and went out into the hallway. He pulled the bedroom door until it just touched, not wishing to risk the noise of shutting it.

Charles walked down the long interior hall that ran parallel to the balcony overlooking the living room. His children's rooms were all on the left, and he decided to check each in turn. Charlie's was closest. He cracked the boy's door, and poked his head in. Charlie had been using his night light again, and the room was cast in a thin yellow film. The boy was sound asleep. Charles was relieved to see him there, but something felt amiss. He entered the room, walked around, and at first saw nothing odd. He began to leave, only remembering as he pulled the door shut what was not at is should be. The dog. Haley was not in bed with boy. But she would come back. Surely. She always slept with Charlie. So he left the door cracked.

Charles hesitated at Trisha's door. Not wanting to barge in, he cracked the door instead, and listened for the sound of breathing. Then he heard it again; the groan in the house. Maybe it was the sort of sound that all houses make, especially at night, when it's cold, and every noise stands out. He heard it once more, and this time he was listening for it. It was *not* the sound of a settling house. And now he was sure that it came from downstairs.

He crept down the interior hallway, but doubled his pace, determined to go all the way around lest he miss Indris. She was probably downstairs, unable to sleep, sitting on the couch with her phone. The hallway made its circuit back to the balcony, and he started down the stairs. Already he could see that there were no lights on. Not even the cool blue of a screen. He checked the living room, the dining room, and the sitting rooms. There was no one here. With butterflies in his stomach, he approached the basement steps. It was utterly dark down there, but it was a walkout basement, and he meant to check the back door. He didn't want to go down, but the thought of something creeping up the basement steps while his back was turned gave him the willies. He went down, checked the walkout door, and found it locked. Charles quickly returned, determined to check all the doors and windows on the main floor.

One by one, he pulled back blinds and tested locks, relieved every time to find them secure, unsure what it would mean if any were not. He didn't know where Indris was, and didn't like to think that she could be outside, wandering around under the dark pines. He suddenly saw her in his mind's eye, not in a dark forest but in some other dark space. He couldn't shake the impression. She was not outside. But where was she? Walking faster, Charles meant to go back upstairs, when he had a sudden thought. He'd forgotten to check his small study. And there was something in that study.

The certainty came to him like infused knowledge in a dream. It was the one room on the main floor that he hadn't checked. Biting back his fear, he strode toward it.

The door to it was slightly ajar. He entered cautiously, half-expecting to find some awful, shadowy thing. But there was nothing. No dark creature of his imagination. No Indris, lying wounded on the floor. The desk chair was pushed in, just as he'd left it. The newly re-filled bookshelf hulked against the wall. The light from his printer cast parts of the room in a soft blue glow. The small leather couch was empty. But the door. Yes, between the couch and the wall there was a narrow black door. He flipped on the light.

The door was still there. The light did not illuminate it. Beams seemed to bend around the rough-hewn, dark thing that should not have been there. The rude knob reminded him distinctly of a reaching hand. It was as if the door had an intention, as if it wanted to be taken hold of. Not all doors were like that. This one didn't respect the conventions of its being. It shouldn't be here. There was no room for it between the couch and the wall.

Looking at the door, he hated it, but something in him wanted to open it. He had the distinct impression that, sooner or later, the brass knob would be turned. It could stand to wait patiently until he gave in. He refused it.

Charles backed out of the room and forced himself toward the stairs. The further he got from the study, the more certain he felt that he had just been in the presence of a predator, one which had lured him there, and was very much on the moment of striking, when its quarry inexplicably looked up, and took flight. Even now, as he forced his legs up the steps, he felt the door calling him back. Tomorrow he would go through the settlement documents, and find the blueprints, or the house inspection, to reassure himself that his own memory was sound. There hadn't been a door there before. There was no room for it.

The struggle to return to his bedroom seemed to last half the night. By then he'd half-forgotten Indris. The dark door dominated his mind. It was in his personal space. Waiting for him there. Had it woken him up, and lured him down, hoping to get him alone in the dark? Something brushed his legs. He jumped, and cried out.

It was Haley. The dog trotted toward Charlie's room, not even bothering to look back. He watched her pass, then turn the corner. Her motion was single-minded, autonomic. Charles shuddered, then turned to his bedroom. Its door was wide open now. He entered the room.

Indris lay swaddled in bedclothes. He studied her, wondering if she'd been there all along, and he'd somehow missed her. But no. Not unless his memory was utterly failing. Then where had she been? He listened to her breathing. It was too regular. He didn't believe she was sleeping. Indris' eyes popped open. In the dark room, they looked black.

"Cuddle up with me," she said.

Her voice was smooth. Almost oily. Far from sleepy.

"Where were you?" Charles whispered.

Her eyes flashed at him.

"Restless," she said. "And cold. Come. Help me warm up."

She was always beautiful. He went to her, suppressing the certainty that nothing here was right.

***

The next day, Charles Sr. received a phone call from his mother. He was at the breakfast table when it came. Hearing her frantic tone, he excused himself, and shuffled toward his study for privacy. He closed the door behind him, and sat down on the couch. Looking studiously away from the black door that was still there, he listened to her panicked talk. She was an old woman now, and Charles' father had passed on.

"It was just a dream, Mom," he said.

Edith Caldwell disagreed. She felt sure she had seen him, bound in strange fetters, and wandering into an open mouth, not knowing that it was a mouth. It reminded her of an angler fish, or one of those snapping turtles that made its tongue into a worm. She could see the danger, but he couldn't. She called to him, and he didn't hear. Charles reassured her.

"We are doing wonderfully. Yes. No. Yes, I will say my prayers. I promise I will. Yes, thanks for the reminder. Indris is fine. I think so. Yes, it won't be long now. UVA. Her chances are pretty good. Well, hard to say. I mean it's still very early. Just getting the ball rolling. Uh-huh. Yeah, well he's talked about community college for a year. Maybe a trade school. Thanks, I'm, sure he will. Charlie is fine. Mom. Yes, look, Mom … I'm fine. I—"

There was a groan and a snap. Charles dropped the phone. It bounced off the cushion, then struck the pinewood floor screen-first. He didn't reach for it; didn't attend to his mother's surprise at the loud noise. He looked to his left, where the door had been. But the couch was again nestled in the corner. There was nothing beside it but blank wall. No door. No space to put a door.

***

Charlie didn't know if he believed in ghosts. He'd never seen one. But in any house, you could feel things before your five senses touched them. In his old house, for example, he'd sometimes wake up and know that Mom was unhappy that day. His old room was in the basement, and he'd come upstairs on eggshells, afraid to set her off. So he knew that that kind of thing—the sixth sense, whatever you wanted to call it—was real.

Seated at the dinner table, he could feel the *wrong* in the air. He tried to pin it down. He compared it to being calm, and someone turning the music on full blast. He compared it to the time when he was four, and he'd set the moth on fire. Charlie had a good memory, and the thing with the moth still gave him the creeps. Brent came home that day with a Polyphemus. He'd had it at school since it was a big green caterpillar, and, when Mom asked him to take Haley out, he'd placed its mesh container on a counter by the stove. God only knew why, at that specific moment, little Charlie had wandered over and turned the stove on. Everything went up. The moth wasn't killed, but its wings were burned. The poor creature was terribly disfigured. The thing was, he'd never touched the stove before that day, nor since. But he remembered the awful feeling in the air, just before he'd done it, like some dark orchestra was playing. Innocent though he was, he'd danced to its tune, and left his older brother in tears. When wrong things were around, they left their imprint on the air. It felt that way now.

Charles, Indris, and Charlie ate in silence. Haley wasn't sitting under the table, like in the old days, waiting for Charlie to drop Mom's pork. She'd curled up in a ball against the large entertainment center that filled the wall where the painting had been. Trisha sat on the couch with her headphones on, watching the big screen. Brent had friends upstairs in his room. So it was just Mom, and Dad, and Charlie at the big table. Charlie studied his father, and wondered if Dad could feel the wrong thing too.

"You've barely touched your dinner, Charles," said Indris.

"I'm not that hungry," said Charlie's father.

Indris looked at Charles with a certain vacancy. She was neither hurt, nor curious. She was a mathematician working out a problem.

"This is a dish that you enjoy, Charles. I followed the recipe precisely."

You couldn't miss the way Dad leaned back in his chair, like he was trying to put space between them.

"I said I'm not hungry," Dad mumbled.

"It does not please?"

Mom didn't quite look at him as she asked, but through and past, as if her words came from a recipe too. His father's eyes narrowed.

"Oh, it *pleases* just fine. But I'm just not hungry."

Indris didn't react to his tone. She turned to Charlie, and her mouth smiled without involving her eyes.

"What did you do today, honey?"

Charlie shrugged. "Just went to school. Not much else."

His mother stared at him, grinning. There was a long pause during which she neither moved nor spoke. Abruptly, she pushed her chair back, stood, and began clearing the table. Charlie and his father watched her, their own mouths hanging open. The glance that passed between them confirmed their mutual disquiet. With unhurried motion, Indris cleared every extraneous item, leaving only the food they weren't eating. This done, she sat, and her body swiveled toward Charlie's.

"You must now go and distract yourself with play, while I take your father upstairs into the bedro—"

Charles Sr. made a loud, unformed noise, and knocked his beer all over the table. "Indris! What are you? … Come on!"

He glanced at Charlie, tossing his hands in an exasperated apology. His face was red. Indris turned toward him. She reminded Charlie of a marionette.

"Don't you enjoy this activity?" she said.

His father's face turned a deeper shade of crimson. Charles shook his head incredulously.

"Just … just *stop talking about it*! Okay?"

Charlie felt confused, and strangely awkward. He didn't know why his father was upset, but he wanted to get away.

"I … I'll go play with Haley," he said. "Outside, okay?"

Dad nodded to Charlie. Mom smiled pertly, as if everything was now in order. Charlie had turned to leave, when there was a loud crash upstairs.

"What on Earth?" said his father, looking at Indris. But if she was curious about the loud crash in her new house, the fact did not register on her face.

"Shall be go up to our room now, Charles?"

Dad stared at her. He didn't answer but walked toward the living room. Brent was bounding down the stairs. He came through the door, breathing hard. His friends trailed him, their faces white as the marble on the dining room floor. Brent struggled to catch his breath.

"We saw … the weirdest … thing in my room … chest with all my clothes … trophies and junk and stuff on top fell … in…"

Like a much younger child, he grabbed his father. Dad took Brent's shoulders, and looked hard at his friends.

"What's he trying to say?"

The two other boys mumbled and looked down.

"What did you see?!" Charles snapped.

"Don't know," said one of the mumblers.

"What do you mean you don't know?"

Charles questioned Brent again, but the boy-man appeared to be on the verge of hysterics. Gone was the bored sarcasm, the perpetual smirk. His face was terrifyingly sincere.

"Look," said the friend who'd spoken, "I think we gotta go."

"What happened?"

"We have to leave," said the boys. The two darted from the room before Charles could say another word.

"It's ... like a door, or something," muttered Brent.

Charlie watched the color drain from his father's face.

"A door, you say?"

Brent nodded vigorously. "It was just ... there. Behind my chest of drawers. And then it just opened. Like, not out, but into the wall. Then the chest fell in. That's what made the crash."

Charles Sr. swallowed. He looked around with wild eyes. "Did you go in?" he said, in a whisper.

Brent didn't answer. Charles shook him, and repeated the question.

"Not really," Brent said. "Just a little, okay? To pick up the dresser. Then we shut it."

"Do NOT go in!" said Charles.

Trisha, who by now had heard the commotion, entered the room. She removed her headphones, and looked at her father inquisitively. Charles repeated his command about the door, making sure each of them heard. Trisha nodded at that, but looked at her mother, puzzled.

"I'll go up there now and board it over," Charles said.

Indris placed a pretty hand on her husband's wrist.

"Is that really necessary, my love?"

"Are you serious?" he said, the sarcasm thick in his voice.

Indris Caldwell looked as if she might argue. Then, glancing up in the general direction of Brent's room, she seemed to change her mind. Her eyeless smile showed, but she pressed her lips together, suppressing it. With a quick nod, she retreated from the room.

"Go get my toolbox," Dad muttered. "And five or six of those boards under the awning next to the woodpile. You know what I'm talking about, Charlie?"

Charlie nodded perfunctorily. Then, realizing that his father was trusting *him* with an important task, he rushed down the basement steps. In a moment he'd returned with the toolbox and two boards. It was all he could carry in one trip.

Dad received the items, and told him to get more boards, and to meet him upstairs in Brent's room. Charlie said he would and steeled himself for a second trip to the basement, all alone. Before he left, his mother spoke from the other room.

"I wouldn't waste my time," said Indris.

Charles Sr. swallowed, and licked his lips.

"Why not, Indris?" he said.

"Because," said Charlie's mother, "the door isn't there anymore."

***

The air was still quite cold and wet. Branches crackled under his feet, but the mountain atmosphere seemed to catch the sounds, swallowing them up lest they should escape the dark forest. The boy had hiked quite a distance from his house, following a small compass that had been in his stocking last Christmas. For several days he'd planned to find a window through the forest, a clearing from which he could spy his old home. He'd found it, more or less. It was an archway in the trees that looked down from the mountain, onto the valley and the river, and across the bridge to the life he'd left behind.

Haley was with him, and not with him. He told himself the dog was sick. She ought to have followed him out willingly, but only did so when his mother caught him begging her to go on the hike. Haley had been unmoved by Charlie's pleas, yet at a word from Mom, the collie rose and accompanied him. Now she stalked about, keeping her distance, not once coming up to press her head against his thigh for scratches behind the ear. So he was alone out here. Several times she'd passed nearby, and he thought of talking to her as he'd always done on adventures, then decided against it. Talking to Haley was confiding in a friend. His furry guardian angel. He didn't want to confide in her now. Haley wasn't Haley.

So he stood there, looking out into the gray and darkening sky.

Through the arboreal archway, he saw into the past. It wasn't unlike looking at stars; great beings that had once been, but might now be nothing but images, photographs from the childhood of the universe. He was only eight, and what he called home was just as unreachable as the stars. But as long as he looked down across the valley and saw the white blur that might have been the outskirts of his old neighborhood, the past was all still real. A branch snapped behind him.

Charlie froze. He knew it was close, and too heavy to be the dog. Anyway, she was off in the nearby trees, keeping her distance from him. Whatever was coming, Haley would be no help.

"Who's there?" he said, without turning.

Something was behind him. He had no illusions about winning a fight with anything big, and already close. But even a dark shadow with red eyes was better than the mere certainty of a presence that had no name. He turned, hands raised to fight. It was Dad.

"Charlie?" said his father.

Charlie didn't know why it was a question. "What are you doing out here, Dad? I thought you were at work today."

His father's expression was unreadable.

"Oh, I am. In a way. Tell me, Charlie ... tell me about your friend Ryan. Ryan Pleise."

Charlie found the question odd, and out of place. Dad knew all about his best friend Ryan. Ryan was just the person Charlie would have liked to have with him now. And, despite Dad's earlier promise, they still hadn't hung out since the move.

"Why are you asking me about Ryan?"

"Just tell me about what he's like. What he means to you," said his father.

That stumped Charlie. He didn't know how to talk about his best friend. And here, on top of a mountain, on the other side of the Montoka River, it was almost painful to think about him.

"Well," he began, "Ryan's the one person other than Haley who gets what I mean the first time I say it. Not like other kids. Like if you mentioned a baseball stat, or a movie, and you said the wrong name or number, even for a second, and corrected yourself, other kids would jump on you and give you a hard time, just to have something to say. That's the kind of thing where Ryan would just wait until you were finished, or nod because he knew what you meant. He was ... he is cool like that. When can we visit him again, Dad?"

His father didn't answer but crept closer over the frosted branches and needles. Now towering above Charlie, he reached out, turned up Charlie's chin, and squinted his eyes. He seemed to relax.

"Not gone through any doors?"

But it was more of a statement. Charlie blanched, and shook his head vigorously from side-to-side.

"Don't ever," whispered his father.

"No! I never will. Dad, how long have you—"

They both froze. At the same moment, Charles and his son noticed, in their periphery, the shape and form of a collie. Haley was standing stock still, as if she were part of the background. They didn't say another word. They knew. They both knew. She was listening.

Charlie looked hard into his father's eyes. There were a dozen questions he might have asked, but a single, pressing question knocked hard against the walls of his skull. *What are you going to do?*

But perhaps words were unnecessary. Charles Sr. squeezed his arm. The pressure was a promise. There was a plan behind it. And Haley, whatever Haley was now, couldn't read *that.*

Charles Sr. looked off through the bent pine archway. His breath was loud and husky on the chill air, and both Charleses stood in the halo of their own self-made smoke, little embers still glowing to spite the coming winter.

"Best to eat together," said Charles. "Best not to go too far into the woods ... without a friend like Ryan."

Charlie nodded. He understood. Dad wanted him close. Safe from her. From *them,* really. And ready for whatever he was planning to do.

***

They sat around a palatial dining room table that glittered under the light of a new and expensive hanging candelabrum. Charles passed the lasagna to Indris. She smiled, thanked him mechanically, and carved out a steaming serving, before dropping it on her plate. Indris had only one smile now— anxious, expectant, and hungry—though not for the food. Her husband watched her eyes dance over each of the children. They locked for a moment on Trisha's, and the two women shared a look that was not for the others, though neither tried hard to conceal it. When had it happened to Trisha? He did not know them anymore.

Charles looked at his youngest child. Even at eight, the boy saw things as plainly as his father. And in his innocent face there was a plea. Almost a command. *Do something!*

He cleared his throat, not knowing how to begin. What he had to say sounded crazy in the light of day. But outside, the light was failing, and night was almost here. Too often in the recent past he'd acceded to a kind of inertia, ignoring his own sense of what was right. And now, here they were. And it didn't matter anymore if he could justify his authority. He must act.

"I want to talk about the doors," he said.

Brent looked up sharply, and his fork clattered against his plate. The young man shook his head and laughed nervously.

"You mean that thing in my room? I was wondering why we hadn't said anything about it."

The women didn't react. The steady attention with which they continued to consume their lasagna was far more telling than any reaction. Haley wandered in from somewhere, and now stood at the alert by Indris.

"*Indris,*" said Charles, more sharply than he'd intended.

She looked up from her plate. Her eyes, darker than he'd ever remembered, glinted in the light of the candelabrum.

"Yes, dear," she said. "I think we all heard you."

One hand continued with never-varying speed to deliver dainty morsels of lasagna to her mouth. The other crept over, spider-like, to stroke his hand. He snatched it way. Trisha saw that, and giggled.

Charles felt his throat constricting. For a wild moment he thought he'd been poisoned. But it was only fear.

"There are doors. Black doors. Or maybe only one. We've all seen them."

Brent crossed his arms, looking skeptical. There was no support there. Nothing in the way of an alliance offered to a co-belligerent. It was teenage bravado, thought Charles. A scared boy-man acting casual. Or maybe not. He hadn't done enough to know his older son, and now, nearly a man, Brent was a cipher to him.

"Brent," said Indris, "eat up. This lasagna is just delicious."

Brent pushed his plate away.

"Not hungry. Think I'll go see what's streaming."

"No!" Charles Caldwell pounded the table. Charlie flinched at the sound. Charles stood, gripped table's edge, and leaned over it.

"We *are* going to have this discussion. Right now. And nobody is going anywhere. Now this door ... no one ... NO ONE is to go into it. Do you understand me? And we are leaving! We are going to pack our bags, and get away from here—"

Indris was whispering to Trisha. The girl snickered, and said something in her mother's ear. Charles gaped at them, unable to form words.

"Care to share you conversation with the rest of us," he finally sputtered, stupid and stupefied.

Indris' eyes were black now. There was no mistaking the color. Nothing to hide anymore. "I think you already know that it's too late for that, Charles."

Again, she reached for his hand. She took hold of it. Her thumb caressed the large veins on the back of his hand. She was a snake gliding over him in the dark. He tried to force himself to speak, but his tongue stuck to the roof of his mouth.

"And as for moving away from it," she continued.

There was a loud crash. Charlie shrieked, and jumped out of his chair. The large entertainment center had fallen forward. No, fallen was not the right word. It had been flung across the room. The wall that had housed it stood naked, except for the narrow black door in its center. Without a sound, the knob turned, and the door swung inward. Behind it, a long dark hallway reached into the wall.

Indris pushed herself away from the table and stood. She turned her back upon her husband, and walked lightly toward the black hallway. The dog trotted up beside her, nestling its head against her rounded thigh. Trisha waited a moment, then followed.

"Trish!"

Charles could only strangle the words out. "Don't go! Don't go!" he pleaded.

Trisha went up to her mother. Indris said something Charles couldn't hear and ushered her daughter past. Girl and dog went under the threshold, and disappeared down the inky corridor. Indris waited until they were well on their way, then turned to address her husband.

"Charles," she said, her voice milky. "You don't really want to be alone?"

She didn't wait for him to answer, but cocked her head, cat-like, and flashed him a look as inviting as it was predatory. Then she turned down the hall and was gone.

"No. No!" he gasped. "Come back, Indris. Please come back!"

He started toward the door, yet with every voluntary step he took toward it, he felt its own dark pull on him. Somehow it was hurrying him along, conforming him to its plans. With every step, he became more the possession of this hungry thing. The doorway wanted to open *him*, and climb inside, as if *he* were the novelty. And that enraged Charles Caldwell. He let the rage grow. It was good and clean. A holy anger, long doused, domesticated, and de-fanged rose up in him now like Nemesis scorned. The whole world had tamed it; styled it pushy, overbearing, and inappropriate. Yet it had a place. Here, at last, was the time to let it out.

He would not just follow her. Would not give in to its inertia. Would not surrender what was his to its silky, easy emptiness. He would kill it. Yes. He would march into its maw, like a dragon slayer, and cut out its insides.

"Boys!

He turned to his sons. His only allies. Brent shrugged, then looked away from him. The little coward.

"Charlie! Charlie, I need your help, son."

Charlie wiped tears from his eyes. He nodded and ran around the table to his father.

"I'm going to save them," said Charles. "There's a big rope down in the basement, in the corner where the tools are. I need it, but I'm afraid to leave this door. I'm afraid it will—"

Charlie gripped his arm, both nodding and shaking his head, as if he'd gone witless. Charlie understood. *Yes, I will get the rope,* and *No, don't say that the door might close on them!*

"Go. Quickly!"

Charlie nodded, and ran toward the basement steps. It was a heavy rope. If only Brent would help him.

"I'll go too," said his older son.

Charles thanked him, relieved and a little surprised. Brent said nothing and ran after Charlie. The youngest Caldwell would be terrified, alone down there, in a house that wanted to eat them. And God only knew what strength they'd need to pull the women out. But they could do it. Yes, he had to believe they could do it together.

He did not face the door. Not yet. He kept it in the corner of his eye, and waited, and waited for the boys to return. After a long time, Charles heard a terrible cry from the lower level. It was Charlie's cry, a cry of fear and pain. Another voice followed it, deeper and more commanding. Finally the two returned, carrying the rope between them. Charlie was hysterical. Beside him, Brent stood ashen-faced.

"A door opened up down there!" cried Charlie.

"It was scary," agreed Brent.

"NO! You tried to pull us in!" said the boy.

Brent shook his head, his palms out defensively. "It was like a black hole, or something. I got confused for a second. But we got away. Here's the rope. What do you want us to do, Dad?"

Charles took his older son by the shoulders and shook him. "Look at me! You can't give in. I need you to stay here and help your brother. Don't look directly at it. I'm going to tie one end around the banister, and the other around my waist. I don't want to get stuck in there, you understand? I don't know what's going to happen. I'll give you two the slack, and you pull if I yell pull. You got that?!"

Brent nodded. "But we'll stay here, right?"

"That's right!" said Charles. "Stay here, and wait, and pull if I say pull. And even if I *don't* say pull. If I don't come out after a while ... then you do your best to haul me out."

He shook Brent again. He wanted to slap the boy. Throttle him out of his perpetual nonchalance, out the softness and slipperiness that he'd allowed to grow within his oldest son. Charles realized now that Brent's coolness was nothing but cowardice, a way of keeping at bay everything in life that might have counted for something. That might have tested him, and found him wanting. He'd failed the boy. Nearly a man, Brent was prepared to face nothing.

He turned from him, and did as he had said with the rope. Then he dropped a length of slack into each boy's arms, showing them how to wrap it about their arms and wrists to reinforce their grip. He clutched the two boys to him, feeling the warmth and love of the younger, and—even now—the near indifference of the elder. Then Charles Caldwell turned full upon the black dragon and plunged down its throat.

***

It was cold in the hallway. Charles kept his focus on his feet touching the ground, letting the contact of sole with surface be his link to reality. He did not know how long he'd walked, but it couldn't have been far. Even now the rope had slack, and it dragged behind him on the strange, smooth ground. The blackness gave way to a red-gray film to which his eyes were finally adjusting. It was cold, and there was a thin scent on the air like standing water. Suddenly he wasn't in a hallway anymore.

Charles found himself in a vast space. Not a room, but a yawning, sloping shaft. He did not want to see it. He felt its size alone would take his nerve. Emptiness was its name. He knew that. It led ever downward. That he knew as well. He cried out for his wife. To his surprise, she answered.

"Come. Sit with us," said Indris.

He saw her somewhere to the left of the ever-declining shaft. She stood with her back to him. Trisha was beside her, seated before a black wall. Her head was cocked up ever so slightly. Something dark and clinging had encircled her legs and thighs, and now crawled up her back, so that she seemed to be in a chair. His daughter stared up into a dark orb that came from the wall. It glistened, obsidian black, and yet it varied, like a rainbow of night. The dog was beside her, encased in the same cords. Indris' arm, thin and shock-white, reached down to stroke Haley's head. The collie's eyes were fixed on the fluctuating darkness before it.

Charles couldn't help it. The bright darkness drew him too. He took small steps toward it, thinking it would be nice to sit down beside his daughter, and to gaze with her at the swirling ink orb, so varied that it seemed, in its own way, just as good as color. He did that. Something felt up his body, and formed around him, clutching first at his feet, then his legs, and thighs, and back.

He was sitting now, if sitting was what it was. He thought it would be nice if Trisha turned to look at him. She did not. Charles looked down at his waist, and broke out into a cold sweat. The cold things that had slithered up him paused. He understood that even now, he must choose this. He forced himself to look away from the orb. Charles tried to see Trisha's face, and only then realized that there were two of her. Two images. Two projections. One, the color of flesh going gray; one shock white with deep black eyes, occupying nearly the same space, fluttering in and out of each other, threatening to merge. He looked past her, at Indris. His wife, or something that was like his wife, watched him watching her.

"Darling," said Indris, in a sing-song voice.

Suddenly she was beside him. Her hand turned his chin toward the dark gem.

"You don't have to be alone."

As he stared at the gem, something came out of the wall. Shuffling, squeezing, and panting, it birthed itself from the horizontal plane. A man. Dark-eyed. Charles. No, not Charles. The Charles-copy shuffled over, and reached out its hand to grasp his. The hand sank in, seeming to meld with his own. The arm went next, then the shoulders, and then the chest. It hurt. One body pushed into the other, squeezed into the same finite space. He was being occupied.

"Don't worry," said the Indris-thing. "This is how it goes."

It came to take away his burdens. This was the easier way. It was the way the whole world was going. And anyway, he deserved it. And there was just no reason to fight it.

Charles felt a small tug at his waist. He remembered the rope tied there. For just a moment, his attention went to little Charlie, back in the world, with only Brent to look after him.

He stood up, tearing himself away from the dark things that cushioned him. With effort, he reached into his body, and took hold of the Charles-copy. For a moment he saw clearly that it would make *him* the shadow, and wear his flesh and blood out in the world. There it could find others. One-by-one, it would bring them all. Charles gripped it with both hands, and hurled it into the black wall. It shrieked, and tore at the surface, like a thing drowning in the deep water.

"No, darling," said Indris, milky, musical, and so sweet, without looking at him. "You can't turn back the clock. This is just the way things are going. You don't want to be alone, do you?"

Charles looked at Indris. He didn't know whether it was his wife, or her shadow, or whether the two had already become one. With bitterness, he tore his eyes from her, unable to suppress the certainty that she could not be saved. But it wasn't too late for Trisha.

"Trish! Trish, can you hear me?!"

His daughter didn't respond. He began to tear at the cords that bound her. They did not resist him, but neither did *she* resist them. As he freed one limb, the other sank back into the enveloping cords, and they regrew to hold her. He put his hands beneath her armpits instead, and yanked her backward. She fell into his arms. He reached into her head, found the shadow, and tossed it onto the floor, surprised at how weak the darkness was, when resisted. Her shadow-self landed on the ground in a wet pounce. Already it had gained much of her substance, and as he dragged her backward, the other Trisha slumped toward her on its own power. But Charles took the thing that was not Trisha, and with a great effort, he flung it back into the wall. It began to sink in there, just like the other, its eyes full of fury and despair.

"Dad?" Trisha said, coughing.

Charles cried, and hugged her tight.

"Hang on. I need to get your mother."

Trisha cried, and shook her head.

"For her it's done. Get Haley."

Charles looked up uncertainly. The Indris thing looked back. She was a voluptuous darkness, and she reached out to him, beckoning.

"Come to me, my love."

Whatever dark amusement she'd worn before, at the dinner table, it was gone. There was now no secret joke between Indris and the darkness. She was so longer a thing with two faces, but a single, dark form. He looked into her eyes, and saw there a hunger that could never be satisfied. Still, he wished to go to her. Charles went to the dog instead. He tore her from black tendrils, and placed her in Trisha's arms. He dealt with Haley's copy in the same way he had his own, and Trisha's. The real Haley buried herself in Trisha's neck, recovering quickly. Then she hopped down, and barked angrily at Indris. That single wholesome sound broke Indris' spell on Charles.

"Come with us!" he pleaded.

"Come with you *where*? This is where I live. This is what I've always wanted."

"That's a lie!" he said.

"No, Charles. You just didn't see. I've always wanted more. Stay here with us. You don't want to be alone, do you, Charles?"

Bitterly, Charles swept up his daughter, and began the long and painful steps toward the light. Haley followed loyally. With every step he wished to turn, and run back, to lose himself in the dark body of the one who had been Indris. In her house of forgetting, where things were easy. But he thought of Charlie, and how the boy had tugged at the rope. Charlie needed him. That gave him strength.

***

"He's been in there for a long time," said Charlie.

Brent glared at the door impatiently.

"We should pull him out," said Charlie.

Brent shrugged. "Maybe," he said. "Give it a few minutes."

"What if he's stuck in there?" said Charlie.

Brent seemed to weigh the possibilities, then shook his head.

"We should let it play out a bit first. Never know if we'd be interfering. Ruining the whole thing."

Charlie shook his head. His Dad should have come back by now.

"I'm pulling. I don't care what you say. Sometimes I don't think you even care!"

Brent looked at him, affecting hurt, but Charlie didn't believe it. Not even for a second.

"You just don't want to make the effort!" continued Charlie. "You're afraid ... afraid of trying and having it not work out. You'd rather act as if you didn't care!"

Brent laughed. It was a condescending gesture, and one very familiar to Charlie.

"So look who knows so much about me," he said.

Charlie decided to ignore him. He began to take in the rope, armful by armful, unsure how he would have the strength the pull his own father back. Finally the rope went taut, but it was heavy, and large, and he could not even keep it tight in the air. How on Earth was a boy supposed to rescue his own family?

"Please, Brent! Help me! Stop being a coward!"

There, he'd said it. This was no time to be nice. He expected a snarl. A biting retort. But Brent only chuckled. Charlie looked up angrily at him, prepared for a nasty retort. But the other wore a small, secret smile.

***

Charles was halfway toward the distant square of light. Perhaps Indris could still be saved. Perhaps not. He must save the ones he could. He knew that if he turned back now, even for her sake, he'd have no strength for the others. And anyway, he could not be sure of himself. His love for Indris was not so pure as his love for the children. Long ago, he now saw, he'd exchanged it for something else that fed his needs.

With Haley following, he continued to lead Trisha down the hallway toward the distant, blurry light of a real, if imperfect, world. She was walking on her own feet now.

"Dad," she said, in a weak voice. "What about—"

"I can't, Trish. I'm sorry, but if I go back for her, I don't think I can save you."

Trisha shook her head. It seemed to require her a great effort to speak. They were getting closer now. Ten, perhaps fifteen steps and they would be through. Then he would take the children, and leave, and face the cold world without Indris. He suppressed that thought. He tried to think of Charlie, and of the twins.

"Dad," began Trisha. This time she faced him, and dug her nails into his shoulders.

"Let's just get to the end first," he said.

"What about Brent?" she said.

Charles stopped. His gut twisted within him. Trisha turned, and pointed to another enclave along the wall just past where they'd been. There was another rainbow of swirling darkness. How had he not seen it before? At its feet, staring up, and all in tendrils, sat his eldest son.

***

Charlie was trying to breathe. Brent knelt on his back. With a kitchen knife, he sawed through the rope that was his father's lifeline. Charlie was crying. He was only eight.

"Shh," said Brent. "I'm not finished yet. Still in the cocoon. You'll see what I mean. When it happens to you. I just need you to stay still. I'm getting tired again. Starting to fade. Need to go back. Just once more, I think."

"Why are you doing this, Brent?"

His brother, or the thing that was like his brother, twisted the knee that was in his spine, and sliced through the last strands of the thick rope. The Brent-thing breathed heavily. It seemed to Charlie to be losing steam.

"You'll see," sighed Brent.

The knee came off his back. Charlie groaned, and rolled over on his side.

"Now," said Brent, sucking wind, "just look into the doorway. Really look."

"No!" said Charlie, squeezing his eyes shut.

"What are you afraid of?" said Brent. *Don't be a coward.*

Chuckling, he lifted Charlie's head by the hair, and forced it up toward the door. The other hand peeled back his eyelids. "I can't make you go in," said Brent. "That's a rule. But I can make you look. At least I can make it hard for you to look anywhere else. Then, when there's nothing else to look at, you'll come. You'll want to come."

Charlie tried not to look.

"Just take a quick look," said the tired shadow of his brother. "That's where everything is headed. Everyone you love. You don't want to be alone, do you, brother?"

Charlie tried not to look, but it was hard. At that moment, the thing seemed inevitable. The doors that led downward knew about him now. Maybe they would follow him wherever he went. His eyes opened, and caught, and remained fixed on the darkness. He thought of his father, and that helped a little. But Dad had gone into the darkness too. Everyone would, when the time came. Wouldn't it be better not to be alone? Who was he to hold out, when the world was rushing all together down one stream? He might have given up then, and forgotten his reasons for resisting, but, quite suddenly, his father was standing in the threshold.

"Brent."

Brent released Charlie, and scampered to the side. There was a pause. A sly look crossed Brent's face. Charlie saw it.

"Dad! Thank God you're here! Charlie was trying to go in. I—"

Charlie tried to call out that it was a lie, but he couldn't find his voice. And anyway, the door lay open, summoning him, and a good part of Charlie wanted to answer. But that turned out not to matter. His father leapt forward, and struck Brent across the face. His brother shrieked, and flung his arms over his head. Charlie felt himself lifted, and pressed into the warmth of Trisha's arms.

"Take him, and Haley. Go to the car. Don't stop anywhere in the house. Just go."

Charles Caldwell had a new voice now. It was animated by a kind of holy defiance. In its own way, this voice compelled as much as the summoning darkness. Trisha heard it too. She bowed her head, like a maiden, and began leading Charlie toward the front door. Haley trotted after them, wagging her tail. Trisha suddenly stopped, and turned back.

"What if,"—her eyes were arching toward the doorway—"you don't come?"

Charles bounded across the room, took his daughter by the chin, and turned her face toward his own.

"Look at me!"

She did, staring at him with a kind of terror.

"Go. Take the car to the bottom of the driveway. Leave the engine running. If I'm not there in ten minutes, or, especially, if you find yourself wanting to return for any reason, then you go. Go right away then. You understand me? You drive away, and never come back!"

Trish nodded. She grit her teeth, turned from the black threshold, and marched toward the door. Charlie glanced back once to see Brent groveling on the floor before his father. Begging. He couldn't hear what Brent said, but something in the scene reminded him of Sunday School, and swine falling into the sea. He saw his father wrap the boy in the rope, and pull it tight about his chest. He heard Charles Sr.'s cold words.

"You are *not* my son!"

Charles hoisted the Brent-thing over his shoulder. It screamed, and beat at him like a small child, but Charles Caldwell kept hold of his vicious burden, and plunged back into the dark hallway.

***

The Suburban hummed at the bottom of the driveway. Somewhere in the valley below the mountain, the sun might still linger above the horizon. Here, under the grave gaze of black pines, night had come, and night had stayed. In the past, Charlie might have been soothed by the SUV's mechanical growl, by its tank-like girth, shielding him from what was unseen; unmade by human hands. Now he had no such illusory assurances. That which pursued them in the house might pursue them here. Human art couldn't contain it; maybe even helped it along. Perhaps even now, it plotted and connived, and looked for gaps and cracks and paths through, burrowing toward them from the other end of their weakness.

Trisha's hands were on the wheel, clutching it, as one caught in a landslide clutched at protruding rocks and brush. Charlie felt the need to talk to her. Every time she looked back over her shoulder, it gave him a fright, and he chattered to keep her with him. The car, after all, was in her hands. Their fates as well. But she was in his.

"If he doesn't come back..." she began.

"If he doesn't come back, then we go, Trish!"

Trisha seemed to waver. "But if he's almost here, and we drive away..."

Charlie was becoming desperate. If she caved, if she turned around now, he knew she wouldn't stop there. She'd already touched the dark thing. It had its claws in her.

"No, Trish," he protested. "You know what Dad said!"

She was silent for a moment. He saw her chewing her lip. She looked back over her shoulder again.

"Stop it!" said Charlie. He was sure that every time she looked, her resolve wavered a little.

"I'm just trying to see if he's coming!" she retorted, but there was a lie in her voice.

The clock on the dash had ticked off nine minutes. Charlie had only his hope. No strength. No grownup power to resist. He stared at the numbers, willing them to never change, so Dad would come, yet also hoping they would change soon, so that they could flee. How he wished to be away from here! Something slammed against the car.

"Open the back!"

Dad's voice was ragged. Trisha sighed so profoundly, he thought she would collapse. Her shaking hands couldn't find the trunk release, so Charlie leaned across her and pushed the button. He turned around in his seat, and watched his father struggling with Brent. The young man looked dazed, and his eyes were tear-stained. Dad lifted him over the back seat, and stuffed him through the gap. Brent dropped on the floor with a thud.

"Is it him?" cried Trish.

Dad looked at her, and nodded gravely.

"Dad," she said. "Please come here. I'm … I'm freaking out. You should drive."

His father shook his head. He seemed still to be struggling.

"You need to drive. I'll stay back here. With her."

He reached down, then lifted a flurrying bundle from the ground. Indris Caldwell was in his hands. Her eyes were black. Her skin, the color of spent coals. Dad had bound her feet and hands. He'd gagged her mouth with his shirt. In the dim light from the open trunk, Charlie saw her eyes darting around. The desperate look of a predator barely restrained. They fell on Charlie. He had to look away.

"That's not her!" shrieked Trisha. "That's the other! Oh God, don't take her with us!"

In a bear hug, Charles Caldwell lifted the monster, and fell with it into the back of the Suburban. Indris slammed her limbs wildly around the back cabin, and Charles could hardly keep her from darting back into the night.

"Shut it!" he yelled.

"But it's not her!" protested Trisha. "That's the other one!"

"Shut it, I said! There's only one now."

Trisha didn't move. She hugged the steering wheel, blocking Charlie from the button that closed the door. He got out and walked behind the Suburban. He had to climb on the bumper to reach the door. As he took hold of it, his mother's feet kicked out toward his before his father could restrain them.

Charlie fell hard, knees first, on the bumper. A fall like that would have hurt Brent, or Trisha, or even Dad. But Charlie was little, and Charlie was light. He got up immediately to try again. Again she kicked, but now he dodged, and leapt to the ground with the door in his hands, slamming it as he fell. When he got back into the passenger seat, he reached across Trisha's back to lock all the doors.

"Go!" shouted their father.

Shakily, Trisha put the car in drive, and started down the twisting road.

***

They didn't discuss the destination. Dad could hardly speak. He kept telling Mom that he loved her. Charlie's mother, or the thing that had become her, beat and kicked his father, bound limbs and all, making the large automobile shudder as it crawled down the mountainside. She must have gotten her gag loose. She shrieked, and cursed her husband. She bit his face, and Charlie heard his father cry out in pain. Still, Dad kept her in the car.

The farther they got from the house, the more Indris' curses sounded like pleas. She begged to be released. She cajoled. She offered terrible things. The things she said to Charlie's father could almost have made Charlie believe that Dad was a bad man, a tyrant or an abuser, hurting an innocent woman. But Charlie knew better. He knew his feelings were being plucked and twisted, like guitar strings, so he ignored those notes, and made himself remember.

As his father held on, the Indris-thing became more like his mother. Even her voice had started to change. Charlie suspected that the spell of that house, whatever it was that had enticed them all there, was breaking. And Mom knew it too.

Just as the car began to exit the mountain, entering the straightaway that headed toward the end of the pine-watched road, toward the bridge over Montoka River that led, eventually, to his old neighborhood, the Indris-thing uttered the most painful of all its terrible words.

"I wanted more than this! I want more than these children! More than you, good ol' Charlie Boy, could ever give me! Don't you understand! YOU ARE NOT ENOUGH FOR ME!"

She said many more awful things, things that even Charlie's thought-catcher, the one that lived at the back of his brain, could not pretend not to hear. And when she stopped shrieking, tearing them all down to atoms, she wept. It was an awful, wrenching, self-pitying sound. Charlie wondered if his father wept too. He thought of the sad expression his father must be wearing, down there in the trunk of the Suburban. Beside Charlie, Trisha shook her head, stung by what she'd heard. Even Brent, now sitting half-collapsed in the row behind them, looked crestfallen. At first, Charlie was also very sad. He'd almost have preferred the Door to the things his mother had spoken out loud. Then Haley, who'd been sitting at his feet under the dash, climbed up and licked his cheek. And it came to him.

As the car cleared the whispering pines, those overlooking watchers whose dark, bent-together bodies made a kind of doorway, Charlie reached out with both hands. He placed one hand on each of the twins' shoulders. The car passed under the threshold of mountain dark, and out under a sky with many stars in it.

"Don't take it too hard," he said to his brother and sister.

He repeated it again, for his father's sake. Charlie's eyes were squeezed shut now. He was trying to find the words.

"Don't take it too personally. It's just … I don't think … I don't think any of us were meant for this place. Even those stars aren't enough for us. It's the way we're made. Our hearts are all too big for any house."

After a moment, he felt Trisha and Brent relax against his outstretched palms. Even his mother's weeping subsided. Across the bridge, cradled in her husband's arms, Indris wept quietly still, but in a different way.

STAY WITH ME

"I love you even more today than I did before, but ever shall it be, oh my greatest mystery."

So I heard her singing throughout the white castle. Her song is like the blood in the veins of that place, and it reaches me wherever I wander. She might be close or far, so much as the geography of the place is concerned, but always she is near. The white castle is not infinite, or so I reason. Each room has its size and limits. Yet, whenever I go looking, I always find another room. When I take my eyes from these wonders—vaulted golden hallways, great stones laid in lovely patterns, colorful tapestries invariably hiding some secret door, itself unveiling more mysteries—when I take my eyes from them, and attend to her sweet song, I long for her. Then a sweet aching, which is the only pain I know, pierces my heart. I do not fear that I shall never see her again. It is *she* whom I fear. Do not misunderstand me. This is another sort of fear, as a buzzing bee might feel before a mountain. I do not understand this at the time. I have not yet learned the bee, only seen him in the garden. As for mountains, they are beyond the thin golden lattice that marks the boundaries. I am thinking of this, and pining for her, and fearing her, and fearing for her, and loving her, when she appears.

Just where my heart seeks her, there she is. Her raiment—I do not say her clothing—is like violet and gold nebulae, were they living. Her body filling it is like a wave captured before breaking in a soft, round net, and her skin is the golden shores of those same far-off seas beyond the lattice. She kisses me, and takes my hand, and I walk with her in the cool warmth of the white castle.

It's some time before she speaks. I think neither of us wants to resort to words. Sometimes I think we do not need them. I have often considered, since the calamity, that it would have been better for me had I never spoken. Or else, had I spoken to her more.

"Did you find new things?" she asks, her voice as musical in speech as in song. How can I answer such a question? Everything is singular, unique, totally itself. It is all so precious, so perfectly beyond my ken. And nothing is so precious as she who sings it into being.

"Some of it is new to me," I say, cautiously, not wishing to appear a fool before her, "but I often prefer to dwell in rooms I have known. I do not find them any less wonderful, now that I know them."

Then I hasten to add, "But I love every new room too. Each swells my heart to bursting. I want to … stay with them. With all of them."

She smiles. I think that her smile is the only thing that could ever break my heart. I would now that it could be broken again, in the same good way, a thousand times.

"Stay with me," she says.

***

I cannot describe that evening, for I would want to say it was the same as every evening. But that is a kind of blasphemy. Same is a vulgar word.

I sit across from her at the crystal table in the great dining hall with the vaulted ceiling. Far above us, the rafter beams are of many colors, catching the white moonlight, and breathing it down upon us in a rainbow glaze. We almost touch, she and I, though there are many places at the long table, and the two of us sit at either end. I know it is better simply to accept this reality, because I cannot doubt its truth. Nothing could be truer than this; nothing more real than her. With such immediate, interior certitude, why did I insist on more?

The other chairs look empty, but I believe they may be full. The room teems with life, and many minds seem to lean in, and to wait upon us, their hearts full of an unnamable anticipation, as are hers and mine.

She passes the golden bowl to me, and our fingers touch. In the bowl is a red ichor. It saturates and overflows the savory bread and meat that rests within. I taste it, and suddenly look up at her in ecstasy. We are in ecstasy. This meal is her work. It is her song. It is her. I eat her. I feed on the life that she sings into being. But there is more. This is but a taste. Strength for the journey; whither, I do not know. That has not yet been revealed to me. But her eyes know, and pine for its culmination.

None of this is spoken. My cumbersome speech would do it no justice. Her own music would never exhaust itself in description of it. I am the poor man; she, a wealth of everlasting being, full of unspeakable actuality. In our inequality of being, we are equal; that is the first thing we have in common. This meal mingles us. It is the second thing we hold in common.

Her dream is to fill me with her song, that is, with *her*. I know that this is the greatest of privileges, and yet, I nurse another dream, one which has slowly taken root. I do not dare tell her. There is nothing wanting, and yet, I allow myself to want this thing. Oh, foolish misery! Why did I not tell her? Could it have been worse to reveal my mind, than to do what I did?

"I love you," she says.

Her eyes are truth. There can be no truth outside of truth. I don't know what to say. What return can I give to this ever-flowing mystery, this voluptuous injustice, that *she* should love *me*?

"From beyond time, I have loved you," she says again, before ending with those same words with which she ends every sweet and precious day.

"Stay with me."

***

I am wandering in the library. I found it yesterday, or perhaps a thousand years ago. I want to know about mountains. I want to learn about the seas that I have seen from atop the white castle, far off past the gardens, and the lattice wall that encloses them. I hunger too for knowledge about the fruit and flowers that grow there. Even the grass. All is precious to me. Whatsoever I wish to learn, I find in a volume bound in golden vellum, within easy reach.

My knowledge is deep and good, yet it stirs a greater hunger in me. For what do I hunger, I who am so satisfied?

"For what do you hunger, my love?"

She is standing beside me now. I did not hear her enter. Her eyes are stars, her body a velveteen archipelago. I am suddenly foolish. I cannot speak, or remember that other hunger. She is all that I see.

"Tell me," she says, and in her eyes I see something distant; something obscure to me.

"Confide in me," she says, more insistently, and takes my hand.

I choose to confide a certain wish that I have sometimes had while standing in the library. It is not that other wish. Oh, foolish man! Why did you not tell her?

"I would like it if there were a stairway from here to the upper limits of the castle," I begin. "One that starts in the jeweled rotunda, and pierces through the ceiling, leading to that balcony that I have sometimes seen above the white castle. I believe it must be just above us here. I saw it when you showed the boundaries. A balcony that overlooks … that overlooks the garden."

She squeezes my hand.

"But it *does* lead to the balcony," she says, with an enigmatic smile.

"Oh?"

"Sing it, my love, and it shall have been."

I begin to sing, and look hesitantly toward the jeweled rotunda. The sun coming off the stone is so brilliant, it seems to form a structure of light. This has always been so. When I sing, I am only conscious of the spiral structure that has always been there, but which was too brilliant to see. Then her voice joins my own. What happens next is the very mystery whose lesson, had I but learned it, would have blessed me forevermore. And you, my son. And you!

When I sing with her, I see the spiral light more clearly. When she sings with me, I see that this light is the most delicate framework of shaped stone; that it, in fact, rises from the colored stone, and swirls upon itself, and climbs like white vines to the ceiling far above, and pierces through an open portal there, and opens to a vast platform. It is the same great balcony that overlooks the garden, and spies out upon the lattice wall that marks the boundaries beyond which I'm not to wander. My song, when it joins her song, traces out the winding stairwell that has always been there. Her song, when it joins my song, becomes—and has always been—that same ornate ladder. My songs, my deepest inventions, are her songs, and it is only their union with her song that brings into them being. No, into *ever-having-been*.

"Let us go and look," she says, placing her soft hand in mine.

Together we ascend the paper-thin stone, and every step with her is joy, so that the journey becomes its own aim, and I almost forget my reasons for the song that discovered the stair. Almost. Would that it had been *all*, and not almost!

Some time out of mind, we gain the top. We stand together on the vast balcony. The wind blows over our bodies, sweeping her hair across her shoulders, and out behind her like wings. Now we stand at the edge, looking off toward the mountains beyond the boundary, and even further toward the seas. My eyes drift downward, back toward the lattice wall, and further in, to the gardens within the castle grounds.

"I wish to walk the gardens," I say.

She squeezes my hand, and there is something in the pressure that feels as if *she* clung to *me* for support. As if I could ever support *her*, She Who Sings.

"I know this, my love," she says.

I chance a look at her eyes, and they are radiant as always. She cannot but smile, for she *is* a smile. The everlasting smile that made the world. But in that smile, and in the stellar eyes that sparkle, there is something like a cool spring rain. She presses me to her, and kisses me more fiercely, I think, than ever she did before that day.

I cannot grasp it. Her. I cannot understand why she loves me. How have I merited such a love? It is a mystery to me, like the mystery of my being. No, no. The two are different. My being is more like the rooms of the white castle, which seem finite, but are always more in the searching. I have no memory before this place. Yet I can understand everything I put my mind to. Nothing in the library is obscure to me. So why can I not grasp this most primal of mysteries, that she should sing me into being, and cling to me, and love me, and look at me, sometimes, with eyes that seem to make her own endless happiness captive to mine, as if she had rendered herself up to me, a victim?

"Stay with me," she says, like always.

***

The next day, my wanderings take me into the gardens. We have walked the castle grounds many times, but today she is not beside me. I tell myself that I do not wish to trouble her. Surely, her perfect happiness deserves some greater object than me, from time to time. So I leave her alone. My curiosity moves me to visit each garden in turn. There are four, but the east garden is always invisible from the castle; even from the balcony. I resolve to see it.

As I walk through the tall grass between the lush rainbow rows of ever-fresh fruit, I think about the kinds, and natures, and growing ways of each and every one. In the library, I have learned what they are, but not *who*. It is my privilege to name them, to bring them into dialogue with those who will come after. Why should I be so lucky as to name the things that she has sung? Is this world for me? Why for me? I see no sense in it. Yet competing with the knowledge of my own infinite smallness is that secret desire, which I have never confided in her, which I have not even admitted to myself. I ought to have done so, but in my mind, my poor son, I had already made one good the enemy of another. I had set her against her own song.

As I round the castle toward the east garden, a thought comes to me from out of the blue. We have always walked the garden together, she and I, but never the east garden. Is it right that I should discover it without her beside me? Should I not call for her, so that my joy can be hers, and hers mine? Something moves in the distance.

I stand silent for a moment. (It was in this very moment that I ought to have turned back, or else called for her!) A figure stands in the tall grass, about a stone's throw off. There are often animals on the grounds, and more far off beyond the lattice, but I have never seen another like myself here in this place. I walk toward him.

His face is turned away from me. He crouches, and his arms are in the flower patch, moving it about, as if pruning it. I cannot see his hands.

"Exploring again?" he says.

His voice is clever, and crisp. There is something in it like the bucking of a deer, or the swift path of the eagles that dive toward the earth, beyond the lattice wall, and disappear into the mist where I cannot see. There is a kind of simplicity in his delivery, as if all that he surveyed were boiled down to a clarity.

"Yes," I say. "And what are you doing here?"

"Here I am, crouched in the garden," he says, gruffly. "What does your own reason tell you?"

I watch him ruffle the flower patch. I cannot see the hands that make the flowers buckle and sway.

"It tells me nothing," I say. "She sings the flowers, and I learn their ways. Sometimes I sing them straight and tall, and she with me. I do not know what your role could be."

He seems to shrug, and though I see but the thin crescent sliver of his face, it pulls back in some expression.

"Will you ask her?" he ventures, and there is a challenge in his voice. It occurs to me that I have never discovered anything all by myself. I have never reasoned alone, without her to aid me. On all my journeys, I leave open to her the door to my heart. I do nothing on my own two feet, for she is always present.

"Who are you?" I press, returning the challenge. "What are you doing here?"

He hesitates. The roses rock in his grasp. I will have to sing them straight later.

"I am the gardener," he finally says.

I did not know we had a gardener.

"But why?" I stutter, for the first time, unsure of myself.

"How do you suppose the flowers and fruits grow?" he asks, matter-of-factly.

I must have frowned then. I ought to have, anyway.

"She Who Sings, and who loves me, makes them grow. You must know this."

He shrugs again.

"Then who grows the mountains, or the thick, dark forests, full of unexplored wonders, or the distant seas, thronging with new things?"

His question stops me. I had always assumed…

"Surely, it must be her," I venture.

He doesn't answer, but he leaves off ruffling the flowers for a moment, and looks out toward the lattice wall.

"It is so great, and so distant," he says. "And wild, and dangerous too. I wonder … who could have the courage to master it?"

My heart catches in my mouth, not at the word "danger"—for I know there must be reasons I'm forbidden to cross the lattice wall—but at that other word, master. *That* is my hidden desire. That I should be a master too, as she is. That I, who am but a speck, should sing my own songs, and shape the world by my own voice. How is it that this stranger knows my secret? Can he know this, and she not know it? But I cannot believe that there is anything that escapes her, for there is nothing but nothing itself that she has not sung. And this thing that burns inside me is not nothing. It reaches deep.

"I do not wish to speak to you anymore today," I say.

He rises immediately and keeps his back toward me. I should turn to go myself, but my eyes move from the flowers, whose petals now litter the garden floor, to the figure who walks away from them through the tall, waving grass that stands between the garden and the lattice wall. And as I watch, the figure reaches the distant lace barrier that marks the limits of my world, and, without pausing, passes through it.

***

That night we eat in silence. It's a different silence than before. She sees that I am troubled. I have never been troubled. She comes to my end of the table, and wraps me in her star-spun raiment, taking me within its folds, but not yet permitting her golden skin to touch mine. There is something else that must happen first. A rush of comfort fills me, and I long for forgetting.

"Confide in me, my love," she whispers into my ear.

But I cannot bring myself to tell her of the desire that the gardener has named. How can I, when she has given me everything, and still I want more? I could not bear to see that sweet face turned toward me in disapproval. That would be a death greater than that of which I have been warned, the death that lurks beyond the lattice wall. Yes, I know now that I should have confided in her. But in truth, I knew it then too. My choice was my own. My calamity—our calamity, boy—was all of my making. And yet, if I could go back to that present moment, that time when all time was actual, would I have chosen any differently?

So I do not tell her. There is a mist in her eyes. Some obscure knowledge comes into them, as though she sees beyond this moment to the next, fateful day. And of course, she did.

"I love you, so very much, my love," she says again, and presses me as close to her as I can be, closer than I have ever been, down to the last layer of her endless raiment.

Why? I want to ask, for I know that love seeks equality, and I cannot understand this love. It will not fit within my mind, but ever overflows it, dashing my hopes of understanding. Oh cursed, oh *damned* be my understanding!

"Sing with me, my love," she says.

We sing together, and there is nothing but beauty in her song. Yet in that beauty there are novel chords; a power like unto the distant mountains; a ferocity, like the distant seas. Yes, there was still only love in her song, and beauty, but there is beauty also in the rain. Then she clings to me so tightly that it is as if *I* were the singer, and she, only my song.

"Stay with me," she says, and her voice is pleading.

***

I am in the garden again. It is the next day. The last day. The gardener fiddles in the brush. He's hunched over, hands and feet buried in the swaying grass, like the apes I have seen in the distant forests.

"Figured it out yet?" he says, without turning to look at me. I can't deny that there is something intriguing in his blunt demeanor. Something bold, and careless, and unencumbered, or so it then seemed.

"I learn new things every day," I say, holding my ground. "I shall know a thousand things before tomorrow."

"But with limits," he retorts.

"I've not reached any limits," I protest, determined to best him; unable to stop listening to him. "There is always something more for me."

He laughs. His laugh is like the hyena's cackle that sounds behind the barrier.

"And why do you suppose that is?" he says.

"What do you mean?"

"Oh, come now, friend. Why do you think she keeps you searching? Digging around inside that castle? Always content. Always happy. Like that slug over there."

He nods, but does not point, toward one of the small creatures.

"It's happy too, you know," he continues. "It's always finding something new."

Again, I'm taken aback. What could possibly be wrong with happiness? But for a man to be a slug … to want so much, and to always be so limited…

"I am happy. I am very happy with her," I insist.

"But are you complete?" he shoots back, hardly letting me finish.

"I am becoming more complete every day."

He shakes his head.

"Impossible. Completeness is not a matter of degrees. Either you have everything, like her, or you really have nothing. Being is being. If she is absolute being, then you are just a dream."

His words shake me. I cannot see around them. I cannot reason past them. If She Who Sings is the source, then what am I? Beside the infinite, all that is finite is equally flat. And at least the slug does not yearn to be all-in-all.

"She has completeness," he continues. "And mastery. And you already know she can give you anything you desire. She can make what's hers, yours. But has she? Why hasn't she? Tell me!"

I don't answer. I don't dare breathe the thoughts that come to me. He's raised the matter of the incomprehensibility of her love for me. A love so easily given. So mysterious. Can it be—I fear to think it—that it is incomprehensible because it is impossible? Is her love given to me so easily, or is it given only lightly, a seeming love, to keep me in thrall?

And I want so much to comprehend, to resolve questions in terms I command. To possess. To master. To sing the world, as she does, but with my own voice. What is the point of reason if not to comprehend? What is the point of longings if they cannot be satisfied? The gardener is still turned away from me.

"Look again at my friend, the slug," he says, with the same casual nod. "It's happy and content. And, so long as it's in this garden, behind those spindly walls, it will lack nothing, but it will also lack *everything*. The everything you want."

My mind fails me. Is the gardener saying what I think he's saying?

"Is the *everything* I seek ... behind the lattice walls?"

He doesn't answer, but shrugs as if to say, "Where else could it be?"

The last thought that came to me, before the calamity, was that, perhaps, the everything I sought was not past the golden lace walls, but beneath that star-woven raiment whose hidden mystery had not yet been granted me. And, my son, if I had run to her then, I know now that she would have taken me within its folds. I know now that *this* was the very thing she longed for; that I should choose to believe in her goodness, the truth I could see, rather than that much smaller goodness which lay within the barriers of my own mind. But I did not run to her. I wanted to stand on my own.

"As long as you're in here, you're her pet," continues the gardener, practically spitting the words out. "Is that your everything?"

"I don't think that could be!" I protest. My very last protest. "Because she loves me!"

He shrugs, and then nods sagely.

"No denying it, and the grass and flowers too. She loves everything in its place."

In that moment, my son, I was gripped by the thought that beside her, I was ultimately no greater than a slug, or a flower, or a speck of dust. Yet in my heart I harbored some destiny even beyond the perfect bliss I knew. To be the master. To be He Who Sings.

I do not remember putting one foot in front of the other. It seems to me that no sooner had I made my choice, then I was already standing under that golden lace that stretched to the sky. I do not know. I never looked up. In that moment, its delicate framework was the spider's snare of a jealous woman, and not the protective boundary of an almost-Heaven. The presences that I had often felt around me while I ate with her at the crystal table seemed to scream out in warning, their cries passing from concern, to outrage, to near despair, as I crossed the threshold into that outer world. Even they could not understand what I was doing. I had passed beyond their paltry world of limits, into my own bold, self-sung world. A world without limits. One of self-making. And I promise you, my son, that the pleasure of it lasted but an instant, before it fled forever.

For in that moment, I turned to look back, and there she stood. Behind her was the white castle, already crumbling into dust. A gray mist spread in from the outer world, creeping snake-like over the swaying grasses, as a man pulls a shroud over a fallen son or brother. And the pain in her face was far, far greater than a man in his death struggle; greater even than your mother's torment, when she brought forth in agony only to lay your baby sister lifeless on the straw. I had struck She Who Sings a blow from which she would never recover. I had wounded the body which I had never touched. Beside her, the gardener cackled, and sniped at her feet, though without daring to touch her. He groveled before her, burying himself in grass that went gray as the mist passed over it.

She Who Sings cast aside her starlit raiment, and it fell to the weeds at her feet. Her raiment too was gray and decaying. For the first time, I saw the mystery that it had always concealed. She was terrible to behold. I had only ever glimpsed her sweetness, her kindness, her generosity. Now I saw the ferocity of love that undergirded it all. It was the infinite justice of love to love, love returned for love, love endlessly poured forth and endlessly received; endlessly yearned for and endlessly increased; a fount that has no beginning; an ocean without bottom. And those eyes of love turned first on me, wet with the shock of my betrayal, and then full upon the gardener.

Before her he still groveled, not daring to raise his head. She turned back to me. Her voice was the White Mountain, distilled into wrath.

"Why did you cross the lattice wall?"

I could not answer. What could I say for myself, child? I was like you, when you stole the sweet rolls, and I found you with them. I brought this thing upon you, this inner contradiction, and for that I am deeply sorry.

Like you, I pointed toward the other. To escape myself. I could not face my shame. She turned back toward the one who'd styled himself the gardener, though I now saw it was absurd that this mewling wretch should make anything grow.

"Look at me," she said.

He looked at her, and began to scream.

"Show yourself," she cried. "Show yourself to him."

The gardener rose, peeling himself from the brush, and I saw that he was faceless, and that he had no hands, and no feet. Still he cackled, seeing my misery. Where his mouth should have been, a gash opened and closed.

"You're no better," he spat, seeing my horror at his appearance. "All is lost to you. She knows it. Even She Who Sings must mind her own song. Else it is but a dream! None of it, of any import! Admit it, Fair One, and then undream us all!"

She threw her arm down, and the handless, faceless creature slithered at her feet. There she held him from a distance. She turned to me.

I expected to see hate there, for I knew, somehow, that this false one had spoken factually. How could the singer of a perfect song go back on her song's perfection? How, if it was real? Even if she could still love me, this song was her word, and her word was truth. Even a grain of sand was but a tiny mirror of that truth, a dark-looking glass, indeed, but a reflection all the same. She looked at me, and knew my thoughts, and—if this is possible—pitied the creeping darkness that coursed through my being.

I looked down. That she did not force me to gaze upon her naked justice, that beauty that I had once presumed to long for, and which was now a terror to me … that forbearance, child, was my only measure of hope. For in permitting me to look away, she spared me from the self-condemnation which would have forced me downward, writhing in a place of my own unmaking, gnawing upon myself until I had neither hands, nor face, but only an endless, vicious, screaming impotence. Only in light of her beauty, my son, and in light of the glory of her whom I had cast aside, can you begin to comprehend the red and thirsty hell that I had merited.

Once more her enemy cackled, even as he screamed in an endless death agony.

"What will you do? What *can* you do?"

I sensed that every defiant scream only increased this being's agony, forcing it deeper and deeper into the earth, its pain redoubling as its distance from her approached the infinite, but could never achieve even that.

She did not answer it, but only looked at me. Still the gardener screamed, and even I who had done such evil was shocked by the temerity of his abuse.

"Why did you make us at all!" he screamed into the earth. "I will not suffer you to make me! I will not suffer to be made by another!"

His screams did not rattle her. She looked at me for a long time, and it was agony to see her. I longed to look away, though her eyes now held me. Then she sighed. A single golden tear escaped her eye, cut a path from cheek to chin, and dropped at her feet. It fell upon her starry raiment, which was already turning brown, subject to the same dead film that now covered the grass. She released my eyes, none too soon. I could only stand to look at her feet, but she crouched down, and placed her hand upon the fallen covering. When her fingers touched it, it changed again. She began to sing to it.

I watched the colors of the world swirl beneath her down-pressed hand. Plant-like, her cloak seemed to drink up the earth. It became a swirl of reds and blacks. It grew thorns and thistles. Vines from her cloak began to grow up about her arms, and to encircle her body. As they did so, the light of her pure justice was dimmed, blocked by the net of terrible thorns that now grew from the vines. They plunged into her fair skin, lacerating her everywhere until she bled upon the earth. All the while she still sang, and yes, even smiled. Then she rose, my child, and wrapped herself in this terrible covering. Her raiment settled, and became her skin. Her flesh, once liquid gold, became a tapestry of ugly wounds. Pockmarks covered her face, oozing and bursting on their own. Her slender fingers grew twisted—yes child, even as mine are now, in my old age. As yours shall also be in the years before death comes to claim you.

But she walked forth, smiling, hiding her painful stumble in a determined stride. Without touching me, she led me out from the place of the white castle, and I felt all become dust behind me, though I dared not look in regret toward that which I had destroyed. We walked for a while along a silent path, made by I know not whom, until we came to a place where the path forked.

She turned to look at me. To my wonder and my shame, she grimly smiled, but her body shook with the agony I had given her. That agony, child, is my only heritage. And it was not mainly to you and your brothers that I gave it, but, especially, I think, to her. I wove a cloak of misery, yet she stooped, and drew it over herself. In that moment, at the parting of trails, I saw that her eyes, once colorful nebulae, were now as dark and as mournful as the yawning space between the stars. She had swallowed the darkness.

I could not bring myself to confess my regret—not even then, while she looked at me. What cheaper thing could there be than my paltry regret? But then came the words that shook me, and the very earth beneath me, down to the root.

"I love you," she said, her voice trembling from the effort. "Even more today than I ever have before. But ever, ever shall it be. Oh, my greatest mystery."

If it was a song, it was without tune, or else I could not hear the notes. For I could not—as I cannot now—remember the sweet sounds of any music from those golden days before. I only know that I have known it once. I could no longer feel the truth of it, for feeling truth is another gift that I took for granted, and lost. But I knew it, boy. And I decided only too late, to believe what I knew. To believe in her love for me. Does it surprise you, my son, that we must decide to believe what we know is true?

"You will see me again," she said. "In the castle at the end of the world."

Then she walked away, up a narrow and rising path that was harder than the one she'd left to me. Often I have wondered what would have happened if I had called for her then. If I had run to her, and fallen at her feet. Often I have wished for one more word with her.

Yet I *do* speak to her now; now that her burning love is at a safe distance. Now that the very sight of her does not torment me. And I hear her also, sometimes, when I am quiet. I hear her on the wind that moves over the White Mountain, and dances upon these mighty waters. And her voice on the wind is always the same. "Stay with me."

ABOUT THE AUTHOR

Joseph Breslin lives in Maryland, where the crabs are good and the spring lasts only one week, together with his lovely wife, Liz, three scrappy sons, and a cat named Frodo. Frodo initially preferred the author over the author's wife, until the latter deviously stole away Frodo's feline affections. When he is not plotting to recover Frodo's heart, Joseph teaches and coaches full-time. For free stories and reflections, to contact the author, and to hear about upcoming books, please visit **joeybreslinwrites.com**.

Scan me to rate and review *Other Minds!*